I Knew You When

Beyond The Wallace's

Carey Anderson

DEDICATION

I would like to dedicate this book to everyone thank you for your constant support. To those who take the time to give me feedback, especially those who take the time out to write those reviews. Thank you for taking a chance on an unknown and then coming back for more.

Cover Design by KreationsK

Join me on Facebook – www.facebook.com/careythewriteranderson

Twitter - @CareyTheWriter

Blog - http://careyanderson.blogspot.com

Website – http://www.careythewriteranderson.com

Editorial – Treasures of Joy Editorial

ACKNOWLEDGMENTS

I would like to acknowledge all of my supporters. I know I say this time and time again. I would not find the strength to continue without your continued support.

I would also like to acknowledge my Beta Readers who take time out of their busy schedules to read my doodles and let me know if I'm talking out of the side of my neck.

Also to my Rough Riders, you all pick up right where my Beta Readers leave off. You all are amazing and I could never thank you enough for your support as you also take time out of your busy lives to not only read my work, but you tell others about me. Thank you so much.

To my loyal readers, the ones who have made yourself known and the ones who are silent. I thank you from the bottom of my heart.

To my literary friends, I would like to say thank you all of your support. A special thank you to Angie Liddell, Ty, and a host of others. Thank you for your friendship and support.

I was the over confident one

You were the shy one

I couldn't remember the words

No one could hear yours

You saw me said I was priceless

I saw your adoration for me

(*Chorus*)

I knew you when all of your thoughts and desires were consumed by me

I knew you when there was a song in your heart and I was the melody

I knew you when

I knew you when

I knew you when

Then one day you touched me

You touched me right down to my soul

Now all my thoughts are of you

I hurt them because they're not you

You say you don't love me anymore

I say that's not true

(*Chorus*)

I miss you

Please come back to me

I promise I'll love you endlessly

This story is supposed to end with you laying next to me

(*Bridge*)

I Knew You When all we could do was dream about making it big

Now that it's a reality, you don't come home to me

Missing you makes it harder to breathe

Please don't leave

ME

I miss you

Please come back to me

I promise I'll love you endlessly

This story is supposed to end with you laying next to me

(*Chorus*)

Chapter 1

Novian

I kissed Shay tenderly as she held on to me tightly. My mom heard about an Agent's open call in Los Angeles and she rented a car to drive out there to audition. I told Shay I would call her as soon as I could to let her know how things were going. "I love you Novian, I don't understand why I can't go to support you." She pouted.

"My momma is barely letting my brother come. He's coming to pay for the room." My mom started laying into the horn. "Look, I gotta go. You know how she gets."

Shay looked so sad as she kissed me one more time and then she walked back to her apartment and shut the door. You would think she would be excited for me. This could be the trip to change my whole life. This could be my big break, the one that launches me to stardom. My mom was loud and rude as she laid on the horn as I walked to the car. *She pregnant yet?* She hollered at me as I opened the car door.

"NO!" I hate when she talks about Shay like that. Shay is not some groupie that dug her nails into me. Shay and I have been together since junior year of high school. She didn't care that I felt I was going to be a star and all the other girls would follow me around like groupies. She actually didn't want anything to do with me because of that. I had to do a lot of listening to figure out how to get next to her. Because of Shay I pay attention to so much more. My momma just wants to get me signed and on the stage selling out arenas. My big brother rejected her idea of stardom for him. He's the one who took care of me while she ran from nightclub to nightclub looking for her big break.

"That girl is going to end up pregnant, mark my words. She knows you're going to be somebody and she wants her cut."

"Momma Shay is going to school, she don't have time for a

baby."

"Un huh! Who you gonna believe? I know females, and I'm trying to teach you the game. You can be stupid if you want to."

"Since you wanna teach him about games, why don't you tell him what you had to do to get this car?" My brother smiled at her.

The look my momma gave my brother made him laugh hard. My momma don't have to say much, sometimes it's the looks that she gives that say it all. "SHUT UP!"

I got my pillow and stretched out across the back seat with my Walkman on and went to sleep. I didn't have to stay up to listen to them fuss for the next five or six hours to Los Angeles from the Bay. I made sure I had enough batteries to last me the trip out here and the trip home.

Earlier today my best friend Amos and I talked about all of the *what ifs*. What if this is it? What if I blow up? I told him I'd give him a job in my entourage. Amos declined saying he already had something lined up. In other words, he couldn't have his child and baby momma waiting on me to make it big so that they could eat. He told me to take care of my family and just to remember to kick it from time to time with my boy and we'd be good.

I woke up as we descended out of the grapevine. Lee had the directions out and he was telling her which way to go. The sun was setting on the day and everything was beautiful. It felt like I was saying goodbye to the old me and hello to my new self. Lee told our momma she had to take the couch cause she snored too loud and neither one of us would get any sleep with her directly next to us. She sucked her teeth and said she would be back. When she left I asked Lee where he thought she was going. He said he saw a liquor store a block or so over. He said he was sure she was on her way there.

Lee took out the herbal tea, honey, and lemon. He asked me

how I was feeling. I told him I was excited and a little nervous. He said nervous was good, he told me to turn in early so that I was refreshed and energized for the morning. The audition wasn't until the afternoon but they wanted to get their super early so I needed to get in the bed. Lee fell asleep almost as soon as he laid down in his bed. I laid in my bed staring at the ceiling trying to imagine what my life would be like in the next week. I was going to go in there and give it my all. I'm going to riff like I've never riffed before. Old skool music played through my head as I laid there staring at the ceiling mentally practicing my performance. Around midnight I heard my momma stumble into the room. Lee woke up and listened to her as well. She was trying to be quiet as she bumped into things and tried to find her way to the couch. She was making noise for a long time when Lee cursed her out and told her to just get to sleep already. Our mother laughed and then she got quiet. I finally got sleepy and then I dreamed about Shay like I always do.

We got to the audition site **at eight o'clock** in the morning. The line was down the street. My momma got irritated cause she was under the impression that I was personally invited to this somewhat private audition. I told her not to sweat it cause no one here was better than me. I don't care how good these people tried to be they would never be as good as me.

When we finally got to the front of the line the girl at the desk barely looked at me as she asked me for my name and invitation. I gave her my name as my momma rummaged through her purse looking for the invitation. When half a minute passed and she was still looking I almost lost it. Lee was busy looking at some girl; he looked confused when he turned around. "What she looking for?"

My momma was cursing and then she dumped her entire purse on the ground as she went through everything. She made sure she had money for liquor and whatever she needed to keep her up. All of that spilled out of her purse. Her one job was to bring my invitation and she has failed me. My opportunity missed, this was my chance to be a star and now look! "My invitation," I said like it hurt.

"Oh," Lee reached in his back pocket. "She left it on the table. I grabbed it as we walked out of the door." Lee handed the invitation to me and then he returned his attention to the girl he was looking at.

Once again my brother has saved my life. I handed the invitation to the girl who looked annoyed as she watched my momma pick up her junk and throw it all back into her purse. In a monotone, the girl gave me my audition number and told me where to wait to be called. People were everywhere nervously pacing waiting for their chance. My momma shoved a hot cup of lemon water and honey in my hand. I looked at my cup; she gave me an embarrassed smile as she told me she forgot the tea bag back at the room. I leaned against the furthest wall away from her as I watched all the people moving about, going into the room, and coming out. Some people came out looking satisfied with their selves while others came out looking devastated. I made eye contact with one of the auditioners; she had long straight hair, and a few freckles. She smiled at me and I smiled back. Just when I decided I'd walk over and talk to her someone tapped my shoulder. "Novian," I turned around. "What are you doing all the way out here?" She smiled.

Torrie had on a white t-shirt that hung off her breast and stopped just above her belly button. Her jeans were ripped in all the right places and her brown skin took me back to yesterday. "Did you really follow me all the way out here?" I told my Johnson to calm down.

"More like you're following me," she followed my eyes as they raced all over her body.

"What are you doing here? You here to tease the Agent as well?" All she ever does is tease me. Get me to the point where I admit that I want her and then she recoils. I told myself to ignore her the next time I saw her anyways. She's always trying to put it in Shay's face that I'm weak for her. Shay's pretty but she's no Torrie. Torrie's got it all hips, thighs, breast, butt and it's all wrapped up in pretty even brown skin. All that and she has the voice of an angel, but an angel she's not. She's more like a vixen, or a harlot. I haven't exactly smashed her yet, but I know that when I do, I'm going to be in big trouble.

"I received an invitation just like you. I've come too far to hold back anything. This trip is not about teasing." She watched my eyes, and then she looked at my hair. "What's with the hair? You auditioning to be the newest member of Special Generation?"

"Ha! Ha! You're very funny looking like a Salt n Pepa reject."

She started to say something when the girl calling the auditioners to their fate called out, "one oh five! You're up next!"

Torrie's face turned innocent. All confidence was gone as she walked to the door. Torrie turned and looked at me she reached for the door. She mouthed, *wish me luck.* I smiled at her and shook my head no.

I was smiling to myself thinking about all the things I wanted to do to her when my momma's voice brought me back to the present. "What's she doing here?"

"Auditioning."

Torrie

"Don't forget the words! Don't forget the words!" I told myself as I tried to get my nerves in check.

"State your name," the balding white guy said as he watched me walk.

"Torrie Rowe," I cleared my throat.

He looked at his paper. "Oh right, you can sing and you can

dance." He didn't sound excited about me at all. "Look at the girl with the camera. Tell her your name, age, where you're from, and what you're going to sing for us." Could he be anymore dry? Ugh! I turned to the camera girl and did as I was told. "Before you sing let me give you one word of advice." I nodded at him. "The music industry is full of divas. The way the industry is heading you're going to see a lot of females taking off their clothes trying to sell their package. You could stand to lose some weight, but you've got a nice body, but so do so many other females. That's not what's going to take you anywhere. You my friend, you have an angelic face. You can glam up or glam down and be the girl next door. Hold on to the innocence in your face. Now sing!" I sang from the bottom of my toes. He didn't seem impressed and I know I did well. He wrote stuff down while I stood there looking stupid. "Oh yeah and you said you could dance. Show me something." Crap! I wasn't prepared to dance. I quickly did a couple of sloppily thrown together moves. He sighed and said he'd be in contact. I wanted to cry as I walked out of the audition. Novian is going to want to know how it went. I took a deep breath as I walked. Novian was up next and I wished I could sit in and watch how his performance goes. I waited close to the door trying to eavesdrop.

"What are you doing?" His nasty and raggedy momma said to me. She smelled like alcohol and sweat. His momma was probably pretty a long time ago, right now she is not cute at all. All of her hair was pulled back into a bun. She was trying to look decent instead of her normal haggard appearance.

"I'm rooting for Novian."

"Yeah right, I bet you bombed in there and you're looking to see if he does better than you. Let me save you the suspense. Novian's going to nail it. He's going to sign with this Agent and then he's going to get a recording contract. Novian's going to be a star, and you're not!"

People were looking at us otherwise I would've cursed her

out. I hate this lady; she really does get on my nerves. I went over to the table where the girl who only knows one volume level was sitting. She was telling the latecomers that they missed the audition and to call the Agency to inquire about future auditions. I took one of the extra pens and I wrote down the phone number to my cousin's place. I was staying with her for the next two days before I headed home to Berkeley on the bus. Novian was coming out as I walked back. I put the paper with my cousin's number on it in his hands while he hugged his momma. I used my hand to tell him to call me. He smiled and then he returned his attention to his momma who was acting like Novian got signed right on the spot.

I walked back to my bus stop, and said thank you when my bus pulled up right behind me. I didn't feel like waiting in this LA sun and heat. I rode the bus back to Adina's place. She pulled up on me as I walked down to her street towards her apartment. She excitedly told me to get in. "How did it go?"

"Fine I guess, I doubt this turns into too much of anything either. Guess who was there?" I smiled at Adina.

"You know I hate guessing." She parked and then she turned her body to me.

"Novian was there with his brother."

Adina gasped, "Lee was there? How did he look? Did you talk to him? Did you tell him I live out here now?"

"I didn't talk to Lee, and I guess he looked fine. I gave Novian your number and I told him to call me."

"Good thing I just paid the bill to get it cut back on. You think he's going to call?"

"Novian's going to call me, you want me to tell him to bring his brother?"

"They're coming over my place?"

"Yes, I need to relieve some stress. And you need to live out your high school fantasy."

"My place isn't ready for that kind of company."

"I'll help you, let's go!" I said hurrying out of the car.

Adina's place wasn't bad; she was just lazy about putting her clothes away sometimes. I get it, she works and then she goes on audition after audition.

When the phone rang she got so excited. It was Novian and he was playing mister nice guy. That's always been his problem, he's too nice. I like when a man walks in and takes charge. When a man owns the room without saying a word. I could see Novian getting to the place where he is that man some day. As for today, he's still just a boy. Fortunately for him, I need to be with someone who makes me feel like a Goddess rather than a mere peasant.

Novian's drunk of a momma was gone in the rental car, so Adina and I picked Novian and Lee up. Novian was quiet in the car as he stared out of the window. Everyone noticed so Adina asked him why he was so quiet and he said he's never been to LA or Hollywood before. So Adina drove her little putt-putt car around showing them everything. We parked so that they could walk on the Hollywood stars and have a look around. Adina kept smiling in Lee's face and he seemed receptive to her advances. Novian would look at me from time to time, but then I could see him feel guilty about looking at me. He's probably still with that ordinary girl. I don't care about any of that. I just want to get served and I'm hoping he's at least decent. Lee bought everyone burritos at the taco truck and then he and Novian went into the liquor store. As Adina and I waited in the car Adina got so excited and she thanked me for making this happen.

When we got to Adina's place the guys sat on the couch while we went in the kitchen. They bought gin and orange juice. Adina said she was taking Lee into her bedroom. Then she bumped me and told me to have fun. I sat on the couch and then I handed Novian his cup.

He thanked me, and then he sat his cup down on the coffee table. "You're not thirsty?"

"Not at this exact moment." He was leaning forward almost on the edge of the couch. "How'd your audition go?"

"Great! I expected him to call by now. How about you?"

"He told me," Novian gestured like the guy making his voice like the man. "You're a good looking kid. Cut that crap off of your head. Do some sit-ups and more sit-ups. Dial up the sexy, play down the gimmicks."

I touched his dyed orange streak in the front of his modest almost too curly high top fade. "You've got really nice hair, I bet it took a lot to make it look like this."

He laughed, "man, Shay fried it with the blow dryer."

I knew better than to roll my eyes at the mention of his girlfriend. "I bet if you cut this off and start over you could grow your hair pretty long."

"It definitely grows fast," he rubbed his head.

I took a big gulp of my drink. Novian picked up his cup and stared at the liquor. I chugged my whole cup, then I told him to do the same, he shook his head no as he put his cup down. I filled up my cup again; eventually he poured his cup out in the kitchen. After another big chug I put my cup down. My lips were starting to feel a little numb. I put my hand in Novian's hair. "Massaging your scalp will help your hair grow." I looked at his face and he closed his eyes liking the feeling of my hands in his hair. So I got up on my knees and put my breast in his face. I rubbed his head as he stared at my breast. He slowly put his arms around me like he was ready for me to tell him to stop. When I kept rubbing his head he moved his hands to my butt, he squeezed and then he moved to my breast. His lips were almost on my left nipple. "Novian, are you going to call me when he calls you?"

"Huh? Yeah sure," he said getting back to his task. Normally he fights harder to be good to his girlfriend. I decided that Novian needed something to look forward to. I wouldn't let him enter me, but I let him eat dessert. I swear this was his first time cause I had to give him direction. He didn't automatically know anything. When it was my turn his eyes crossed and he watched me blow his mind. I guess him and Shay only get down in the missionary position. He couldn't contain himself. The walls in this place are super thin, so we could hear everything that was happening in the room next door. Lee was definitely experienced and from the sound of the rhythm in there, he knew what he was doing. When Novian acted like he wanted to keep going, I told him I was tired. A bold faced lie, but I needed him on the hook.

Chapter 2

Novian

"I like you kid, I see you took my advice and you cut your hair. How's the workout coming along?"

"One hundred push ups, two hundred sit ups!" I smiled proud of myself.

"That's good, however I want you to feel the burn. Make it three hundred and five hundred. Don't forget about your legs and your lower body. You'll look ridiculous otherwise."

"Ok," I smiled big.

He adjusted in his seat as he sat back. "I like you kid. You definitely have a marketable quality. We're going to make a demo to shop you around. In six months if I don't see evidence of you working out, I will drop you like a hot potato." He looked down at the papers on his desk. "I need you to prepare five songs, but we'll only use three for your demo." He moved his finger up and down the list. "I need to find a studio for you to record in. Do you have a place to stay out here?"

"Here? How long will this take?" My momma rudely interrupted.

He opened his hands, "it depends on his work ethic. I'm willing to put a little extra in my budget for the studio. Since I will be putting up the money, I will own the demo. Once we get him signed if he wants to buy me out for the demo he can. Sound good?"

"You still ain't said how long. Every time we come out here it cost us money. We can't just lay up in LA like that. We got jobs!"

"We do?" I looked at her with a smirk.

"Shut up!" She said under her breath.

He picked up his paper, "I'm familiar with the pricing of the studios out here. You're in Northern California, let me see what studios we can get out that way." He scanned the list and called out names. My mother suggested some studio and he found it on the list. "I'll need to have my secretary call and confirm pricing for studio time. I'll call you with a name in a couple of days."

"That's it? You could've had this conversation over the phone." My momma said all huffy.

"Yes, but I needed to see him. See what his physical progress looks like. It's not enough to know how to sing. You've got to be a package deal. As long as he continues to work on it, he'll be fine." Then his eyes went to my hair. "What are you doing here?"

"I'm growing my hair out."

"Why?"

"Women love men with nice hair, so I'm growing it out."

"I don't know about that."

"Just watch, it's going to work for me."

He sighed then he pushed a contract towards me. "This repeats everything that we've said. I will own the demo until you buy me out. Sign and then I'll call with a studio near you."

My momma pinched me as I signed, "what is wrong with you?"

She gave me an evil smile, "don't you want to have someone look at that first?"

"Someone like whom? You?"

"Lee could look at it."

"Lee's not a lawyer, it'll be fine." I finished signing. "I look forward to your call."

"OH SO YOU SO SMART NOW? YOU KNOW WHAT SHOULD AND SHOULDN'T BE IN THEM CONTRACTS! If my life ain't taught you nothing you don't sign without knowing what you're looking at!"

I stood up and got ready to leave, she wasn't going to stop. She was going to keep going and I didn't want this here. "You want to talk about this, we can do that in the car. It's over, I signed and I'm leaving."

Why did I say that? This woman yelled most of the car ride home from LA. Fortunately her voice gave out and I had peace for the last two hours of our five-hour drive.

Instead of taking me home before she dropped the car off she took me with her. She pulled over on the street and took out a pen. She wrote on a paper bag. "When we get to the gate ask for Brad, if they say he ain't there tell them you need Darius. Tell them we're returning Brad's car."

She drove up the hill in Hayward like she knew this road like the back of her hands. When we pulled up to the gate a guy looked in the car. "What do you want?"

"We're here for Brad."

"Who are you?"

"I'm Novian and this my momma Ursula."

"Ursula? Why you so quiet?" He shined the light in her face.

She angrily pointed at me, "she been fussing."

"You know Brad can't see you right now. His wife is home."

My momma slapped the steering wheel then she looked for the bag she wrote on earlier. She wrote her question down. "She came back?" My momma started crying. Then she pointed to the other name. "She wants to see Darius."

"He not gon' tell you nothing different." The guy called someone and then he said he was coming.

My momma was crying and carrying on. She couldn't say much but I think I understood the story. This tall big guy came out of the shadows looking annoyed. "Ursula why are you here now? You always trying to start mess."

"She came to return the car."

Darius looked at me, he smirked. "So this is the boy you been bragging about?" He stared at my face. "I guess it could be true, but you know how it goes. Innocent until proven guilty." Then he looked at my momma, "stop crying you already know." When she kept crying he sighed loud. "Move over, I'll take you home."

The sound of my mother's tears were the only sounds in the car. So just in case I doubted it before, whoever this Brad guy is must be her sugar daddy. She had to have hooked up with him when she looked like something worth noticing. I told the guy how to get to my place, and then he looked back at my momma and asked her if she moved. She shook her head no and then she climbed in the front from the back. I stood there watching as they drove away. Her tears annoyed me, and I wrestled with feeling bad for her.

Shay said she was going to come over as soon as she got off of work. Lee was in the kitchen washing dishes when I walked in the door. He asked me how it went and I smiled at him. My irritation lifted as I told him about our meeting. His smile dwindled a little when I told him I signed Alec's contract for my demo. He agreed that he was not an entertainment lawyer. However, he said I needed to have all contracts reviewed before I signed them. I don't make enough money as a security guard to afford much of nothing. How am I supposed to afford a lawyer? We talked for a little bit then the phone rang. Lee answered it and then he smiled. When he asked what was up with her cousin I knew it was Torrie. I didn't have a lot of time to talk to Torrie before Shay got here. So I told Lee I'd get the cousin's number for him later.

Torrie said hi and then she wanted to know what happened with Alec. I told her that he wants me to record a demo. Torrie started breathing hard. Alec hadn't called her back or returned any of her phone calls. Then she asked me what I was about to do. I told her my girl was coming over and then we were going to chill. "Ditch her and come hangout with me."

"Sike! I'm in no mood to be teased tonight."

"Who's teasing? I'm ready, are you?" She made her voice sound all sexy.

"If you're ready tonight, you'll be ready tomorrow. Or the day after that, I'm not worried."

"Seriously Novian? I'm ready why you playing?"

"I've known you since what? Middle school, and you've always been a tease. Junior year you finally let me suck on a titty, Senior year I got to put a finger in. Now you finally gave me some head and I guess I'm supposed to drop my faithful and loyal girl to dry hump you? Get real! If you serious about doing this hit me up tomorrow. Otherwise, PEACE! I don't have time for the games." I could hear her breathing but she wasn't saying anything. "Talk to you later Torrie." Then I hung up. I jumped off the couch celebrating my victory. Girls be thinking just because we want in, we supposed to bend over backwards to get in.

Lee came out of his room with his things to take a shower. He had his robe on, slippers, towel over his shoulder, soap on a rope, and toothbrush in his mouth. Looking like someone twice his age, he stood looking at me like I was the crazy one. I replayed my conversation with Torrie to him. Lee smiled and then he bumped me with his elbow to say I was the man. After a few minutes in the bathroom, Lee turned on the shower. Shay knocked on the door just as Lee started to belt out his tune. Shay smiled and hugged me, and then she listened to my brother sing. "Aren't you glad you don't have to go against him?"

"Ha! Ha! That was so funny I forgot to laugh." Then I went in for a kiss.

"How'd it go today?"

"He doesn't see my vision for my hair, but he's white what he know? He told me to increase the intensity on my workouts." Then I picked Shay up, "and he wants me to record a demo."

"Really?"

"Yep! We about to do this!" I said excitedly, "you spending the night?"

"You know I can't."

"You eighteen now, what's the problem?"

"I still have to respect my momma's rules. She'd have a fit if she knew I was here right now. I've only got an hour."

I kissed Shay, "that's ok. As soon as I get a place you coming to live with me."

"You're not going to be worried about me when you start hanging out with celebrities."

"I'm always going to love you, no matter what." Then I kissed her. Shay is the only real thing in my life. With the exception of the random groupies, I tell Shay everything about my life.

She knows all about my momma, how she's chased a singing career her whole life. How she was married at one point to Lee and my sister Leona's father. How she tried for years to be content with their family and the life she had. The stage kept calling her. Singing for her is like breathing for everyone else. She left her family to return to the stage. She left her family to go back to what she loved. Her quest for stardom came at a price. I don't know who my father is, and I know her to be drunk more than I've ever seen her sober. Lee tells me stories about her when they were a family and I try to imagine her as a loving and caring parent. That's just not our reality. The only thing she's done for me is teach me to sing and push for me to have the career she never did. Lee has been my parent, my caregiver, my support, and my family since he's known about me.

I remember meeting Lee for the first time. I was sitting in a chair swinging my feet at the police station. The way Lee looked at me when my momma pointed to me. I'll never forget the look I had never seen on anyone's face towards me. It was the look of concern, the look of love. I was about four years old and Lee was eighteen. The age I am today, I can't imagine assuming the responsibility of a child at my age. I'm so grateful that my brother is always a better man than me. I would be so lost without him.

I've told Shay about it all, she never made me feel bad about any of it. She told me about when her mother died and how lost she felt. I could relate to that feeling. She said she was angry when her father started dating. She was even angrier when he remarried. She said she was passively angry with her stepmom as if it was her fault her momma was gone. Then one day Shay got sick and her stepmom left work to come get her. Her stepmom stayed with her and took her to the hospital because she was convinced something was wrong even though her father kept saying she only had a cold. Her father was complaining about the hospital bill until they told him she had pneumonia. Shay said her stepmom almost lost her job behind staying with her and making sure she was ok. Shay and I bonded over our losses and our feelings of uncertainty. I love this girl from the bottom of everything that I am.

Torrie

All the anger and frustration I felt earlier subsided. I was surprisingly in a state of euphoria. Novian came over here strong and determined. It was time for me to put up or shut up. Well I thought I was going to put it on him and have him eating out of the palm of my hands. Boy was I wrong! This fool tapped a nerve I didn't know existed. Novian had me over here folded up like a pretzel unable to move and calling out to God or any power beyond my own to help me live to see another moment cause this *right here*! I've found my crack! I wasn't looking for it, but man did I find it. I laid there with my face buried in the pillow while Novian laid on top of me catching his breath. My leg was still spasming and at first it scared me until I realized the feeling that came along with it was a good one. I thought doing this was going to make him a slave to me. I didn't expect this to backfire on me.

When Novian backed up he smacked my naked behind, then he took his condom off. He tied it up and put it in the trash. I wanted to go again, but suddenly I was afraid to ask. I told myself to stop acting scared, this is just Novian. The guy who's had a crush on you since you were kids. He should be feeling like I feel right now, not me. I sat up and then I reached for my spiral notebook. I clicked my pen and then I let my hands do what they do. Novian watched me as I wrote a poem. I wanted to be embarrassed, but then he'd know the power he possessed over me at this moment. I acted like he wasn't sitting there as I continued to write what was now pouring out of me. Two pages front and back later Novian patiently waited for me to finish. Then he took my notebook from me. Normally I would fight someone to the death over my notebook. Even my mom who ain't got it all knows, DON'T TOUCH MY NOTEBOOK! But like I said Novian just did something to me that rendered me meek and mild. He carefully read everything then he smiled and said they were songs. I corrected him and said they were poems. "What do you think music is? It's poetry turned in to music." He kept his eyes on my notebook. "I had no idea that you were such an amazing lyricist."

I blushed so hard I thought my face was going to catch on fire. "You really like it?"

"This is stupid fresh yo! All you need are beats." I leaned forward and kissed him. We already had sex and he gave me a compliment. I wanted him again! When our kiss kept going he pulled back. "I only brought one jimmy."

"Can't you go to the store?"

"Naw! I'll just go home." He tried to stand.

"No!" I grabbed his arm. "It's ok, just pull out."

"I don't..." I jumped on him and kissed him.

I was so lost in how well I was working him that I was completely gone. He was telling me to stop, he even tried to move me, but I clamped down on him cause this new feeling was so good to me. Completely covered in sweat I looked at Novian who looked so conflicted. He looked a little mad and that was when I realized I didn't let him pull out. "I'm sorry!"

"Get off of me! You did that on purpose!"

"No, no I didn't Novian. I'm sorry!"

Novian stumbled when he stood up; his legs were as weak as mine. "I can't believe this! I can't have no babies right now, especially by you!"

"I don't want a baby right now either!"

"You could've fooled me!" He took a deep breath. "Torrie I swear to God if Shay finds out about this I'm going to get you!"

My good feeling was dwindling. My body was recovering faster than I wanted it to. "Novian please! We can talk about this later." I turned my back to him before he saw my tears. "I've never done it without a jimmy, I forgot."

Novian was quiet for a minute, "are you crying?"

"No!" My tears betrayed me.

Novian grabbed my shoulder and turned me towards him. I tried to hide my face but sobs kept escaping my lips. "You're crying! Torrie doesn't cry! Torrie is a cold piece of work. I thought Torrie didn't own tears! I'm sorry!" He sat on the bed and put his arms around me. "I'm not that messed up! But now that I see you're crying I guess you weren't plotting on me."

I could stay like this all day! His arms were strong but gentle and I was eating it all up. "I'm sorry Novian I really am."

He kissed my forehead, "okay."

I glanced at the clock and we didn't have much time left before people started coming home. We got dressed and then I grabbed my backpack. I packed things for over night. I didn't know where I was staying tonight, but I knew I was not staying here. I love my cousins and family, but sometimes it's too many people in this little townhouse. Novian asked where I was about to go, I shrugged cause I really didn't know. He looked me in my eyes and said if I could behave myself I could come with him. I chewed back my excitement and refused to release my smile. I let a very unimpressed acceptance of his invitation out. Novian put his arm around my neck and told me to stop faking. He said he saw me losing my mind cause I didn't expect him to get me like he got me. "You are a lot better than I thought you'd be. Don't go getting all big headed."

"You cried," he smiled at me.

"Shut up Novian! If I find out you told anyone I cried I'm going to tell your girlfriend every detail about today!"

"What's wrong with crying, girls cry all of the time."

"Not me! Weak females cry, not me."

I asked Novian if he had more condoms at his place. He smiled and said yes, my body started tingling at the thought of it. Novian said we couldn't sit together on the bus, just in case we saw someone who knew us or his girlfriend. People got on the bus and then they got off. I followed Novian off of the bus and to his apartment. I asked him who he lived here with cause it was only one bedroom. He said he lived with his brother. He slept on the pullout bed in the couch for now. He said as soon as he can afford it he was going to get a place for him and his girl. I felt disappointed that he didn't think about me like that.

When his brother came home I was in their kitchen cooking while Novian worked out. "What are you doing?"

"You should be hungry, I'm making dinner."

He looked at Novian who was in a zone and completely tuning us out. "How long you been here?"

"Novian came over my place after he got off of work. We've been hanging out all day."

"How's your cousin doing?"

"She's missing you, she's waiting on you to give her a call."

"I lost her number, I told knuckle head to get her number from you."

"I can call her right now if you want?"

"Hold on," he disappeared into his bedroom. "I don't have long distance on my phone. Write down her number and as soon as I have another calling card I'll call her."

Then their phone rang, Lee answered it. Then he told Novian the phone was for him. I tried to pretend like I wasn't listening, but I wondered if it was his girlfriend and if it was if he was going to send me out on the first thing smoking. Novian got excited and he scurried to find a pen and paper. He wrote excitedly and then he said thank you a few times. When he hung up he said that Alec booked him for studio time at *Silent Chaos* in Oakland. Novian was so excited as he went over which buses to take to get there tomorrow after he got off of work. Novian excitedly went back to his workout and Lee went into his bedroom. I called out that dinner was ready when I put the pot on a towel in the middle of the table. "Spaghetti? You watch her make this?" Lee said eyeing my food.

"She didn't go to the bathroom if that's what you mean." Novian sat down, "you mix your sauce with your noodles."

"What's wrong with that?"

Lee touched Novian shaking his head at him. "It looks good, thank you for making this meal for us."

"Naw, what was he going to say?"

"I prefer to mix my own sauce and noodles on my plate is all. That's the way Lee makes it."

"Say thank you Novian," Lee was trying to redirect his brother.

"Thank you for cooking for us." Novian ate a little, but he was too excited. He and his brother were talking about music and the songs he was going to record. "Show me that scale again, I want to use it."

Lee opened his mouth and I was floored. I didn't know he could sing like that. His voice was *WAY* better than Novian's. "Why aren't you out here trying to get signed?"

"I like driving buses too much," then he smiled at me.

"Seriously, your voice is amazing." Novian cut his eyes at me.

"All gifts aren't meant to be shared. Besides there are thousands maybe even millions of people on this earth with beautiful voices and ranges. Not everyone is looking to be a star. Some just want to enjoy their gift in peace."

Novian sucked his teeth, "and some people are too afraid to try."

"We have a living example of someone who has chased that dream their entire life. I'd rather live my life then waste it waiting for something that will never come."

"That's her story, it doesn't have to be yours."

"You really want to talk about this right now in front of her?" Lee nodded at me. Novian picked up his fork and started chewing. "Practice your breathing and you'll get it. Keep your eyes open little brother. Your journey doesn't have to end up like anyone else's."

"Thanks," Novian's energy was completely gone.

Lee finished eating and then he said he would be back later. Novian kept his eyes on his plate as he stared hard. I reached out and touched his hand. "Is it your momma?" Novian shook his head no like he didn't want to talk about it. I rubbed his hand, "my momma is literally mentally retarded." Novian looked at me, no doubt trying to remember if he's ever met her. "Apparently some men think it's funny to sleep with a retarded girl cause she don't know no better. We stayed with my Grandmomma until she had a stroke and died. Now we live in that townhouse with my uncle and his family. Sometimes it's too much, cause my momma don't always understand when they're making fun of her. She doesn't get their sarcastic comments. Then she have her own issues. I started writing when I was little cause everything used to bother me. Shoot! It still does."

"But I've met your momma."

"Barely, I don't let her have long conversations with anybody. It's not like you can tell by looking at her."

"Does that mean that any kids you have can be retarded?"

"It's a possibility I guess."

He stared at me, "you better not be pregnant."

Novian

The building wasn't big and it was all white. Something about the white paint made it stand out and sparkle right here in the middle of all of these buildings. There were bars on the windows and a screen door. I banged on the door and a big guy came to the door. "Yeah?"

"I have an appointment."

"Who are you?"

"Novian Murphy, I was sent by the Talented Tannibaum Agency. I'm supposed to record my demo here."

The guy opened the gate and stood to the side so I could enter. He looked me up and down then he mumbled, "New Edition wanna be's." I looked around the entry way and it was all white, but not like the bright white outside. When we turned the corner everything in the building looked way nicer than the outside let on. I followed the big guy who wore only a tank top and jeans. His arms were huge and he was solid every which way around. His face said don't even think about messing with me. "This is Novian, he's our three-thirty."

The other guy who wasn't as big but also had a don't mess with me look on his face looked at their list. "Right, you've got three hours today and seventeen more hours to schedule. Did you bring music, or are we creating music?"

"You can do that?" I was stuck taking in the whole place. It's way bigger in here than it looked.

26

"Isn't that the point of coming to a studio? Otherwise you can make demos at home on a boom box. Don't ask stupid questions." The second guy said.

I took out my tape; "I have the music on my tape. I recorded it from my brother's record. I don't know how we should do this."

The second guy looked annoyed, "this has to be your first time in a studio. Give me the tape."

The big guy watched me to see how I took the second guy's disregard for me. I mean, I could have pride or I could get this demo done. It's not like he was wrong, this is my first time in a studio. He just didn't have to call me out on it. I handed my tape to him; he flipped the tape over and over. Then he stood up, he told the big guy I was going to be on board three. I followed him to the right and we went through a door. There was a master board, which covered a big table with two chairs in front of it. Behind the table was a recording booth with all the stuff on the wall to make it sound proof. I couldn't believe I was actually here. I tried to hold back my excitement, but I was grinning like a stupid cat. The guy looked at my face and started laughing. "So what, this is my first time in the studio. I don't even care."

"Well get used to it, if this is the career you want, you're going to spend a lot of time in places like this. This is where all the hard work starts. You record then you promote, then you record some more."

He played my tape, he wrote down the song titles and original artist without me telling him. He asked me if I wanted my music to sound exactly the same or slightly different. I said slightly different cause there was no point in sounding exactly the same. Once he had everything written down, another guy came hurrying in. "Sorry I'm late." This guy wasn't like the other two. He seemed like an everyday person like me.

"This is Novian, I wrote down your notes for you. Make sure

you log your time. His time started twenty-three minutes ago. He has three hours. He needs to schedule his next appointment before he leaves, and he only has seventeen hours left. Got it?"

"Got it," then the guy hung his jacket on the hook next to mine. "I'm Swift," he stuck his hand out to shake mine.

"Novian, nice to meet you." I looked at the other guy, "I'm not working with you?"

The guy smirked at me, "you can't afford me. Swift's got you and he's almost as good as me."

Swift shrugged him off, "thanks for the vote of confidence." He told me not to pay Dame's jabs too much attention. Then he went over my list, "alright. So I suggest that we spend these first three hours getting your music together. You really think you're going to get five songs out in 20 hours?"

"20 hours isn't enough time?"

"Depends on you, even some of the best people I know need more than 20 hours. We'll see how you do."

Swift recreated the music on his keyboard. He looked at my list; he didn't even need to hear the song. He had it locked down in his memory I guess. He played each instrument on his keyboard and eventually we had instrumentals to all of my songs. I could tell Swift knew his stuff cause he even asked me what key I was going to sing each one in and if there were any riff progressions so that he could play that out in the music. I felt like I was in the right place for real. When my time was up, Dame came back. He said he needed our booth for the next client. Then he asked how it went. I told him it went good and that we had all the music together. I shook Swift's hand and I told him I'd see him in a couple of days. When I walked out of the booth I saw that guy Darius and a whole bunch of other guys. They were drinking and making noise. Darius pointed at me and a few guys looked at me. Darius then waived me over. "You're

Ursula's son right?"

"Yes," I didn't know which way this was going to go.

"This is the one she be talking about all the time?" The big dope looking one asked.

Darius looked at him like he was stupid, "I swear sometimes. Who else?"

The idiot smiled at me, "you ever heard of Mr. MC?"

"Of course," who hadn't? He put Oakland on the map for real. Well him and a few other artists.

"What you working on?" Darius asked interrupting whatever the dope was going to say next.

"I'm recording my demo."

"Who they got you working with?"

"Swift."

"Swift is cool, but you must be working with a small budget. How many hours you got?"

"20."

"For how many songs?"

"5."

Darius frowned like that was ridiculous. "When are you coming back?"

"Friday night," I didn't know what was wrong with my time, but I guess I was about to find out.

"I'll be back, I want to see if you're as good as Ursula says you are."

******

"This is it?" Lee said looking at the building unenthusiastically.

"Wait until you see the inside." I said as I excitedly got out of his car. I knocked on the door, and the big guy opened the door again. He asked who my brother was and then he let us in.

There was a big guy with a kid standing on either side of him. His skin was as black as night, and he looked mad for no reason. Like he was probably mad all of the time. The little boys were quiet as they stood next to him. He was looking at the list and standing in front of Dame. All three of them looked at Lee and I when we entered the room, then the black guy looked at Dame to explain who we were. Dame pointed at me, "that's Ursula's son. I don't know who the other guy is."

"My name is Novian, and this is my brother Lee."

"Why should I care who you are?" His voice was so deep it seemed like it rumbled the building.

"I'm just saying, my name is Novian. My momma doesn't define who I am."

He squinted his eyes at me, "so you're saying you don't want to be affiliated with Ursula?"

"I'm saying she don't define who I am. I..." Lee grabbed my arm.

"Please excuse my little brother. You know these kids miss the big picture half of the time."

Dame and the other guy looked at the black guy who was looking between Lee and I. "Right, well consider this your first lesson in hard knocks little idiot. I'm cancelling your studio time today and charging you for one hour as a cancellation fee for being an idiot."

"What? You can't do that!"

"I can and I did." The guy said watching me for a reaction.

"I CAN'T BELIEVE…." Lee jerked my arm telling me to calm down.

"When can we come back?" Lee asked.

"You can stay, that little punk can't come back while I'm here."

Swift came out of studio three, he looked at my face and then everyone in the room. "What's wrong?"

"That one has no respect for nothing. I'm cancelling his session for today. He owes me an hour for the short notice, and he needs to reschedule."

Swift whistled, "that's cold Malcolm. Let me get my schedule. Can he come with me to reschedule?"

"When he starts running his mouth send him out. Doug will throw him out if you need him to."

The big guy smiled, "he ain't going to be that stupid."

"Come on," Swift told us as he walked back to his studio. When we walked in he closed the door. "Don't be stupid Novian."

"Who is that guy?"

"That's Malcolm, he owns this studio."

"How he know my momma?"

"Ursula comes and sings backup and educates all kinds of artists in this studio. Everybody around here likes her, she's crazy but who isn't?"

"Why Darius tell everybody she's my momma. Even you

knew who I was talking about without me saying who specifically."

"Cause Ursula was going to be your key to fitting in around here. You just messed that up and put yourself on Malcolm's radar. Wrong move young person but you'll see."

"So I'll just go to another studio, this isn't the only studio in the Bay Area."

Swift smiled, "if you want to be dumb and try. The world is your oyster, go discover it. I'm willing to put money on it that you'll be back."

"Who's this Malcolm guy, for real?" Lee asked.

Swift looked at the door like it was going to open at some point. "Stay out of his way, don't get on his bad side. He has no patience for dumbness at all. If you were thinking of manning up, take a pass with that one. You already stepped off the curb wrong with him. Everything you do now he's going to look at it as if you're bucking up at him. Especially when he has his kids, stay out of his way. He's protective like any dad would be when it comes to them. You chose the wrong day and the wrong time to try to exert yourself." Then Swift told us to come back tomorrow at eleven.

When we walked out of the studio Malcolm was talking to Darius. They stopped talking and looked at me. I walked up to them, "I want to apologize for the misunderstanding." I stuck my hand out to shake Malcolm's. He looked at my hand and then he tilted his head to the side.

Swift slapped his face to say I was an idiot; and then Lee said goodnight as he pushed me out of the door. I really don't get how I was wrong. Lee and I went back and forth all night about it. True, I jumped the gun a little about my momma. Now that I think back on it, it wasn't a negative that he referred to me as Ursula's son. However, I tried to apologize and he looked at me like I was the weakest person ever.

The next day when Lee and I pulled up Darius was outside leaning against a sparkling beamer. He watched me as I approached them; he asked me what was wrong with me. Lee told me not to try to explain anymore, to close my mouth and listen before I spoke. So it was now time to put that advice into action. This studio was such a minor stop in the big scheme of things. One day I'd be rich and famous and I wouldn't have to deal with stuff like this. I told Darius it was all a misunderstanding. He told me the same thing Lee was telling me the night before. To close my mouth and open my ears. Doug opened the door for us, Dame checked us in, and then Swift took us into studio three. Darius and Lee sat in the chair and couch getting comfortable as Swift and I went over which song I was going to work on first. My heart started pounding as I walked into the booth. This was my moment, I finally made it. I put the headphones on and then I waited for the music. Everyone was looking at me waiting for me to sing. I opened my mouth and I choked. I was dry, flat, and just plain ole horrible in the first bar. Swift opened his mouth and let it hang open. Darius put his hand up to his head and grabbed his temples. Lee told me to stop. Then he came in the booth. He told me to take deep breaths and to remember that I own this moment. It was time for me to perform; I needed to get out of my head and to leave all that other nonsense at the door. I thanked my brother and then we started over. I could see all of their eyes afraid to hear what was going to come out of my mouth. "Sunshine, blues skies, please go away! My girl has found another and gone away..." There it was! There was my groove. My rhythm, my sound! I could see Swift nodding his head as I sang. Swift stopped me at the three-hour mark and told me we had to stop cause he had another client coming in. As I got my stuff, Swift told me not to ever waste time with insecurities like I started off with. He said he was about to cancel everything and send me packing. Darius said I did well and that my momma is going to be so proud of me. Then he asked me why she wasn't here with me. I hadn't told her. He told me it could only help to get my momma on board while I was at the studio.

******

"Please Novian!" She clasped her hands begging me.

My eyes were still crossing from the head game she just put on me. I knew Torrie was holding out on me. I let my head fall back on the couch as the memories of what just happened danced around my mind. Torrie was begging me to take her to the studio with me. Now I'm asking myself what my name is. She's talking but I'm still recovering. To say Torrie is a freak is an understatement. I will never say she doesn't pay attention to detail.

I exhaled and then I told her she better be invisible while we were there. The owner didn't like me and he was difficult at times just because he could be. I've lost three hours messing around with him. I get it punctuality is important to him. It's never been my strong suit. I can't wait until this part is over.

We got cleaned up and then we hurried out of the door. Someone was smiling down on me, the bus was on time. Torrie rode on the front of the bus and I rode in the back. I don't know what that girl just did to me, but I can't wait for her to do it again.

Doug asked who Torrie was through the screen door. "My other girl."

Doug sucked his teeth then he opened the door. Torrie's eyes got big as she looked around the inside. Dame looked up then he sat back in his chair. "Who's this?" Doug told him what I said, and then Dame looked Torrie over. "You sing too?"

Torrie smiled with her shy girl put on. "How can you tell?"

"The same way I can tell you're trying to figure everything around here out." Then he looked at me, "you've got yourself a real vixen."

"What? Why would you call me that?"

He looked Torrie up and down, "just telling him what I see."

Swift came out of studio three, he looked confused when he looked at Torrie then he looked at me. "You ready?"

Torrie

I blinked my eyes when I saw Swift walking towards us. He was just as handsome as the last time I saw him. Swift is a good guy, so good that when he found out I lied about my age he dumped me. He was mad at me saying he was not that guy. The guy who enjoys taking advantage of little girls. I was only fifteen then, but I told him I was almost nineteen. He disappeared into thin air. I couldn't find him for nothing. When Novian went into the booth I could see him battling with himself on whether to speak to me. "I'm eighteen now, as of a few weeks ago actually. I've got a California ID to prove it."

"It's probably fake," he grumbled.

I reached in my purse, "here." I handed it to him while Novian focused on getting ready.

"You're here with Novian," he handed my ID back to me. His conflict was visible all over his face.

"He got a girlfriend, we're just friends."

"I've already had you, I'm not looking for a fun time. Groupies come to this studio all of the time."

"Ok, so what are you looking for?"

"The real deal, come find me when you're ready for the real thing."

"I can't just abandon Novian. I do love him," what a difference two and a half weeks can make. I was only supposed to be using him to find a way to promote myself. I never should've gave him none. He went from Novian. To oh my freaking GOD **NOVIAN**! Like I've been asking myself if I would actually have his baby. When I know there's no way I can have a baby right now.

"Guess you'll have to choose. I've got work to do." Then he turned his back to me.

I sat back quietly weighing my options. Who am I kidding? Of course I choose Swift. He had a car and his own place. I bet I could move in with him. I need to create my own demo, and focus on my career. Swift is the logical choice, but Novian. Novian is good sex, and a totally different connection. I can choose Swift with my head, my heart chooses Novian. Even though Novian won't care anyways. He acts like Shay is so great! She's plain and beneath ME! Shay better be glad Swift came up, I was about to take her man.

Novian barely laid down the track for his fifth song. He threw it together and slapped it on the tape. Swift handed Novian two tapes and wished him luck with his demo. Then he handed both of us business cards.

When we walked outside a guy was leaning against a Beamer waiting for someone. Novian told me to wait and he went over to the guy. They spoke lowly and then the guy looked at me. They talked for a minute then Novian walked back to me. He was scrunching up his nose and rubbing the back of his head. He said he was going to take off with the guy and he'd get back to me later. I looked at Novian like he had to be kidding. He reached in his pocket and gave me a bus transfer to get home. He kissed my forehead and told me I understood. The guy smirked at me and then he got in the car to wait for Novian. I grabbed Novian's jacket and asked him why he would leave me? Novian removed my hand and told me he'd catch me later. I stood there stunned as he walked away from me. He got in the car and they drove away.

I told myself not to cry. I wasn't going to cry about this. Novian's not nobody worth my tears. I didn't want to go home, but I had nowhere to go. I turned back around and I knocked on the door. They big guy came to the door and asked me what I wanted. I asked him to let me talk to Swift. The big guy slammed the door in my face. I hung my head and walked to the bus stop. I don't know who Novian thinks he is! Just because he has an agent and I don't doesn't mean he's better than me. How dare he treat me like a groupie when he's been panting after me for years.

When the bus pulled up Novian's momma was getting off. I sucked my teeth and stared at her. When she saw me she spit at me and then she walked towards the building. I used my transfer and then I watched out the window as she knocked on the door and then walked right in.

****

"I did my chores! You need to talk to your nasty son who be pissing all over the toilet!"

"Torrie! You need to get a job. Trying to figure out how to become America's next Whitney Houston isn't work. You need to do something with yourself!" I sucked my teeth. The first thing people want to do is knock my music. It's not good enough that I enrolled in school. Since my momma is *disabled* I get a full ride. No, they want me to work like a dog at a job that will never provide me with a future. "I don't want to have to put you out. I don't care if my son pees all over the bathroom, if I don't see it clean you haven't done a thing. So I suggest you stay on top of your chores." My uncle gets on my nerves. One minute he's like the father I never had, I live for those moments. Then other times like now, I could walk out of this door and never come back. He knows his son is nasty and he be on him too. Since he ain't here and he left this mess behind my uncle's going off. I only come here when I have to. Novian hasn't been taking my calls! I threw up last night. Can my life get any worse? I told myself not to think about it and that I'd deal with it today. This morning I told myself I'll deal with it tomorrow. I need to get through the day.

I very angrily scrubbed that bathroom down like I did earlier and then I showered and left. I needed to sleep, but none of my friends were home. So I caught the bus to Eastmont mall in Oakland. I sat on a bench in the middle of the mall trying to think of my next step.

I saw her at the same time that she saw me. She stopped walking for a minute. I could tell she wanted to drop his hand but it was too late. She had that just sexed look all over her. I didn't say anything, I just stared. Novian swears she's so faithful and so loyal. Well look at little miss cheater. She's so dumb, we live in Berkeley. Oakland is not so far away that she should expect not to run into anyone who knows her and knows the guy she was just all over isn't Novian. This guy looked like he had a little change and I was hungry. Shay stopped walking as I approached them. She was trying to read me. She doesn't know whether I still talk to Novian anymore or not. "Hey Shay how you been?"

"Fine," she burned me with her eyes.

"I wasn't aware that you moved on. Who's this sexy drink of water?"

Shay tried to mask her irritation. "This is my boyfriend."

I smiled at her, I had her squirming and she knew I knew it. "Wait until I tell Lee I saw you with your boyfriend. I'm sure he'll be so happy for you." I saw imaginary smoke shoot out the top of her head. "Listen, do you have that money I loaned you? I didn't want to hound you about it, but I do need my money back."

Shay's mouth literally fell open. "Sorry, I don't have any money on me."

"What about mister sexy over here?"

"How much you owe her?"

"Twenty dollars," Shay was trying to play me. My silence

couldn't be bought for twenty dollars.

"Yeah that was the first loan that you never paid back. You owe me two hundred."

"Two hundred dollars?" She shook her head no. "You're crazy!"

"Do you owe her or not?" Mister sexy asked Shay.

"Of course she does, remember we were at Lee's house. I made that quilt for you. I called it the stitches of Novian's heart. You said you loved it and you'd pay me next time you saw me." I took a step back and smiled, "I see you, do you see me?"

Shay looked away as she told her boyfriend that she owed me the money. Mister sexy pulled out his wallet and gave me all but five dollars out of it. I gave Shay a hug to say thank you. She whispered in my ear that this wasn't over. I patted her back and told her I was counting on it.

As I walked away mister sexy told Shay he wanted to see the quilt. I wiped the sweat off my nose as I counted out the two hundred dollars. She's stupid, I would've told my version of the truth and been done with it.

****

"Can I speak to Novian," I said just above my tears.

"Who dis?"

"Torrie!"

"Um! Um! He's going to have to call you back."

"LEE! It's important! Please let me speak to him."

Lee was quiet for a minute like he was putting it together. "Hold on," I could hear soft music in the background. A door closed

39

and the music was gone. "He can't talk to you right now. How far are you?"

"The doctor said four weeks."

Lee cursed and then he said we were careless kids doing way too much. "What are you going to do?"

"I barely have a place to stay, I can't have a baby right now."

"How much?"

"Four hundred!"

"Where are you going? To the celebrity clinic? You've got to be on Medi-Cal, go to Planned Parenthood, or something. I can't give you that much for an abortion."

"I went to my doctor, Planned Parenthood is closed on Mondays. I can go tomorrow."

"I got two hundred, that's all I can spare right now. If you two idiots end up in this situation again I can't help you. Understood?"

"Understood, can I come get the money now?"

"No, I don't have it on me right now. I can bring it to you after work tomorrow."

"You are a good brother Lee, I'm sorry and this won't happen again." Then we hung up. I called Adina, "I got two hundred. I'll get on the bus tomorrow night. See you in the morning."

"Where'd you get the money?"

"Don't worry about it, just know I'm coming." I drummed my fingers on the table as I tried to control my anger. Novian hasn't been taking my calls. I don't know who he thinks he is. I took deep breaths until I was calm. I looked in the mirror and waited for the pissed off look to leave my face. Once I was cool I stood up and went out to my girls. We were dressed up and hitting the streets with our fake ID's. I wanted to do anything tonight other than think about how Novian hasn't been taking my calls and how he left me completely hanging.

I've called Swift a few times each time I was talking to his machine. In an effort not to sound desperate I stopped calling. I guess Swift was fed up with me. He was good to me when we were together. He showed me off, took me out, and let me crash at his place whenever I wanted. Maybe he and Novian compared notes and they both threw their hands up. All I know is Berkeley has brought me no joy as of lately and my hometown used to always find ways to cheer me up. Berkeley always made me feel special and like I was a part of something grand. Now it's cold, dirty, and bitter.

This morning my uncle came in the room and banged on the door. He told us we needed to clean up cause my Aunt Gail and my cousin Chandra were coming out tomorrow and they were staying for a week. All you could hear were sighs and moans. My Aunt Gail was fine, a little messy but fine as far as Aunts go. Her daughter was a nasty somebody. She got me when I was little, so I can't stand being around her now. I don't know if she continued to prey on little girls, but I steer clear of her because the sight of her makes me cry. I called Adina in a panic this morning on my five-dollar calling card. I just about panicked when she didn't have the money to pay for my bus ticket. I spent all day trying to come up with a way out. I don't want to be around my cousin that much. That's why the conversation I just had with Lee was my ticket to freedom. I was getting out of Berkeley, I needed room to breathe.

When we walked inside the club, no one was dancing. People were all sitting around like everyone was too scared to go out on the dance floor first. We ordered our drinks and then we all huddled around our little table gulping down the only drinks we could afford. Somebody was buying me more drinks tonight. I wanted to deal with anything other than my stupid life right now. "Let's go dance," I told my group. Everyone looked scared, "how you all going to be my backup dancers when the time come if you can't go out here on this dance floor and get the party started. They were still quiet. "Come on you guys, let's show them how Berkeley girls do it!" Of course they all acted shy still so I told myself it was all up to me. Stuff like this is exactly why I don't want to be a part of a girl group. All it takes is for one person to be scared or off and then there's problems. I went out on my own and started dancing and singing along to the music. My Long Island felt stronger than usual. I knew why, but I ignored it. I pretended like this was my mini concert. People got so pumped up by my one-woman show that others quickly joined me on the dance floor. Pretty soon I was dancing alone in the middle of a crowd. A guy danced up to me and asked me my name. When I told him he asked me to come with him. I didn't know where he was taking me, but I hoped he was buying me another drink. He led me to a table to the side where a woman was sitting and watching everyone. "Mick, get her another drink." She said to the guy.

The first thing I noticed about this woman was how long her nails were. They were long and red. She told me to have a seat. Mick came back with another long island, he sat it in front of me and then he went back out to the dance floor. "Thank you," then I gulped down my drink. She watched me for a minute, and then she looked away.

"I like what you did out there. All these scaredy-cats in one room. I'm not going to beat around the bush. Come back every Friday. I'll pay you $40 a night plus all the liquor you want. I want you to keep the party going. A club without people dancing is not a club. Deal?"

"Deal," then she slid me forty over the table and said it was for tonight. "I'm going out of town for two weeks though, will that be a problem?"

"Can you send someone in your place?"

"You saw my group, they were too cute and scared to go out there."

"What's your name?" She watched me gulp on my drink.

"Torrie."

"Well in that case Torrie, you better hope I don't find someone else to do your job within two weeks."

"What's your name?"

"I'm Fancy."

Chapter 3

Novian

I couldn't believe I was sitting in the sitting room of Mr. MC's house. Talk about plush! This place makes the house Lee is buying look like a shed. Darius took me to sit on the green sofa. Man! I sat on it and it felt like I was sinking. This couch is so comfortable even with all these pillows. As I adjusted and got really comfortable Mr. MC appeared in the room. He was smiling at me as he wrung his hands together. He stood there for like a whole minute just taking me in. "So you're Ursula's son, it's nice to meet you."

Darius came back to listen to our conversation but he didn't say anything. "Yes, I didn't realize my mother knew you until the other day."

"Yeah, we go way back. So she tells me you sing?" I said yes. "Let's hear it, sing something for me." So I did, I sang tracks of my tears by Smokey. Mr. MC sat down on the couch facing me while he listened. "You're good, but what else would I expect from Ursula's son. Who recorded your demo?"

"An agency in LA."

"Are you under contract?"

"Only for the demo he fronted for me."

Mr. MC nodded his head. "I'm going to sign you to my label. I'm sure Ursula has instilled a good work ethic in you. You're starting at the bottom; I'm not going to instantly make you a star. You can start by singing the intro and a few hooks on my songs. I'll put you on some of my other artist's projects. We'll get your face and name out there before we put you out on your own."

He started to say something else when a door opened. "Brad!" A woman's voice called out.

Darius hurried to the door to help her. Darius and a preteen girl came back with bags. "How long is she staying?" Mr. MC stood up and walked towards them. He hugged the little girl. "How you doing baby?"

"Ok," the girl said sadly.

"My sister is fine thank you for asking." The female snapped. I could hear her voice but I couldn't see her.

"Don't start, I got company. We're talking business right now." Then he walked back to the living room. He gestured for me to come to him. The woman was fumbling with something in her purse. She was beautiful! I don't know if that was weave or not, but it looked beautiful on her. Her hair on the left side of her face was tucked behind her ear showing off her blinding diamonds. She glanced at me then she did a double take. "This is Novian, he's going to be apart of my label."

She scanned me head to toe. That made me stand up straight. That made Mr. and Darius chuckle. "He needs a style."

I caught myself before I licked my lips. This is a real woman! She was like a Torrie times ten. I had to tell my Johnson to calm down. She took off her long trench coat, and then she turned to hang it up. Aw man! She's bootiful! Her small waist made everything else stand out. I don't think I've ever drooled over a woman this thick before. Never to be mistaken for a little girl, this is a woman in a woman's body, and I wanted in. I wanted to be suckled, comforted in that ample bosom, while palming her backside like I was holding Spaulding himself. "What does he need?" Mr. asked her.

She looked at my hair, "are you growing it out?"

"Yeah, I mean yes," I cleared my throat. "I've been told I have nice hair, I figured I'd grow it long."

Then she walked up to me staring at my hair. Dang! She smells so good! I bet everything on her body smells just as good. She reached out to touch my hair and all I could do is stare at the large breast coming towards me. She put her fingers in my hair. "When was the last time you deep conditioned?"

"Huh?"

"Your hair is dry and brittle, you gotta take better care of it if you're planning to grow it long."

"Baby, what he need?" Mr. asked, reminding me that we weren't alone.

"Does he have time? I can do it for him."

Mister pulled her back by her arm. "You trying to keep your skills up for any particular reason?" He looked pissed off.

She snatched her arm from him. "You made me quit! I'm telling you what the boy needs. You can have your jealous fit later. Let me change my clothes and you can stand and watch." Then she grabbed a bag by her foot. "Sandy baby, let me show you which room you'll be sleeping in."

I forgot all about the little girl who was standing there quiet the entire time. Darius picked up the other bags and then he stared at the woman's butt as they went up the stairs. Mister didn't see that though. When they were gone I looked at Mister who was looking around the room trying to calm himself. "So that's your wife?"

"Ex-wife, about to be wife again." Then he exhaled, "when you love a woman never lie to yourself and say it doesn't matter. Everything matters! Camille is my weakness! I try to fight it, but everyone knows it. If you only learn one thing from me know that love is uncontrollable." Pain spread across his face, "we'll talk more later. She took all my energy just by walking in here. She's gonna do something to your hair then Darius will take you home."

"How can I reach you?"

"I'll get your number later on from your mother." Then he walked closer to me. "For now, let's keep it between us who your mother is. They got bad blood between them." Then he patted my shoulder.

Camille and the little girl came downstairs. I swallowed as I took a look at Camille in her tank top. "Brad, did you offer him anything to drink?"

"Hospitality is your department."

Camille shook her head then she looked at the little girl. "He is so rude. Come on suga, I got drinks in the fridge out here."

She headed back towards the door she came in through. Darius started to follow and Mister asked him where he was going. Darius said he was going to watch. Mister told him I was harmless and to come with him. I followed Camille and the little girl out the door. We walked past three nice cars and through a door on the other side of the garage. She had her own little shop set up out here. She had two of everything. Two chairs, two sinks, and two chairs with half bowl looking things at the top. Camille patted the chair and told me to sit, and then she walked to the fridge. She called out to us, telling us the types of sodas she had. The little girl and I said we wanted ginger ale. She handed the little girl her can and then she opened mine. She drank a little then she pulled a bottle of vodka out of the cabinet. She poured it in my can, then she swirled it in her hand and then she handed it to me. She didn't even ask me if I was old enough to drink. I don't drink so I held the can. Then she walked up to me and moved my hair around. She pulled my head back so that it rested on her extremely soft breast. She asked me what I wanted her to do for me. I looked at the little girl who was watching us. "I can grow your hair out for you, but you'll have to do exactly what I say. Can you do that for me baby?"

"Yep!"

"Tell me your name again."

"Novian, I'm Novian."

"I'm Camille and that's my niece Sandy. You don't mind if she watches us do you?"

I was confused about the do me part. "Watch?"

"I keep telling her there's money in cosmetology. I want her to watch the process." I agreed, "so you got that baby? Remember, there's no such thing as an ugly man. There's only strong men, mild men, and weak little boys. You don't ever have to guess either. You let him show you who he is. Use your God given gifts to stay ahead."

"What kind of cosmetology school you sending her to? The madam's house of training?"

She ignored my comment, "tonight we're going to deep condition you and then I'm going to braid your hair. Wear your cap at night, and come back in a week. Once your hair is long and you decide to wear it out you need to comb it. You're going to have to do better than whatever you were doing." She put her fingers in my hair again. "This don't make no sense!"

****

That little girl is always around but she don't say much. She watches everything and she's even caught me staring at her aunt when she bends over or something. Camille knows exactly what she's doing when she does stuff like that too. Sometimes I swear she wants to start something with me and she flirts to see if I'm open. I don't say anything while that little girl is in earshot, which is all of the time. "How you liking school?"

"It's ok," she watched as her aunt greased my scalp.

"How you like living in a house this big? I bet this feels amazing."

"I'm going home in a couple of weeks, but it's ok here I

guess."

I tried to mask my excitement, that means weekly Camille and I would be in here alone. "Where's home?"

"The city, I live in San Francisco with my mom. She's about to have a baby and she's been in the hospital this whole time."

"Are you excited to have a little brother or sister?"

She shrugged, "having two older brothers hasn't helped my life. I don't see how it will matter."

"Do you ever smile?"

Camille's hands stopped moving and then the little girl watched whatever she was saying. "What's my name?" She asked me.

"Huh?"

"You want me to smile show me that you know my name."

"Your name's not little girl?" I was relieved when she laughed. I thought real hard. Ding! Ding! Ding! "Sandy," then I watched her smile spread across her face. "That's a beautiful smile, I hope to see more of it."

"Hey!" Camille pushed my shoulder. "Stop flirting with my niece before I get jealous."

"You trying to get me in trouble with my girlfriend with that smile."

Her eyes got big, "you got a girlfriend?"

"Look at me and ask me that again."

Camille laughed, "you're a mess."

"You don't have a boyfriend?"

"No, boys seem to always look past me."

"Stupid boys, men are going to lose their minds just looking at you."

Sandy blushed hard and then she stood up as if her aunt was directing her. She walked up to me and stuck out her chest that I had never paid attention to. "Will you be one of them?"

Camille had her chest poked out on my left and now Sandy was on my right. It was a Novian middle sandwiched between my favorite. Two slabs of soft and succulent breasts. "Stop messing with me, you've had your fun."

Sandy laughed taking a seat a little closer. Camille went back to my hair. Everyone was quiet and then Mister walked in the room. In that moment I was relieved that none of my fantasies about Camille were occurring. He asked how much longer with my hair. She told him I'd be out in a little bit.

When I was done I thanked Camille and then I went back in the house. A big guy was flowing in the middle of the kitchen while Mister stood at the counter keeping the beat going. The guy was good, but he lacked certainty about his lyrics. Mister told me to come in the kitchen. "This is Ursula's son Novian, Novian this is Ricky. Novian's going to be on this track with you." Mister looked at me, "what do you think of the song?"

"I like it," I didn't know what he meant.

"Before I start investing in production for you, you got to show me it's worth it. Who did you buy this from?"

"This cat from around the way. I gave him a couple of C notes and I told him I'd acknowledge him in the credits."

"WHAT?" Mister's sudden outburst only seemed to startle me. "YOU BIG DUMB IDIOT! Now you gotta keep paying him. You have absolutely no head for business. You can't write, you don't have a flow unless I give it to you. I don't know why I even bother!"

Ricky hunched over a little and then he hung his head. "I'm sorry, what should I do?"

"You're going to record the song if it catches then we'll deal with it then. Novian, listen to the song we need a chorus." Mister had Ricky spit the song from the top for me. I listened for the tone, and then I asked them to slow it down. We went back and forth for a long time spitballing ideas. Mister was thinking up-tempo dance music. I was thinking laid-back cruising music. Something you could ride up and down East 14th with this song bumping out of your car. Mister said he'd see if he could get 2Short to make a cameo in the video. Ricky got excited, he had good ideas. Mister told him he needed to slow down. He said the majority of his video budget would go to getting someone like 2Short to do a cameo in his video. He told Ricky to scout out parks and public locations where they could film quickly and bypass permits to film. I took everything in as he spoke. Then Mister told us to go to the studio **tomorrow** to start recording.

Torrie

I touched my stomach; I was going to have to do something. There's something in there with my eyes and Novian's mouth. I told myself to suck it up. I can't allow myself to want it. I can't allow myself to think about Novian when I know he's not thinking of me. He thinks Shay is so great, she's so wonderful. Why would she be faithful to him when she knows he cheats on her. I don't blame her for having somebody, I just can't stand her. "Why are you sleeping so much?" Adina said hitting me with a pillow. I laughed but I didn't respond. "So this audition is for a part in a sitcom. They want a young African American female age range 20 to 22. About my height five foot five to five foot seven."

"The audition notes are that specific?"

"Girl, you have no idea. One time I had everything they were looking for except that I wasn't a lefty. I walked into the audition with hundreds of me's and most of them were lefties. Or they faked it really well."

"Wow!"

"The music industry is worse, watch. Get dressed you're coming with me."

"To your audition?"

"Yes, then we'll go to the taco truck or something."

The waists on my jeans were becoming uncomfortable. I left them unbuttoned and chose a shirt that was long enough to cover my opened jeans. On the bus I listened to my heartbeat. Wondered what my baby's heartbeat sound like. I wondered if my baby would be like my mother. An innocent soul that everybody runs game on. Would my baby be like Novian? Who until high school was adorably sweet and innocent. He was the guy who panted after me in the shadows until that day. I knew his little known secret. That he possessed a voice that made you want to drop your panties and forget everything except getting next to him. I was in music classes with him all through middle school. He used to be shy about singing in front of people. He used to sing low and almost unnoticeable. It wasn't until I interrupted his one on one session with our teacher after school that I stumbled on his gift. Of course I didn't make a big deal out of it. I waited until it wouldn't feel like he had power over me to tell him his voice was *nice*. I swallowed air as I argued with myself. I can't raise a baby on my own. I can't be anybody's mother. I tried not to cry as I told myself to make a decision.

All these buildings start to look the same. Cold and uninviting as you approach them. The guy with the trendy hair wrote Adina's name down with his left hand and then he gave her a number. A tall and slender woman walked out from the back. Her eyes scanned everyone in the waiting room. When she got to me I told her I was only there to support my cousin. Her eyes looked angry as she moved on. I asked Adina if she needed me to go outside. She ignored my question and gave me the script to help her run lines. The tall lady watched the floor like she was taking in everyone's practice as their actual audition, then she went back into the room.

When they finally called Adina I hugged her and I wished her luck. I put my arm up and as soon as my face touched my fist I was knocked out. Adina nudged me while the tall lady watched. "Where are you two off to?" She asked as she stared at me. I adjusted my clothes as I stood.

"We're going to get something to eat and then we're going home." Adina answered.

"How about the two of you join me for dinner. Did you drive?"

"Actually we caught the bus. I need a new battery for my car."

"Great, ride with me." Her tone was all business.

I asked Adina if this was normal with my eyes. She shook her head no, but I knew she was as curious as I was. I grabbed Adina's hand as we followed her to her ridiculously expensive car. I sat in the back silent as I memorized every feature of this fancy ride. When I make it big, I'm going to have a car just like this. This car was so expensive you barely heard it purr down the street. We pulled up to a place where people were lined up down the street to get in. The line looked like a line in front of a club where people were waiting to get in. She got out of the car and left her keys in the ignition. A guy in a red vest hurried over and gave her a ticket. She looked back at us as we sat frozen in the car. She told us to get out of the car as if we were being ridiculous for not knowing what was going on. We followed her inside and she walked in front of the people waiting for the hostess station. The girl smiled a fake smile at the woman and then she asked the person she was talking to, to wait one moment. Then the hostess showed us to a table in the back corner of the restaurant. The woman ordered a glass of merlot as she took off her jacket and handed it to the hostess. She sat down and then she looked at us. "So little Miss Adina wants to be a star?" Adina smiled but she didn't say anything. "How do you think you did on your audition today?"

"Hopefully I nailed it and I land the part."

"Look at the menu and choose your meal before our wait person comes." Then she looked at her menu as well. When our waiter came she ordered something that sounded amazing. Adina and I said we'd have the same. She watched me eat a breadstick and then she focused on Adina. They spoke candidly about her audition, while I wondered what this lady was building to. "So how do your men feel about you all chasing your dreams?"

"We're single," Adina volunteered.

"Oh?" She kind of looked surprised.

"Yep, we're focused on our careers right now. We don't have time for men."

"What about..."

I cut her off, "I'm sorry. Maybe Adina caught your name during her audition, but I don't know you."

She tried to hold back her smile. "What do you want to know?"

"Can you start with your name?"

She stuck her hand out to me. "I'm Bonita Fairchild, I'm the casting director for the show Adina auditioned for." We shook hands, "and I know people that could be an asset to you in your career."

"You haven't even heard her sing."

"Sing something," she sat back and folded her arms.

I looked around the restaurant and then I took a deep breath. I leaned forward and then I sang as quietly as I could. She smiled and then she asked Adina if she had any other observations. "Are you married?"

Bonita took a deep breath and then she took a sip of her wine. "Divorced," she said that with so much venom. Her eyes burned me and then she looked away. I didn't know what I did, but she was upset.

After dinner she told Adina to come back **tomorrow** for a second audition. She reached in the back seat and then handed Adina a script. She told us to bring bathing suits and we could have dinner at her place afterwards.

I was tired and all I wanted to do was sleep, but Adina stayed on my case begging me to help her memorize her lines. Adina grabbed me by my shoulders and told me this was her opportunity. If she couldn't sleep neither could I. She said the people who stop to rest get left behind. I sucked it up and ran lines with her until she had her script memorized and polished.

When Bonita called her name Adina walked with her head high. I fell asleep before the door closed. Adina woke me while Bonita watched from the exit doorway. I rode in the back watching the scenery change from Hollywood to Beverly Hills. You could tell the difference immediately. The streets were clean and all of the apartment buildings looked expensive. I imagined the lives of the families in these houses. Bonita used the remote on her visor to open her gate. She parked under the carport in front of her garage. Adina asked her if she lived in this big ole house by herself, and Bonita said yes with a plastered smile on her face. The smell of delicious food greeted us in the face when we entered the door. The house was beautiful with modern furniture and almost white everything. She told us to take our shoes off. Then she watched as we stepped on to the carpet with our bare feet. This carpet felt like pillows under your feet. Immediately I felt sleepy. I've never seen an all white kitchen. The thought of it scared me. She took food out of the oven and set it on the counter. She opened a bottle of wine then she asked me how old I was. She looked me over when I said I was 18, and then she pulled a bottle of sparkling cider out of the refrigerator.

I ate my first curry dish in life and I fell in love with naan. She took out the next script and asked Adina if she was ready. Adina excitedly said yes. Bonita told Adina to change into her bathing suit first. Adina took off her top and shorts right there. We laughed cause she was ready. Adina took the script then she went out by the pool. Bonita looked at me. "You have a beautiful voice."

"Thank you."

"A voice like that could take you far with the right people backing you."

"I'm trying to find the right people."

"This business can be pretty cruel, how do you plan to survive?"

"I write songs, music is good but if it's not telling a story what is it doing? I want to make people dance, and I want the conscious people to listen."

"So I take it that you have samples?"

"I've got notebook after notebook full of songs."

"So how does your baby fit into all of this?"

I looked at Adina like she could've heard her although she was on the grass on the other side of the pool working. "I don't know what you mean."

"Are you going to keep it?"

I swallowed, "as soon as I go home I'm going to the clinic. I..."

Bonita waived her hand to tell me to stop talking. She sat back and took another sip of her wine. "My ex husband and I bought this house to raise our family. Turns out I can't have babies. There went my marriage."

"The father doesn't want it and I'm too young."

"Who knows you're pregnant?"

"The father, and his brother." She frowned at me, "he gave me the money to get rid of it. I came out here instead."

"Tell me about the father."

So I told her about Novian, I normally know better than to talk to a stranger like this. I needed to get all this stuff off my chest. Bonita listened then she told me to come get in the pool. I put on my bikini and then I grabbed the pool chair and floated around the pool. Now all I could think about was Novian and how much his rejection hurt. I kept wiping my face with pool water to hide my tears. Bonita floated across the pool in her pool chair like she was a queen. With her face pointed towards the sky she asked Adina what she would give up for stardom. Adina joked that she already sacrificed our sleep last night and she'd do it again. Bonita waited for my answer but I didn't know. After a long pause she said when she came to Hollywood she wanted to be a star. She came from a little city on the corner of Texas and Arkansas. Fresh out of college she was ready. She met a guy, and then she met more. She said she wasn't proud of the things she did or the baby she sacrificed to be herself. She frowned and said you can't change what's done. She said once she had a name behind herself she met her ex. She said he was her dream guy, everything she wanted. They had plans for a family by day and taking on Hollywood by night. She said then they found out she couldn't have a baby after they exhausted all of their options. She said he didn't want to adopt, he wanted a biological child. She said he then found someone who gave him a child and he divorced Bonita.

Adina asked her what she was going to do now. She said she's adopting.

The next day at the audition Adina went to the back and I fell asleep. Bonita woke me up and told me to follow her. We went outside by her car. "How do you feel?"

"Fine I guess."

"I don't see the point in beating around the bush. I want to adopt your baby." My mouth hung open, "I want to have my physician check you out. As long as she verifies that you and the baby are healthy, I will pay for everything. You can stay with me to have the baby."

"Why would you want my baby?"

"Cause you don't. What's the difference between doing it this way or going through an agency?"

"I didn't consider carrying it in my body."

"Adina will get this job and my help to continue working. I'll help you with your career as soon as you're ready. Even if you blow it and only go out as a one hit wonder, I promise I can make that happen for you."

I looked down at my flat stomach. "Won't people know?"

"I have a plan if you're in?"

I shrugged, "I don't want it no how."

Bonita told me to tell Adina I was going home. Adina was going to be busy working. She said I could call her from time to time to check in. My uncle and mother didn't know where I was so I would continue that way. Meanwhile she would wear a prosthetic belly when she had to go out in public. Her doctor and I would be the only ones who knew for a fact that she wasn't pregnant. When I asked her about Adina remembering the story she told. She said she would simply say that this is her miracle baby.

Novian

I looked around trying to check my embarrassment at the door. Mr. MC was all relaxed leaning back in his seat letting the jets work their magic on his feet. While I sat forward like somehow my posture was going to give me a more manly appearance in this all woman environment. "Look son, I already told you. You need to sit back and relax, they're going to take good care of us here."

I shook my head, "I don't know. This feels awfully girly." I shook my head as I told myself guys do this all of the time.

The worker walked up to him with two bowls of liquid, one in each hand. She put one on each of the tables next to his chair. He put his hands in them and exhaled like he was the guy from the 7up commercials. "You're about to be on camera. Everybody's about to see you. You're a good-looking kid and we need to use that to our advantage. Look at Babyface, I mean he's an alright looking brotha. It's his polished look in addition to the lyrics that he croons that have these females dropping their panties. You're getting a facial, manicure, and pedicure. A well-polished man takes care of his appearance. These girls can run around here saying a man does this and a man does that. How they like the rough look of a man, and that bull. Then as soon as a smooth cat comes sliding in all you hear is how smooth his skin is. Or how good he smells. Or look at all of his muscles."

"Muscles," I glanced at my aching body in the mirror. Mr. has had me working out like crazy with Darius, Ricky, and him whenever I'm not in the studio or in-between breaks at the studio. I thought I was doing well before but these fools are crazy. Especially Ricky, he's a mountain of muscles, but dumb as all get out. Last night I was checking out the fruits of my labor though. Cuts on my arms, rock hard stomach, cuts all in my legs. Shay has been all over me, so I know what he's saying is true. I just never thought of myself as a pedicure kind of guy. "Can I go without the polish though?"

Mister looked at me, "say something dumb to me like that again and I'll knock you out myself. What I look like talking about putting you out as a pretty boy and then I do some girly junk like have you walking around with polish on your nails? Huh? Huh? Stupid little kid asking dumb questions! Man! Shut up and say thank you!"

Camille walked into the room of the spa where we were. She just got her hair done, but my eyes immediately went down to the high heels she was wearing. She was either barefoot or in heels; I don't think this woman owns a sneaker. She walked like she was trying to turn the women on too. They kind of stopped what they were doing and watched her. I imagined them wishing they were her. Jewelry, hair done, expensive clothes, heavenly body. "Brad," she waited for him to look at her.

"What?" He frowned.

"I need to go get the baby and you haven't said anything."

He exhaled, "I'm too old to be dealing with a new baby. This is supposed to be our time together."

Camille exhaled irritated air, "look! I want this, please do this for me. It's not like I ever got to have a baby of my own. Wait until you see how darling she is. I guarantee you'll love her."

"I didn't want any more babies for a reason You're sticking me with another man's baby as if that's going to make me feel better. Won't Sandy feel abandoned?"

Camille held back an eye roll as if what he said was ridiculous. "No, because she will still come over from time to time. Please baby, I need this." She walked up to him and gave him a juicy kiss like they were alone. I looked around at the spa workers who were shamelessly watching like they were mesmerized. Camille reached down to mister's crouch and rubbed him gently. In a heavy voice she said, "please baby. Do it for me."

"Ok," he swallowed as he surrendered. "But we get one more night just me and you."

"But I'm supposed to get the baby today."

"Tell your sister she can deal with the mess she's made one more night. I want one more night free from baby distractions."

I could tell that didn't exactly go the way she wanted it to go, but she chose to pick her battle. "That's fine, when will you be home?"

He leaned back in his chair, "late. Tell this fool ain't nobody about to turn him in to no girl. You see him over there questioning his manhood because he got his feet in water? School him!"

Camille smiled at me, "remember how you were your first time. Cut the boy some slack." Then she walked all slow and seductive towards me. I looked at mister to see if he saw the way she was walking up on me. He was watching her, but I think he was hypnotized. "Novian, the way to a woman's heart is through her eyes. By the time I'm done with you, all the ladies will think you're irresistible.

****

I looked at the clock, I had to be up in four hours, but I couldn't sleep. Thoughts of Torrie ran across my mind last night before I laid down, and all I've been doing is laying here ever since. I've rolled over so many times trying to fall asleep, but I can't. Lee got on my case so badly when he had to take the money out of his furniture fund to give it to her to get rid of the baby. The first paycheck Mister gave me, I paid my brother back. He looked like he didn't expect to see that money ever again. He told me to invest in condoms and to never leave home without them. It was kind of amazing to me that just like that she was pregnant. That was too easy, but I guess it doesn't take much to make a baby. She hasn't called since Lee gave her the money. Sometimes I swear I hear her cursing me out in the back of my mind. I keep thinking I'm going to run into her somewhere, some how, but I haven't seen her yet. I try to not think about the fact that I don't know my father and that my mother could've done the same thing with me. I don't like to think about not existing. Then I wonder if I've brought anything to anyone's life? Lee wouldn't have had to grow up so early if it weren't for me. Maybe he'd be married with children of his own by now. I owe my big brother everything, and I can't have him worried about my life. When I make it big he ain't gonna worry about nothing, not on my watch.

I got up and did push-ups until I couldn't anymore. More thoughts of Torrie flooded my brain! I rolled over and did sit ups instead of crunches hoping that the extra effort would tell my brain to back off. Nope, nothing was working! I worked out until I couldn't move; I laid on the floor out of breath begging my brain to shut off. I took a shower and got back in the bed, thirty minutes before I had to get up I finally fell asleep. My alarm taunted me with its amusement at my expense. I brushed my teeth again and hurried down the stairs to Darius' car. He watched me and then he asked me what was wrong with me. I told him I had a rough night. Darius was quiet for a minute and then he looked at me. "You about to shoot your first video, you excited?"

"Yes, I'm ready! I can't believe this is happening."

Darius nodded his head, "what's your plan?"

"Plan?"

"You going to be a background singer your entire career? Waiting for someone to ask you to sing their hook?"

"Naw, Mister's going to work on my album next."

"What did Ursula say about all of this?"

"I haven't talked to her."

Darius looked at me like I was crazy. "Why would you make a move without her? Ursula could be a real asset to you in all of this."

"What am I missing? Why she get so much respect around here?"

"Brad wouldn't be Mr. MC without her. Your mom has been at this for a long time. She's the one who worked things out at Silent Chaos so we could record there. She's golden, why don't you know that?"

I was quiet for a minute, "she know that cat Malcolm?"

"Of course she does, they go way back."

"What's his deal?" I was trying not to get angry about how he did me.

"Deal? He's nobody."

"I guess he decided to flex his muscles with me then."

"Oh you mean your studio time?"

"Yeah, he had me jumping through hoops and I don't like him for that."

"You ain't gotta like him. You're a part of Brad's Team. We bow down to no one. Brad has connections everywhere. Malcolm's a small time hustler. We feed him little pieces of chump change here and there, but ain't nobody worried about him."

I wish he would've told me this sooner. That whole interaction way back then would've gone differently.

When we got to the set there were lights everywhere. A camera crew, music bumping, dancers, and fans on the sidelines. The first person I spotted was Malcolm. He was standing to the side watching the dancers specifically. I told myself not to pay him any attention. The director for the video told me he liked my look. He went over what he wanted me to do and when. Mister came out of his trailer in a zone. Whenever we were in the studio he was different like he is now. He was almost gentle, definitely not intimidating like he normally is. He looked at me and smiled. I asked him where Ricky was and he said he was throwing a tantrum cause Mister won't put his song out yet. The kid that wrote the lyrics is trying to demand a bunch of money that Mister refuses to pay.

"Ok everybody that was good, but let's take it from the top. 5, 6, 5, 6, 7, 8!" A girl called out. The music poured out of the speakers and the dancers fell into their routine. My eyes went to her butt first. The back of her head says she's Mexican or maybe she's Puerto Rican with a butt like that. She got those power legs that probably feel heck of good when they wrapped around you.

I was trapped in my own mental fantasy when Mister hit me in my chest. "What's wrong with you? Are you paying attention?"

I shook my head yes, "I was just thinking about the song." A girl hurried to me and put a coffee cup in my hands and then she hurried away. "What's this?"

"Tea, in case we need you to sing." Mister focused on the choreography of the dancers. The way he was staring at one of the young dancers made me look around for Camille. "Where's the misses?"

"She doesn't come to shoots." Then he smiled at the girl who might be eighteen.

I returned my attention to the girl calling the shots. She was dancing when someone bumped me hard. It was my mother, "long time no see stranger." She smelled like alcohol already.

Immediately I knew at some point she was going to

embarrass me. "What are you doing here?"

"Calm down Renee, I'm always on set for video shoots."

I held back my scream, "why would you give me a girl's name? Don't call me that!"

My mother smiled at me enjoying my frantic check to see if anyone heard her. "I guess I did it to give you a crisis to overcome." She moved in closer, "what's this I hear about you trying to deny me or something?"

I looked at my mother; she had her hands on her little hips. "He ran back to you and told you that?"

"Of course he told me about it. Malcolm is my friend, I got friends all over that you don't know."

"Whatever, he overreacted. How was I supposed to know he knew you?"

"I'm the reason you were even at that studio. I'm the reason you're working with Brad. You better open your eyes little boy. Without me you'll only ever have dreams." Then she walked away angry. She walked up to Mister breaking his attention from the underage girl. He smiled big and picked my mother up as he hugged her. She screamed that he was going to make her sick. Mister gestured to the girl who brought me my tea. She opened a bag and hurried over with a flask, she handed it to Mister. My mother got too excited as he said something as he handed it to her. I had no idea her friend Brad all these years was Mr. MC. I was lost in thought when the girl tapped me. She asked me if I was hungry. I guess I took too long to answer cause she pointed at the table where food was all laid out. The choreographer gave everyone a ten-minute break, and then she spoke with the director, and then Mister. When she started toward the food table, Malcolm stood in her path. She smiled big at him and then he said something to her. She looked at the table with a big smile, she pointed at something then she walked back in the other direction. Malcolm eyed me as he approached the table. I was mad that he knew her. He got a cup of orange juice and a pastry. He acted like he paid my watchful eyes no attention until he got everything he needed. He took two steps and then he looked at me. He said, "don't make me have to kill you too." Then he walked away.

Torrie

Bonita's cook was making dinner and it smelled delicious. The cook made all kinds of delicious healthy dishes all day. Bonita has gotten on my case one too many times about skipping meals. When I told her I was afraid of getting fat she had the doctor address my concerns during her next visit. The doctor explained that I was going to gain so much weight regardless of what I did.. Bonita told me to exercise daily to give my baby what I needed to be able to bounce back.

Adina thinks I went home and my mother thinks I'm with Adina. I call Adina to make sure she has no reason to call my uncle's place looking for me. After the pilot ran for Adina's new show, it was picked up by the network for a full season. Adina has been busy promoting the show and working really hard. Bonita keeps saying how proud she is of Adina and how hard working she is. Adina has been meeting people and working towards her future. Bonita got Adina signed to an amazing agent who has Adina going on auditions during her *downtime* and booking her for all kinds of jobs. Commercials, a little modeling, and things like that. Bonita said my child has paved the way for Adina and I.

Once I hit five months Bonita had the nursery set up. The room is decorated in very light colored pastels and she put all of the latest gadgets in there. Weekly the doctor adjusts her prosthetic stomach to match mine. The doctor comes out to the house to do all of my test and exams. They've tested me and the baby for every imaginable thing under the sun. The doctor says the baby is healthy and strong. Normally I stay pretty detached from all of it. I watch television eagerly waiting for the moment when it's my turn to be on there singing and dancing. The first time the baby kicked me I froze and looked at Bonita with big eyes. She was concerned at first and then I told her I felt it. Bonita cried the first time the baby kicked her. She kept telling me thank you and she kept telling the baby how much she loved it and how she couldn't wait to meet them. I don't say anything cause I can't relate to how she feels.

I was watching YO MTV Raps with my feet up. I was rubbing my feet when they said the latest from Mr. MC was out today. I was watching and nodding my head. Bonita came in the room when she heard the music, Novian was there! I gasped as I dropped my feet and stared. His hair has gotten longer and he looked so good. I pointed to the TV and I couldn't get it out. Bonita asked me what I was pointing at. I pointed at Novian and then I pointed at my stomach, I couldn't let the words cross my lips. Bonita got excited as she then stared at Novian like I did. I wanted to cry as soon as the video was over. I wished there was a way to rewind the exclusive debut and watch it again. Bonita asked me tons of questions about Novian. I cried, as I was honest for the first time ever about him. I told her about how he started verses how he is now.

"So both of you sing and are good looking kids. My child is going to be an amazing kid." She had stars in her eyes. I left the TV on MTV and then I listened for the music from Mr. MC's song, anxiously waiting to see Novian's face again.

That night I caressed my stomach as I thought about Novian. He was living inside of me; he was growing inside of me. Proof that once upon a time he loved me, was with me, and growing from within. I doubt Novian even thinks about me anymore; he was about to be famous. Everybody knows who Mr. MC is, and everyone will be asking about that guy with the beautiful voice and smooth skin.

****

The doctor gave me a shot of something and she said it was

going to help me relax so that my body could do what it needed to do. Bonita fed me more ice chips, as I wanted to cry behind the pain. The doctor was always calm and she used a soothing voice with me during this time. I liked that she explained everything to me so that I would understand what was going on. I heard her tell Bonita that the hospital was on standby just in case there were any complications. I was delivering this baby in Bonita's house. When Bonita initially told me the plan I was scared, I asked how would they manage my pain in a home birth. The doctor assured me that everything would be fine, and that she knew what she was doing. After the doctor gave me the shot, my body relaxed almost immediately and I fell asleep. I awoke to pressure and I cried out a little. Bonita jumped up out of the chair and the doctor came hurrying in. She checked me and said the baby was crowning. Bonita got so excited as she kissed my forehead and told me I could do this. After two pushes Bonita left my side to help the doctor with the baby that was now screaming. I could hear Bonita crying as she said the baby was beautiful. The doctor told me I did really well as she stitched me. I watched Bonita like I was dreaming. She was crying as she looked down at the baby and she sang some song I never heard. The doctor explained next steps to Bonita in the same soothing tone she used when she talked to me during the delivery. I laid on the bed watching Bonita and the baby. Bonita was so happy and excited. Even if I chose to keep that baby I never would've been able to love that baby like that. I had no doubt that Norie (the name I gave the baby in my heart) would be safe and sound with her.

Bonita smiled at me, "thank you Torrie! Thank you!"

"What is it?"

"It's a girl," Bonita smiled and then she walked out of the room.

In the morning the doctor took me to a hotel and checked me in. It was a nice room, and she explained that my apartment would be ready in a week. She came twice daily to check on me and make sure that I was fine. I kept the television on MTV and every time Mister's video came on I tried not to cry as I watched Novian.

After a few days I started exercising as much as I could which wasn't much compared to how much I used to. The doctor said they got the newest and hottest trainer on the market. Josie Kage was going to bring me back to my former glory. I stood in the mirror looking for a sign that I gave birth. I couldn't see anything although every time I went to the bathroom it was a reminder. I was surprised by how quickly my stomach went down. The doctor told me how to express the milk from the baby and she gave me something to help my milk dry up faster. She strongly encouraged me to get on birth control to avoid a future incident, and I complied.

Chapter 4

Novian

Mister said that his single with me singing on it has done so well that he was going to invest in me next. Meanwhile, I've been singing hooks for a lot of his artists. I've been at Silent Chaos so much; you would think that I was on the SC payroll. Mister had me open a checking account and then he put me on his payroll. My first paycheck I paid Lee back the money from the whole Torrie situation. Lee thanked me for honoring my word, and then I took him out to dinner.

As we ate he asked me if I saw Torrie's cousin on TV. I've been so busy I hadn't had much time to just sit down and watch television. He told me he's been recording the episodes, but once his girlfriend found out that he knew her the episodes have suddenly gotten recorded over.

I didn't like his girlfriend and it seemed like as soon as he bought his house here came this female. She walked in the door like she owned the place and she always got something to say. Lee has always been a smart man, but I can see how he's weak for her. She have him in that room calling out to the heavens and then the next thing you know he's bending over backwards to provide her with whatever she smiles at. She's not horrible, I just don't like when she feels entitled to speak to me like she's an authority on anything.

When I offered to start paying rent Lee, declined. He told me to save the money I would pay him for rent for a place of my own. His subtle way of telling me it was time to move. I wanted to be mad, but he's carried me since I was little. I had to think about how much he wants a life of his own. He wasn't going to stop being my brother just because I moved out. I had to check my selfishness at the door and thank my brother for everything he's done for me. For being the only person I've ever been able to rely upon in my life.

Like Lee taught me I wrote out my budget and determined my bills and my savings, then I tried to be controlled with my mad money. That wasn't easy because suddenly I was faced with so many wants and the means to buy them. I bought a few clothing pieces, but a lot of my stuff was provided by Mister and I got to keep them since they were tailored to me.

I found a cool little one-bedroom spot near Fruitvale, not too far from the Grande Lake Theater and everything over there. Shay just about moved in as soon as I got my keys. I didn't want her there as much as she was, but how do you tell your girlfriend you need space so you can cheat on her? I will say that it was nice coming home to her warm body in my bed. A brotha was getting served up regularly for once. On the nights when I couldn't shake the thoughts of Torrie it was nice to roll over and fall in until thoughts of Torrie disappeared.

"You and Darius seem pretty tight." Swift said as he touched controls on the board.

"Yeah, we cool. He been giving me rides until I get my own whip."

"I've been meaning to ask you, what's up with you and Torrie?"

The mention of her name made me uncomfortable. "I haven't talked to her in a long time."

"So you two ain't together?"

"Naw, you've met my girlfriend."

"Your girlfriend don't mean you and Torrie wasn't together." He looked me in my eyes.

"Right, we not together no more. I ain't talked to her in months."

He turned his body to me, "I'm confirming her story. We've been talking over the phone for a minute. I was just making sure she was free before, well you know."

Yeah I knew, and what could I say about it. Part of me wanted to see her again, but the other part of me was ashamed for how I did her. I couldn't face her. "Yep, she's free."

Torrie

Once Bonita came back to work after her six-month maternity leave she set up a meeting between she and I. I had one more month out here and then I was going back to The Bay, back to Berkeley. We mapped out our plan of attack. I want to write my entire album, I want to tell a story with my music. Music is supposed to say something, inspire you to something great or speak to the feelings you've experienced. Bonita said I was asking for a lot of creative control and usually artists don't get that much power when they debut. She told me to figure out which songs I wanted to record and build my plan of attack. She said if push comes to shove I would need to record my entire album and then shop it around. I was fine with that cause that meant I could record my music the way I wanted it to be.

I was surprised the first time Swift answered his phone. I expected him to try to get off of the phone quickly with me. To my surprise and delight he stayed on the phone with me. I didn't hide from him my main reason for calling him. I told him when he never returned my calls or answered his phone before I understood and it actually worked out for the better because I made some great connections.

Swift said he was with someone at the time, and he didn't want the distraction of me. I asked him what his status was now, and he said he was single. I told him when I came back we needed to link up to go over what I needed from him. Then he agreed and added that he would show me what he needed from me.

I didn't feel good about leaving Norie out here but it's not like Bonita lets me see her. Her nanny called once during our meeting, if I didn't hear her call Norie, *Angel* I wouldn't have known what she named her. I held back my smile; I liked her name although she would always be Norie to me.

******

When I walked down the ramp Swift was standing there. I was so happy to see him, and it felt like someone cared. When I called my uncle and told him I was coming home he sighed and then he got off the phone with me. Bonita gave me a few thousand to help me when I came out here, and then she said she would see what she could workout for studio time for me. I didn't tell her about Swift just yet cause I wanted to see if he would really help me or if he was just looking to get laid. Either way I was tired of the memory of Novian and I did not want him to be the last person I slept with anymore. Swift hugged me and then he delivered a powerful kiss. I hadn't been kissed in so long that I think I immediately got excited.

Swift drove me to my Uncle's place. My uncle was outside when we pulled up. He wasn't happy to see me at all. He immediately asked me how long was I going to stay cause the place was full of people as it was. I was totally embarrassed and caught off guard by his lack of enthusiasm about me. My momma came out of the door and she ran to me and hugged me tight. She told me she missed me and to never stay away that long again. "Momma this is my friend Swift."

Swift corrected me, "boyfriend. It's nice to finally meet you."

My momma smiled big, "he's cute Torrie."

"Thank you," I blushed as I looked at Swift.

"Torrie's going to live with me. She just came by to get her things and leave a number where you can call her." Swift said looking at my uncle.

"You're going to leave me?" My momma's eyes looked so sad.

I hugged her and immediately felt guilty for my long absence. "Only for right now momma. As soon as I can afford it, you're moving in with me."

"Good, that will be one less person sleeping on my couch." My Uncle said as he got in his car to drive away.

My momma helped me get all of my things, which barely filled up the back of the car, and then I gave her Swift's phone number. Swift made room for me in his closet. While I got situated in there he cleared a couple of drawers for me too. While I put my things away he left and came back with food.

That night when we had sex, it was like my first time all over again. I told Swift it had been over a year since I had sex, I don't think he believed me until then. Once I found my rhythm again it was on.

Novian

Everybody keeps asking me if I'm nervous. What I got to be nervous about? All I've got to do is go out there and sing. All during rehearsal I kept telling everyone I had it and I knew what I was doing. I've been on the stage before with Mister's artists, this wasn't any different. I did pause when I saw Mister on stage rehearsing hard. I told myself he needed more rehearsal since he does all that sequential dancing with his dancers. When it was time I got a little nervous but I was ready. Mister and Darius stood over to the side and he told me to get the crowd warmed up for him.

I rubbed my hands together as the MC introduced me. My music started and my background singers swayed to the music. I slid out on the stage and danced to the microphone. The audience was still arriving. Some people clapped, I paid that no never mind. I sang my song, did my moves; I thought I was killing them. So what if they didn't know what I was singing. I was Novian, the guy everyone has been loving on these hooks. They've seen me on TV with a little bit of everybody. People were still walking in and out of the auditorium. One girl towards the front looked at me like, *so what*? As the music started for my fourth song, I said, "one more song and then Mr. MC will be out."

The audience went wild. My heart fell out of my chest. They weren't in to my performance. I tried to finish my song, but half way through I threw my hands up. I walked off the stage in the middle of my song. Mister was frowning at me while Darius covered his mouth as he cracked up laughing. I stormed past them and slammed the door to my dressing room. I put my hands on the table as I leaned over trying to catch my breath. My eyes watered as I tried to get it together. Mister slammed the door behind himself as he tried to calm his temper. "So now you just some little punk sissy who runs away crying when you get rejected?"

"You heard them, I bombed!" I stood up and faced him.

"Boy! Everybody's not going to love you! Every performance isn't going to knock the socks off of the crowd. This is your fault! You the one walking around here like you're a star. You need more humility! I offered to go over your set up with you, but you were so convinced that you had it. Big headed behind singing a few hooks! When you finish walking around in your panties bring yourself out here! This is a business! You need Ursula! Stop acting like she's beneath you."

"You don't know what it's like to be her son."

"No I don't! Be a man and get over that. Ursula knows her stuff! Musically it gets no better than her, and when she loves you." His voice trailed off for a minute. He took a deep breath. "Look, I'm man enough to admit that tonight was a test. You are talented, but you developed an ego too fast. Wipe them sissy tears out your eyes and come out here like a man. Leave your pride in this room, and next time leave it at home. Tonight we're changing your whole line up. I'll tell Ursula to forgive you."

I laughed, "oh and just like that she does what you tell her to?"

Mister stared at me for a minute, "you aren't very observant are you?"

"What's that supposed to mean?"

"Nothing," he shook his head. "If I tell Ursula to forgive you, she will."

Mister knows how to put on a show. Then I noticed my mother running around back stage. She had a headset on; she pressed a button and told someone they were off. I never paid attention to how she was running things in the background keeping everything on point. When I changed my clothes and went out with Mister it was like a brand new stage. There was energy, crowd participation; this was what I was used to. Mister had the whole house rocking. People were in the aisles dancing along, doing the steps from his videos. I had to give him his props; he knew how to work a crowd.

After the show we signed autographs. It was like no one realized I was the same person from before. I got in the car with Darius, Mister, and my mother. "Where are we going?" Darius asked Mister.

Mister exhaled, "I'm tired and I don't feel like playing the restaurant shuffle. Let's go to my house."

"Brad," my mother said weakly.

"La La, I'm tired and I don't feel like faking. I don't have it in me tonight."

La La? I looked at my mother like her nickname disgusted me. "Maybe we should wait until the morning then. We could..."

Mister cut her off, "we're doing this tonight!" He pounded his fist on the door.

The rest of the car ride was drop dead silent. When Darius pulled up to the garage I wondered if Camille was home. This was only business so I didn't see what the big deal is. Mister works with all kinds of people male and female. We're always at the house at all hours of the night so I didn't see why there was all this tension. Mister told us to go into the dining room, and when Darius asked why we couldn't go in his office. Mister told him we needed space to spread out and he seemed annoyed by the question. My mother sat quietly at the table and then she took out her flask and took a good chug on it. Darius put the teapot on as he busied himself in the kitchen.

My mother explained that although my songs are very good no one has ever heard them before. So to the audience I could've been speaking French as far as they were concerned. He told me until the world became familiar with my work I needed to stick to established hits to warm the crowd up. She said I walked on that stage like everyone should know who I was like I forgot they weren't there to see me. Truth of the matter is that I did forget that they weren't there to see me. She handed me a list of songs, she told me to practice them tonight and in the morning we'd start working with the band to arrange them to my pitch. Great this meant I wasn't getting any sleep tonight. At least I'm getting used to not sleeping. As we were finishing up, Camille's voice made all of us jump. Her voice was angry as she asked Mister what he was doing. It wasn't until that moment that I noticed that Mister wasn't saying too much. He was drinking his tea and listening over to the side as my mother gave orders. Mister waived Camille off and told her to go back to bed and that he would be up in a little bit. He rubbed his chest as he frowned. Camille started screaming at him, telling him she couldn't believe he brought my mother into her house. My mother didn't say anything she just watched Mister with sad eyes as she waited for him to say something.

Mister was letting her fuss, but you could tell he was getting more and more irritated. He warned her to stop one more time, but she kept going. Mister jumped out of his chair and charged at Camille, he almost had her but Darius grabbed his arm asking him to calm down. Mister spit choice words at Darius as he jerked his arm away and went after Camille. Mister caught Camille by the ankle on the stairs, he grabbed her and made her fall then he drug her back down the stairs. Camille screamed telling him to let her go. Then I heard the sound of thunder as a part of Mister's body collided with Camille's. Camille stopped screaming but she continued to cry.

I hopped out of my seat and I ran behind Darius, my mother stayed put at the table as she looked at her hands. Mister had Camille's weave clutched in his left fist as he punched her in the face with his right fist. Lee taught me that you aren't supposed to hit women; he told me that we're supposed to protect them and when they push our buttons we're supposed to walk away. Clearly no one taught Mister this lesson, and I couldn't believe I was seeing this. Why would he hit a woman as fine as Camille, and in the face of all places? Darius stopped and I ran to Mister, I grabbed his fist before he struck her again. He stumbled backwards as he yanked Camille with him. He let go of her and swung at me. I didn't even feel it; my adrenaline was pumping too hard. I grabbed Camille and pushed her out of the way as he and I started fighting. This old man ain't no joke. He's probably spent his life fighting or something, because he was throwing them and I was trying my best to hang with him. My mother ran in the foyer and told us to stop. Mister stopped swinging and I backed up. Darius helped Camille standup and then he walked her to the kitchen. "BOY! I'm gonna tell you this one time and one time only. You never get in the middle of a man and his woman. That one could've got you killed."

"Brad! Over my dead body! You better NEVER lay a finger on my son AGAIN!" My mother said getting in his face.

I stood up straight preparing myself to fight again. He went after Camille for less than this. "Tell your son to stay out of married people's business!" He flexed and unflexed his hands.

"I'll talk to him about that, but never again! You hear me!"

Mister looked at me like he wanted to finish me. Then he walked towards the kitchen. Darius was visibly upset but he wasn't saying anything as he put ice on Camille's face. Mister told him to take us home and that he would deal with everyone tomorrow. Then Mister put his arms around Camille like he wasn't just whooping on her.

We walked out of the door behind Darius who was marching like he was angry. When we got in the car Darius put his keys in the ignition but he didn't start the car. He started hitting his steering wheel and growling. My mother rubbed his head as she told him she knew and for him to let it out. Darius started screaming about he hates when Mister does stuff like that. Then he started blaming himself saying that he knew Mister was in a mood, and he shouldn't have let him bring us to the house. My mother said Mister was already in a mood because the concert didn't do as well as he thought it would and so he was going to be a little short. Darius asked why Camille had to be his punching bag. My mother said that's what Camille signed up for.

Then she turned and looked at me. She told me to never be that stupid again. She said Mister could've killed me tonight and if it wasn't for her he probably would've. Then her hand shook as she put her flask back up to her mouth. I told her no man should ever hit a woman like that. My mother said we were talking about Camille, and what happened between Mister and Camille was none of nobody's business. Darius calmed down and then Mister opened his front door. He was shirtless in his underwear and slippers. Any other time I might've laughed, but tonight I couldn't help but think this fool is crazy.

Torrie

The ring of the phone brought me back to life. When I tried to move to answer it Swift had me entangled in all of his limbs as he slept peacefully. At first I thought this was endearing and it was truly what I needed…. at first. Now, it's getting old. I gotta ask for permission to pee it seems like. I pushed Swift's head as I moved up the bed to answer the phone. He started grumbling in his sleep like I was messing with him. "Hello?"

"Why do you sound sleep? It's the middle of the afternoon." Adina laughed.

"Long night at the studio, even longer night once we got here. Why you sound so chipper?"

"I GOT THE PART!" She screamed into the phone.

I removed the phone from my ear, "dang Adina! Why you gotta scream in my ear?

"BECAUSE! BECAUSE! I HAVEN'T TOLD YOU THE BEST PART! I NEED YOU TO FLY OUT HERE FOR A PARTY!"

I sat up, "party?"

"Yes gurl! The cast from the last movie I did is all going to be there, and even a few record executives. You need to put on your good girl act and network."

I chuckled then I looked at Swift who was looking at me through one red eye. "Let me talk it over with my man and then I'll let you know. When did you need me?"

"Preferably tonight, but at the latest tomorrow afternoon. I have dresses, how's your hair?"

"Swift just paid for me to get it done. Let me talk to him and then I'll call you back."

"When we hang up, give him some so good that he has no choice but to say yes. Remember my coaching."

"Bye gurl, I'll call you back." Swift was scowling at me when I hung up the phone. "What?"

"What is it?"

"Adina needs me to network with her at a party tomorrow night."

"No!" Swift put his head back down facing the wall.

I scooted up to his back, "aw come on baby. It'll be one night and we'll both benefit from all the connections I make."

"Those parties ain't nothing but big ole orgies disguised as everything else. I could take the night off and come with you."

"Adina only has a plus one. Besides your clients rely on your help to help them be the best artists they can be." I kissed the back of his neck. Then I pushed my body against his, "please say you're ok with me going. Everything I do, I do it for us."

Swift didn't want me to go, so I spent the night with him. Then when he left for work I caught the bus to the airport. Adina had my ticket waiting for me. I thought about Norie, I wondered if she was talking yet. If she looked more like Novian or me. Thinking about her made my chest ache in a spot I have never felt hurt in before. When I watch Novian on television he clearly is not thinking about me. I'm sure he's forgotten all about me as if I never happened. He would die if he knew about Norie. That all too familiar feeling of depression washed over me. I looked down at the magazine in my lap as tears fell out of my eyes and I pretended that the magazine was so interesting.

When I got off the plane Adina was waiting at the gate. She looked great; the difference between working and looking for work was all over her. She kept asking me what was wrong and I told her I was tired and that I missed Swift already. She smiled and said she hoped she was like that after two years with her man. She was rounding off the time we spent apart and now. I let her comment ride on the air.

Adina excitedly pointed to her brand new Honda Civic. I smiled at the car as a courtesy, but I didn't understand why she wasn't driving a car like Bonita's. Her new apartment was ten times better than that ran down place she stayed in before. However it was still only averagely nice. She's on television for crying out loud, I expected her to be living in an expensive apartment and driving a phat car. You could tell she took pride in this place though. It was clean and she even decorated. She said we needed to eat before the party. She said that there would be food there, but it would be ridiculous stuff and the people judge you when you eat as if you're not supposed to be hungry. So I volunteered to cook while she went to take care of some things. She actually had food options in her refrigerator. So I made grilled chicken salads for us. We sat at her table and ate. Adina kept staring at me so I asked her why. "I don't know, you look different."

"How?"

She stared harder, "I don't know. You just do. I guess your face changed."

"Am I ugly now or something?"

"It's not even like that, you're just different. You're just.... just...... just." Then she laughed, "If I figure it out, I'll tell you."

When I went to the bathroom I stared at my face in the mirror. My skin was a little lighter, simply because I hadn't been outside all that much since I was pregnant. A good walk outside would fix that for me though.

As we drove to Beverly Hills I couldn't help but think about Norie, she was nearby and I couldn't see her. She has no clue that I exist. My depression was back and I couldn't shake it, so I got quiet. Adina introduced me to lots of people. I couldn't turn on my charms so I would say a quiet almost seemingly shy hello.

Then I saw him, he was average height and dressed very nicely. An established man about his money. I saw him look me up and down and then he went back to his conversation. Our eyes met a couple of times, and they connected as he walked towards us. I was preparing myself to speak when Adina stepped towards him and then they kissed. He rubbed her back and then he asked her to introduce him to her friend. Adina pulled back her excitement as she told him I was her cousin. She introduced him as Matt. While Adina smiled at me, Matt looked me up and down again. He asked me if I was an actor as well. Adina answered for me telling him that I was a singer. He smiled, and then he told me to sing for him. I knew he was testing me. I belted out a tune right there and then he smiled at me. A few people listened, some looked jealous while others smiled. Matt said my voice was amazing, and then he asked me whom I was with. I gave him the name of the agent that Bonita set me up with. Matt smiled and said he'd see me soon. He pointed to someone on the other side of the room and he told Adina she needed to meet them. When she started walking he looked back at me and smiled, so I did the same. I felt like crap anyways, so what difference did it make. I met people that night, and at one point Adina was talking to some people. Matt came over and he touched my shoulder. I smiled at him again, Matt handed me his card. Then he asked me when we could get together to discuss my *talent*? I asked him if there was any time like the present, and he smiled. He stared at me for a moment like he wanted to make sure I understood what he meant. He said it was a little crowded at the party and he'd like to go somewhere to talk. Then his eyes trailed off to Adina as she networked. I shrugged and I told him I went home in the morning. I looked at his card and my eyes got big. I asked him if he really represented this major label. He smiled as he continued to look around. Then he looked at me and said a moment alone with him could change my life.

As soon as I looked at Adina that depressed feeling came

back. Once again I was facing a moral dilemma. Adina has always been there for me. I didn't know what the story was with this guy. She didn't mention him before we got here. How do I know that she doesn't kiss other associates? They only pecked each other on the lips, it's not like they swapped spit. Matt told me to keep an eye on him and he'd tell me when we could sneak away. I walked around talking to people and accepting their praise as they told me how much they enjoyed my voice. I saw Matt talking to someone and then a girl approached Adina and I. She introduced herself and then she told Adina that she wanted to step outside to discuss a future roll she felt that Adina would be perfect for. Adina asked me if I would be fine without her. I smiled at her and I told her to go get them.

I watched Adina disappear then I watched Matt. He told me to go out to the garage and he'd join me in a minute. He pointed at the door then he walked away. I went to the bathroom; I asked myself if I really wanted to do this. I could see the depression growing over me by the second. I took a deep breath, maybe he didn't want sex. Maybe he only wanted to talk. I looked at his card again. I took a deep breath and then I told myself to see what happened.

When I stepped into the garage I was greeted by the view of a guy going in on a woman. They acted as if I didn't exist as they continued. I walked to the front of the garage where I could still see them, but not obviously. Matt turned red when he walked into them. He searched the garage until he saw me. He motioned for me to follow him. I quietly walked behind him out to the little house by the pool. Someone was already in the living room, which meant someone was in the bedroom. Matt smiled real big when he discovered the bathroom was empty. He locked the door behind me. He took out a notepad and pen from his inside jacket pocket. He wrote my name, my agent name and number down. He told me this was my pre-audition. He said if I did a good job he'd setup my official audition for the label. Then he unbuckled his pants and let them fall. I took a deep breath and then I got on my knees. Matt sat back and let me do all of the work. I rode him like I was a cowgirl. I had this white boy speaking in tongues.

As I readied myself in the mirror to go, he was still trying to get it together. Then he said I needed to give my cousin some lessons. It felt like he injected depression straight into my brain. I told him if he ever told her I'd come looking for him. He laughed and then he smacked my butt and said until we meet again. He walked out of the bathroom and I was left with a reflection I couldn't face.

I stayed in the bathroom for a long time holding myself and hoping this was all for something.

****

I couldn't sleep, my mind was racing with thoughts I didn't want to have. Adina was so excited about her conversation last night that she ran her mouth all the way back to her place. As we undressed for bed she asked me where I disappeared to. I told her I went outside to get some air. She said we must've missed each other cause she went outside looking for me. She said Matt looked concerned for half a second and then he suggested that you might've hooked up with someone. I watched her eyes and then I asked her what did he say when she told him how in love I was with my boyfriend? She said he shrugged and assured her I'd surface before she was ready to go. I guess that's why she looked relieved when I approached them.

I jumped when the phone started ringing. The sun was barely coming up and someone was calling. I could hear the sleep in Adina's voice as she answered the phone. Adina walked into the living room with sleep in her eyes as she handed me her only phone. "Hello?"

"Torrie, Hollywood is calling are you answering?"

My heart sped up, "what do you mean?"

"I can't stop thinking about your *talents*, and you can sing too." He laughed at his joke. "How soon can you come back to audition?"

"Talk to my agent, she knows what I'm looking for."

"What you're looking for?"

"Contracts and things like that. She has quite an impressive business plan for me. You witnessed my *talents* last night." I looked at Adina who was putting a pot of coffee on. "She can tell me whether you're just yanking my chain or not."

"Baby, as long as you and I are good, I'll make the deal as sweet as I can." I didn't say anything to that. What was I supposed to say to that? "Where's my girlfriend?"

I told him to hold on and then I gave the phone back to Adina. She immediately started smiling. She thanked him for looking out for her little cousin. Then she started going on and on about how good he's been to her. Depression was stabbing me in the chest. Doesn't matter that I didn't know they were seriously together. He just propositioned me for future hook ups and I didn't reject him. I cried into my pillow, this is going to blow up in my face. I can feel it.

When Adina got off of the phone, she told me that Bonita introduced them. She said she never pictured herself with a white guy before him. She went on and on about all of the things she loves about him. They've been together for almost a year. They're even talking about moving in together. Adina floated on a cloud as she drove me to the airport. She said Matt was disappointed that she didn't come home with him last night. She said they were getting lost in the sheets as soon as she dropped me off. I couldn't get on that plane fast enough. Swift picked me up from the airport, but he was quiet the entire ride and only giving me one-word answers. I didn't have the energy to chase him through this fit he was throwing. When we walked in the door, he grabbed me and kissed me before the door closed. He kept grabbing me and pushing me. He pushed me on the couch and yanked off my pants. He roughly took all of my clothes off and then he roughly bent me over and took me from behind. He had me in a choke hold as he pumped me hard. Before Novian I thought Swift was good. This was fine, I couldn't feel anything anyways. I was too depressed to think about anything but the pain that I was in.

Chapter 5

Novian

"I'm late Novian!" Shay protested as I kissed her neck.

"Its just a study group, you can be late." I kissed her neck some more.

Shay's whole body froze over. Her cheeks and ears started turning red. "When are you going to grow up? Eventually at some point you're going to have to let this music thing go. I should at least enroll in school and take some classes. You let your momma and Bradley tell you what to do and when to do it. You don't even know if Ursula is on your side or his." I let her go and then I walked back to the bedroom. Here she goes with this nonsense. "You don't even know if they're paying you what they should. All those people are making money off of your voice, and they throw a couple of dollars your way. You have no idea of how badly they're screwing you over."

"You can leave now," I hate when she starts talking to me like she knows more than I do. I don't tell her my every move. Lee and I have an entertainment lawyer on retainer. All of my contracts have been verified and I get my little royalties checks. I'm not making the money I want to make, but I can afford this apartment. I can afford my car, when I'm footing the bill I live simply. Fortunately I'm always with Mister. He lives, well he was living lavishly. He downsized from the big house with the security gate to a nicely modest house in the Oakland hills. Ok well, it's still huge to me. Compared to the mansion that he lived in before he downsized tremendously. Ever since Shay moved in, it's been tension. I thought having the kitty on hand when I came home was going to right all the wrongs. It was nice at first but now… She runs her mouth too much with opinions about everything. Like my life is a joke to her or something.

"I only tell you these things because I love you."

"Problem is it don't feel like love when you're talking down to me like that."

"I'm sorry, what I do, I do for us. One day you're not going to be in the studio. We need a plan B." She kissed my lips and then she left.

I looked at the time, I was going to be early, but I figured I'd hang around the house until it was time for my appointment with Camille. Camille was pulling out of the driveway as I drove up. She rolled down her window and told me I was early, when I shrugged she told me no one was home and to follow her. I've been here before; it was Camille's special store where you had to have a license to shop here.

When she got out of the car I whimpered. If Shay would've stopped playing I could be mellow right now, instead of pent up. I would've noticed Camille's curves and then turned my eyes. Right now I feel, I feel…. hungry. Like I'm dying to eat. Camille stood there smiling at me as she waited for me to get out of the car. I wasn't going to get out, but she was waiting. When she hugged me her soft body melted into my hardness. I told my Johnson to calm down. Camille smiled at me and then she took my hand and pulled me along. "Did Brad tell you about his heart?" She asked as if she asked if he told me what his favorite color was. I shook my head no. "That's why he hasn't been going as far during his performances anymore. Hammer seemed to pick up on Brad's slow pace and he's taken off. Bigger entourage, bigger productions, he's younger and better." She shook her head as she picked up a bottle from the shelf. "He has to take all these pills, and they mostly take the life out of him." Then she watched my eyes like she waited for the point to sink in. "Even with all of that," she set the bottle down and picked up another one. "Where is my husband?" I shrugged, "the little bit of energy he has he uses it on those dancers or her."

"Her?"

"Every now and then I know he gets a taste for old school." I didn't want to think about it so I looked away. "I get horny just like the next person." She smiled at me. "I need your help Novian. If I'm frustrated somehow I end up irritating him by breathing, and well we know how he holds back with me." She rolled her eyes as she put the bottle down. "I know you want to, and you'd be helping me."

"Mister would kill me," I was trying to think with my other head.

"He's not going to know."

"I didn't take you for the cheating kind."

My comment irritated her, "cheating kind? I wasn't aware that there is a certain kind. My husband steps out on me regularly. Look at me! Do I look like the kind of woman who's going to sit around waiting? You think your girlfriend waits on you?"

"Yes!"

She smiled at me, "to be young again. Honey you run around here from county fair to small arena with your ding-a-ling hanging out. She knows you mess around on her and she's most likely messing around too. Gone are the days when Lucinda walked with her head down and cried because you weren't faithful. Shoot! Lucinda's got a new bag and she goes by Lucy."

"Who is Lucy? You're always talking about Lucy."

"You're talking to her, Camille is married to Bradley Caruthers. Camille makes sure he takes his meds, washes his clothes whenever he comes home from being on the road. Camille loves her husband and takes his crap like a helpless Lucinda. Lucy takes care of Camille and looks out for her."

I shook my finger at her. "I knew you were crazy. Thanks for confirming." Then Camille grabbed me and pulled me in for a kiss. Her body was soft and she had more curves than Shay.

When I got into the kiss she backed up as she smiled at me.

"Nope not today, hear me Novian. When Lucy comes for you don't waste time talking." Then she picked up the stuff she needed. She told me she needed to make a stop before she went home, and then she drove off.

Left with nowhere to go, I decided to stop by my mother's to kill a little time. She was standing outside talking to a guy. I couldn't gauge the tone of their conversation. My mother's arms were wrapped around herself as she spoke with him. He stared at me as I approached them. She excitedly put her arm out to me. "You remember Renee," she stood so proud I chewed back my irritation.

"Of course," he was not impressed with me. "How's jumping around on a stage working out for you?"

His tone wasn't friendly and I didn't like him just from the look of him. I turned to my mother, "you got anything to eat?"

My mother's eyes turned sad, "please say hi baby. This is Eugene."

I looked at him with a so-what expression. "You need to learn how to respect your elders. You got a real bad attitude problem." I didn't say anything to him, I just looked at him. He squinted his eyes at me, "these little punks always wanna flex. I otta break you down right now!"

"You could try, but..." He punched me in the mouth and I didn't see it coming.

"Learn some respect!" My mother pleaded with him not to hit me again, as I was trying to get around her to fight him. Eugene stood there waiting for me, his expression and demeanor never changed. "If you really wanted me she couldn't hold you back." I moved my mother out of the way and he grabbed me by my neck. This man's hands were fast and strong. He had me and instead of fighting him back I was forced to try to release his grip on my neck. My mother pleaded with him to let me go. "You've done him no favors." He squeezed harder.

"Eugene please! I'm sorry! I'm sorry! I've got my ways; it's all my fault. Please let my baby go!"

"Next time I see your little punk behind you better have a respectful tone or I will kill you. I don't care who your mother is! You hear me?" I couldn't speak, he had my throat. "You hear me?"

"Eugene! Please!" My mother pleaded, "he doesn't know you."

"Why should he have to know me to respect me? He keep on like this and your son will be dead. I'm doing you a favor." Then he released my throat. He kissed my mother's lips as she cried. He walked away.

"Who was that?" I held on to my neck as if that would lessen the pain as I tried to regain my breath.

My mother stood there watching him walk away, "Eugene."

Torrie

Matt drummed his pen on the table as he looked at his colleagues and waited for their response. Swift was sitting next to me and he looked impatient while no one spoke up right away. Bonita, my agent, and my entertainment lawyer sent my acceptance conditions day's prior, and Swift and I were flown out here to meet with Matt's label. There was a lot of back and forth because of the list of demands I had. The label countered with the fact that I was an unknown. Armed with a complete album, mostly produced by Swift and I. I was ready to go and all they had to do was say yes and provide distribution and rotation.

The woman told me that the label was very impressed with my presentation and even my representation. She said they were very excited to work with me on my project. The problem was that as an unknown even though my album was great I needed to be launched before my album hit to drum up interest in my work and me.

They proposed some grunt work, I wasn't happy, but everyone on my team seemed to out vote me and agree with the label. I cut my eyes at Matt, cause he was the one telling me I could have anything I wanted. And after everything we've been through here he is agreeing with them when he's supposed to be on my side. Bonita noticed the looks I was shooting Matt, and in the end so did Swift. I kept my eyes to the ground after that. Matt was going to hear my mouth the next time I spoke with him. He's been promising all these things that he can't right away deliver on. Matt fell to the back as we left; he had to know I was upset. Bonita and my agent were excited though. They said no one got a deal like they were crafting on their debut album. Swift sat over to the side watching me. I had to take their word for it that my deal was anything good. It surely didn't feel like it. Bonita got a call that she took at the table and then walked away. My agent smiled at us, "her little girl's got a cold. I tell Bonita all the time that I don't know how she manages her career and being a single mom."

"It helps when you can afford the help." I took a drink of my soda.

"I'm sure money helps, but she's arranged her whole life to be with her baby. She's such a good mother."

Bonita came back to the table and she told us she had to go. I asked her if everything was ok, she smiled and said her baby was asking for her. I know that shouldn't have hurt, but it did. Bonita left and then my agent paid the bill.

Swift was quiet the entire time, only speaking when he had to. When we got back to the hotel he looked at me. He asked me who Matt was to me. I told him that Matt was Adina's boyfriend and that I met him at the party he didn't want me to go to. "How long have you been doing him?" If looks could kill I would be dead.

"I'm NOT!"

Swift grabbed me by my neck and threw me up against the wall in the bathroom. I grabbed my head from the impact. "DON'T LIE TO ME!"

"I'm not lying!" I tried to remove his hands from my neck. "Let me go!"

"Or else what? You going to call the police? Just remember, without me you go back to sleeping on the floor in your uncle's too crowded apartment. I could hold up your whole album. I MADE YOU! A clever lyricist you might be, but a song is NOTHING without a melody! You've set your lyrics to my melody and now you want to act like this!"

"Swift calm down, I don't know…"

He slapped me; "you insult my intelligence when you try to play me for stupid. I know how to read you. You forget that I'm actually in love with you; I can read your mind. You're the idiot who's never stopped long enough to pay attention to anyone other than yourself!" He squeezed my neck again, "and Novian!" He banged my head up against the wall again and then he released me. He marched into the bedroom and threw himself around. I fell to the ground crying and holding my neck. I didn't know how he knew, but I decided to be quiet.

After a while Swift came and picked me up off of the floor. Tears were still seeping out of his eyes as he carried me to the bed. He kept kissing me and then he took my clothes off. He kept telling me he loved me and that he was sorry. Every stroke was matched with an apology, every kissed was followed by a declaration of love. I didn't know what to think.

Novian

"Listen up little boy, class is in session." Camille stood in front of me completely naked. "I don't know what you think you've been doing, but it's my job to teach you something. This is a vagina. It's not a chew toy; it's not a pounding mechanism. It's a beautiful flower with layers and layers of petals. You can't drool all over it and think you did something. You have a nice sized package but it's a waste if you don't know what you're doing with it." She opened my legs, "pay attention class is in session."

When we were done, my eyes were blurry, and I was seeing double. Camille was trying to catch her breath. I asked her how I did on my final, and she started laughing as she tried to catch her breath. She patted my back and then she told me to keep it like that. She looked at the time and then she said she had to go pick up the baby. She said my homework was to practice on Shay. Lately in his major hustles to stay afloat, Mister hasn't been working with any of the artists that he was nurturing. He brings me into the studio from time to time to sing hooks and things. I haven't heard my voice on the radio in a minute. I guess I should be happy cause he's still paying me. However I feel like this could all end soon if I don't make moves on my own. Camille says he should be working on developing his artist instead of trying to compete. She said he doesn't listen to her cause he feels like she doesn't know what she's talking about.

****

I went over Mister's house to work on some new material and get my hair taken down, washed, and re-braided. My hair has gotten pretty long, but Camille warns me about playing in it. So I don't mess with it too much. The house was quiet and Camille opened the door with knuckle imprints on her bare shoulders. She didn't say too much as she took my hair down and combed it out. As she washed my hair in the washbowl drips of water hit my forehead. I opened my eyes and realized she was crying silently to herself. I asked her what was wrong and she said nothing was wrong as she looked at her niece who was quietly playing in her play pin. I stared at her face and I reached up and wiped the tears from her eyes.

As I sat in the chair in the family room, she sighed slowly and she said she was getting too old to be dealing with Mister's crap. She was uncharacteristically sad and hurt. That's when she told me he flew out that afternoon and wouldn't be back until the end of the week. She said Mister was upset because he lost the choreographer that he had been working with and he couldn't find anyone to match her quality of work and pricing. When she asked him how he lost the choreographer, she thought he was going to say he hit on her or something like that. She said all he said was **MALCOLM**. She didn't think anything of it until his insults of Malcolm sound like the Malcolm she knew. She said they put together that he was talking about the Malcolm she knew at the same time and he flew into a jealous rage. I asked her how she knew him, and she didn't answer. She just kind of stared off into the distance. She said she's been dealing with random punches and kicks ever since then. She said his last night before he left he made her sleep on the floor next to their bed. He told her he was treating her like the female dog that she was. That's when she started crying. I looked at the baby, who had fallen asleep. At first I was only trying to calm her so that she didn't wake the baby. Then she kissed me and pulled up her dress as she pulled down my pants and draws. She rode me raw and I was utterly speechless. She gave me a few minutes to recover and then she brought me back to life again. I felt guilty about the whole thing until she started telling me the things he says about me behind my back. About how stupid I was and how if it wasn't for my mother he'd walk all over me without any remorse because it was my fault for being so dumb.

Camille and I have been going at it every chance we get since then.

******

I don't know how she does it. Camille was calm and she

looked at me like there was nothing between us. She never carried herself any differently and I guess now I see how she's always been a flirt. Watching how ruthless Camille is has made me look at Shay completely different. Sometimes she's just missing in action and when I question her about her whereabouts she has no real explanation. Sometimes she throws my accusations back on me. She asks me why all of a sudden I'm suspicious of everything she does. She has a point when she says she's consistent. So I've been trying to chill out.

I wanted to work on new music, but nothing was coming out right.

When Amos called I was excited to hear from him. We've been playing phone tag for a minute now. Amos told me to get dressed and to come out for the night like a normal person. He told me not to wear any shiny clothes or jackets with medals on them like Mister does sometimes. I couldn't stop laughing.

Amos came inside; he smiled as he looked around. "Your girl keeps your place nice."

I looked around, "you know I clean my own place. Ursula may not have taught me much, but she showed me how to keep a clean place. Shay ain't neat at all."

"Where she at? She can come with us if you want."

"I don't know where she is," I waived my hand like I didn't want to talk about it.

"Yo! How come you didn't tell me Lee got married? I saw him and the wife walking the mall trying to get the baby out."

"Probably cause she ain't my favorite person. I understand he's postponed his life long enough behind me." Then I looked at Amos, "man you ain't been here five minutes and you pressing all the buttons. You want a drink? Cause I need one right about now." I pulled the bottles Mister gave me out of my cabinet.

Amos hurried over, "what is all this? Since when you drink? The Novian I know wont touch the stuff."

"Mister gives me all kinds of stuff. Pick your poison light or dark?" I ignored the rest of his statement.

He thought about it for a minute, "we don't need my darkness tonight. Let's go with light to keep things upbeat."

I raised an eyebrow, "tequila?"

"Heck yeah! Oh it's on!" Amos got excited. I went to my room and I got the flask I brought back from Michigan for Amos. I put both of our flasks on the counter and then I filled them to the brim. "Novian, when you start drinking?"

I knew he was asking because of my mother. I hate the look of her drunken stoopers on her. "You remember Torrie?"

He smiled, "of course I do."

"I drank with her, now I do on occasions."

"Where she at now?"

I shrugged, "don't know. Let's go!"

Amos was talking about his drama with his baby momma as we drove. I was running from thoughts of Torrie while he spoke. I'm almost certain Shay is cheating on me and I turned my back on Torrie for her. Amos shook hands with the bouncer and then he let us in ahead of the line. The lights were low and music was pumping out of the speakers. We sat at a table on the side. Amos looked around as he leaned back in his chair. Then he smiled and stood up. He shook hands with a guy then he hugged him. The guy was older than us; he looked like he was in his thirties at least. I liked how his beard was perfectly lined, and his whole appearance was smooth. "I want you to meet my boy, this is Novian. We go WAY back. Novian, this is Vic I put in work for him."

Amos was smiling; even though the guy was grinning he was scanning everything about me. "What's up?" He nodded.

"What's up?"

"Where you from?" Vic stood up straight as he stood in front of me.

"Berkeley."

"Why you look familiar?"

"Oh! He be singing with Mr. MC."

Vic started laughing, "that's right. I remember booing you off the stage once."

My smile dropped, "everybody's a critic until it's their turn."

Then a group of girls walked past us barely dressed and making my mouth drool. "Yo! Your Pops is here tonight?"

"You know the freaks can't get enough of him. We in the house deep tonight. Let me know if you need anything." Then Vic went to the VIP section where a bunch of equally groomed men and women were.

"All of those females for his father?"

"Naw, that fool got like a hundred sisters, nieces, and nephews."

"Which one is the dad?"

"The one in the suit, that's Big Vic." Big Vic was looking in our direction when I looked at him. Whatever his son said to him made both of them laugh. He was probably laughing at me again.

"What kind of work you put in for him?"

"A little of this a little of that." He looked around the room.

"Looks like I spotted Shay." He pointed on the dance floor.

I don't even remember standing up. Shay was grinding with this guy like they were alone. She didn't see me until I was in her face. "Shay!"

Shay screamed as she tried to catch her balance. "Novian? What are you doing here?"

"What are you doing? Who is this?"

"What are you doing here?" Shay stammered as she tried to push past her buzz.

"Who are you?" The guy asked me, as he looked me over.

"What's up Bishop?" Amos came over with his hand extended. "This my boy Novian, it looks like you two been banging the same hoe."

"I should care because?" Bishop looked irritated, "you can have her back tonight after I'm done with her if you two were supposed to be in love or some junk like that."

Amos raised his eyebrows at me like he was waiting for my answer. "Shay you fired! Why would I want her back?"

I looked up and Malcolm was walking towards us. He had two young guys with him and a slightly older kid. I frowned at him and his face didn't change. Both of the young cats looked at me and then at Malcolm for a reaction. "Bishop," he shook his hand and ignored my presence.

"What's up Malcolm? You know this cat?"

"He's Ursula's son."

Bishop's head whipped back to me real fast. "Serious?" He put his hands up like he was surrendering.

Shay was fighting her intoxication, "Novian can we talk about this later?"

One of the guys with Malcolm started laughing. "She's funny."

Shay's head snapped as she looked at the kid. "Dude?"

He laughed harder, "what's up girl? Why you all sloppy drunk in the club before eleven?"

"You know her?" The other guy asked her with no amusement in his face.

"Chickenhead," then he looked at Bishop. "This your girl?"

"Freak of the night, he's the one acting all heartbroken behind this."

"What do you mean by Chickenhead?"

"I mean, I've tossed her before. So have a lot of people after me. What? Were you two in love?" He smiled while the little one batted his eyes at me as he smiled.

"Shay! A freaking kid? For real?"

"I didn't know he was as young as he is until after." She had a goofy smile on her face as she looked at him.

Malcolm watched me for a reaction and I couldn't react. My girl has been cutting up and I was too blind to notice. I guess this explains why she just wasn't in the mood sometimes, no matter what I did. She was too tired after all of her escapades with all these fools. Malcolm started to walk away and all of his boys followed him, "daddy. You think he's going to hit her? I wanna see if you think he will."

"He's not going to do nothing, he'll probably still be with her **tomorrow**." Malcolm walked over to the VIP section and then he shook hands with both of the Vic's.

"You know him?" Amos asked me with his eyes fixed on Malcolm.

"I can't stand him! He always flexing at me."

Bishop stared at me, "you really are stupid aren't you? You don't know who Malcolm is?"

"You should ask me if I care who Malcolm is. He can't do nothing to me, I run with Mister."

Bishop cocked his head to the side, "Brad?" I nodded yes. "What makes you think Brad has got anything on Malcolm?"

"Malcolm ain't nobody! I'm not concerned with him!"

Bishop nodded towards the VIP, "all those Cardell's run Oakland. Amos you ain't school your boy on the Cardell name?"

"Chill man, dump this hoe and let's go." Amos pointed towards the door.

"You can't be Ursula's son, you heck of whack!"

Amos sucked his teeth and looked at Bishop, "come on man. Let's just be cool and part ways respectfully."

"This fool had one choice to make and he's standing stuck like a female. I don't have time for this. If it wasn't for Ursula!"

"If it wasn't for Ursula what? My mom's not here, you want some?" I opened my arms.

"Um! Novian, you don't want to do that…"

"Naw man! He got something to say he can say it. He got something to prove, he can try and prove it."

Amos put one finger up to Bishop, and then he walked up to me so that I could hear him over the music. "Novian! If you don't stop! Did you not hear Vic say that his family is deep in here tonight?

I work for the Cardell's I don't need them getting mad at you and ordering me to put a bullet in your head. You are the only odd man out over here, you need to calm down and learn some respect. You making me regret not staying home with my baby momma. Chill out man!" My chest started pumping up, I shook my head no. "Let me put this in perspective for you cause I see you going in the wrong direction. If you don't back down, you will die tonight, regardless of who your momma is." Then he looked me in my eyes to make sure I heard him.

I took a deep breath and then I lowered my head and walked towards the door. I could hear Malcolm's son laughing as I walked. I HATE THAT KID!

****

"NOVIAN!" bang, bang, bang! "Novian!" Shay had been banging on my door all morning. I imagine that my neighbors are all at work, otherwise why wouldn't they have called the police by now. I sat back with my feet up as I wrote the lyrics to a hate filled song. I heard car doors and then hurried footsteps from the parking lot. I looked out the kitchen window and my mother's bucket was out there. Shay stopped making any noise for a minute and then I heard arguing. Then I heard the sound of my mother cursing her out like only she could. My mother's mouth can be down right vicious at times. This was the first time that I was relieved that she was using that deadly weapon on someone. Normally I would be embarrassed when she went off. Shay was covering her ears and then she ran away leaving all of her things at the door.

My mother marched into my apartment looking me over. She asked me if I was ok. I asked her why everyone keeps saying that I'm Ursula's son like that means something. She looked at me like I had to be kidding. She said most people know her from Santa Rosa to San Jose, the Peninsula to Sacramento. When I asked her how, she said music. "Music unites people on levels you wouldn't understand. The only time I tried to give music up was for Lee and Leona's daddy. I wasn't being true to myself. And well you see it didn't last. I wasn't built to play Suzy Homemaker. I really loved their daddy and I feel horrible about breaking his heart like I did. He knew about my love of music before we got together. He was the one stupid enough to actually believe that our love would be enough."

"Who's my father?"

She couldn't even look at me, "it don't matter Novian. Knowing about him doesn't change anything about where we are today. Why aren't you out with Brad?"

"Ever since Mister started struggling I haven't been working as much."

"He still paying you?"

"Yes, but for how long? If he's not putting me out, how am I supposed to maintain a following?"

"I guess you'll have to figure that out with your manager."

"You want me to beg?"

"I'm not no manager Novian. All I know is the music, the performance. I don't know nothing-about managing talent and booking gigs. That's why we were in LA remember. I didn't really want you under Brad's strings. Can't cry over spilled milk." I gave her puppy eyes, "all I know is that there's an audition coming up for background vocalist. It's not glamorous playing backseat to someone else, but it's work and the particular artist loves to showcase everyone who supports her. I can get you an audition, but you'll have to get the job on your own."

"Thanks," I hugged her. One day she might realize that I don't really care to know who my real father is. He never cared enough to make his presence known why should I care about who he is? I only ask her about him to guilt her in to helping me. I stopped caring when I was a little kid.

Torrie

"I just need you all to be there clapping for me when she introduces me. Make a big deal about me so that people notice. Got it?"

"Yeah, we got it." Sinclaire popped her gum. "Thanks for the tickets girl, it's been a minute since we hung out. Fancy still be asking us what happened to you."

"I've been grinding paying my dues."

"Excuse me Torrie. It's almost time to warm up." The stage producer said.

"Thanks, I'll be right there." I hugged my girls, "thank you all for coming. I feel better knowing you're here."

I took a deep breath then I walked back stage, the musicians were moving about and going out to the stage. I imagined that everyone was here to see me and it was about to be the Torrie show. I hated that we were all told to practice on our own and this would be our only practice. What if I practiced the wrong pitch or something? I didn't know who the other singers would be. The stage director was showing everyone their marks on the stage. He pointed to me and confirmed that I was Torrie, when I said yes he told me to stand in the middle. I stood next to this tall model looking chick. She was cute, but never as beautiful as me. She scanned me just like I scanned her. She stared at my eyes while the director watched me take my spot. He told me not to be nervous and that if I was there that meant I had a pretty good name behind me with someone. I smiled and thanked him as I took a deep breath.

Then he stepped onto the stage. He didn't even see me and I was speechless. Novian looked like he gained muscle and his hair was neatly braided in four long and thick braids that went down his back. His skin was smooth like clay and his goatee was perfectly lined. The director pointed to his microphone and he lost all color when he looked at me. He stood there stuck for a minute; at least I knew the feeling was mutual. When he stood next to me I could feel the heat from his body all over me. Novian stared at the director while the girl next to me checked him out. As we practiced I couldn't help but notice how well Novian and I harmonized together. The other girl was good too, but never as good as me. The director told us to go rest our voices and wait for showtime.

Novian wasn't going to walk around here like he got the best of me, even if he did. I will not make the mistake of sleeping with him ever again. "So how have you been?" I smiled at Novian like we were old classmates.

"I've been out here grinding, how about you?"

"I recorded an album, I'm just passing time building a name for myself until it drops."

"A whole album, that's good." He looked around the room like he wanted to be anywhere but here talking to me.

I took a deep breath and then I walked away, he didn't have to make small talk with me. I could feel depression washing over me, I took deep breaths and I sat in the corner trying to get a handle on my mood. We were about to go out tonight and it was going to be my time.

When The Diva arrived, she was completely decked out in designer clothes. She walked into the room and scanned everyone then she smiled at us like she was giving us permission to worship her. She asked her assistant if we all signed our nondisclosure agreements yet. When her assistant showed her the short stack of paperwork, she smiled as she looked around. Her eyes landed on Novian, "don't I know you?"

He smiled, "you listen to rap?"

"Oh I listen to it all baby. How else you gonna stay on top of the latest sounds if you stick to one genre? What's your name again?"

"Novian."

She stared at him, "what's your whole name?"

He hesitated, "Novian Murphy."

"Any relation to Eddie?"

"Not that I know of."

"I'm not your agent or publicist but I think people would remember your last name a lot easier than they would Novian. Think about it and let me know before I introduce you tonight." Novian agreed.

"Diva! Diva! Diva! We don't have time for this! We got to get your makeup done. Come on!" Someone said as they ushered her into her dressing room.

Novian came and sat next to me, "what do you think?"

"I think she completely ignored me!"

Novian smiled, "about my name. You think she got a point?"

"I don't know Novian, you trying to start all over?"

"Novian is signed to Mr. MC's label, Murphy isn't. I think I kind of like the sound of it."

"Good for you! I don't care!"

"Look Torrie," he started gesturing with his hands. "I'm sorry about the way things went down with us. I thought choosing my girlfriend was the right thing to do. I hurt you and I've got nothing to show for it." I didn't say anything, I stared at him. "I know you probably don't care and I'm assigning more to anything between us than you ever would. I just want you to know you've always been TORRIE to me not just some girl."

"Then why did you desert me like that?"

"I choked, there's no excuse."

"I think you really liked me."

"Whether or not I liked you has never been the question. I just wasn't going to fool myself into thinking that you cared about me. I know you were probably mad at me for knocking you up. Like you would ever go through all of that for somebody you were just kicking it with." I didn't say anything, I wanted to tell him that he had it all wrong but he was giving me all the power right now.

When he touched my hand, I looked at his fingers, "where's Shay?"

"We broke up."

"Really? What happened?"

He took a deep breath, "she was cheating on me. You still with Swift?"

"How do you know about Swift?"

"He asked me if you and I were together. When I said no, he said he was confirming your story."

"When was this?"

"A long time ago."

"Yes, we're still together and he won't like seeing me talking to you. So do me a favor. After the show go your way and I'll go mine." Then I stood up and walked away.

****

I put the key to my storage unit in my momma's hand. "Momma, protect this for me. Swift is not my boyfriend anymore, no matter what he tries to tell you. Don't give him this key."

"Ok, but what if he says he wants to say sorry?"

I put my hands on my momma's shoulders, "look at me momma." Her eyes glided over my swollen face. "It's never ok for a man to hurt you like this. He's not a man and there's nothing he can say to me to make this up to me. I don't care if he loves me. His love isn't good enough. Do you understand?"

"Ok baby, I'm sorry he hurt you."

My eyes watered, "when I come back I will have enough saved for an apartment. You're going to have your own room." Her eyes lit up when I said that. "You're going to have your own bed like you did at grandma's."

"Really?" She smiled really big at me.

"Yes! I promise momma! I promise!"

"Ok baby," we hugged.

I walked back to Sinclaire's car. My momma stood in my uncle's doorway watching me walk away. Sinclaire blasted music as she drove. "I can't believe you let that nigga hit you! What happened to the Torrie I knew? The one who would kick butt first and ask questions later."

"So you're an expert on fighting men? I didn't let him hit me, he did it anyways. It's not like it happened all the time either. Only when he got jealous, and when he found out I was going to be working with Novian he lost it."

"Novian ain't nobody. Why would he care about Novian? If he had any sense he'd be concerned about that keyboard player you're going to be traveling with."

"It's not like I care what he thinks anymore. Thank you for letting me crash at your place tonight."

When we got to Sinclaire's place her sister was too excited and telling me that we had to go to Fancy's club tonight. I didn't feel like going out clubbing, my face was swollen and my body was sore. I felt obligated to go though. Sinclaire and her sister were going and I was sure their momma was going to feel some kind of way about me still being here when they left. I reluctantly got dressed. I popped Advil, which helped with my soreness all over. When we walked into Fancy's it was just like before. A room full of people and everyone afraid to be the first person on the dance floor. I downed my drink and then I went out on the dance floor. After a game of follow the leader the dance floor filled up and there was that guy again. He took me by the bar where I ordered another drink and then he took me to Fancy's table. She greeted me with a hug and then she asked me where I disappeared to. So I told her I spent some time in LA and that I've been working on my album. I told her about my gig that goes on tour tomorrow. She congratulated me and then she told me I could come and promote at her club whenever I wanted to.

Chapter 6

Novian

Torrie is different now. When she thinks no one is paying attention she looks so sad. Everybody likes Torrie except the Diva and the other background singer. Torrie goes out of her way to be nice to them and they act like she's trying to steal from them. The rest of the band and I think it's too many women in one space.

Torrie was ignoring me until she saw the Diva hanging around me too much. During our down time she comes wherever I am and she cuddles into me and then she writes. We don't talk about anything in that space. We just spend time together like that. One time I tried to kiss her and she did everything but run. Torrie made sure she told me that it wasn't that kind of party. I couldn't blame her for being guarded; I ditched her when she needed me the most. Being this close to her brought me peace, and I think it did the same thing for her. Torrie was different, no more pretenses at least with me. She was wounded and she only wanted me to hold her. When Diva found us like that the first time she just kind of stared at us. Then she started asking all kinds of questions about Torrie and I.

"Next time you come home to get your hair done Mister wants you to come to the studio. He has a song he wants you to work on."

"Why didn't he call me himself?"

"He's been all over the place."

"Never stopped him before."

Camille exhaled, "he's been in and out of the hospital. They put him on a new medication for his heart so he's been feeling a little better. He's had to slow down a lot." Her voice smiled, "he's been home more with us."

I guess she thought something about that statement was supposed to make me happy. "Look, I only have the weekend. When are we going to have our time?"

Camille giggled a little, "can't say you're not anxious. I'll work it out. You miss me that much?"

"You know I do."

"You haven't found a fill-in while you're on the road?"

"I've hooked up with The Diva a few times, the other background singers ain't messing with me like that. One doesn't like men, and the other one isn't interested. I miss you, and I need you."

Camille's voice smiled. "I'll see what I can do."

There was little kid noise in the background and then Camille started talking in the background. When she said it was me I could hear Mister's voice. He took the phone from Camille. "How's the road life treating you?"

"I'm making money, I'm getting exposure I can't complain too much."

"That's good son, did Camille tell you I got a song for you when you pop in?"

"Yeah she told me, guess who's out here?" I didn't want to talk about who's raggedy song he wanted me to sing on.

"Who?"

"January!"

I could hear his smile through the phone. "Serious? What she doing out there?"

"Working like the rest of us. She's got the Diva's timing down to a science. She asks about you all."

Mister's voice grinned, "like she cares. She was under your momma kind of like a mentorship. That's a feather in your momma's cap right there." When I didn't say anything to that, he said a few more things then we got off of the phone.

******

I know everyone was panicked but I was getting a kick out of watching January handle all this chaos. The Diva was on one of her power trips and she was being difficult. The promoter told her the house was already packed he could have her backup singers put on the show and no one would be the wiser.

The Diva reminded everyone that the cameras out front would be looking for her. The Diva dug her heels in and refused to go out. January turned to us, "the show must go on. Torrie are you up for the challenge?"

"Why did you ask Torrie, Novian and I are just as qualified!" The other background singer said.

"We don't need egos right now." Then she turned to Torrie, "are you?"

Torrie took a deep breath then she said, "yes."

The Diva laughed as she spun around in her seat to face the mirror. "She's going to bomb! It's over ten thousand people out there and cameras."

Torrie and everyone walked out to get ready. I wanted to see if they were going to fight so I stayed. January calmly told the Diva she was in violation of her contract and then she would have legal heat raining down on her. She told the Diva to pack her bags cause she was done.

January told Torrie to call her manager cause they had a small window to work out the paperwork. Torrie's hands were shaking as she handed January her phone.

The other background singer was seething and the bass player was trying to calm her. During rehearsal Torrie's voice was cracking and at one point she just stood there and cried. January walked over and had a conversation with her that none of us could hear. Then January said rehearsal was great and she'd see us in two hours. When she walked past me she told me to follow her. I walked outside with January to her car. She stopped walking and then she let out the loudest scream I've ever heard. I stood there and stared. January started crying as she screamed. She said there are millions of dollars on the line and the Diva picked the worst night to do this. She said she knew this was coming though which is why she didn't want to work with her in the first place. She said she personally thinks Torrie and I are better singers but she had to pick Torrie because of the way the show was set up. Then she dropped her knees and clasped her hands together in front of me. She asked me to help Torrie get it together. She said I had a calming affect on Torrie and that rehearsal was horrible. She needed me to do whatever it is that I do that makes Torrie step up. I had no idea that she noticed. She said if she can get the promoters and folks behind Torrie she'd make sure there was a bonus for me and she would never forget my favor to her. Even though she didn't say how much of a bonus I agreed.

Torrie

I can't stop waiving my hands! I paced the floor! This is a lot of pressure! How do they expect me to pull this off? This isn't right! This is so wrong! That rehearsal was horrific! I looked at the clock and it was almost time to go out on stage. Heat flashed all over my body and I felt like I was going to be sick.

There was a knock at the door and then January and Novian walked in the room. January had her headpiece on and she partially listened to whomever she spoke to through that headpiece and talked to me. She said when I introduced everyone I needed to introduce Novian as Murphy and she needed me not to forget. "Diva gave him that name why does it matter?"

"Novian is under contract with Mr. MC. Murphy can perform in this showcase. This is a televised show so we need to have everyone's names stated correctly." Then January put her hands on my shoulders. "I believe in you Torrie, that's why I picked you. You can do this. This one performance is going to open so many doors for you. Just remember that I picked you." Then she patted my shoulders, smiled, and walked out of the room.

Novian smiled at me, "are you nervous?"

"Scared!"

"What's the difference between tonight and any other night?"

"I'm going to be in the front. I'll be a leader, I'm not following someone else's key."

"You want me to tickle you?"

Everything in me froze up. "NO! You know I hate to be tickled!"

"I know I'm the only one you let tickle you." He smiled.

Flashbacks of the tickling session that turned into the sex that brought Norie flashed through my mind. "I remember where your tickles got me. Nowhere and fast."

Novian moved closer to me, "this is your moment. You've worked very hard to get here. Think about that notebook full of songs. This is your chance to show everyone who Torrie Rowe is and that she's here to stay." Then he kissed my lips. All of my anxiety melted away. I pulled Novian back in for another kiss. This kiss was long and it was juicy. The best kiss of my life!

Someone knocked on the door and I could tell Novian forgot where we were. I smiled at him and then I thanked him. We walked out of the dressing room hand in hand. January was on the stage speaking to the crowd, informing them that I was going to be performing tonight instead of Diva. Novian squeezed my hand then he let me go and he went to his microphone. He's performed in front of audiences this big before, so it's no big deal for him. When the music started my stomach dropped and I forgot all of the words. A tear fell out of my eye as January told me it was time for me to go out on the stage. I guess he knew I was going to hesitate cause Novian started singing the song. I took a deep breath, I told myself I got this. I started my riff before I hit the stage. By the second stanza the audience was clapping and grooving with me. When I broke the song down at the end singing from my toes. The audience was UP and on their feet. People were screaming and sending me MAD ENERGY! I sang everything that Diva had planned, and I knew I did it better. The audience never responded to her like this. Then when I started dancing with the dancers everyone went crazy! You would've thought this was the Torrie Rowe show. Diva may have known how to sing, but she couldn't move. I had seen these routines so many times over our time out here that I knew the routines by heart. WE KILLED IT!

At the end of the show I had a standing ovation! When the curtain dropped I ran to Novian and wrapped my legs around him. I kept kissing him as I thanked him. Everyone froze as they watched us; I had been doing a good job of keeping to myself. Tonight I couldn't help it, I was bursting with energy. January congratulated me on a job well done. She told me I was taking over the Diva's suite at the hotel and then **tomorrow** we were on our way to the next location. On the bus we all celebrated and everyone said that I did better than even they thought I could. The other background singer didn't say anything. She sat over to the side looking sour. I went to our room and I quietly took all of my things out. When she realized I was leaving she got even more irritated but I didn't care.

Diva's suite was huge and expensive, I ran from room to room as I laughed to myself. Diva wasn't even all that mainstream. She had a couple of hits a while ago and this was supposed to be her comeback tour. I picked up the phone, I took a deep breath and then

I dialed Novian's room. When someone picked up you could hear all of the roommates talking about something. I asked to speak to Novian. When the person said that the call was for Novian the room fell silent. Novian said an unsure hello, and I told him to come spend the night with me. He asked me if I was sure. I told him I was sure and to hurry up. As he hung up the phone I heard everyone erupt into excited chatter. I kept fidgeting with the nightgown I bought on one of our trips to the mall. It was very sexy and the thought of it made me feel grown and sexy. I thought I wouldn't wear it until I got my own place. It was perfect for tonight. When I opened the door Novian's eyes got big and he swallowed hard. I invited him in and then I kissed him. Novian carried me to the bedroom and he laid me on the bed. I wanted to run this show, but Novian showed me that this was his show. He was so strong, he was so powerful, and he was so, he was so… GOOD!

******

Bonita told me that she had a two-bedroom apartment set up for me when I got home **tomorrow**. She said I was going to be picked up at the airport by a car service and taken there. She said she'd give me a call the following morning to go over money and everything I needed.

As I thanked Bonita for everything it happened. A little voice in the background called out to her. You could've heard cotton hit the floor I was so quiet and trying to hear the voice. Bonita, very lovingly spoke in the background. She told Norie that she would be right with her. She didn't say anything right away; she was probably trying to grab her composure. I looked at Novian as he did his push-ups on the floor. I didn't know how mad he'd be about Norie or how he felt about any of it. We never discuss it other than him apologizing for leaving me high and dry like he did.

Bonita apologized for the interruption as if I had no idea who the little voice belonged to. She spoke as if the whole scene didn't even just happen, then she got off the phone with me.

Novian's hair has gotten really long, and even though he mostly keeps it braided it's beautiful. I wondered who's nose Norie had, did she have Novian's flat face or my round face. Did she have Novian's eyes or mine? His red undertones or my orange undertones. Novian asked me why I was staring at him. "Do you ever wonder what our child would've looked like?"

"All of the time, that baby seems like it stays on my mind."

"Really?" My eyes got big.

"I never truly thought about the reality that I could impregnate someone. I guess it's a good thing that you spoke with Lee. I might've wanted to keep it."

"Really?" I sat up straight in shock.

"Dumb huh?" He looked embarrassed, "I mean we wouldn't be here right now doing all of this. We'd be working normal 9-5's trying to make ends meet for our child. Too much responsibility for two eighteen year olds. Do you think you would've kept it if I asked you to?"

Tears came to my eyes, "I don't know Novian. I guess you would've had to have taken one of my phone calls for me to even gauge that." I stood up.

Novian hopped off of the floor and he jumped in my way from leaving the room. "Torrie, I'm sorry!"

"I know!"

"I'm really sorry!"

"I know!"

"Do you forgive me?" I crossed my arms and I didn't say anything. He kissed my neck, "we could have another baby right now if you like."

"Don't be stupid! I've got a lot of work ahead of me. I can't have a baby right now."

"Let me know when you're ready, we can try again."

"Novian, you are not my man."

He spread his palms over my butt and then he gripped it as he pulled me into his sweaty body. "Who is then?" He kissed my lips.

"Not you!" I turned my head.

He started sucking on my neck, "I'm your man Torrie. Nobody will ever know you like I know you. All your diva put ons are for them, I know the real you. No one will ever know you like I do."

"I'm a star!"

"You're still TeTe, the girl who always forgets the lyrics." Then he carried me back to the room. "Don't forget I knew you when this was a dream."

Novian

When I walked into my apartment it was clean, and dishes from this morning's breakfast were neatly in the sink. My comforter was different on my bed and female toiletries were all over the bathroom neatly put away. I stood in the bathroom looking around, and then I heard the front door. I walked into the living room to see my mother walking in going to the bedroom. She screamed to the top of her lungs when she saw me. "WHAT ARE YOU DOING HERE?"

"What are you doing here?"

"I had to put my stuff in storage, Lee told me to stay here until you came home and then we'd figure something else out. Why didn't you tell me you were coming home?"

I ignored her question as I walked to the bedroom, "thank you for keeping up on my bills. What happened with your place?"

She shrugged as she sat on the edge of the bed. "I got behind and then I couldn't bounce back."

"Your beloved Brad didn't help you?"

"I didn't tell him." She tried to move alcohol bottles as if I wouldn't see them.

"Please tell me you've had that jug for months." I pointed at the empty bottle of rum.

"Novian! I don't need your judgment! It's been a lot going on."

"Oh yeah? Why don't you tell me about it?"

"Brad is losing it. He's decided that he hates my friend; we got into a big argument about it. I wonder if his wife is giving him more than just his medication. He gets stuck on tangents and he won't let them go. He's not sounding anything like the Brad that I've always known and loved. "

"Meaning?"

"For one he hates my friend Malcolm, and he…"

"Can you blame him! I hate that guy too!"

She gasped, "how can you hate someone you don't even know?" I told her how he did me at his studio. "That was in defense of me."

"He's just mad at the world because he's so black."

"God didn't make no mistakes on that one, you don't know what you're talking about." She waved me off.

"What would you know about it? He's a little boy to you."

"I ain't never personally went there with him. But these other little girls, they talk." She smiled, "he ain't got no reason to be mad about nothing."

I squinted my eyes at her, "do you have any idea of how gross that sounds? You're my mother! You can't talk about someone close to my age like that."

She put her hands up, "let's change the subject. How long are you home?"

Torrie

"I want to put flowers right here! Don't you think that will be nice?" My momma asked me with a smile.

"Yes momma, that will be nice. Do you like your room?"

"Oh Torrie! It's beautiful! Where did you find all of the butterflies? You know they're my favorites."

"I know momma. When I start making real money you're going to have a bedroom bigger than mine."

Her eyes got big, "you make fake money?"

"No, I mean when I make more money."

"Oh, that makes sense." She looked around the empty living room. "Swift came by a couple of times while you were gone."

"What did he say?"

"He said he was sorry and he asked for your number so he could call you."

"What did you say?"

"The truth that you were on the road and he couldn't call you. He gave me something." She went to her room and came back with envelopes. "He asked me to give them to you."

"Thank you momma." I took the envelopes and I put them in the trash in the kitchen. "Don't talk to him anymore."

"You're not going to read them?"

"No."

"It looked like he practiced writing your name on the envelopes."

"I don't care." Then there was a buzz on the intercom. "Momma this is my friend Novian. He's going to spend the night in my room. I'm going to lock my door, but if you need anything just knock ok."

"Ok, I'll go watch a movie." She walked back in to her room.

Novian greeted me with a hug and kiss. He said my place was really nice, nicer than his. I thanked him and then he picked me up and carried me to my room. He shut the door with his foot and then he laid me on the bed.

Even though I orgasmed Novian continued to eat dessert as my eyes crossed. Suddenly I heard my momma's voice and it didn't sound like she was on the other side of the door. "Torrie are you ok?"

I opened my eyes to see my momma coming in the door. "No momma! I'm ok! Please go back in your room!"

Novian moved so that I could get up and lock my door. My legs were wobbly as I tried to get back to the bed. That was a great reintroduction to my momma.

******

When we pulled up to the building I looked at it

unimpressed. Matt picked this choreographer based on *demographics*. I wanted someone good, and Matt said she was the best as he sent me the short list of the artist she's worked with. When I saw that she worked with Mr. MC I was impressed. His videos and performances were always high energy, so it doesn't matter when she worked with him at least I knew she could keep up with the pace. The guy at the receptionist desk greeted us and then he showed us to the conference room where people were waiting for us. "This is Amber Wallace the choreographer." Matt introduced her proudly.

I held back my frown, maybe this girl could dance. I expected someone black by the way Matt talked about her. I looked at the few people she had with her at the table and then the guy in the seat behind her caught my attention. He was quiet as he observed everyone. He saw me looking, he looked at me then he turned his eyes. I wondered why he wasn't sitting at the table with us, but I told myself to focus.

Amber said she saw some of the footage from the tour and she was so happy to work with an artist who knew how to dance. I smiled, but my eyes kept darting back to the mystery man in the corner. He was listening to everything and I liked how he observed everything about everyone. He noticed when I touched my earring, and when I crossed my legs. He noticed everything about everyone but he said nothing.

"My album isn't just a compilation of songs, it's a story. Each song talks about a piece of that story." Then I looked at our observer. "Mister, would you do me the honor of being in my video?"

Amber's eyes narrowed at me and then she looked at him. "What do you mean?"

"I think he would be perfect for my song, *Power*. I can tell you are *powerful*, and I like your whole vibe. You're handsome, and you exude power even though you're trying to be tucked away."

Amber looked at him and asked him if he was interested. "I have no desire to be paraded around on television as anyone's boy toy." KILL ME! He has a deep voice too. "Amber should be able to recommend some actors or models to provide you with what you're looking for."

"You're not a dancer?" I grinned at him.

"Amber can help you find whomever you need."

Amber was looking at Matt like I said something wrong. Matt looked annoyed with my exchange with the guy as well. The guy sat back and watched me for a minute then he excused himself and left, I pretended like I was interested in the legal back and forth that happened after that. I wanted to know how that guy was connected to the project cause then I was making sure that our paths crossed again. The way he looked at me completely turned me on. That fast the curves of his face were burned into my brain. He was so FINE, SILENT, and **SMOLDERING**! I needed to know more about this man as soon as possible.

Amber and her lawyer walked us out of the building. I was hoping that the guy would come back or I could at least slide my number to Amber to give to him for me. As we slowly walked down the path to the parking lot Matt and the lawyer were talking. I slid my arm under Amber's. "Level with me girl, how do I find that dark chocolate hunk of delicious man?"

Amber stiffened, "do you mean *my* Malcolm?"

"If Malcolm is the name of the guy who left our meeting, then yes."

"Why would you need to find *my* Malcolm?"

She was cock blocking for real! "I guess if it's meant to be it will be." She wasn't going to be any help. That's ok, cause I was going to find him.

Novian

I can't ever say this girl don't work hard. Sometimes when I come over she's on calls, or about to pass out from rehearsing. She's had to fly back and forth between here an LA a lot lately. I'm hoping it all pans out for something for her. Her first video for her first single was this sultry song. It was in black and white and it was shot all over Berkeley. It was her and her love interest confessing their love for each other. The song made me think of the first time we connected. When I saw the video all I could do was blush. She focused on where Lee and I used to live. She was singing about me. She said for her up-tempo songs she said she had to come out hard and show that she can move as well as sing. She came home extremely excited after her first rehearsal with her choreographer. She was sore all over, but she still turned on music and practiced the routine some more. She even had her mother dancing with her. Her mother picked up the routine very fast and the two of them blew me away.

When I asked her if I could come to the set the day of shooting, at first she hesitated. Then she said a slow yes, she asked that if she got too nervous with me being there that I wouldn't be offended and just leave. I thought it was ridiculous, but I agreed. Her cousin Adina came into town the night before the shoot to be in her video. Even though she's been on TV all these years seeing her in person was like old times. She looked a little confused when she saw me. I saw her try to whisper and ask Torrie what happened to Swift. Torrie told her she didn't want to talk about it. Then she tried to hide the sadness that flashed across her face.

On the day of shooting, January was there making things happen in the background. Only this time she wasn't in charge of the go-for task. This time it was this little girl who recognized me and acted like I was a huge star when she saw me. As everyone took their places I recognized the choreographer. It was little miss thunder thighs. She was on the side holding the starting position as she watched the dancers. As the director got ready she yelled out to the dancers that this was it, it was their time to shine. They had the routine and now it was time to kill it! I recognized a couple of Torrie's friends mixed in with the dancers. When the director yelled action, everybody turned on. I stood to the side watching as Torrie turned on like she did that night on stage. Her cousin stood next to me giddy with excitement for her cousin. I couldn't take my eyes off of thunder thighs. She was focused and not paying anyone else any attention. She was hitting the moves on the sides and telling them to hit their marks. At one point she danced out to the dancers in celebration of their victory. Her silly little dance had all of them cracking up. I was hypnotized; I couldn't take my eyes off of her body. I hope Torrie works with her again, I could get used to seeing this girl. It was dark out when they finished all of the dance scenes. Thunder thighs walked over to the food tent in search of food. I stared at her until she looked at me. She didn't smile she just looked at me and then she went back to her task at hand.

January was smiling from ear to ear as she watched the shoot come to an end. "Everything to your liking?"

"Un huh! We have more than enough footage between today and the other days. I'd say today is a success."

"Who's the choreographer?"

"Oh that's Amber, she's the sweetest. I really like what she did with what we gave her. I think she somehow made Torrie even step up."

"Torrie has been practicing nonstop."

"Well her hard work has paid off. Did you see her out there looking like a star? I have a wonderful feeling about this. I think this is only the beginning for Torrie."

"So when it's my turn you think this Amber girl will work with me?"

January smiled at me, "Novian can you even move?"

"I'm no Mr. MC or Hammer, but I can do a little."

January held on to her smile, "you haven't signed on for Torrie's promotional tour. Why not?"

"Mister's got Novian tied up in legal tape. I don't know if I want Murphy tied up too. I want my own name out there, I don't want to be stuck singing backup for my whole career."

"Look at it this way. We build Torrie up and then you can launch from her. I think I see a duet in your future. Let's get her out there and then we'll get you out there. Meanwhile, it can't hurt anything to continue to work with Mister."

****

I was actually pacing the floor; I don't remember this girl taking this long to get ready for anything. "Torrie! Seriously?"

Torrie's mother came out of Torrie's room and she said she was almost ready. Then Torrie slowly opened the door and then she posed in the doorway. She put her hands on her hips as she stood there letting me take her in. I gasped as I looked her over. Her hair was nice, her makeup was beautiful, and the heels she wore made me stare at her legs. I approached and just as I was about to kiss her she put her hand up. "You're going to ruin my lipstick. Down boy!" Then she looked at her mother, "we'll be back later. Call me if you need anything."

"Ok baby, have a good night."

I stood there mesmerized as I watched Torrie walk towards her front door. I forgot I was supposed to be following her out. In the elevator Torrie looked at me looking for approval, "do I look nice?"

I like when her true innocence is on her face. Not that fake stuff she does in interviews that people seem to eat up. That's the look that lets me know that I've gotten her like no one else could ever get her. "You look amazing, I told you to do it up and you did." Torrie smiled at me satisfied by my answer.

A tribute for Mr. MC was being filmed tonight. They interviewed me earlier in the day and tonight was the after party that was being filmed as well. I felt like the man walking in the door with Torrie on my arm. Ricky didn't even try to play it cool. He came over and smacked my hand as he asked me how in the world did I pull Torrie? He openly drooled all over her. Torrie didn't say anything she didn't even smile, she held on to my arm as she looked at him. When Ricky excused himself, Torrie looked around and asked me if Mister only worked with thugs. I gave her a dirty look but I didn't say anything. Mister works with mostly people from the area. A large part of the population in the Bay Area is black. Recently some thing's have come up to make me wonder what all Mister has his hands involved in. However, the fact that the majority of his crew looked like me always brought me comfort. How could you knock a brotha who was providing jobs to our people. I asked Torrie if she was scared of black people now? She said she has no problem with black people, she just didn't expect so many thugs. I shook my head at her little snooty comment.

Then they changed the music and put the spotlight on the double doors. When the doors opened Mister entered with Camille on his arm. Again I had that stuck feeling, I've never figured out how old Camille is. She must be using that Oil of Olay stuff cause she doesn't seem to age. Torrie took my breath away, but Camille made my heart stop. I made sure I didn't show an outright reaction to her cause immediately Torrie looked at me when the entire room roared at Mister and Camille. I was clapping as well until I saw him.

Torrie

Men are such dogs! They see a pretty woman and they lose

their minds. Mister's woman was pretty, but the way these idiots were falling all over themselves was ridiculous. Yes, she's pretty and she's spoken for. I was watching all of the retarded fools act a complete fool about this woman when I noticed Novian's face. He was frowning at someone so I turned my head as he approached us. My heart stopped and I felt butterflies in my stomach. "Novian." He said with no smile in his face.

"Why are you here? Mister don't want you here."

"I was invited, this your woman?" He looked at me.

"This is Torrie," Novian said like he was annoyed with the question.

"I know who she is, I asked you a direct question."

"You need to go question somebody else. I don't answer to you."

"One of these days you'll learn who you should flex at and who you should know better than to. I stay off of you because of your momma. Test me again and I'll gut you like a fish. I don't have patience for little spoiled brat kids." Then he looked at me, "Torrie. I'll see you around." Then he walked away.

Novian was so mad; he started to walk away when Darius approached us. "What was that?"

"Why is he here?"

"It's that whole love hate thing him and Mister got going on."

"Love hate?"

"You never heard the saying keep your friends close and keep your enemies closer?" Then Darius looked at me, "don't you shine up nicely."

"Is that supposed to be a compliment?"

Darius looked at me like I said the wrong thing. "Don't come over here trying to act like you wasn't hopping from booth to booth not too long ago looking for anybody to carry you. I know all about you hopping from Novian to Swift and probably everybody in-between. I saw you on TV jumping around. You're not anybody yet, so keep the diva attitude to yourself. I don't have time."

"Who was in-between?" Novian looked at me.

'Really Novian? You want to do this right here?"

"Who?"

"Why does it matter? I didn't stress you about all the tricks you ran through. How many of these girls in here tonight you been with? Leave me alone!"

Novian sucked his teeth and walked away from me like I was nobody. A few people were looking in my direction. Even though I knew they didn't hear us, their looks looked like they were looking down on me. That was it, I didn't have to stand here and take this. The old Torrie would've waited for Novian to come back and then tried to explain. However, the new Torrie has nothing to explain. My past is none of his business. It's not like we were together. As I walked towards the payphone he was coming out of the bathroom. He looked at me and then he scanned my body. His eyes landed on my face. "You leaving?"

"YES!" I folded my arms in complete irritation.

"Goodnight." Then he walked back towards the banquet hall.

I wanted to talk to him, be in his space for a little bit. I walked down by the payphone and then I remembered, that my momma doesn't drive. Who was I supposed to call at this hour to come all the way over here by the airport to take me all the way back to Berkeley? I could call a cab, but I didn't have cash on me. Maybe mister *my* Malcolm will take me home. That would be exactly what Novian gets, to watch me walk out with the guy who clearly ruffled his feathers. I walked back to the banquet room and I looked around the floor. Novian still had that same cup in his hand. He's not much of a drinker; he holds cups to appear to fit in. I know he's afraid of becoming his momma. I was standing there looking around. Ricky was trying to get me to come out on the dance floor, but I refused. Then Malcolm walked up to me, "I'll take you home."

I didn't even mask my smile, I smiled really big and then I looked at Ricky who was now standing like he was about to run and tell. When I walked on Malcolm's side he openly looked me over, but he didn't say anything. So I returned the favor and looked over Malcolm. I could tell by looking at him that his stomach is rock hard. His shirt didn't cling to him so it's not like he works out to show off. This is a big man! He had the build of an athlete and the charisma of a everyday working blue-collar man. He's tall and his black skin makes him seem meaner than I'm sure he is. He pointed to his car as we approached. "Are you in a hurry to get home to someone?" He didn't answer me he just looked at me. "I was going to suggest we stop off somewhere for a drink." He looked like he was debating. "My treat, I just want to thank you for rescuing me."

He looked back at the building, "fine." Then he chirped his car.

Novian

Torrie was right, I just don't like having her past thrown in my face. I did a lap around the room looking for Torrie to invite her to dance. "Dog! Your girl left with Malcolm!" Ricky watched my eyes.

The room fell silent in my head. "Are you sure?"

"I saw them talking by the door. Then I watched them get in his car. I came back to look for you and warn you. You can kiss her walls goodbye once he hits."

I frowned; I didn't even want to know what he was talking about. I looked at the clock, Torrie gets on my nerves. She better not touch him! I had to perform in twenty minutes then I was going to her house and she better be there alone.

Torrie

"Malcolm! It's good to see you man!" A guy said coming to greet him. Then he looked at me. "Lawd have Mer-Cey! You're a very lucky man! Your booth is open."

The guy led the way, I made sure I swayed as I walked cause I could feel Malcolm's eyes on me. When we sat down a girl walked up to us. She kept her eyes on Malcolm. "The usual?"

Malcolm nodded yes, "what's the usual?"

"Martell Cordon Bleu neat." She looked at me with no amusement in her face.

"What's that?"

"Cognac, you need it dressed up? In something like a side car or something?"

"No, I'll have it just like him." Then the waitress walked away like I just irked her nerves. "What is this place?"

"A lounge," he sat back in his seat.

"Yeah, but where are we?"

"You should always pay attention to where you're going. What if you needed to find your way home?"

I didn't like the sound of that. "So... How do you know Novian?"

"Know him? How do you know him?"

"I asked you first." I smiled and when he didn't return my smile, I exhaled. "We kick it from time to time." He didn't say anything he watched me. "We went to school together. We've always been friends."

"Here you go Malcolm, please let me know if you need anything else." The waitress ignored me. She put our drinks down then she walked away.

"I guess she likes you." I picked my shot glass up. I could smell how strong it was. I looked at Malcolm. He took the shot like it was nothing. I took a sip and my throat burned. The little bit I tasted was smooth. I never drink anything straight. I waived the waitress back over and I asked for some apple juice. "How do you know Amber?"

Malcolm's eyes burned a hole in me. "Don't let me hear you say her name again!"

"I was just..."

"MALCOLM! WHO IS THIS? How you going to bring some female to my spot?"

This woman was big, and very pretty in her own way, but I was confused. "B! Calm down!"

"Naw! You calm down! I'm tired of you bringing females in here like my loyalty is supposed to be to you."

"Where else would your loyalty lye?"

"Keep testing me and you're about to find out."

"She's a paying customer."

"Bring me the tab for this table so that they can get on their way!" Our waitress walked over slowly with pleading eyes. This B lady snatched the billfold from her and slammed it on the table in front of me. "Pay and get on your way!"

"I guess the customer isn't always right." I said as I picked up the bill. It was almost two hundred dollars. "What in the world?"

Malcolm leaned back, "you got it or are you going to need to wash dishes?"

I had it, but I had no intentions of spending that kind of money tonight. "What do you do Malcolm?"

"A little bit of this and a little bit of that."

I put my card on the bill. The B lady came over and snatched it. I didn't understand what was happening so I told myself to calm down. "Sounds like you hustle for a living?" He shrugged at me. "You must have a good hustle to afford your car?" He shrugged again at me. "Only thing about hustling is that there are down swings. How do you keep afloat?" He didn't say anything. "How do you afford almost a hundred dollars for one shot of liquor?"

"You see who's paying." Then he watched the woman come back to the table.

"I suggest you encourage her to tip appropriately." She slammed everything on the table in front of me. "I don't understand you Malcolm, what happened?"

He exhaled, "Bernie please don't push me. I need time and she's playing with her boy toy."

"You mean she's still with that guy? You're ok with that?" She put her hands on her hips.

Malcolm squinted his eyes at her. "I warned you. Keep talking!"

The B lady turned on her heels and walked away. I couldn't help it, I smiled at him. He looked me up and down then he looked away. I tipped the waitress even though I didn't care for her level of service. Malcolm told me it was time to go, so I stood and led the way out. I tried to walk like I didn't know but I wanted him to watch me walk. I looked back at him and he was looking at my butt. I smiled at him then I smacked my butt to make it jiggle. When we got to the gravel covered parking lot I noticed that we were the only cars. I'll probably never see Malcolm again and I didn't want to go home to wait for Novian. Malcolm chirped his car; I stood by the passenger door. He looked at me. I asked him if we could go back to his place. He said no flatly. We couldn't go to mine cause Novian was going to show up. I wanted this and I wasn't above climbing in the backseat. I pointed at his backseat and he frowned at me and asked if I was thirteen. I asked him to take me to the Marriott that we passed on the way here. In the car I put my hand on his thigh. He didn't say anything he drove. I went inside and got the room. I threw my jacket and purse down in the middle of the floor. When I went in for a kiss Malcolm walked to the bed. He took a condom out of his pocket and then he sat down. I unbuckled his belt and pants. He wasn't even at attention yet and my eyes got big. I backed up scared, Malcolm watched my face. I panicked! Where was that supposed to go? Malcolm looked like he was used to this song and dance. He stood up and fixed his clothes. He handed me a card and told me to use it when I was ready for him.

******

"How big was it?" My girl was laughing so hard she couldn't breathe.

I held my hands up, "he wasn't even hard and it was like this."

"I've heard stories, but I've never seen one. I would've done it out of curiosity."

"It looked like it hurt, besides when I came home in the morning Novian was there waiting. We didn't talk about anything. He went in right away probably looking for evidence of me spending the night with Malcolm. There would've been no way to play that off."

She leaned in, "have you called him yet?"

Butterflies hit my stomach, "you think I should?"

"You only live once! You've got to try it at least once. I mean if you're not woman enough to say you even tried then that's fine too. Pass his number over here and I will gladly slam dunk him."

"I don't know, I think that liquor was messing with me. He knows Novian and he knows Amber. That's mixing business with pleasure. I..."

She put her hand up, "stop! Stop it!" She put hands on my face, "who's the star?" I smiled as I looked at the floor. "You are the talent! Amber and Novian better recognize that if it weren't for you they wouldn't eat. They need to get on your level."

I smiled but I didn't say anything cause I felt like she was right, but there was a little voice telling me not to do it.

I got dressed for my dinner with some people that my agent set me up to meet. They want to interview me, so she and I are going to Millbrae by the airport. My momma was focused on her crotchet needles when I left.

My agent talked the entire time. She was excited about all of the requests she was getting for me. The people were waiting for us when we arrived. Another boring dinner where I have to play nice and innocent while these idiots eat it all up. They were going on and on, praising me for everything. I was halfway listening when I saw Amber walk in. Her hair was done and her dress hugged her nicely. I guess she really is a sistah with the way she's filling out her dress. She could never be competition for me, but we are on two totally different ends of the spectrum. She looked good within her own right, but she could never be me. I swallowed when I saw the guy with her. He was gorgeous! He held her chair out for her and then happily sat across from her. He kept smiling at her and he kept laughing. That smile wouldn't let me turn away; it was such a pretty smile. I normally don't like smiles on men, but his was delicious. I wanted to know what she was saying to make him smile like that. "Is that Dwayne Reed?" My agent said in my ear.

"I don't know, who's that?"

"If that's him, he's the hottest thing to hit the field since... since.... Shoot! I don't even know. Women who weren't into football now watch just to get a look at his fine behind, and he's not even a player." Then she sucked her teeth. "Figures he'd be into white girls."

"That's my choreographer."

My agent looked confused for a minute. "So what is she then?"

I shrugged, "I'd have to care to know. I think she's black though, but like I said I don't care." We returned to the conversation at our table.

After awhile Dwayne got up to use the bathroom. He knew one of the guys at our table so he stopped to say hello. Everyone noticed him notice me. He said hello and then he left. "Looks like Torrie has an admirer." I blushed but I didn't say anything. "Torrie fits the type though."

"What do you mean?" My agent asked.

"He's got a thing for chocolate, and Torrie is the superb chocolate soufflé'!" One of the guys kissed his hand as he gestured towards me.

"Thank you, you certainly know how to make me blush." I glanced at Amber's table where she was unconcerned about anything happening around them. "Why do you say he has a thing for chocolate?"

"Whenever he's out he has a delicious woman like yourself

on his arm."

"When he's out? Who is he?"

"He's one of the assistant coaches for the Forty-Niners. He went to one fashion shoot with a model and everyone has been asking who he is ever since. The man has good fashion sense; even his loungewear is on point. Even the women who are on his arm are always..." He kissed his hand again.

"What about the woman he's with tonight?" I nodded towards Amber, "that's my choreographer."

He stared, "can't tell much by the back of her head. She's nothing like the women he's normally out with. Normally they're almost as beautiful as you."

Dwayne walked back to his table and he happily sat down. I don't care what they say; he's looking at her the way Novian looks at me. I know that look. When Amber got up to go towards the restroom, Dwayne's eyes stayed glued to her walk as she sashayed towards our table. I put on a smile, "hey Amber girl. Imagine running into you in a place like this." I said as I stood to hug her.

She didn't look overly excited to see me, she seemed like she was taking in my whole table. "How you doing Torrie?" She hugged me then her eyes swept the table. "Looks like you're handling business. I'll leave you to it."

"And it looks like you are here on pleasure." I smiled at her.

She looked at my smile and then she looked at everyone at the table. "Enjoy your meal." She patted my arm and then she walked to the bathroom.

The men sat quietly when Amber walked away until one of them redirected everyone back to business. When she walked past our table all three of them looked even though one was at least trying to act like he wasn't looking. Dwayne watched their eyes and then he turned his attention back to Amber. The sound of Dwayne's laughter made me turn around as he held on to the table laughing about something. I never knew Amber to be so funny. Well maybe she's a little silly sometimes, but she ain't that funny. He's acting like she's a comedian, and her demeanor doesn't say that she's said anything all that funny. I don't know why I was paying so close attention. I guess I was looking for signs that she was into Dwayne so I wouldn't feel bad if I was ever brave enough to give *my* Malcolm a call.

Chapter 7

Novian

I can never say that Torrie hasn't worked for all of this. When I'm not working with Mister, I'm with Torrie. I never asked her what happened with Malcolm that night. Everything was normal when she came home. I told myself I didn't want to know.

"Murphy, when the music starts we want you to look up. When you see Torrie I want you to smile. We don't want a big cheesy grin, rather..." The assistant put her finger to her chin. She looked at the director.

He chuckled, "smile like you would normally smile. Don't over think it."

That guy from the label is out here again. You can see his thoughts when he looks at Torrie. I've seen him look at all the women that way though. None of them pay him any attention. When my portion of filming was over I approached him. Immediately he was trying to figure me out just like I was. I reached out for a handshake; he cautiously extended his hand to me. Everything on his face said he was guilty. I made small talk, and he only answered my questions. You could tell he wanted to be anywhere but where I was. His guilty expressions were beyond being caught staring at my woman. When I looked in his eyes there was no honor. Nothing but guilt. When I looked at Torrie she was looking in our direction, but she turned her eyes as soon as she saw me look at her. Anger burned in my stomach as I stared at the guy, he calmly walked away and I was left standing there. When January arrived, she was all business talking to the director and all the staff. I gently led her by her elbow back towards the cars. I asked her if there was some part of Torrie's contract that I needed to know about. January put her hands on her hips and asked me what kind of a dumb question was that. I pointed at the whiter than white white-boy, I asked her to explain him. She said he represented Torrie's label like it was nothing. I asked her why was he here. She looked me in my eyes. "Um, Novian if you don't understand how music videos work, I don't know what to tell you."

"Don't give me that! He doesn't have to be here!"

"Matthew put his neck on the line to get Torrie signed under her amazing contract. You should be thanking him instead of whatever this is."

"Did Torrie sleep with him?"

All of a sudden, now she can't look at me. "I can't answer for Torrie. I'm not in her personal business like that."

"January, you're my girl. Tell me what's going on."

She put her hands up like she was surrendering. "Look Novian, all I know is there is a reason why everything went down like it did with Diva. Someone wanted you there and with Torrie, I was told that the moment Diva broke down to push Torrie. I was given an incentive to make sure she was ready when it was time to push her. You came through and you made sure she delivered. I don't really know the story, but I know that the type of support and backing that Torrie has isn't normally given to a fresh new face. If you need to know more that's on you."

Torrie

I looked at my finished product in the mirror. I looked good and I was so happy to think so. My momma walked into the room in her pants and top. She looked very nice. We went to the shop together and got our hair and makeup done. The label decided to throw a party for me in celebration of the success of my debut album. Matt said my album was impressing everyone by the way it is selling. Adina flew out with Matt for the party. Matt dropped her off here about ten minutes ago so she could arrive with me. He went

141

ahead to the club to make sure everything was set up to their standards. "Where's Novian?"

I rolled my eyes, "don't know and I don't care. I'm trying to catch a new fish tonight."

Adina stared at my face in the mirror, "you're changing. This little bit of stardom isn't going to your head I hope."

"Torrie says you've been working on a bunch of movies lately." My mother changed the subject.

"Yes auntie, I've been working so much. I had to do a bunch of juggling to be here today." Adina glanced at me and then she walked away.

"Momma do you think I'm changing?"

"We're all caterpillars, we only become butterflies just before we die. Everybody changes, that's how we grow." I smiled at my momma, moments like this is why I love her so much.

Malcolm said he would think about coming when I sent the invitation out to him. I did such a good job of selling myself; I have no doubt that he's going to be there. Tonight I'm not running from him. I'm too curious to know if I can handle his *gift* or not. I have to prove to myself that I can handle this. Sinclaire told me to breathe through and I would be fine. The door buzzed and my momma called out that my girls were here. "Oh my goodness! I know who you are! You were in that movie I just saw!" I heard Sinclaire's sister exclaim.

When I walked into the living room Adina was looking uncomfortable as my friends spoke with her. I cleared my throat and my girls screamed as they took me in. They immediately started pumping my head up about how good I looked and how Malcolm would be a fool not to take me home with him tonight. In the limo my girls were hyped up and having a good time. Adina sat over to the side clutching her purse and turning her nose up. I didn't know what her problem was, but she used to be just like this when we went out.

Just because she's finally making some money and got a name behind her she don't got to act like she forgot where she came from. I told everyone that I appreciated the tribute to me all over this club. There were life-size cutouts of me everywhere looking like the tightest looking female ever. My momma looked at the pictures and smiled like she was proud of me.

I looked over the crowd and I got butterflies as I saw him gliding through the crowd. Tonight was our night and everything was perfect. "He's here! He's here!" I loved the way that black fedora sat on his head. I wanted at least one round with him still wearing the hat. I smiled at Adina trying to get her attention as she people watched and kept an eye on her man. When she finally looked at me I nodded towards the corner of our booth where Malcolm should've been approaching from in any minute. Adina gave me a confused look when he didn't show up. I looked back out at the club and I didn't see him anywhere. Lets face it, it wasn't bright in here so I could've over looked him in the darkness, but I didn't see his hat either. I stood up looking around the dance floor trying to spot him. I sat down; maybe he went to the bathroom. I decided to give him a few minutes to surface. Adina watched Matt with the most interesting look on her face. I asked her what was wrong with her tonight and she shrugged my question off like she didn't want to talk about it. After quite a few minutes of trying to get her to talk to me about it. I decided to let it go, Malcolm hadn't showed up and I needed to go find him.

When I walked around the corner, I stopped at the booth next to mine. I paused as soon as I saw Malcolm, I was about to throw major attitude until I realized he was sitting with Amber. "I thought you weren't coming!" She looked me up and down. No doubt taking in how good I looked. I looked at her in her green dress trying not to show that I was doing the same. She looked good, but it didn't matter, Malcolm came here to see me. "I changed my mind at the last minute." Then she crossed her legs.

"Malcolm honey, I have a booth for us over here." I said

pointing next door.

"Honey?" Amber looked at Malcolm like she was jealous.

Malcolm shook his head, "why would you say that?"

"Malcolm!" I said through clinched teeth.

"I'm talking; I might get over there eventually. Go talk to somebody." He said shooing me away. I was completely embarrassed and enraged. If he wasn't so fine and commanding and my guilty pleasure I would've left him sitting there looking stupid.

Then the guy in their booth started laughing loud and exaggerated. He irked me immediately. "Who are you?"

"His son!" He said as he pointed to Malcolm.

There was no way he was telling the truth, was he trying to say Malcolm had him when he was like five or something like that. "How is that possible?"

"He is" Malcolm said, "Now get!" The look on Malcolm's face stopped any more questions from me. I turned on my heels and walked away.

I went back to my booth and no one was there. Thank goodness! I grabbed a napkin and dabbed my eyes as they started to leak. Who does he think he is? Nobody dismisses me like Novian did! I'm the star, he must've forgotten who I am.

The guy and one of the girls from the booth went back to the dance floor. I watched them dance for a minute. He didn't look like Malcolm to me. He wasn't no skinny paperweight, he had a solid build like Malcolm but that doesn't mean that they're even related. I couldn't hear what was happening next door in Amber's booth the music was too loud. The seats were too high, I couldn't peak over so I sat back brewing.

After a couple of minutes Amber went out on the dance floor.

I waited to see if Malcolm was going to follow her. When I didn't see him get up I walked over. Malcolm was watching Amber dance. I needed to pull his attention back to what mattered, so I put my hand gently on his thigh. Malcolm had no expression on his face as he picked up my hand and moved it. I stood up and asked Malcolm to dance with me. He acted like I was bothering him as he waived me off. I could feel my heart beating in my chest, how could he do this to me? Doesn't he know this is my night?

The waiter came to the booth to collect the empty glasses. Malcolm asked the waiter to pass along a song selection to the DJ. The waiter started to say the music was preselected. Malcolm was about to say something when I told him if the song wasn't about me it wasn't getting played tonight no matter who he thought he was. His head jerked in my direction and I jumped. Malcolm was glaring at me like he wanted to choke me so I left the booth. I don't know what his problem is. When I saw Malcolm go out on the dance floor it felt like my heart was going to explode. Malcolm caressed her gently and they danced passionately, I dabbed my eyes again.

I looked around until I spotted Matt talking to Adina. I interrupted their conversation and I asked him why no one told me that Amber changed her mind about coming. Matt looked at me coldly and asked why it mattered if she came. I continued to go off. The lack of appreciation was overwhelming and I went in hard on Matt. Adina cut her eyes at me after awhile. She put her hand in my face and then she took Matt away by the hand. I tapped a guy and told him to come dance with me. He eagerly said yes as he followed me to the dance floor. I tried not to show how pissed off I was as Malcolm bumped and Amber grinded on the dance floor as if they were alone. I wonder how that guy she's dating would feel knowing about this? I stayed on the dance floor until I saw them leave together. The thought of Amber going home with him pissed me off.

I tried my best to enjoy my party and then I told everyone that I was going home. I regretted not inviting Novian, at least he would've let tonight be about me. When I stepped outside the club,

Malcolm and that young guy were standing against a car drinking something in Styrofoam cups. I exhaled in relief because I didn't see Amber anywhere. I guess he sent her home and he was going to wait out here for me. I did my sexiest walk to them. You know the one the vixen always does in the movies and videos as she slowly walks towards the guy. Malcolm and the guy watched me as they sipped their cups. "You know they have drinks inside, you too cheap to buy in there?"

The guy looked at Malcolm waiting for his response. "You supposed to be buying for us."

I smiled, "the party's still going. You want to bring your friend back inside?"

The guy smiled as he raised his cup towards me. "I'm trying to sober up now." He swirled his cup towards me. "Coffee, Malcolm's making sure I'm cool before I get in my car."

I smiled at Malcolm, "I thought you left."

"I'm leaving as soon as he's cool."

"Can I go with you?"

Malcolm sucked his teeth as he looked away. "I don't have time for scary females."

The guy held his smile as he watched me. "She scary Malcolm?"

I rolled my eyes, "you can't reveal something like that with no warning. I choked," the kid started laughing. "Not like that," he laughed harder.

"Drink," Malcolm told the kid.

"So?" I was waiting for my yes.

"No, but thanks." Malcolm took another drink as he watched

me.

Inside I wanted to scream, but I decided to play it cool. "You want me to chase you, fine."

"I want you to leave me alone, but I can tell you're not that smart." Then he poured out his cup. I could see the steam from the hot liquid as it rouse up off the ground. "This is taking too long, I'll drive you home." He walked around to the driver side of his car as he chirped it. The guy kept smiling at me until I felt embarrassed. Then he got in the car and then Malcolm drove off.

****

I've been restless and irritated since that night at the club. I told myself not to call Malcolm and that he would call me. It's been almost two weeks so I doubt he's going to call me. I took a deep breath and then I picked up my phone. I dialed Malcolm's number. There was noise in the background, it was a Whodini song. "Hello?" His deep voice sent chills through me.

"Malcolm, its me."

"Me who?" His tone didn't change.

"Torrie."

When I didn't say anything after that he sighed, "what do you want Torrie?"

I instantly felt like I wanted to cry. "I want to see you."

"You've seen me, and you couldn't handle it. I don't have anything else to offer you."

"Are you mad?"

"Should I be?"

"You sound mad, I'm just trying to be near you tonight. It

doesn't matter where. I just want to be near you."

He was quiet for a minute, "I'm going to club Action."

I sat up, "the strip club?"

"How you know about it?"

"One of my girlfriends works there."

"Who's your friend?"

"Her stage name is Sensuous."

"Oh," then it got quiet on his end.

"You know her?"

"I know who she is."

"You slept with her?" Then the phone disconnected. I tried to call him back and it just rang and rang. I decided to go down there and see what he was doing. I put on a catsuit with high heels big accessories and I pulled my weave up in a ponytail on the top of my head. I grabbed a little jacket then I went down to the garage.

Every time I walk up to my leased beauty I feel like I've arrived. My car was a luxury vehicle and so was my building. Nobody could tell me I'm not a star. I parked across from Malcolm's car. I took a deep breath, and no matter what he did, I wasn't going to let him play me again like I'm nobody.

When I got to the door the bouncer did a double take as he looked at me. He asked me where my bodyguard was. I told him I was flying solo tonight. He let me in and then he told the guy and girl not to charge me a cover. They gave the bouncer funny looks as I walked past them. The lights were low and there was a girl up on the stage doing her thing. I stood in the middle of the floor looking around.

An older woman approached me, as she looked me over. "You must be looking for a job. Otherwise I don't know why you're here."

"I'm looking for somebody." I kept searching.

"Well we mind our business at club Action. If you're not here to work or enjoy the show then you're going to have to leave. We don't need angry wives and girlfriends showing up here."

"I'm neither one of those, I'm looking for a guy though. He told me he was coming here tonight and I saw his car outside."

She started to say something when a girl rushed up to her leaving a trail of glitter behind her. "Coco, Paradise is sick and she won't stop throwing up in the back."

"Is she pregnant? I don't have time for this!" She exclaimed as she hurried behind the glitter trail.

"Hey sweet chocolate, how much for a lap dance?" A guy said licking his lips at me.

"Calm down, Ms. Rowe don't work here. She's our guest of honor tonight." This man said to me. He was average height and light skinned, his black hair was curly and he had a whole Latin vibe to him. He knew he was fine and he knew he was smooth. He also knew who I was.

"And you are?" I put my hand out to him.

He kissed my hand, "I'm Vic. Why don't you come have a seat at my special table." As we walked I continued looking around the room hoping to spot Malcolm once again in a room that was too dark for him to ever stand out in. "What would you like to drink?"

"A Southern Comfort and Cranberry."

He gave my drink order to the waitress and then he looked me over. "What brings you out tonight?"

"I was looking for Malcolm, have you seen him?"

"Malcolm? Malcolm who?"

I had no idea, "Malcolm! Malcolm! You know, the Malcolm!"

"Do you know how many Malcolm's come through here? Seems like everyone's name is Malcolm these days."

"Tall, dark, and handsome? The black Malcolm."

"Oh, you got something against light skinned brothas?"

"You're Latin aren't you?"

"Nope, one hundred percent African blood over here." His eyes danced to the music.

"I have nothing against light skinned brothas, tonight I have a taste for dark meat is all."

"You like playing with fire don't you." He watched my eyes.

"Depends on the flame." I took a sip of my drink and then I smiled at him.

He looked up and he sucked his teeth. There was a woman standing where I had stood before. Her dress was perfect for her. It hugged all her curves and showed off everything tastefully. Her hair was short and it looked like she had just come from the shop. The woman looked around the club like I did. Vic excused himself and then he went over to the woman. Neither one of them smiled. She wasn't happy about whatever she had to say, and Vic was not happy to see her. They went back and forth for a little bit and then Vic walked away with her on his heels. They disappeared in the back and then they came out after awhile. From where I was sitting she looked mad, but it was too dark to see her face clearly. They were in a heated discussion as they walked towards me. Vic was using very strong and unapologetic words as he spoke to her. I couldn't make out what he was saying, but I did hear him call her Yvette. She stormed out of the club and then after Vic spoke to the people at the door he gathered his composure then he walked back to my table. I was halfway watching the girl on the stage perform. Some of her moves could be incorporated into my next dance routine. "Everybody wants Malcolm tonight and he's not even here." Vic said as he chuckled.

"Yes he is, I saw his car in the parking lot right outside this door."

Vic's eyes were on the stage, "go and see for yourself." I walked to the door and a new car was parked where Malcolm's car used to be. In order for him to leave he had to see my car. I blew out irritated air. When I turned around Vic was standing there looking me over with a smile. "Are you in the mood for some cinnamon instead?"

I was so frustrated that I couldn't see straight. I don't remember what I said or how I agreed. Somehow Vic and I ended up in the owner's office on her couch.

Novian

"Torrie! It's Novian, is there a reason why you aren't calling me back? I know you're busy, but you can stop to say hello or something. You know what, forget it. I hope you're having a good time. I guess our paths will cross again when they cross." I slammed the phone down. I looked around the room. It feels like everything is spinning out of control. Amos keeps telling me that he keeps seeing Torrie and Malcolm in the same circles. He says they don't come together and he can't tell if they leave together or not. However, Torrie is definitely throwing herself at him whenever their paths cross.

One thing that seems consistent across all these females' lips is that that tar baby is working with a serious package. One girl was like it was too much. She didn't get a dreamy look about it. She was more or less horrified. She said she tried to give him head, but her mouth is only so big. She actually had me cracking up about it. I will say that the females who speak from personal knowledge… whoa! Torrie fits the type too. Gorgeous, banging bodies, chocolate skin.

I told myself not to think about Torrie anymore. Ever since her career has started taking off and mine, while it's going and I'm getting checks for my contributions to Torrie and other artist's projects. I'm not getting the notoriety. I want my face and name on the screen too. I took a deep breath and I told myself to get over it. I had a meeting in a hour and a half anyways.

I did some push ups to work off some aggression and then I got in the shower. I let the water beat me in the face for a few minutes. I'm not thinking about Torrie like that anymore.

I took the elevator up to the twelfth floor. "Hello Mr. Murphy, we've been waiting for you. Right this way." The receptionist said as she stood as soon as I stepped off the elevator.

Ok, well I like this greeting already. When I walked into the conference room that guy Matt was there and he was with two women. I recognized Torrie's agent, I gave her a hug and friendly kiss on the cheek. The other woman held a slight smile on her face as she watched me. "Hello Novian, I'm Bonita Fairchild, it's so nice to finally meet you."

"Finally?" I shook her hand and then I found my seat.

Bonita sat down and crossed her legs when I could see them. "Yes, you're the muse in Torrie's last video and I've seen your name amongst the list in her projects."

"Would that make you a fan?"

She smirked, "in more ways than you know." Then she passed me papers. "I asked to have you brought in so that we could come to an arrangement."

152

"Arrangement?" I looked at the small stack of papers.

"I would love to represent you Novian," Torrie's agent interjected.

"Well I can say that I like what you've done with Torrie's career so far."

She smiled, "you like that? Wait until I really start to put in work."

"The problem Novian is your contract with Mr. MC." Matt chimed in like the women's energy towards me annoyed him.

"Our work around for the Diva's tour was work with me under my last name."

"Un huh, right! But is that the name that you're going to be willing to work with us under for the duration of your time with our team?"

"My name is Murphy so it's not like it's some sort of crime."

Bonita pointed to the papers she gave me. "Go over the paperwork with your lawyer. We're going to need you to think this through. When you return your paper work to us, we're going to need a one-song demo to shop around. Novian you will have to continue to pay your dues. Torrie has paid a hefty price to work with all three of us. Of course we can't ask the same things of the two of you. I just want to make sure you understand that you will not be an overnight success. If you're in this for the love of music then you will ride the waves with us. The kids that are in this for the fame and the money may have one hit, but they don't last. You have to decide who you're going to be."

"Ok," I picked up the empty folder on the table and I put it in my backpack.

"Now that that's out of the way, lets go to dinner." Bonita

smiled.

"We can't, we're flying out tonight. I could've sworn I thought you were flying with us?"

Bonita looked at Matt, "I guess there was a mix up. I thought we were all flying out in the morning. That's why you brought your baggage here." Matt looked annoyed as he looked at Bonita. "Well Novian, I guess that leaves just the two of us. What do you say?"

"Smooth Bonita, that was real smooth." Matt walked out of the door like he was irritated.

The agent got her things and then she left as well. "Well I have reservations if you'd like a free meal." She stared at my hair.

I shrugged, "sounds good to me. Is Matt your man on the low or something? Why's he all upset?"

Bonita grinned, "I'm sure he and Adina are very happy together."

"Torrie's cousin Adina?"

"Don't say it like its so shocking, white men do love black women you know." She stood up and smoothed out her skirt. "Shall we?"

"Should I drive?"

"No, I have a car service coming. No point in paying for parking. I'll have the service bring you to your car later." She kept looking at me like she was studying every aspect of me.

"Did Torrie tell you something about me? Why do you keep looking at me like that?"

Bonita smiled and then she sat back after she gave the waiter her menu. "That girl is so in love with you. I'm looking at you trying to understand why."

I couldn't stop the blush that came over me. Just when I was done, this woman made everything come back to me. "She told you she loves me?"

Bonita smiled at my blushing, "I'm a woman, there are certain things that don't have to be said. Anyways I'm sure she doesn't want me over here blowing her cover. So tell me about you Novian. What do your parents think about your career choice?"

"It's just my mom and she used to sing too. She's so proud whenever she sees me on stage. Its like I'm accomplishing something she never could."

"Did your father die?"

"I'm not concerned with him." I looked her in her eyes as she searched my face.

"Do you have any kids?"

"No."

"I have a little girl, her name's Angel and it fits her whole personality and everything."

"That's nice," I was wondering why I should care.

"She's got hair just like yours. Who does yours?"

"Brad's wife is a former beautician. She takes care of my hair for me."

"It's so long and pretty! I guess she's not taking on new clients huh?"

"No, she only does my hair and her nieces."

"Lucky nieces," Bonita kept watching everything about me. Sometimes she would just smile. This had to be the weirdest seduction scene ever. I played along to see where this whole thing was supposed to take us. I took a bite of my salad. I frowned as soon as the taste of arugula hit my mouth. I picked up my napkin and spit the salad into it. I got our waiter's attention and I reminded him that I asked for a salad without arugula. I asked him to bring me soup instead. Bonita's eyes got big as she smiled at me. "My daughter hates arugula too."

"Smart kid, that mess is nasty no matter how they try to dress it up."

"Do you have any allergies?"

"I'm allergic to penicillin, nothing other than that. Why?"

"Asthma, sickle cell, diabetes?"

"None of those that I know of. Why?"

"I was just wondering..." then she changed the subject.

Bonita kept staring at me and making mental notes about me all evening. When it was time to go, she invited me back to her hotel. I don't know why, but something didn't seem right so I declined. I decided to trust my gut.

As I drove home I thought about everything that happened in our meeting and that weird dinner. What did she mean Torrie is in love with me? You wouldn't know it by the way she's running behind Malcolm these days. It's like she wants the D so bad she's willing to jeopardize everything to get next to him.

******

I was listening to the music Mister was playing when Camille and her niece sashayed into the music room. She was bolting for her uncle; she stopped and ran back to her aunt when she saw me. I smiled, "you don't remember me?"

She smiled and then she hid her face. "Uh oh babe, she's not in love with Novian." Camille laughed.

"What does that mean?" I looked at Camille.

"Baby girl has got a thing for the bad boy." Camille teased.

"I wouldn't say all of that. If anything all of this time with her uncle has made her aware of killer instincts. She naturally gravitates to the guys who are ruthless."

"She's smiling at me though, that counts for something right?" I waved at her.

"I guess you could say that." I started from her feet and made my way up her many curves to her face. Camille stood to the side like she was proud of her mini-me.

"Sandy?" I couldn't believe how much she's grown up in these short few years.

Darius walked in the room, "stop looking at that little girl like that." He kept walking to the kitchen.

"Yes, stop!" Mister glared at me like he wanted to knock me for looking.

Sandy smiled proudly like she made the entrance she was shooting for. "It hasn't been that long since we've seen each other has it?"

I looked at Camille who was smiling big at us. "It's been long enough for me to be caught off guard by this."

Mister pulled Sandy by the arm to make her stand on his other side. "She's still a little girl, don't let me have to say another word about it."

I looked at Camille, "Brad. We're leaving."

"Goodbye angels, you be good." He kissed the tops of Sandy and baby girl's heads. "Darius is going with you all, right?" He asked Camille.

"I guess so," she slightly sucked her teeth.

I looked at Darius who looked wounded by her reaction to him. "Baby please, you know how tough everything has been. I'm working on a plan to beef up security. Please cooperate, I trust Darius, you can too."

"I can cooperate, doesn't mean I have to like it." Then Camille kissed Mister, when she turned around she looked me in my eyes. "You're due for a deep conditioning and rebraid right?"

"Yes," I said with a straight face.

"I'll look at my books and then I'll text you with a date. Take care Novian."

I watched them walk out of the door. Sandy's body hadn't filled in completely yet. She was on her way to being every bit of a brick house like her auntie. I watched her booty strut to the door as they left. When I looked at Mister his eyes were burning me. "Keep it up, and it won't matter who's son you are!"

"About that, I need to know. What's the deal with you and my momma?"

Mister walked over to his bar and poured a drink. He offered me a drink and I declined. "I knew Ursula when she was just a housewife trying to juggle your brother and sister and her husband. What stood out to me is that she wasn't just a pretty face, or a heavenly body. She knows her music, she taught me how to read music. How to listen to it, how to perform it. She turned this little nightclub in the city from a hole in the wall to the place that everyone wanted to be seen at. Your momma got deep roots in the music scene all over The Bay and the Peninsula. Without her I wouldn't be who I am today. She even saved my life before. Why do you act like it's such a burden to be her son?"

"She was never there for me. My brother raised me. The only time I could count on her to get her hands dirty is if music was involved. Even then she couldn't do it sober."

"Do you know why your brother had to come get you?"

"She got in trouble and had to go to jail."

Mister poured more liquor then he sat down on the couch, he rubbed his chest and then he looked at me. "I used to be a hot head like you, not listening to nobody or thinking anything through. I thought I knew it all. I wrote a check my butt couldn't cash. Have you heard of the name Briscoe Martinique?" I shook my head no, "Briscoe is this cat from around the way. I know you heard of them Wallace's." He looked at me.

"Who?"

He put his glass down from his mouth, "you ain't ever heard of the Wallace family? They run just about everything around these parts. Some people think its just Oakland. I call them the idiots, its so much more than just one city. Just remember the name, if you hear it in the future throw your hands up and walk away. They aren't just black either, it's like they recruit all nationalities to be a part of their family. The Latour and Cardell families are related to them too. Their arms are long." He took a drink, "anyways this cat that I HATE to this day runs parallel to the Wallace's. I can't pinpoint his direct involvement with that family but he's connected. Anyways this cat named Eugene and Briscoe run tight, always have as far as I can remember. Briscoe and me ain't ever got along. I can't even tell you why other than I ain't ever liked the look of him and he I. I called myself trying to take on Briscoe; at the time I didn't know how connected he was. In the beginning, your momma and I were always like brother and sister. Our relationship caused problems when she left your brother's daddy and then she got herself a boyfriend. The same way she protects you is how she used to protect me when I was young and dumb. I went up against Briscoe and he was coming for me. Your momma lost her boyfriend over me, well that night at least. He could've killed her too, thank God he had some kind of love for her otherwise none of us would be here."

"Us?"

"You would've died that night as well."

"You two were like brother and sister even at that point?"

Mister smiled at his glass, "yeah sure." Then he swallowed the last of his drink.

"So I guess you really aren't my father." I smiled.

While Mister choked, "warn me next time you decide to say something so stupid. I don't have any kids." He looked so guilty.

"Brad, we both know that ain't true. You got kids all over this country that you running from."

Mister laughed as he continued to choke, "I plead the fifth!"

"Fifth?" I couldn't stop laughing. "Why Darius had to go with them?"

"I got a little war going on." Then he snapped his fingers. "Which reminds me. I need to send you back to Silent Chaos to record." He got up to get the tape.

"Why can't I record in your studio?" I watched him put the tape in.

"Malcolm's studio is better than mine, and you're the only person I can send in."

******

They were staring at me like I was crazy to be standing here. I stood tall as if I had no idea of what was going on. "Brad thinks he's so smart. You supposed to be a suicide bomber or something?" Dame looked like he was looking for a reason to shoot me.

"I don't even know what you're talking about."

Malcolm walked in the door with two guys. He looked me up and down then the guys with him did the same. "Brad's got jokes." Malcolm reached for the time book. "Four hours? This is a waste of my time." He dropped the book and walked in my face. "What are you here for?"

Malcolm doesn't scare me. "To make..." He punched me in the mouth. I bent over holding my mouth.

"Aw! Come on, that was just a little love tap." One of the guys said smiling.

"Let me work with him. If he's here about music he'll get what he's paid for. If he tries anything, I'll kill him." The other guy said in the same dry tone that Malcolm speaks in.

"I thought the Twin Terrors were coming?" The guy with the stupid grin said.

"They are," the first one replied dryly.

"D-Rick, don't kill him. I like his momma. Remember she sang that song for me that time." He smiled up at the ceiling.

"Whether or not I kill him depends on him."

"Kill me? For what?" I stood up straight even though my lip was throbbing. "I'm going to let that one go Malcolm. I don't know what your problem is with me. I should be the one pissed off with you."

"One of these days being Ursula's son isn't going to be enough to save you."

I wanted to ask him what being her son was saving me from, but the coldness in Malcolm's eyes wouldn't let me ask. D-Rick asked Dame which studio was open. Then he led me to studio number two. The silly guy moved on to the next thing to laugh about as we went to the studio. "Swift doesn't work here anymore?"

"No," D-Rick said turning on the board and setting up for me.

"Did he quit, get fired, what happened?"

D-Rick looked me in my eyes, "really? Is that what you and Swift used to do in here? Gossip like some little girls."

"No, but we did talk about stuff."

"If you need conversation I suggest you bring a friend along. I'm here about music, and nothing more."

"You seem a bit young to work here though." He's definitely a teenager; I just don't know how old he is.

He stopped touching the board and turned towards me. His eyes held no smile, and he looked irritated beyond believe. "These boards don't care about my age. I know music and that's all you need to be worried about. People pay thousands of dollars for minutes of my time. Because you're Ursula's son you'll get a sample of my work today. Keep asking me dumb questions and talking to me and I will shoot you." The look on his face said he meant every word. I nodded in agreement.

I played the tape for him, he asked me questions specific to the music. Whenever I went on too long about anything he blank stared at me. Malcolm came and stood in the window watching from time to time. That other guy came and would make stupid faces in the window, or pretend like he was playing music on a keyboard while he pretended to sing. Halfway through our session two guys walked into our booth. I could see them talking to D-Rick, but I couldn't hear what they were saying since I was in the recording booth. The music stopped and one of the guys spoke over the speakers. "You're rushing it at the end, relax. Let your voice drop and sit on the final scale."

"Huh?"

The funny guy nudged him, "show him Dresser!"

The guy on the microphone and the funny guy laughed. While D-Rick and the other guy looked like they wanted the nonsense to stop. Then the guy on the microphone demonstrated what he was talking about. SHOW OFF! Everyone sat back and waited for my reaction. "You can have that one."

When my session was done, I walked out of the booth and Malcolm was standing there with the tape in his hand. "As long as you're linked up to Brad, don't come back here. Your life was only spared because of your momma. Brad knows I won't let it slide again."

I reached for the tape, and everything went black. Last thing I remember was seeing knuckles coming towards my face.

Torrie

I drove up to his shop; my desire pushed me here. I didn't care about anything else, I felt like I needed to have him. I sat in my car waiting for his car to show up. After an hour his car pulled up next to mine. He sat there staring at me for a minute. I got out of my car and I waited for him to get out of his. I apologized as soon as I thought his ears could hear my words. His face didn't change, he just looked at me. "Come to my place."

"No," he stared at me.

His stares always make me squirm. "Malcolm, cum with me." He moved his eyes away from me, and I knew I had him. "Follow me," then I got back in my car. He stood there like he was debating with himself. I held back my smile when I saw him get in his car. I started my car and then I waited for him to start his car. He was moving real slow. Didn't matter cause once I put it on him, he was going to be mine. All of his movements were slow, he drove slowly behind me. At times it looked like he was going to drive away. I put my hazard lights on and then I waited for him to resume. When we got to my place I told the guard to give Malcolm a visitor pass. I parked my car and then I hurried to his. He sat there for a few minutes and then he slowly got out of his car. I waited for him to follow me. I made sure my hips swayed with every step. In the elevator he purposely stood on the opposite side of the elevator as he stared at me.

Malcolm threw his hands in his pockets as he stood in the middle of my living room. "Now what?"

"Make love to me," I started unbuttoning my dress.

"I can't, I don't love you."

"But you will."

"I can't offer you love, I don't even want to."

"Then why are you here Malcolm?" I let my dress fall to the floor.

"This whole seduction scene may be turning you on, but it's not doing anything for me. I don't have anything for you."

"I want you Malcolm, and I know you want me."

"I want to give you the dick, that's about it."

"You want me Malcolm," I unlatched my bra.

"You are an idiot," he watched my bra fall to the floor.

I stepped out of my panties, and then I stood there as he stared at me. I walked into my bedroom and then I climbed in the middle of the bed. It took him a few minutes and then he walked into my room. He took his watch off, and then he took off his shirt. I closed my mouth as I drooled looking at his body. His skin was so dark and strong looking. He took off his shoes, and he placed them next to his folded shirt. He put condoms on my dresser next to his watch. He took off his pants and folded them and placed them on top of his shirt. He put his gun on the dresser next to his watch. I didn't realize he carried a gun, but at this particular moment it didn't matter. When he took his shorts off, my eyes got big. I swallowed as I looked at him, when I gestured for him to come to the middle of the bed. He said no, he told me to come to him as he reached for a condom. The closer I got, the bigger it got. Close up on it I almost wanted to change my mind. I've never seen one this big before. No wonder he's not talking a bunch of mess about what he can do. With a package like this you don't have to say anything. I watched him put the condom on and then he told me to come to him. Now I was moving slowly, and as soon as I got within reach he pulled me to the edge of the bed. He pushed me on my back and he grabbed my legs. I was already excited, but it didn't go unnoticed that he didn't delay with foreplay. I yelped when he put the head in. That thing was huge from the tip onward. I asked him to wait a minute, he looked at me and then he pushed again. I backed up; I was having a flash back of losing my virginity all over again. I asked him to wait as I had a pep talk with myself. I could do this. I could do this. Malcolm said he didn't have all day and he could leave if I was having second thoughts. I took a deep breath then I asked him not to grab my legs. Malcolm leaned over me and hovered. He put himself in the position and then he pressed in on me. He was too big! He had to work to get in while my body immediately reacted to him in my space. It HURT! He was just past his head and I felt him inside my stomach. I put my hand on my stomach as I tried to back away. Malcolm told me not to run, this is what I wanted and it was too late for that. I clamped my legs on him. He said if I didn't want him to hold my legs I needed to open them. As soon as I opened them he pushed further. I couldn't take it; I backed up as my legs shook. Malcolm pulled me back to the edge of the bed and then he didn't try to go in any further, but now. OH GOD! OH GOD! OH GOD! My legs started shaking again. Malcolm's rhythm picked up and that confirmed it, he's trying to kill me. Every thrust hurt, but it felt heavenly. I couldn't believe how many times I busted in the past couple of minutes. OUCH! OUCH! OUCH! OUCH! He told me to open my legs, but I couldn't. I screamed to the top of my lungs when he grabbed my legs and pressed a little further. He started to nut and he pulled out. I didn't know why he did, but I was thankful to be disconnected. He grabbed the dresser behind him as he caught his breath. He took his gun with him to the bathroom. I heard the toilet flush as I gently touch myself. I was sore to the touch. I heard water and then Malcolm came out a minute or two later in his boxers. He put his clothes back on as I laid in the middle of the bed throbbing. I don't even know how to explain what just happened.

Malcolm looked back at me in the middle of the bed; he looked like he was thinking of what to say. "A smart person would leave me alone, but since that seems not to be you let me say this. If you say anything to Amber about this, I will personally mess up your entire life."

"Why are you talking to me like this? Come back to bed Malcolm."

"For what? I was just getting started and you can't hang. It will frustrate me to mess with you."

"That's not fair, you didn't even warn me."

"You're an idiot, I've said it time and time again." Then he turned towards the door.

"Where are you going?"

"Don't ever question me, if I feel like breaking you in I'll be back." Then he walked out.

Every movement on my bed hurt, I ran bath water and put Epsom salt in the water, then my bubbles. Even wiping with tissue was a challenge. I couldn't get in that bath fast enough.

****

Sinclaire fell over laughing as she held her stomach. "You look so confused."

"I don't even know how to feel about it. No one has ever put in such little effort and turned me out." I made it sound as funny as I could, but I really wanted to cry. Malcolm hangs up in my face, stands me up, and calls me stupid at least twenty times every time I see him. It doesn't matter what he does I come running back. He never pays for anything, and he barely even wants to be seen with me in public. If we go out and someone notices me he leaves. He says he doesn't have time for my celebrity status stuff. As bad as he makes me feel, I hold my breath until we can get to it. When I'm on the road traveling all I can think about is getting to him.

I thought I was doing a good thing. I saw him looking at this car one time when we were out. He kept looking back at it. I had my assistant search and search and search until she came up with a picture that resembled the car he was looking at. I used my star power to have one customized with gold "M" emblems all throughout the car. I hadn't even bought myself anything as expensive as this car. Malcolm likes expensive things, his liquor choice. His clothes, cologne, everything. His stuff is so expensive that I didn't even know what it was until I had my assistant look stuff up for me. No wonder he doesn't have any money. He spends it all on his appearance. I had the car delivered to his house. I sat on the hood and waited for him to come home and see it. I just knew he would be appreciative and maybe finally let me spend the night.

When he pulled up to the house a white guy got out of his car and stared at me for a minute. I ignored him and I watched Malcolm. Malcolm looked like he always does but his words were short. He told me to leave! I asked him if he liked the car. I slid off the hood and held out the keys for him. The guy sarcastically told him to thank me. That made Malcolm madder and he told me if I didn't take the car away he was dumping it in The Bay. I started going off because now on top of everything else I was embarrassed. I couldn't take this car back. I spent a lot of money on it, and now it was all for nothing. Malcolm and the man walked inside his house and he slammed his front door. I fell down in the middle of the grass on my knees and I sobbed. After awhile someone walked up to me and handed me tissue. I knew it wasn't Malcolm. I looked up and it was the white man. "Wipe your face, you about to scare the neighbors."

"Why doesn't he like it? I spent a lot of money on this just for him."

"Money can't buy you love darling. I don't know what possessed you to think that this is the way to a man's heart. You need to pick yourself up and be on your way."

"What am I supposed to do with the car? It's customized for him."

He looked at the car, "where would he even drive a car like that? It wasn't practical for you to buy that at all. You better think of someone else, try and sell, or give it to them."

"I don't know why I love him! He's not even good to me." I wiped my knees as I stood up.

"You don't love him, you're running from something else. One day you'll get it together and you'll be fine. Until then you'll do foolish things like this."

"You don't even know me. You don't know what I feel!" I put my hands on my hips.

Malcolm opened the door and stood in the doorway. "The truth makes you angry I see. Clearly you're the type of female who can't be handled delicately. So let me give you the message my son sent for you."

"SON?" I gave this clearly white man a get serious look.

I saw impatience flicker in his eyes. "Get off of my son's property before I have to remove you!"

I was going to say something else but the look in his eyes told me to shut my mouth and get while the getting was good.

I saw that day playing out a different way. I got in the car and

I drove down the hill. I pulled over and fixed my face. I thought for a minute then I thought of my plan. I parked just outside of the gate for Novian's condo. His car was in his spot so he was most likely home. I called him on his cellphone and he let me go to voicemail. So I went to the intercom and laid on the buzzer. I didn't even care if he had a girl here. I just knew he wouldn't turn me away. "WHAT?"

"Uh Novian, can you come down here please."

"FOR WHAT?"

"I have a surprise for you." I tried to sound as cute as I could. I haven't seen or spoken to Novian in over a year at least. He stepped off of the elevator in basketball shorts and a wife beater. He was a sight for sore eyes. His eyes went to the car, my eyes stretched big when I saw his face. "What happened to you?"

"I don't want to talk about it. You called me down here to look at this?" He was completely annoyed.

I held up the keys, "it's yours."

He froze, then his eyes stretched as he looked at it. "What?"

"I owe you everything Novian, you know if you wouldn't have been by my side I would've forgotten the lyrics to the songs. I would've fumbled through my big break like I did at that rehearsal." I put my arms around him as he looked at the car with big appreciative eyes.

"This is amazing, I'm speechless Torrie. I really didn't think you cared."

"I'm always going to care when it comes to you. Do you like it?" I put the keys in his hand.

"Like it? This is amazing! I LOVE it Torrie! Thank you!" He kissed my forehead.

"Good! Now take me for a ride."

Sinclaire was still laughing in her own world. Then she said she heard he was messing around with this girl off of 35th. Everything in my soul tensed up. I kept asking question after question. Sinclaire and I picked up her sister and her sister's friend.

We drove over to 35th and MacArthur. Novian was there leaning against the car I bought him kissing on this girl. Everything inside me turned RED and I didn't let Sinclaire stop the car before I got out. I marched up to them and I grabbed the girl by her weave. Her hair went flying in one direction and her body went in the other. Novian yelled at me asking me what I was doing. I kept hitting him in his chest asking him how he could ride in the car I bought him with some random female. Sinclaire called out to me to watch out. The girl was charging at me. I beat that girl down on that sidewalk with every bit of rage I could muster inside of me. I beat her for everything I was angry about before. The things I was angry about now, and the things I would be angry about in the future. In the end the girl used her bloodied hands to cover her head as I tried to stomp her. Novian told me to stop, and then I told him to go home!

Sinclaire grabbed me and pulled me away. As we were getting in the car that kid with the dread locs stood across the street openly staring at me. He was going to run and tell Malcolm. I took off running and I ran between the cars on the busy street towards the kid. He didn't even flinch which is what I guess I thought he would do. He never moved he just watched me. I reached back to swing on him and he caught my fist in the middle of my swing. His hand felt like a wall and I fell. He looked at me with no concern in his eyes as he asked me what was my problem. Then he looked around to see who was looking at us like he was going to kick me or something. I tried to kick him and he grabbed my foot and threw it behind me, which made me flip over. I hit the ground again. Then he stepped on my back and his foot felt like a ton. "Why are you trying to hit me?"

"WHY ARE YOU OVER HERE WATCHING ME?" I screamed

between breaths.

"You're the one running around here creating scenes like no one would recognize your face. You're about to be sued for everything you got." He stepped harder, "Swing on me one more time and I will forget the way I was raised and I will have to defend myself." Then he took his foot off of me. He didn't walk away; he stood there staring at me like he was waiting for me to make a decision. Novian was helping the girl up and not paying any of this any attention. Sinclaire ran towards me as the guy calmly walked away. She asked me who he was, and I couldn't remember his name to save my life. All I knew is that he was going to tell Malcolm.

Chapter 8

Novian

I'm so happy to be out of Oakland. Everything is so crazy right now. Once Bashell found out that she had a fight with Torrie things blew up. Torrie's team dished out a lot of money to keep the story from leaking. Torrie's people got on my case as if we were in a relationship. Torrie showed up out of nowhere, with an over the top car. Then she disappeared again. Amos is still telling me about Torrie running behind Malcolm. Amos said she acts like a strung out female. After all these years if he hasn't acknowledged her I don't understand what she's supposed to be doing. Meanwhile her career has skyrocketed! She's everywhere I turn. I've done background vocals for a lot of her material, but we're not even in the studio together.

I flew out here two weeks ago. I brought my songs and my agent had me meet with a lyricist first. I took notes as we went over my songs. The things that he suggested seemed like they would've come to me automatically. When I got frustrated he told me to go easy on myself. He said it's easy to point things out after the fact. He said while you're creating you can get so lost in the creation of your project until you become more seasoned.

My songs were good, but with his help my songs were golden. When I stepped out of that conference room that guy Matt was walking by. As usual he avoided me until he had to interact with me and other people were around. When I got to the elevator I was surprised to see Adina as she called my name. "What are you doing here?"

"I came to have lunch with Matt but he can't go. Are you available?"

I smiled at her, "of course." I sat in Adina's car and smiled. "Look at how far we've come. Driving around in fancy cars, living the lives we always dreamed of."

"Paying the ultimate price for it all."

"We all have to pay our dues, some people never get this far."

Adina exhaled loudly, "how's Torrie?"

"I should be asking you the same thing. Don't you two talk regularly?"

After we were shown to a table. "Torrie's not the same person anymore. I haven't spoken with her in years. I'll see her from time to time, but we don't talk."

"She hasn't changed all that much. You're finally seeing who she is. I've always been an after thought to her. All those years in school when I was chasing her. She was the same way, you're just now getting a taste of what I've always gone through."

Adina looked me in my eyes as she twirled her fork in her hand. "How could you still love her?"

"I guess I know her better than anyone."

Adina gripped her fork. "She slept with my man!"

I shifted in my seat, "ok. You're still with him though."

Adina dropped her shoulders as she cried. "I feel so trapped. She won't admit it, but I'm not stupid. It's so obvious, but it makes no sense. None of this does. Why would she hurt me like that?"

"Torrie's selfish."

"So she gets with every guy she wants. There are only a couple of guys at the label she hasn't gotten with. I don't know what's wrong with her. Why was I stupid enough to think she wouldn't do that to me?"

I moved to the seat next to Adina, I put my arms around her.

"It's my fault. I'm sorry Adina."

"How? How could you defend her? How could you take responsibility for her wrongs?"

"She didn't tell you what happened?" Adina shook her head no as she stayed on my shoulder. "I got her pregnant, it was an accident of course. I avoided her; Lee gave her the money to take care of it. She said she had it done out here. I thought you knew."

Adina sat up, "when was this?"

"Years ago, before she was with that one guy."

Adina was quiet as she thought, "Swift?"

"Yeah, Swift."

"How's Lee doing?"

"He's good, he's married with kids. Still driving the bus and doing it proudly."

"Does he ever mention me?"

"He used to, once his wife found out about you he's not allowed to watch anything you're on."

"Is he happy?"

"Lee doesn't complain. He gave up his youth for me and he never mentioned it. He's like his dad; they step up to their responsibilities. His dad never complains about my mother either."

"Sometimes I wish we could've found a way." She stared at my eyes. Then she rubbed my hair. "You are handsome Novian."

I politely took her hand off of my head. I kissed her hand then I moved back to my seat across from her. "It's my fault, I'm sorry."

"So when did Swift come into the picture?"

"I don't know, I don't want to think about all of the details. How many projects you got coming out this year?"

Adina smiled weakly at me. "My agent says I'm such a hard worker. When I looked at my list, I've got four films just this year. Some of the others are staggered over the next few years."

"When will you rest?"

"When I don't need Matt and his team in order to be me."

"So no wedding bells?"

She blew air, "he gets so many pats on the back for having a black girlfriend. He's asked and I refused."

"You're still together?"

"Only for show, once I figured everything out I refuse to let him touch me. It's been years, the cold part is that he'll at least own up to it. Torrie has resorted to avoiding me."

I reached over the table and I held her hands as she cried. When it was time to go Adina walked into my arms as she cried into my chest. I held on to her as she cried heartbroken tears. I felt like garbage. Adina dropped me off at the label, but I was drained. I couldn't work anymore, I needed to relax and think about my life. I told the lyricist that I would connect with him on Monday. I told him I needed to shut down for the day. It didn't matter to him; he was getting paid for today regardless.

As I walked out of the building Bonita was there talking to Matt. She was talking to him, but she was watching me. I wasn't in the mood to dodge her subtle seduction scenes either. I nodded at her and kept it moving. When I got to my hotel I called Lee. I needed to talk to my brother and refocus myself. Of course! He wasn't home from work yet. I talked to my nephew for a little bit. His little sister was in the background trying everything she could to be included in our conversation. My niece can talk your ear off about nothing, so neither one of us wanted her to take over our call. When I couldn't take the baby crying in the background any longer, I told my niece and nephew that I would talk to them later.

I was about to fall asleep when there was a knock on my door. I exhaled cause I knew I didn't want to see whomever it was. I opened the door and Bonita was standing there. She looked from eye to eye like she was looking for something. Then she told me to come on. I exhaled cause I was tired of fighting this. We sat in silence as she drove through the city. I told her that her house was nice, and then I asked her how long she's lived in this house. She thanked me and then she hurried to her front door. She told me to take my shoes off. Her house was spotless! Bonita turned to me and asked me to join her in the pool. She took off her clothes and dropped them along the way to the pool. Her body doesn't look like any mother I've ever seen. Who knows what the women out here in LA do though.

I stopped walking as I looked at the huge picture on her wall of her daughter. I couldn't take my eyes off of this little girl. She was precious, adorable, and all around beautiful. Bonita always says that her daughter has hair like mine. Looking at the picture I could see why. I found myself looking at all of the pictures covering her walls in that room of her little girl.

When I went outside by the pool Bonita was doing laps. She stopped in the middle of the pool and asked me why I wasn't getting in. I sat on the lounge chair and I told her I had a long day. Bonita stared at me for a minute while water ran down her face. Then she asked me what was wrong. I told her that all I can see around me are ripples, affects from dumb choices that I made in the past. She asked for an example. I used Torrie's fight as an example. I told her that Torrie and I are not together, but I know at some point I'm going to be with her. I told her I needed to exercise more discretion. Bonita said Torrie needs to grow up and to stop letting her temper drive her to act out. She said Torrie and Meredith Bling came to blows because Meredith walked in on Torrie coming on to her man. She said Torrie has been acting out a lot lately and fortunately for Torrie she's become a real asset to the label and marketing executives. I heard what she was saying but I needed to own up to the part I play in her acting out.

When Bonita tried to kiss me I turned my head. I told her I couldn't; she was too close to Torrie. Bonita got frustrated as she said Torrie doesn't care. She said Torrie's been running around with the morals of a screwdriver. I changed the subject, I asked her about her daughter. She stared at me for another minute, and then she walked away and wrapped a towel around her naked body. She went inside and then she came back with a bunch of picture books. She opened one and stared at the first page. "Angel is my miracle baby. I didn't think I would ever get to be a mom. All of my life I wanted nothing more than to be a mother. Then as life would have it I thought I missed my chance. Angel is my blessing and reward for all of my hard work. Whenever I get stressed out, I look at her and I say this is all for her. It's always been for her. I know every mother must think that her child is the most beautiful child in the world. Look at this baby, have you ever seen a more beautiful child?" I looked at the picture and smiled at the baby. "I haven't dated since she was born."

"So then what was this?"

"You're different Novian." She didn't look at me when she said that.

"Where's her father?"

"He's not in the picture, to be completely honest with you he doesn't know about her."

"Why?"

"Part of me fears he'd try to take her from me. Call me old fashioned but I don't think it's healthy for a child to go from parent to parent. I doubt that he'd want to be with me, but it's not really fair to speak for him huh?"

I traced the picture with my finger. "Why wouldn't he do

whatever it took to have her with him everyday?"

"Yeah and then I end up with nothing cause he took her from me."

"Why would he do that? My mother wasn't really around when I was growing up. My brother raised me the best he could. He was just barely eighteen when he took me on. My mother isn't the mothering kind; well she wasn't while I was growing up. She does try harder now that I'm grown. You're a great mother, I can tell by these pictures. He'd be crazy to walk away from you."

"Thank you for that, I hear you, but custody can get tricky. It would kill me."

"Is she coming home soon?"

"She'll be home this evening after her class. You're going to be gone by then."

Torrie

I had my smile plastered on my face as I pretended to enjoy signing autographs for some of my fans. I brought my momma out for champagne brunch. She likes to put fruit in her champagne. She doesn't drink it, but she eats the fruit. When the girls walked away I sat back in my chair holding on to my smile. My publicist has warned me that people are always watching once I've been spotted. So I need to keep pleasant expressions on my face when fans are around. I looked around the restaurant and his profile caught my attention. If I ever doubted that someone was him, his skin was so unique to him, how could I mistake him?

Malcolm hasn't been taking my calls especially after that night at the Motown Review. I felt my blood pressure go up as I looked at the woman at his table. She was beautiful! I've seen her

178

before, I tried to remember where. She did not look happy. I could tell by their body language they were having stern words with each other. When she stood up I scanned her from head to toe. This woman had curves on top of curves. I wondered if she's had surgery, nowadays women don't come that built and that beautiful naturally. I adjusted in my seat as I watched Malcolm stare at her as she walked out. I told my momma I'd be right back. When I stood up Malcolm turned his head towards me with disgust all over it. "Well hello to you. How have you been?"

I watched him pick up his glass. Of course the standard champagne wasn't good enough for him. "What do you want?"

"Who is she?" He shrugged as he watched my eyes. "She the reason you've been missing?" He shrugged again.

When she came back the look on her face told me that she knew why I was standing here. "Who is she?"

I pointed to myself, "Torrie! Who are you?"

She looked at Malcolm and he shrugged again. "If you're smart you'll get away from our table."

I chuckled, "you must not know who I am."

"You should ask me if I care." Malcolm took another drink as he looked between us.

I glanced at her arms and I saw how toned they were. She wasn't skinny but not too big where I couldn't throw her around. Her hair was short so there wasn't too much to grab on to if we did fight. I cut my eyes at Malcolm and then I walked back to my table. When I glanced back Malcolm was watching me walk and she was pissed. Talk about insecure.

I watched Malcolm and the woman walk out. She made sure he walked behind her and now she was switching extra hard.

When my momma and I walked out of the restaurant I was looking around hoping Malcolm was waiting for me.

I dropped my momma at my uncle's place. Then I drove to Malcolm's shop. His car was here so I parked. When I got out of the car I heard a woman fussing and it was coming from around the back. When I peeked around the corner it was that woman standing in the doorway fussing. "After all these years, this is where we stand? You would let some little girl step to me?"

"Why would you fight anyone over me? I told you about that."

She put her arms up, "after all these years this is where we stand?"

"I don't have time for this."

"She's moved on to a guy with money. You're seriously going to sit here and wait for her?"

"Verses what? Play stepdad to your kids? I want you more than I want them and you know how much I want you."

"You want me Malcolm, and I don't understand why you try to fight it."

"Because after I'm done with you, you act like there's something else to be had. If you're looking for love you need to go back to your man."

"I know you care about me. We were together all those years!"

"You might've been with me in the best way you know how. I was never with you."

That was all I needed to hear. I walked around the corner, "you need me to handle her for you?"

He squinted his eyes at me, "at least there's someone on your level."

"Excuse you! We're having a private conversation!" She wiggled her neck at me.

"My man don't want to talk to you." I walked up to Malcolm to walk inside.

He used his fingers to push my forehead. "I don't want you here either!" I was so embarrassed that I didn't think. I started going off! Next thing I know me and this woman were tussling. I guess I expected Malcolm to stop us but he stood there and watched. I underestimated her strength, and I know she underestimated me. She got up screaming she wasn't in high school and how ridiculous it was to be fighting over a guy. My knee was throbbing where I hit the ground. My hands and knuckles were scraped too. I sat on the ground in a trance as I watched her cry beautiful tears from a broken heart. It was at that moment that regret hit me. We didn't love Malcolm the same way or for the same reasons. She literally looked like her heart was breaking. Malcolm looked like he could careless. I wanted to apologize, but my pride wouldn't let me.

Malcolm told both of us to get off of his property before he called the cops.

She limped to her car and then she started screaming like she was mad at herself. "Nothing but DRAMA!" She looked at me with beautiful heartbroken tears that leaped out of her eyes. "One day you're gonna learn! This is FAR FROM OVER!" I stood up as she drove away.

Novian

"What the heck Novian!" Torrie screamed into the phone as soon as I said hello.

I didn't know what her problem was but I was not in the mood. I hung up the phone and then I tried to write again. Then my buzzer for the front door sounded. I mumbled a curse and then I went to the intercom. "WHAT?"

I could hear Amos laughing, "calm down Romeo. Let me come up." I buzzed him up and then I went back to my ringing phone. I picked it up, and hung up again. Then I took the phone off of the hook. Then my pager kept going off. Torrie was blowing me up. I sucked my teeth then I turned it off. "What's wrong with that girl?"

Amos picked up my remote and turned the television to a celebrity gossip station. "When we come back from commercial, more on Adina Vaughn's new suitor."

Amos gave me a goofy grin. "You dog!"

"They're not talking about me," I frowned at him.

Amos started laughing, "who has an affair that they don't even know about?"

"What are you talking about?"

"You'll see," Amos gave me a toothy grin.

When the show came back from commercial a guy in an ascot and glasses grinned really big at the screen. "So just in case you've been under a rock and haven't heard. Adina Vaughn appears to have moved on to a new young tender. I guess the saying is true once you go black, you will be back." He sucked his tongue as he smiled deviously at the camera. Pictures of Adina and I holding each other. My mouth fell open. I didn't even feel like anyone was watching me. "It took a little digging but it appears this is one of the back up singers for Torrie Rowe. We tried to contact Ms. Rowe for comment. We couldn't get her yet, but we'll keep trying. I can smell the drama unfolding. As soon as we have more information, you'll be the first to know. This has been Red Rick bringing you The *Juice* first!"

Amos looked at me and started laughing out loud. "You dog! Ain't that her cousin?"

"It wasn't even like that, she was caught up in yesteryear. Thinking about my brother and what could've been."

"That one picture looked like she was throwing it at you."

"She was just brokenhearted." Then I thought about Lee. I put my phone on the hook and then I called him to make sure there were no problems. I didn't even say hello back, I asked him to let me explain. Lee hadn't heard the gossip, and then he started laughing as soon as I told him. I told him the truth, that she did try to go there kind of. He held on to his laugh as he reassured me that he knew I wouldn't go against the code like that. We chatted for a while and then Amos made himself comfortable in the kitchen.

When I got off of the phone with Lee, I called Torrie back. She was screaming like a crazy person. I let her yell and scream and then I told her to get out of my ear with all of that noise. She actually opened her mouth to question me as if she has the right to. I decided to let her stew in it. I refused to confirm or deny that anything happened between Adina and I. After all the stuff she does, she needed to think I was capable of being as ruthless as she is.

Torrie

My phone kept ringing and I was trying to sleep, so I turned the ringer off. I did not want to talk. I rolled over and then there was a pounding at the door. I couldn't believe the doorman let someone up without my consent. I got up irritated and grabbed my robe. I opened my bedroom door as my momma answered the door. "I'm so sorry Ms. Rowe, Ms. Fairchild would not leave the front desk and I don't know what she said to the police for them to demand that I come up and either bring Ms. Rowe down or let her up."

"It's ok, send her up." I called out and then I walked to the kitchen. "Momma leave the door cracked for her. You can go back to bed, I got this."

My momma looked uneasy as she sat on the couch like she was nervous. I put on the coffee maker and then I took mugs out of the cabinet. I sat them on the counter as I opened the refrigerator Bonita came storming in my front door. "TORRIE!"

"Well hello Bonita how are you?"

Bonita looked around and then she focused on me. She laughed an angry laugh. "You know, I don't say anything when you throw your little diva fits. I don't say anything when you spread your legs everywhere you go. You start fights constantly and you can be so unprofessional at times. I say nothing; I know you're an angry child throwing fits all over the place. However, when you mess with my money, my job, that's where I draw the line. You are going to work with Novian!"

"No I'm not!" I shook my head calmly.

Bonita looked at me and then she looked at my momma. "Who is this?"

"That's my momma."

"Can you give us a minute, we need to discuss business. Your daughter doesn't seem to understand what I'm saying to her. I need the space to explain it." My momma got up and went into her room. Bonita shifted her weight from leg to leg. Then she dropped her head. She dropped her purse and coat on the floor by the door. When she lifted her head her eyes were red and she walked into the kitchen. She walked up on me and started choking me. When I tried to reach the counter to grab one of the mugs she moved me away from the counter and continued to choke me down to the floor. Bonita was freakishly strong and her eyes looked so crazy. She was focused on me and by the look in her eyes she felt nothing about trying to kill me. I tried to hit her, kick her, I scratched her but it didn't stop her. Suddenly she let go and I started coughing. She watched me like she was trying to figure me out. "You're stronger than I ever gave you credit for being." She tilted her head as she kneeled next to me as I gasped for air. "Maybe you have no idea who I am, but you signed your life away to me a long time ago. The only control you have is over whether you live or die. If you choose death I can help you with that." Then she stood up and made herself a cup of coffee. "Get up, fix yourself up, and come have a cup with me."

"No!" Then I coughed.

She kicked me hard in my thigh; "I said get up and come have a cup of coffee with me. Keep testing me and I will kill your mom and your cousin! Oh but that's after I confirm her suspicions about you and Matt for her. Let her come after you and then I'll let her in on the deal you made with me. How you sacrificed everything so that the both of you could have your flourishing careers. How you let your love for her and everyone else turn you into this bitter little spoiled brat. Let her sit there confused and then I'll kill her. GET UP! GET YOUR COFFEE! COME SIT!"

Bonita looked so crazy, and clearly I was no match for her crazy. I slowly got up and did like she said. I didn't want to sit next to her, but the look she gave me made me come directly next to her.

She said she didn't care why I didn't want to work with Novian. She told me I was going to do it. She told me I didn't have a choice. She said with the flip of a button my career could be over. I could carry the financial burden of all of the lawsuits against me. Or I could remember my place and do as I'm told. When I hesitated she asked me if I had a backup plan? Did I possess any employable skill set? Then she told me I wouldn't even be employable at a burger stand once she was done with me. She said the same hand that built me up could tear me down.

She looked at her watch and then she told me I had thirty minutes to pack my bags to go to LA. She said Novian would be at the studio tonight to record. I told her I couldn't leave my momma. She didn't believe me, so I reminded her that my momma always travels with me. I told her I don't like to leave her behind. She told me to ride in coach with my mom then. She told me the clock was ticking. I told my momma to pack her bags and then I cried as I packed mine. I didn't have a good reason for refusing to work with Novian other than I felt so out of control. The label MADE me work with Amber when I didn't want to and when I found out about the details of the deal they negotiated with her I was livid. She didn't deserve anything other than her fee for jumping around on beat. Little miss white girl wanna be black so much. I want to beat her face in. Everybody's protecting her, making sure she has what she wants. Who's protecting me? Making sure I have what I want? I want to destroy her. I can't stand her! She always walks around like she's so innocent. Shooting me dirty looks whenever she can. At least the feeling is mutual, I don't like her and she doesn't like me. I don't care if it's fair or not, I'm going to kick her butt the first chance I get.

Novian

"What's with all the security?" I asked Mister as I took a seat.

"Same ole enemies, just a new day." Mister said as he turned in his chair to face me. "So Murphy huh?"

I exhaled, "you've got Novian caught up in so much red tape. I've got to make a living too."

"Lamont!" Mister called out. A young guy with dreads walked in the door with papers in a folder. He handed them to Mister and then he turned to walk away. "Hold on Lamont." Mister looked at me. "This is Novian." The guy nodded then he looked me over. "Novian this is Lamont."

"So! Who is he supposed to be to me?"

Mister sat back and smiled, "this is a copy of your contract. You want it back?" Then he handed it to Lamont. "All you got to do is take it from him."

The kid looked at me with no expression on his face. "You want me to fight some kid over paperwork?"

Mister opened his hands, "Novian already has a following. It might not be all that big. Absolutely no one knows who Murphy is. All you got to do is take the paperwork from Lamont."

I tapped my hand on the chair. "You called me over here for this?"

"Did you honestly think you could cut all these side deals and I wouldn't have something to say about it at some point?"

"You're only mad about it cause you must think something is about to pan out for me. All these years you have not cared about me doing business as Murphy. I'm not stupid. Is Lamont some kind of ghetto karate king or something?" Lamont didn't say anything he just stood there looking at me. "You sent me to Malcolm's studio knowing that you and him are at an all-out war. How could you set me up like that? Talking about Malcolm ain't got nothing on you, but you did nothing about what he did to me. I don't know what your problem is but I'm not about to play this game with you. You can't use me anymore so now you gonna have this kid beat me up.

Mister smiled at Lamont. "He's not as stupid as I thought he was." Lamont's plain expression never changed. "Change of plans then. You're going to add me on as your agent. I'll handle all of your bookings and affairs. If you need convincing Lamont will convince you."

I exhaled, "you want this kid to beat me up so badly. I'm not stupid and I'm not going for this. You must have some kind of foresight of big things for me. Otherwise why would all of this be happening?" Mister didn't say anything he just stared at me. The kid's expression never changed. I bet he was waiting for me to do something so he could karate chop me across the room. "That contract ain't worth all of this! I thought we had a mutual respect for each other. I thought…"

"Respect for you? If it wasn't for your momma you'd have been dead a long time ago. Don't nobody care about Ursula's son who has no clue as to who to respect and who to flex at." Mister looked pissed then he looked at Lamont. "Do we let him go?"

"How would you be showing Ursula honor by hurting her son?"

"This is business!"

"It's up to you, you know I don't care. However, you will have to deal with Ursula afterwards. You know he's going to go running back to his momma. If you touch Ursula, Malcolm will not hold back his reaction."

Mister stroked his chin, "let's deal with Malcolm and then we'll loop back around to this. How soon before Darius brings my girls home?"

"Camille is still at the spa. Darius is with your niece at her mother's. As soon as Camille's ready he's going to bring them home."

Mister looked at me, "when I call you. You better come, if you run from me I will kill you!"

Torrie

I was beyond irritated! I stood at the bottom of the stairs staring up at that picture. I knew he was going to get mad but I didn't care. "I THOUGHT I TOLD YOU TO GET RID OF THAT PICTURE!"

"Get out Torrie!" Malcolm didn't even look at me, as if he

knew I was going to march out of the door just because he told me to.

"YOU ARE MY MAN!"

"I'm not anything to you, you need to leave."

I took off up the stairs, it was my intention to pull the picture down and punch a hole through it. Halfway up the stairs he grabbed my ankle and after I fell he drug me down the stairs.

Novian would never touch me like this. Malcolm would be gentler to a snake than he is with me. I don't know what he's mad about but he didn't take it easy on me a few minutes ago. He didn't care when I asked him to slow down. He didn't want me to come over, but I needed to see him. I couldn't wait to come home and see him. I should've popped up on Novian instead. This session was harder, faster, and rougher than ever before. Malcolm told me to wash-up in the sink in the downstairs bathroom like I was a whore. When he walked away clearly not caring about my well being, I pulled my pants up and walked slowly towards the bathroom. I looked up at the picture of Amber and got angry.

"LET ME GO!"

"I told you not to come over here and you gotta be hardheaded!"

"AMBER IS NOT BETTER THAN ME!"

He was about to let go of my ankle but he grabbed it tighter and drug me to the front door. "I TOLD YOU TO KEEP HER NAME OUT OF YOUR MOUTH! YOU THINK THIS IS A GAME? I TOLD YOU NOT TO COME HERE AND YOU CAME ANYWAYS! I'VE EXHAUSTED ALL OF MY PATIENCE WITH YOU! YOU COME OVER ACTING LIKE YOU COULD EVER QUESTION ME ABOUT MY GUEST! YOU BETTER BE HAPPY I DIDN'T SNAP YOUR NECK THEN! I'VE EXHAUSTED ALL OF MY PATIENCE WITH YOU! LOSE MY NUMBER, AND YOU BETTER NOT COME BACK HERE!" Then he picked up my stuff and me. He tossed me on the grass and slammed his door shut before I made contact with the ground.

I laid on the ground crying and crying. I was so angry that I couldn't pull it back even though I was trying.

"Hey!" He kicked my foot, "you need to get going."

I didn't recognize this guy at all. He was tall, Mexican, and CUTE! "Who are you?"

"Don't matter, he's pretty upset. If I was you I'd get out of here before he comes back." I got up slowly and now everything hurt.

I called Sinclaire as I drove away. Sinclaire hung up after she said she was coming over. I thought about calling Novian. I shook off the thought.

"YOU ARE TORRIE FREAKING ROWE! WHO DOES THIS GUY THINK HE IS?" Sinclaire barked as she paced back and forth. "Does he have any idea of how much of a blessing it is for you to even pay him any attention?"

"Why does he have a picture of your choreographer up in his house?" Sinclaire's sister asked as she rolled the blunt.

"I don't know what his thing is with her. She's got a man. Dwayne is in love with her, he don't mess around on her either. I tried remember."

"I don't get it?" Sinclaire said as she watched the blunt.

"Torrie?" My momma called from the living room.

I got up and closed my bedroom door behind me. "Yes momma?"

"My brother is taking me out to an early dinner. I will be back late tonight. Do you like my dress?"

I smiled at her innocence, "you're beautiful momma." My

uncle was only going to ask her for money. That's why I only give her a little money. Well little compared to what I could give her. She says he took us in so it's not right to forget about him now. "Have fun, and I'll see you in the morning."

When I walked in to the room Sinclaire and her sister were pumped up, talking about Amber was trying to show me up and take my man. As I puffed I listened, they were right. I stood up and started getting dressed. It was going to feel so good beating Amber's face in. Maybe if I wasn't high and overly emotional I would've thought about it before I left.

Novian

"Where are you?" Amos sounded excited.

"Home," I was sitting on my couch trying to write.

"Torrie's on the news! I'm coming to get you!"

"Get me? Is she ok?" My heart started pounding.

"I'm coming man! I'll buzz when I'm down stairs."

I turned on the television, and then I turned to the channel two news. There was a reporter on the screen talking really fast. Torrie's picture was on the screen in the upper left hand corner. "We just received word that the third person they pulled from this mangled wreck has died." I didn't understand what was happening, but I stood up immediately. "For those of you just tuning in, I'm reporting to you live from in front of the North Star Dance Company. Where crazed fans followed the talented and young singer Torrie Rowe and some friends. It appears that they were outside talking when the gunmen opened fire on them. Torrie has been rushed to the hospital. We're told that her condition is stable, but we don't know much else at this time. Torrie's bodyguard returned fire and the car lost control. You can see the police are measuring the skid marks on the ground as well as the ammunition on the ground. The car wrapped around this pole and two of the four men died immediately. Stay tuned as we bring you more information as the story unfolds."

I ran to my room and pulled on clothes quickly. I grabbed my wallet and keys and then I met Amos downstairs. "You cool man?"

"Why would fans want to shoot her?"

Amos looked at me like I was crazy. "Why would four men get in a car full of ammunition to shoot a celebrity? Please don't tell me you believe everything you see on the news."

"So what happened?"

"I don't know exactly. Vic told me to take you to Torrie. I'm supposed to stay with you two while Malcolm has the rest of them strapping up their boots."

"It's the least Malcolm could do."

"What do you mean?"

"He's going after them for coming after Torrie."

"MAN NOVIAN! I SWEAR! OPEN YOUR EYES! Malcolm don't care about Torrie! He never has and he never will. I don't know what happened, but somehow Torrie got caught in the crossfire."

When we got to the hospital there were police everywhere. One of the nurses watched me as I approached with Amos. She didn't say anything to me. She moved things around on the desk then she handed us visitor stickers. She told us to put them on immediately then she called someone and told them we were here. A police officer came and told us to come with him. He got on the elevator with us and he didn't say a word. There were police at the door when the elevator opened. They checked the officer who brought us up and then we were told to go to the nurse's station and tell them whom we were here to see. I looked at Amos who did not look comfortable being around all these cops. I told the nurse we were here for Torrie, and she told us to follow her. I could hear Torrie crying as we approached her room. "LOOK AT MY FACE! LOOK AT MY FACE!" When we walked in the room Torrie was in the mirror crying as she looked at her face while the nurse was tending to her. "OUCH!" Torrie was crying and crying.

I swallowed as I looked at her. Her eyebrow was gone, and the whole right side of her face was raw. "Torrie, I'm here."

"Novian?" She turned to face me.

"What happened?"

"You've seen the news don't come in here to ask me stupid questions. Look at my face!"

"Hold still! I need you to calm down. If they need to go out, then so be it."

"They're fine," Torrie closed her eyes as she tried to sit still.

"I don't understand how this happened to you."

"When I hit the ground I fell face first. I didn't fall, I skidded on the ground."

"That explains the burned appearance of your scar. The plastic surgeon will be here in the morning. As soon as that sedative kicks in you will be able to get some rest." Then the nurse looked at me. "Are you taking her home?"

"Can he spend the night with me?" Torrie didn't even let me answer.

"Yes, I'll get you a blanket and pillows. How about the other one?"

Amos backed up, "let me make a call. I'll be right back."

"There's a payphone in the waiting room." The nurse bandaged up Torrie's face and then she left.

"What happened?"

Torrie shook her head. "I don't want to talk about it. Just hold me Novian." I climbed on the bed and I held Torrie in my arms as she cried. I fell asleep holding Torrie who cried in her sleep all night long.

In the morning, Torrie and I jumped as Bonita came bursting through the door. She jumped when she saw us laying in the bed together. If looks could kill we would've been dead. "What's this?"

"Don't ask stupid questions, you should be surprised if he wasn't here." Torrie sat up slowly.

"Novian, what are you doing?" Bonita asked like she was hurt.

Torrie shot me an evil look with her one good eye. "I'm here for Torrie."

"Would she be here for you?"

That was a good question and I couldn't honestly answer that. "Doesn't matter. Why are you here?"

"To check on her obviously. Your mother is downstairs with some man. They won't let her up."

"They won't let my mother up, but they let you up?"

Bonita gave me a crazy look, "who's going to stop me?" Bonita tossed her hair and then she sat down in the chair on top of the blankets and pillow that were brought for me. "So what, are you two supposed to be back together?"

"That's not any of your business."

Torrie and Bonita fussed for the next however long. When the surgeon came he removed Torrie's bandages and examined her face. He was asking her question after question. Then he looked at Torrie's file. "You tested positive for THC." He looked at Torrie.

"Seriously Torrie? We talked about this!"

"Whatever!" Torrie shrugged Bonita off.

Bonita sat over to the side being quiet for a minute. Then she turned on the television and started watching the news. When the newscaster showed the dance school Bonita looked at Torrie evilly. As soon as the doctor walked out of the room Bonita got in Torrie's face. She spoke real low and evil. "This is all over that guy isn't it? You got high and went to Amber's school." Torrie watched Bonita, "did a guy do this to you?" Torrie didn't say anything she just stared at Bonita. "Please tell me you're not that dumb to try to protect a man who's hit you?" Bonita snapped her fingers. "Who's the guy you were going on and on about?"

Torrie looked at me and then at Bonita, "you want him that bad? Why? What has Novian done for you to want to take everything from me? Leave me alone Bonita!"

Bonita snapped her fingers, and then she raised a finger when she remembered, "Malcolm!" She smiled evilly at Torrie.

Torrie looked at me, "he didn't do this to me."

"He was there?" I asked her.

"Not at first, it's complicated Novian."

I stood up, "explain it."

Torrie looked at Bonita who was now smiling and satisfied with herself. "I can't!"

Chapter 9

Novian

"I don't understand what's going on."

My mother was drunk, "it's an all out war going on right now. Stay away from Brad!"

"Now you tell me, I went over his place a few months ago and he was in straight muscle mode. What's wrong with him?"

"He's got a lot going on, Malcolm told me to stay clear of Brad." She shook her head as a tear fell, "I can't save him no more."

"MALCOLM!"

"Yeah Malcolm! And Novian you need to pick your enemies better. Malcolm is not your enemy!"

"How would you know what he is?"

"I know any enemy of Malcolm's don't stand too long."

I shook my head and then I looked away. He was staring at me when I looked at him. I looked away until I recognized that blank expression. The kid watched me as he approached us and then he sat down next to my mother. "Ursula, you know it's not safe to be out like this."

"I can't take this Jeremy! I'm tired of hiding! I want all the fussing and fighting to stop." My mother rocked herself as she took another swallow of her drink.

"Jeremy?"

"Say something else and I will kill you." He said calmly to me and then he returned his attention to my mother. "Are you still staying with him?"

"It's only temporary, I'll bounce back on my feet in a minute."

"Ms. Ursula I need you to go back indoors, Malcolm's orders. It's not safe for you to be out like this. Especially right now."

"Brad is going to get himself killed, Malcolm said he's done. I told him to leave Malcolm's baby momma alone, but he won't listen to anybody."

"You've done all you can do for him. You need to stay in doors and out of the way."

Then a white man pulled out a chair at our table I don't even know where he came from. He gently touched my mother's shoulder. When she looked at him she gasped then she sat up straight, "Tim?"

He smiled tenderly at her, "I know this hurts but it's not safe for you to be out here. Go back inside."

"Who are you?" I asked him.

"What you need to be concerned with is getting your mother to safety." He said very sternly to me. "It's not safe for her to be out until..."

"Come on Ms. Ursula I'm going to get you home."

"Is your name Jeremy or Lamont?"

His head snapped at me and his locs swayed with his head jerk. "Question me again! It's none of your business who I am!"

I looked at the other guy, "look kid. Don't be stupid. Go home, and don't come out again until someone tells you it's ok. All you need to know is your life depends on it."

Torrie

My agent pumped me up so much. I was prepped on how to handle this exclusive interview. A camera crew came to my condo to connect me to the show. The interviewer and the audience were all eating it up. How I survived the attack of crazed fans. Suddenly I was the victim in the whole incident. I wasn't the aggressor. What I didn't really know, is who the gunmen really were. Why they were shooting at us, and how I got mixed up in this mess.

When I tried to call Malcolm, he told me that if it wasn't for his sister, I would be dead. I started to ask him how that woman was supposed to be his sister. All I could remember is how crazy and angry he looked the last time I saw him. He told me to NEVER call him again! Then he hung up in my face.

My interviewer was very gentle with me as she asked questions about the incident. She kept praising my courage to relive the experience. When I broke down at the memory of the events moments before the bullets rang out; the interviewer ate it up drumming up the drama. "So you were outside speaking with Amber when you suddenly heard screeching tires?"

A tear fell, "yes."

"What were you thinking when you heard the first shot?"

"Everything happened so fast. I fell, we all did. It was loud as bullets flew back and forth. It didn't register that I was hurt until someone gave me a napkin for my face."

"What was your first reaction when you saw your face?"

I started crying, "this is all too much."

Novian told the people in the room I was done. They looked stuck like they didn't know what to do. The interviewer went to commercial and then she asked us what was going on. Novian pointed to me as he said it was too soon and he was pulling the plug on the rest of this interview. Everyone was shocked, but no one could be more surprised than me. He made them leave and then he held me for as long as I needed him to. It was right then that I decided to leave Malcolm alone.

Novian

I heard voices in the living room as I walked out of my bathroom. I put on shorts then I walked out in the living room. That guy Eugene had his arms around my mother as she cried into his chest. His eyes were on me as soon as I walked into the room. He kissed her cheek as he kept his eyes on me. "Are you sure? Could it have been someone else?"

"I know, I know."

"What's wrong?" I asked my mother.

"Brad's dead!" My mother cried out from her broken heart. "How could Malcolm do this? Brad didn't mean it, he should've let me talk to him."

I stood there not knowing how to feel. "Mom? Malcolm did this?"

"Ursula you weren't there, you don't know what happened. Don't tell this boy what you're assuming."

"We've been hiding out in this apartment for the past I don't know how long because Malcolm told us to. What else am I supposed to believe?"

"All I'm saying is you don't know what happened, don't spread assumptions as facts."

"Is Camille ok?"

My mother sucked her teeth and then she stared at me. "Why do you care?"

"Is everyone else ok?" I asked Eugene.

"As far as I know," then he turned his attention back to my momma. "You're coming with me."

My momma hesitated, "I..." she tried to pull sobriety out of the air. "I can't!"

Eugene got mad, "why can't you? He's gone and good riddance! You're coming with me. Go pack your bags."

I watched my momma as she looked at him past her buzz. I never saw her look at anyone like that before. Torrie looks at me like that sometimes. "For how long?"

"We'll see, stop wasting time asking dumb questions."

She deflated, "Malcolm will be mad."

"What that troll got to do with us? I don't care what he's mad at!"

"Malcolm looks out for me, he made sure I was ok when you could've cared less."

Eugene squinted his eyes at her, "forget Malcolm!"

"You don't mean that."

"If you don't come with me, I'll go kill him right now!"

She searched his eyes, "you wouldn't!"

He stared at her, "you know I would. Go pack!" I watched my momma slowly walk to her room as she kept looking back at Eugene. His face didn't change as he watched her. She went in her room and shut her door. Eugene turned his attention to me. "Stop staring at me."

"Where are you taking her?"

"If you don't know, I don't know what to tell you."

"Who are you?"

"You know who I am."

"Who are you to my momma?"

"Eugene!"

Torrie

"Hello?" His voice was heavy.

"Novian are you ok? It's all over the news."

"I don't understand, the police have been over here. Questioning me as if... as if I could do something like this."

"I'm coming."

"No, you need to rest."

I took a deep breath. "I didn't have the surgery."

Novian was quiet for what seemed like forever, "I'll come to you. I need to get out of here anyways."

As soon as I hung up my phone rang. "Hello?"

"PLEASE EXPLAIN TO ME HOW MY DAUGHTERS END UP IN JAIL IF YOU WERE THE VICTIM OF A HATE CRIME?"

I knew Sinclaire's momma was upset but goodness! "Police were called and they had warrants. Everything happened so fast."

"I'M GETTING A LAWYER!"

"You and everyone else. Go ahead, get in line." Then I hung up the phone.

I had already decided I needed new friends. I wouldn't have been there if they hadn't pumped me up in the first place.

When Novian got to my place I met him at the door with a key. He looked at his hand and then at me. I thanked him for taking care of me as much as he could. He looked exhausted as he kissed then thanked me. He plopped on my couch, and then he told me to come to him. He pulled me into his lap and asked how I was doing. He was looking at my scars.

Novian

My heart feels heavy and I can't explain why exactly. Lee has always been my father figure. So I don't know what that means about Brad. I hate the way we left things; I don't really know what to think about what happened to him. I mean they found him beaten to death. My momma thinks it was Malcolm, I'm not so sure. With the way that Eugene guy swept in and took her, who's to say they didn't get in it over her and he did it. He definitely didn't feel anything about Brad being gone other than he was coming to take my momma home. I wanna feel sad, but there's a part of me that is relieved that I won't have to deal with him. I want an opportunity to be great; all this drama is nerve racking to say the least.

Torrie setup transportation for my family to the funeral. With everything she's going through, she actually remembers to be there for me through this. I think she's needed me as much as I need her right now. My phone rang, "hello?"

"Renee, I mean Novian." I took a slow deep breath. "Baby, I'm going to ride with Eugene." My momma's voice shook.

"Are you sure?"

"Eugene won't let me drink and this is too much! I need a little something to help me get through this. Do you think you could bring me something?"

"Who is Eugene? Is he your man or something? You've never listened to anyone about your drinking."

Her breathing got heavy, "he's an old friend. Can you?"

"I'm sorry I don't have nothing here. You drank everything."

"Could you go to the store and get me something? I'll pay you back."

I laughed sarcastically, "yeah right! You drank all of your money. I don't have time to run to the store. Torrie will be here any minute."

"Torrie? Why is she coming?"

"To support me, why you always act like that with her?"

"I don't trust her no further than I can spit on her. She's the kind that will do you in as soon as you turn your back on her."

"I think we do that to each other. I guess I'll see you there."

"Baby I got the shakes, I don't know if I can do this." I could hear tears in her voice.

"Somebody at the funeral is bound to have something. All you've got to do is make it through the ceremony."

"Bye son, I love you!" Then she hung up in my face.

When I got in the limousine Torrie looked very pretty in a plain kind of way. Her makeup was a little heavy cause she was trying to hide her scars. When we pulled up to Lee's house, he was waiting at the curb with his family. I paused for a minute when I realized his father and my sister were with him. Lee and Leona were definitely their father's children. Those African and Asian features were too strong to miss. I asked Torrie if she knew they were coming. She didn't know who she was looking at but she said Lee gave her a count. I got out of the car and Lee's father greeted me with a sympathy hug. He gave me his condolences. My sister Leona did the same. Leona lives in Vallejo with her husband and children; they live a quiet life. I don't see her much since she got married. I haven't seen Lee's father in years. Not since I started working with Brad. Mr. Dozier looked at me, "where's your mother?"

"She's going to come with a friend, she will be there."

Mr. Dozier looked at me, "how you holding up?"

"Fine I guess, I just wish they'd hurry up and find out who did this so we can all get some closure."

"These things take time. The truth always comes out in the end."

I nodded my head in agreement then I watched Leona enjoy our nieces and nephew. Lee and his wife looked on with big smiles as they held her pregnant stomach. When I looked at Torrie she was staring at my sister in-law's stomach as well. She looked kind of sad, I was happy that she didn't turn on her diva persona. When we pulled up to the mortuary media was outside snapping pictures of everyone as they entered. As we got out of the car I spotted my momma walking with Eugene and a few other guys. She looked very pretty in her hat that drooped over one eye. She cleans up very nicely, and since I've never seen that dress before I assume Eugene was behind it. My momma stopped walking when she saw Lee and Leona's dad. Her mouth hung open as she waived a solemn hello. Lee's dad walked over to her in the middle of the men and hugged her tightly. He kissed her cheek and he told her he was sorry for her loss. Eugene watched them but he didn't look bothered one way or another. One of the guys had a smile on his face as he spoke to Eugene. Eugene grinned but they let my momma and her ex-husband have their moment. Eugene looked at Torrie and I then his group and my momma walked inside. There were reporters everywhere and all kinds of celebrities. Some were still relevant and others were has beens. They were all there to pay their respects. We found seats in the pews in the middle and then we waited for the ceremony to begin. When we stood for the family, Brad's family procession was long. A lot of them I had never seen before in my life. Sandy walked the aisle holding her little sister who filled the auditorium with her heartbroken cry. Camille looked sad, but not devastated as she walked with a woman down the aisle. After everyone sat down, I saw Darius slip in in the back of the auditorium. He stood against the wall with his arms folded and no expression on his face. I imagined him trying to be strong and not break down, Brad was his everything. I remember when I asked him if Brad was his father; he told me he knew exactly which cemetery to visit his father in.

When our row went to view the casket I glanced at Camille and her nieces. Baby girl was torn up and she continued to cry as if she was going to run to the casket and jump in if Sandy let her go. Camille was staring off into the distance. When she looked at me her expression didn't change, but she focused on me. Like she was trying to tell me something. As we went back to our seats I spotted Malcolm sitting in the back. THE BALLS ON THAT GUY! It takes a man who truly feels he's untouchable to return to the scene of the crime as if he's innocent.

At the grave, my momma had a flask that she held like there was actual gold inside. Eugene wasn't paying her any attention; he was too busy talking to that one guy. Leona and my momma watched each other for a little bit. Then Leona exhaled and walked over and hugged her. They talked for a while and then we left to go to the repast.

One woman tried to get in Camille's face and she was swiftly removed. People were talking, but everyone was solemn. My momma said something to the Eugene guy and then she walked to the front of the room. "Excuse me!" Everyone turned their attention to the front of the room. "I know we are all here to pay our respects to Brad, but I also thought we were here to celebrate his life. If any of you ever knew Brad you knew he was all about the music. We don't even have his music playing in the background." She shook her head, "we need to celebrate his memory. Celebrate that we were blessed with his presence while we had him. It's time to celebrate, we can all be sad when we go home. Leave the sad stuff for the behind closed doors stuff. Ricky baby give me a beat that I can sing to."

Ricky looked surprised that she called him out. "I don't have a beat machine."

"Baby you got two hands and a surface to make music on. You know that pounding you used to always do that Brad would eventually tell you to stop? All of that is just percussion. Now I need you to start a beat, and then anyone who can follow him do it on the surface nearest you."

Ricky looked around, "you want me to do this?" He hung his head, "I can't!"

My momma walked to him, "yes you can baby. You're sad, well pound it out. You're mad, well pound it out. This is your moment to set it off up in here. Come on baby, you can do this." She said gently to him.

Camille looked at me like she was slightly annoyed, but she didn't say anything or outwardly object to my momma's scene.

Ricky dropped his head and let his shoulders move up and down as he cried. Then he took a deep breath and started pounding on the table. The camera crews started zooming in. Then he let out a loud scream, and then he started pounding on the table. It was actually a cool little beat. A few people followed his rhythm and she applauded them. Then she asked the left side of the room to stomp their feet on the beat. She demonstrated for them. Then she told the right side to clap and she showed them how she wanted it. The room suddenly came alive with music.

Ursula didn't need a microphone. Her riff started slow and deep, then it progressed to a loud roar. She was singing from her heart. People started cheering her on and pretty soon the entire room was consumed by her. I've never seen my mother like this. I remember when I was little and she used to sing. I was really little so I don't think I grasped her energy like I was right now. Torrie and I were trying to keep quiet, I looked at Torrie and she stretched her eyes at me. We were trying not to sing but the energy in the room seemed to call us. Just when I thought I was going to break, Lee shot up. He held on to his wife as he belted out a riff that gave me Goosebumps all over. At the end of his tune Leona came in with her own and equally beautiful riff. Torrie grabbed my hand and I nodded yes. We stood together and joined in. People started jumping and screaming at us to keep going. At one point my momma's voice cracked cause she was crying so hard. People told her it was ok and to keep going. When we were done Torrie and I stood hugging each other. She rubbed my back and told me she was sorry for my loss. As I held on to her, I saw Bonita watching us. I didn't know she was even here. Adina was with her, but Adina did not look at us. I turned my eyes and then I saw Camille watching us. The rest of the night Brad's family came over and said hello and they thanked us for coming and for showing out like we did. "We all needed to scream! Thank you two for being the voice tonight." Brad's sister said.

I walked over to Camille and I gave her a hug. I asked her how she was holding up and she glanced at Darius who was watching every word that came from her lips. "I'm still your beautician." She touched my hair, "I nurtured this hair, don't let anyone else do it. You hear me?"

I smiled, "yes I hear you."

"Give me a minute to get myself together, then I'll tell you when to come." Then she turned her back to me.

As I walked away Eugene and his friend watched me walk. "Look at little Renee all grown up." Everything inside me cringed when I heard him call me by my first name. "You don't remember me do you?"

I shook my head no, "why should I?"

Eugene smirked then he looked at his friend. The friend stared at me for a minute. "At least Barb's kids know who to flex at and who not to."

"This one is still behind trying to catch up."

"I never thought Ursula's son would turn out like this." The guy said like I wasn't standing there.

"I told her she did him no favors raising him all sheltered. He is who he is now, he'll wise up one day or die trying." Eugene looked me in my eyes, "you got something you want to say to me?" I wanted to go off. I wanted to curse him out and create a big scene where everyone saw me roasting this man. Remembering our interactions before I turned on my heels and walked away. There were cameras here and everything. The last thing I needed was for everyone to be up in my business. Then having the whole scene immortalized for the world to see.

When I sat at the table Lee pulled up his chair next to me and his father sat on the other side of me. "That didn't look friendly."

"He's a bully! I don't have time for him."

"They've always been like that. They like to test your manhood for sure." Lee's dad said.

"You know who they are?"

"You don't know who they are?" He looked surprised.

"Eugene just appeared one day out of thin air. I don't know who that guy is with him. They too old to be acting like some little kids flexing at everybody."

"You mean to tell me you don't know who Eugene and Briscoe are?"

"Dad, remember Novian was with me. She never had him around them."

"They never came?" He looked irritated.

Eugene and his friend watched us. "No, she didn't want them to."

Eugene and his friend walked over, "Leroy! You still heck of wholesome and good I see. How's it hanging my brotha?" Briscoe stuck out his hand.

Lee's father looked beyond angry; in that moment for the first time ever I wanted to know which one he was angry with. Neither one of them looked a thing like me. I couldn't see a reflection of me in either of their faces. Shoot! I look more like Brad than either one of them. Eugene was a little taller than his friend but not by much. Briscoe has a James Evans straight from the motherland nose. I bet when he gets angry he snorts from it. When he talks he uses his nose to put emphasis on his words. He was a different kind of brown from Eugene. His voice wasn't deep like Eugene's. I sat there staring at this man looking for any trace of me whatsoever in his face, build, or anything.

Lee's father shook Briscoe's hand. "I'm a little surprised that Novian doesn't know who you two are."

Briscoe frowned at Eugene, "that's what they call him?"

"Yep."

"You can thank Renee's momma for that. We've always been around though."

My momma hurried over, "what are you all talking about?"

"Why doesn't Novian know them?"

My momma put her hands up, "Leroy please!"

"Oh don't worry about me. I'm so over you and what you did to our family. I'm floored by the fact that Novian doesn't know them."

"Dad, you know she's been battling alcoholism all these years. Please let it go."

"I just don't understand how a man doesn't stand up for his own."

Briscoe smiled at me like he was amused with my lost expression. "Ursula, you better get your boy before I have to handle him."

"Fighting me today won't change what you did yesterday, or who you'll be tomorrow. You're too old to be running around here fighting like you're a little kid. And it won't change the fact that a man steps up. I am so disappointed in both of you."

Eugene and Briscoe stared at Mr. Dozier. When Briscoe started to smile, Eugene grabbed his arm. "Naw! He always got some soapbox speech to give. I'm sick of you! Why aren't you dead yet? Older than Methuselah trying to tell us how to be."

"That was in the past, let it go." Eugene told his friend.

I stared at Briscoe, our hairlines were even different. This man can't be my father, I don't see it. Clearly Mr. Dozier was talking to him because he was the one taking it so hard. So what they do, pass my momma around their click. I got up and walked away. This was too much. I walked over to Torrie and Bonita who were talking about something. Torrie stopped talking and looked at my face. "Are you ok?"

"I'm ready to go, are you ready?"

Bonita stared at me while Torrie said she was ready when I was. Lee put his hand on my shoulder, "are you ok?"

"What was all of that?"

"Three old men arguing about what happened yesterday and using you as the reason to argue." Lee patted my shoulder, "you going to be ok?"

I forgot Adina was here until she stepped to us. "Lee?" She smiled really big, "Long time no see stranger."

Lee swallowed, "Adina, I had no idea you were here." Then he turned around to see his wife watching him like a hawk. Adina moved like she was going to try to hug him, Lee quickly put his hand out. "It's good to see you."

Adina looked so disappointed, she shook his hand. "You have a beautiful family."

"Thank you," he turned to me. "I'm ready to go when you are."

Lee turned around to return to his wife. He had no idea Adina was following behind him. "Hi I'm Adina Vaughn." She stuck her hand out to my sister in-law.

My sister in-law took a deep breath as she rubbed her belly. "I know who you are."

"You have a beautiful family!"

"Thank you," my sister in-law said as she watched Adina's eyes. She looked like she was about to jump up and forget she was pregnant.

"Woman to woman, I wanted to come over and shake the hand of the woman who captured Lee's heart. You will never know how much I envy you."

"Oh, I know. Thanks for saying it though." She continued rubbing her stomach as she stared at Adina like she wanted to hurt her.

Adina walked back over to us, Torrie was staring at her. "You can speak to her, but for me you don't have one word?" Adina blank stared at her. "Why are you even here?"

"She came to support Novian, we honestly didn't know if you'd be here."

Torrie started to say something and I grabbed her arm. "It's time to go. Get the car, and I'll go get everyone."

****

"Novian, it's time for an appointment, can you meet me?" Camille's voice said lowly in my ear.

I glanced over at Torrie who was knocked out sleep. "In an hour, I'm still in bed. Where?" Camille's been spending a lot of time in San Francisco with her sister and her nieces.

"Meet me at the house."

"Ok." I told Torrie I was going to get my hair done and I'd be back. I knew she had appointments today so she wouldn't have time to be worried about what I did. When I got to the house Camille was in the driveway in her car. She was staring at the house and she jumped really hard when I tapped on the window. She said she can't go in there yet. She followed me back to my place. I put my car in the garage, and then I got in her car.

We drove to Pinole and we pulled into the Brookstone Condominium complex. She put her car in the single car garage, and then she told me to come on. The downstairs unit was right by the parking lot. When she opened the door the condo was fully furnished. I asked her where we were, and she said this is one of the places that Brad used to bring his women to. She smiled as she said he thought she didn't know about it. Camille took my hair down, and then she washed it. As soon as she put the processing cap on for my deep conditioning treatment we went at it for a round. Then she rinsed my hair. Once she braided it, we were back at it. We were all over that condo.

"CAMILLE!" I woke up to Darius screaming her name. "CAMILLE! Baby PLEASE!"

I looked at Camille, "how did he find you?"

She looked a little scared, "it doesn't matter. He can't know I'm here."

"If I open the door, he's going to push his way in. What should I do?"

"Lay here with me and don't move. Eventually he'll go away."

"CAMILLE!" He wasn't even ashamed that he was crying. "CAMILLE! BABY JUST TELL ME IT ISN'T TRUE! WE CAN FORGET ALL OF THIS! CAMILLE! CAMILLE!"

"What is he talking about?" I whispered to her.

"Malcolm," she laid there like she was afraid.

"Malcolm?" I frowned like she was trying to feed me rotten eggs. "What about Malcolm?"

She cut her eyes at me, "you don't even know him. Why are you looking at me like that?"

"How well do you know him?"

"Like you care! Me being with Brad didn't stop you from being here. Don't start acting like there's something that's going to stop you from coming back to me. You don't need to know my business!"

"You used to mess with him or something?"

She didn't take her eyes off of me. "I'm going to give you a courtesy I didn't give him. I see Malcolm whenever I can. Nothing or no one has or will ever stop me from being with him. Brad knew this and that's why he's dead now."

"Brad is dead because he loved you and he trusted Darius to always be there and protect him."

"Loving me didn't kill him, putting his hands on me did. That fool has beaten me from the top of my head all the way down to my feet. One time he beat my feet with a belt. He treated me like I was an animal!" Her cheeks turned red as she stared at the ceiling.

"Where did you meet Malcolm?"

"I was running from Brad, and I found myself wandering around the mall. When I saw him he was watching me. He didn't approach me, he just watched me from a distance. I was in no hurry to get back to my life so we played the staring game for some time. He wasn't moving he sat back and watched me. So finally he called me over. He invited me to sit down and then he didn't say anything else. It was different with him. I was used to guys trying so hard to impress me. He didn't do any of that, he just waited. Finally he asked me what happened to my face. I told him I had a fight, and he just watched me as if he knew what I was saying without me even saying it. So I don't remember what I said to get the conversation going, but I just talked and talked. Eventually I bought us lemonades, and I really appreciated how he just let me vent. I knew he was younger than me, but I didn't realize he was so young at the time."

"How old was he?"

"Let's just say it wasn't legal. Here I was thinking I was about to put something on this little guy and I found myself doing everything I could to get back to him. Sometimes we'd meet up just to have sex in his car." She was quiet as she reminisced. I couldn't help but feel some kind of way about her getting lost in her thoughts about Malcolm when I just put in work. I felt like this was another, *I'm teaching you something lesson.* I laid there listening to her go on and on while Darius still screamed his heart out outside. "I started spending nights with him, and Brad tried to come after me. He didn't know it was Malcolm but he knew it was someone. I ran to my sister's and filed for divorce after he beat me up pretty badly. I worked for Malcolm for a few years after that."

"Worked for him or worked under him?"

"It was all the same to me, I was in heaven." She smiled at me.

"How did you and Brad get back together?"

"He got to me through my sister, the only one who was always in his corner no matter what he did to me. He gave me money and anything I could ask for as long as I would come back." A tear ran down her cheek, "my sister needed the money. She had mouths to feed, and well I can't have children of my own." She put her arms around herself as she cried a little harder. Her sobs matched Darius' screams outside. "He never hit me as badly as he did when I left, but who wants to be hit period? I talked it over with Malcolm before I went back."

"What did he say?"

"He understood why I needed to go back. His shop was doing well, but he couldn't compete with Brad's money, and we both knew he wasn't going to ever make money like Brad has. Besides, he was with that girl Yvette, and having babies by that other girl. His money was stretched as far as it could go. Brad gave me a lot of money just to come back. He paid for everything for my sister, gave my nephews jobs. He didn't lay a finger on me for the first few years I was back. Until I spilled the beans about Malcolm."

"How did you do that?"

She shrugged, "I told you about it. I guess I was too interested in the conversation or something. Brad knew and there was no way to deny it. That was the first time he hit me again. That's why I wasn't allowed on set for video shoots. That and the fact that your mother was always around." She stared at the ceiling, "he never hit Ursula. I guess I always felt like the abuse was what I got for taking him from her."

"CAMILLE! CAMILLE!" Darius continued to scream, and then he got quiet. Camille looked at me like she was waiting for me to tell her what happened. I got up and went to the window. A couple of police cars were now outside, and the neighbors were out openly watching.

Darius was always this rock and a smart brotha. I never would've imagined seeing him like this, especially over a female. Camille picked up her cell phone and called someone. She told them that Darius showed up screaming and the neighbors called the police. She started crying, as she said no, no, no. Then she got up and put her robe on. She told me to follow her as she put the phone in her pocket on speaker as it was still going. She opened her front door and told me to come on. I only had on my boxers, but I did as she told me. Darius' back was to us as he spoke with the officers. "Darius why would you come here?" Camille said with tears in her voice.

Darius spun around and his eyes got big as he looked at Camille's morning after face. His brows moved and then his eyes went to me. I can't even describe the look of anger, hurt, and murder that filled them. He started to charge at me, and two of the officers grabbed him. The other officer moved quickly to her car and called for backup. "I'M GOING TO KILL YOU!" Darius yelled as he struggled with all his might to get free. "I DON'T CARE IF YOU'RE BRAD'S SON! YOU GON DIE TODAY!"

I couldn't move, I stood there frozen and it felt like I couldn't breathe! Darius was giving the two officers a run for their money as he tried to get to me. The third officer was hurrying back to help the others. Camille screamed when he said it, "WHAT?" She fell down on her knees holding her stomach.

Everything seemed like it was happening in slow motion. I watched the police rough Darius up until there was blood. Darius stayed strong as long as he could, but I could tell he was broken. More police cars came and the officers hurried to help. "All of this for me?" Darius said as he let blood drip from his lips.

"No! No! No! Darius say it's not true. Please tell me you only said that to hurt me?"

Darius bowed his head, "I give up! I can't do this any more! Camille how could you hurt me like this? After everything I did for us, after all of this!"

"I never asked you to do anything, I loved my husband and you were mad because I wouldn't leave him for you."

"Are you saying that he's responsible for the death of Bradley Caruthers?" One of the officers yelled.

Camille stood up and dusted off her knees. She wiped the tears from her face and she stared at Darius. Darius stared back at her with a menacing expression. "I didn't say that." She pointed at me, "you knew he was Brad's son and you said nothing?"

"How long have you been doing him?" Then Darius spit blood on the ground.

Camille walked away from him and then she grabbed my hand and gently pulled me inside. She shut the door behind me. I looked at her with big eyes, "is it true?"

Camille stared at my face like she was dissecting every feature. She put her hands up and covered her mouth. "I never saw it until now, but you'll have to ask your momma baby." Then she took her phone out of her pocket. I forgot about the running call. Tears started running down her face and then she spoke. "So now what?"

Chapter 10

Torrie

My plan was to tell Novian about himself. I didn't expect to see him for a couple of days. He came to me that night. My momma and I were sitting on the floor watching the people on TV cook. He was visibly upset and then he said he couldn't find his momma. I kept asking what was wrong until he told me everything. I wanted to be mad about him openly telling me he left me to go be with another woman. Let's face it, Novian and I don't have a traditional relationship. I let it go. Even though I won't talk about what happened in that parking lot, he has to know I've slept with Malcolm. I fell on the couch when he said that Mr. MC was his father. Novian plopped next to me then he put his head in my chest. "Who died?" My momma asked as she watched us.

"You remember, the guy that put Novian out."

"Oh, he's your daddy?"

"That's what one person said. I need to ask my mom."

"Torrie doesn't have a daddy. She's my baby though, I saw her come out of me." No one said anything I continued rubbing Novian's head. "My momma tried to take Torrie away from me. She said I didn't know how to take care of her. I proved them all wrong. She was mad cause she kept asking me how I got a baby and I kept telling her I didn't know."

Novian looked at her, "my mom let my brother raise me. I don't have a father either."

"Just like Torrie," she nodded her head.

Novian shook his head no. "Torrie has a mom who wouldn't let anyone take her away. I was sent away."

"And now you sing just like Torrie. If your momma kept you

do you think you would sing?"

Novian chuckled then he started laughing. "Probably not, she raised my brother and my sister and neither one of them want anything to do with singing." Then he started laughing hard. He went down to the floor and then he hugged my momma. "Thank you, I think I needed to talk to you today. I looked that man in his face and asked him if he was my father and he said no. For all I know he lied to my face. Why would I worry about someone who didn't want me? As long as I can sing, I have everything I could possibly need."

My momma smiled innocently at Novian. That night I could tell Novian was awake by how heavy he was breathing. When I rolled over to look at him he looked at me. "I love you."

I smiled, "I love you too."

"When do you think we should have a baby?"

I closed my eyes, "we already had one."

"I want to try again."

"Our careers."

"You're established, and after this whole setback I'll be on your level. You could take a year off to be with me and have the baby. You've been working so hard."

"But this industry is so demanding. What if people forget about me?"

"How could the world forget about their angel?" Then he started laughing.

"They will forget about me just like they forget about everybody else." The thought of it made me really sad.

Novian pulled me in closer; he put his face in mine. "If that was the case, then maybe for once we could be on the same page and go all in at the same time."

"Like no more secret rendezvous with your hair dresser?"

Novian looked at the wall, "ok. But I will need to replace her right away with someone of the same hair caliber. Remember when I was trying to grow it out, and now it's thick and goes down my back. It's a part of who I am now."

"There's all kinds of stylists in LA, I'm sure you can find someone to do your hair."

"Ok, but what about you?"

I held my breath, "what about me?"

"All of your craziness stops too. No more Malcolm or any other guy."

The mention of his name hurt. Malcolm refused me and then he turned on me. He was telling someone to kill me like my life didn't matter. Novian has nothing to worry about. "I'm done with Malcolm."

******

Novian and I have been tucked away in this love cave. Jumping on each other every moment we get. When he has to go to LA, my momma and I go with him. As quietly as we can be we have been out everywhere. I don't want the media getting wind of us. They made such a big fuss about Adina and Novian; I don't want to know the story they'd tell about us. Sex with no barrier is great. Sex with the thought of life coming from it has been amazing. The first month I was a day late, and I almost screamed behind the fear of getting pregnant that easily again. Even though it was what we wanted, I was still afraid. I was a little relieved when it didn't happen right away. After the second month though? What if that quack did something wrong and I'm scarred forever! What if I can never get pregnant again?

"What if I can't get pregnant?"

"You will," he rubbed my back.

"You don't know that for sure."

"Maybe you're taking the test wrong."

"It's a stick, you pee on it. There aren't too many ways to mess that up."

Novian walked into the bathroom. He came out reading the instructions. "Lets practice."

"Get real!"

"A! Your man said get up, that means you get up." I pretended like I didn't like him telling me what to do. I got up slowly as he read the stupid instructions out loud. I took a deep breath then I acted annoyed. He stood in the doorway as he read more of the instructions. After I washed my hands, I walked away as he counted down the time. "And there you have…" he got quiet. "TORRIE!" The bass that escaped him made my hair stand up. I ran to the bed and threw the pillow over my head. "Baby come look at this spider! Its heck of big!"

I snatched the pillow off of my head. "I'm not coming in there for a spider. You're supposed to be watching the test."

Novian came out of the bathroom with a devious grin and balled up tissue in his hand. "You gotta see this!" He dove on me on the bed. I told him he plays too much. He kissed me, "by the way we're pregnant too."

I stopped smiling, "are you serious?"

"Yes!" Then he yelled, "I'm going to be a dad!"

"You're going to be a great dad!" I chewed back my guilt.

Novian excitedly ran to the phone. He called his brother. He had the biggest smile on his face. I was frozen on the bed watching him. None of this seemed real. That night we had the best sex to date. Novian kept kissing me and telling me he loved me. Afterwards my guilt consumed me. I almost told him about Norie; instead I told him I didn't know how to feel which was the truth. Novian held me tenderly as he told me I was going to be an excellent mother. I guess he doesn't know me after all.

****

I sat outside of the booth while Novian dazzled the DJ during his radio interview. He looked so happy and I could tell he was charming her. It didn't bother me today, but when I'm big and ugly it was going to piss me off. I caught a glimpse of my scarred profile in the mirror. My listening ears turned off and I started staring. As the scars heal they're fading. One day they won't be completely noticeable. There's just an obvious difference in my fresh new face and my face today. The world applauds my bravery, when I know I shouldn't have been there. I could've died behind my stupidity.

I thought about Malcolm and I got sad. When I saw him at Mr. MC's funeral he flipped me off. That hurt so much! How we go from... from... Ok well we were never Novian and Torrie. He did have kind moments here and there. I touched my scars; they were my reminder to slow down on all my craziness.

"Why haven't I heard from you?" Bonita's voice came out of nowhere.

I jumped, "I've been spending time with Novian."

She examined my face; "I know the work of a man when I see it. You're so stupid for protecting him."

"What do you want?"

"I'm checking on my money." I rolled my eyes as she watched my face. "You and Novian have been looking pretty cozy." She traced the back of Novian's head with her finger on the glass. "You think you two could give me one more?"

I don't even remember standing. All I know is I was in her face cursing her out from the bottom of my soul. "Ms. Rowe, please! They're on the air." The show producer said as she hurried towards us.

"She needs to get away from me!"

"Ms... I'm sorry, I don't know your name."

Bonita looked me up and down. I don't think I've ever known evilness until I met her. "We're fine, Torrie is overreacting as usual. Torrie's going to behave herself. Her everything depends on it." She looked at me sternly. When the producer walked away Bonita looked at me evilly, "come have dinner with me!" I shook my head no and she walked into my face. "You will or else I'll tell him that you've lied to him all of these years. I will end your career, and your cousin's. I bet that will give her another reason to hate you." I hung my head but I refused to give her the satisfaction of one tear. "We'll have dinner at your hotel." Then she touched the window, "I want him!" I didn't say anything.

Bonita left and I sat there in turmoil. She could not have my baby unless I gave it to her. She already has Norie, I want this baby. Novian wants the baby too. He's so excited, there's no way I was giving this baby up.

When Novian came out of the booth he was all smiles until he saw my face. He asked me what was wrong and when I said nothing, he asked me how I was feeling. I told him I was tired and I needed to lay down. The producer came out to talk to him, he asked her to walk with us to the car cause he needed to go. She completely ignored me as she told him he did a good job. She told him he needs to keep his energy and his excitement about his music up. She said that was the only feedback she had for him. When Novian kissed my cheek and then put his arm around my neck her eyes got big. She said she didn't know we were together. Novian smiled at her and I didn't say anything. She said a fake congratulations and then she told Novian to come back anytime to promote. When we got off of the elevator she stayed on to go back up. I told Novian it was only going to be a matter of time before people started gossiping about us. He smiled at me and said he didn't care.

When we got to the hotel there were messages from my assistant. She was telling me that she had four out of the nine confidentiality agreements back, and it would take a few more days for the final agreements and then the process of elimination until she had the choice down to one realtor. Novian frowned at me as he listened to the message. I told him that I've been thinking about a condo or townhouse in LA since I spend so much time out this way. He didn't say anything, I told him I started the process long ago and it slipped my mind to mention it. As soon as I started to relax I immediately tensed up. I told him I needed to have dinner with Bonita. Novian watched my face and then he asked me why I was so upset about it. I honestly said I didn't feel like going, but I knew I had to go.

We cuddled on the couch for a little while then my momma came in the room carrying lots and lots of bags. My assistant had even more bags on the luggage cart. "Torrie this is definitely your mom. This woman can shop her butt off."

"I saw so many pretty things, I couldn't help it." My momma set all of the bags out neatly. "Go sit down by them." She told my assistant. Then she cleared her throat. "I thought about everybody today, so I got something for each of you." Then she opened one of the bags. "I got this coat for my brother so he could be warm in the rain when he goes to work. They said it would keep him really warm."

"I like that, it's nice." Novian said complimenting my momma's taste.

"I got this for you because you're always thinking and asking questions." She handed a bag to my assistant.

My assistant looked surprised then she opened the bag. She pulled out a leather jacket and a little hat. Then she pulled out a box the size of a manila envelope. Inside of the box there was really nice stationary and the pen was gold. "Oh my goodness! Thank you so much! Thank you! Thank you!" She jumped up and hugged my momma.

"You weren't there when she bought this?"

"She was on the phone with my brother asking what size he wore when I got this for her." My momma smiled at my assistant, "see I can be sneaky too."

"This is cute, but if I'm paying you to be with her, you need to be with her." I snapped at my assistant. Her smile dropped and she sat there looking scolded.

"It's not her fault Torrie, don't be mean to her." I blew air as I looked around the room. What would my momma know about what I was saying. "I got this for you." She handed me a small box. Inside was a gold and diamond pennant.

I frowned, "a worm?"

"It's a caterpillar, you're not a butterfly yet. You're still a caterpillar. When you wear it, I want you to remember."

I couldn't even pull it back, I started crying then I went into my bedroom. I heard Novian telling them I needed to rest. Then he came in the room. He put his arms around me and he kissed the back of my neck. As I drifted off to sleep I told him I needed to have dinner with Bonita.

******

When I awoke I suggested that Novian take my momma and my assistant out to dinner. I went down to the restaurant where

Bonita was impatiently waiting. She stared at me as I approached our table over to the side. "It's time for you to tour again."

"What did you have in mind?"

"We could start promotion now and you could start in six weeks. We'll include England, Paris, and Tokyo."

"I can't!"

"Why not?"

"I'm supporting Novian's launch."

"You can't be so blindsided by his rising star that you forget to make sure yours continues to shine bright."

"We've discussed it, you and Matt said I could have this year."

"Business suggests otherwise. You've already been off all of this time."

"I've still been promoting and interviewing though. I haven't been forgotten."

"Memory is subjective," then she looked at me hard. "You don't deserve him."

I tried not to slouch. "You have no idea of what I deserve and what I don't. You don't even know me."

"I know that I've spoiled you rotten. You cause more problems than someone of your caliber should. You run around causing problems and never have to deal with the consequences of your actions. This last one, she refuses to sign the confidentiality agreement. She's been non responsive to all of our attempts to contact her."

"So!" I took a sip of my water.

"So?" Bonita tilted her head. Then she kicked me hard under

the table. It hurt like crazy but I refused to give her the satisfaction. I took a deep breath. "If she decides to go public with her allegations, your career as an innocent could be over."

"So what do you want me to do about it? The damage is already done."

"Why were you fighting her?"

I remembered the way Malcolm looked at her. His words were mean, but there was a look in his eyes for her that he's never had for me. "Same reason, different female."

"All over a guy?" She shook her head. "How did I end up with such a basic female? Novian deserves better."

"Than what? Than me? Novian has been in love with me since he was a child. Since he ever opened his mouth and showed anyone he knew how to sing. He's put in work just to be with me. He..."

"Yes! Yes! All of that and you were going to kill the best part of both of you. You were pregnant and he never went looking for you." When I didn't say anything she sat back with her glass of wine in her hand as she brought it to her lips. "Did you know Novian and January had a little thing going on for a minute there?"

I shrugged, "I don't care! Matt said I could have my year off and I'm taking it."

"Which brings me to my point. I would like to have another baby. I'll give you two years off so that you can get your body back."

I waited for her to say she was kidding but we both knew she wasn't. "No! You took the last one when I was too young to know any better. I will never ever make such a deal again."

Bonita smiled evilly at me. "Those are awfully strong words for a dumb kid."

"Call it whatever you want, I refuse."

The waiter sat Bonita's plate in front of her. "I know you're pregnant Torrie. If I can't have that baby then no one will." Then she picked up her fork and started eating like she just wished me well. I stood up, "cross me Torrie and I will kill you." Then she ate some more.

My heart was pounding as I walked away from her. I was scared, but I refused to show her that I was. I went back to my room and ordered room service. I only ate a couple of bites of my salad cause it tasted funny. I think I've adopted Novian's aversion to arugula. I ate my burger and thoroughly enjoyed my milkshake. I was so full I could barely keep my eyes open. I awoke to Novian and my momma coming in the door. As soon as I stood up my mouth watered. I ran to the bathroom as I erupted like a volcano. I was spraying out of both ends. My body kept trying to empty it's self when I was completely empty. I was in pain and the lights seemed like they were sitting on me. Novian called for an ambulance, and I was rushed to the hospital. As soon as they got liquids in me they were violently coming back out. The first nausea medicine did nothing to help me. After almost two days they got me stable. It was too late because my body had rejected everything.

****

MY MOUTH! Novian stood there staring at me like I just pushed him too far. I stood there with my hands on my hips with a look that said I could care less about his feelings. While inside I was cringing at what I said. Novian was quiet for what seemed like forever, and then he told me that I didn't mean what I said. I got on my tiptoes and got in his neck cause I didn't reach his face. "I don't care what you do! I can't stay around here feeling sad with you. Obviously it wasn't time for us to play momma and daddy. I can't sit around here feeling sad anymore. I need to work, make sure the one thing I can control still works for me. You of all people should understand it. Mister runs to the studio to run from me! I don't need you to take care of me. I've been taking care of myself since my grandmother died. I DON'T NEED YOU NOVIAN!" I poked him in the chest with my finger.

Novian grabbed my wrist and moved my hand firmly away from his body. "Look! I know we're both still hurting about the baby. There's no sense in us fighting about it. I love you Torrie, and you love me, otherwise you wouldn't be trying so hard to push me away."

"What does love have to do with my money? Love doesn't pay any bills for me. Yes, I'm still hurting about that baby, I wanted it. Sitting around here with you is not going to bring it back. I'm not ready to set my heart on trying again right now. I…"

"You're just scared, I'm scared too. We can do this Torrie."

"What do you mean by we? What do you have to do? All you have to do is be present for the fun part. The rest is all up to me. You weren't the one up there with your essence pouring out of you. Going crazy as you felt life leaving you. You don't have to sit here and look at you, feeling like I let you down. I saw how excited you were. The whole world knows about my failure and I just want to forget about it."

Novian put his hands on my shoulders and then he hugged me tightly, "don't leave me right now Torrie. I need you!"

"Novian I can't stay around here. My momma and I are going to the rental in LA and then I'm going on my tour. I can't be with you right now, it hurts too much."

"You said you were going with me to the awards ceremony."

"I'll be back in time to go with you to that. I just can't do the Bay right now. There's too much pain here." I broke free from his embrace and then I walked towards the door. "I'm sorry for everything I said. I guess it would've made me feel justified if you would've hit me. Probably would've made it easy to find a reason to hate you. I just can't right now Novian. I've got to go." Then I walked out of the front door to his place. My uncle and my momma were waiting in my uncle's brand new Cadillac. My momma keeps upgrading his car every time I allow her to have enough change to buy him one. She tells him it's a gift from us, if she were smart she wouldn't buy him nothing past the first car she bought him. He took us in out of obligation. Never out of a sense of loyalty for family. "Momma is your passport at the rental?" I looked through her purse.

"You took it last time, I don't know."

"You going somewhere nice?" My uncle asked being nosey.

"Its not any of your business where we're going." I continued looking through my purse.

When he stopped at the light he turned around in his seat. "I don't care how big of a star you're supposed to be, get smart with me one more time and see if I don't back hand you!"

"I'm not a child anymore, I don't have to pretend to respect you. The only reason you keep the lines of communication open with my momma is so that she can give you money. You're a leech just like everybody else." I stared in his face daring him to think he could hit me.

My uncle flinched at me as if that was supposed to scare me. "I took you in when you had nowhere else to go, where's the gratitude for that?"

"And you treated us like we were animals. We had to sleep on the floor, on your piss stained and ruined mattress. But when your other sister came out she got to at least sleep on your pull out couch. Your son would piss all over the toilet and you would hold me accountable for his lack of aim. You never made him clean up behind himself. We were your live in Cinderella's and now you wanna act like there was love to be had? Please! My momma may forgive real easy, but I don't. I remember everything, every time you were annoyed when I came home. You didn't care that I tricked that grown man into thinking I was old enough to stay with him. All you cared is that I was gone. Now look! Everybody looks up to me and wants to be me, and you so proud to tell people that I'm your niece. When all you ever did was ignore me. We are only related by blood. You've never liked me and I don't like you!"

He smirked at me, "I saw your father the other day. Did you ever figure out who he is?"

I kept trying to swallow but nothing was happening, finally… "I DON'T HAVE A FATHER! IF YOU DON'T WANT ME TO CRASH THIS CAR YOU WILL SHUT UP AND DRIVE!"

"Torrie doesn't have a father." My momma said.

"Exactly momma, please tell him to stop talking to me." My heart was pounding in my chest. It was like a loud noise stopped me from hearing anything else he had to say. I could see his lips moving but I couldn't understand him. I didn't want to understand him. I don't have a father, I never have and I never will!"

Novian

I watched January get dressed; she thought she was sneaking out. I had her shoe in my hand, as she searched all over the dimly lit room. When she saw I had her shoe she sucked her teeth. "Going somewhere?"

"Novian I have to go, and this will never happen again."

"That's what you said last time."

"I mean it this time."

I smiled, "don't you mean it every time?"

January sat on the bed and then she rubbed my shoulder, "I

know you're upset about Torrie. But look at everything that's happening for you right now. You're taking off just like I always knew you would. Focus on your career, stop all this bed hopping and focus."

I turned over and exhaled, "I'm focused. It's just hard right now."

January sat on the bed next to me. "You guys could try again."

"I think she's scared, I can't blame her. That whole situation was scary. It was the most helpless feeling watching her go through all of that. It's my fault though. I know better than to want something like that so badly. It's probably what I deserve."

"Why would you deserve to lose your child?"

"Cause I didn't speak up the first time and I let her get rid of it. In all honesty, I wanted that baby too but I was a scared kid. I feel so disconnected right now. My mom is off with some guy and I need to talk to her. She's the only one who can confirm the million dollar question." January wasn't going to press me to share. "I mean I asked him directly and he said no. I also know that he was always lying about his kids. He wouldn't own up to any of them. You know how Brad was."

January put her hand on my stomach as she stared at my face. "Bradley was your father?"

"That's what Darius said as they took him away to jail. I don't know cause my brother's father seemed to imply that this guy named Briscoe is my father. It never really mattered to me before. I just want to know the truth. If Brad was my dad, it puts a whole new spin on our time together. Even though the last time I saw him he threatened to kill me. I just want to know."

"I'm sorry," January said like her apology could alleviate my pain.

"You know your father?"

"Yes, we went to live with him when my parents divorced."

I looked at her, "you didn't have a mom?"

"We still had our mother, she was always present in our lives."

"I didn't have either, I had my brother. I owe him everything."

"You had Ursula, she's amazing."

"Maybe as a person," I don't know why that was hard to say. "From what I'm told she was a great mother to my brother and sister. I seem to have gotten the leftover rotten parts of her. She was barely around once my brother took me. I just want a family of my own. I want to matter to someone."

"You matter to Torrie, she's just as misguided as you are."

I pulled January down to kiss me. "Thank you for understanding. I need you to stay."

January whimpered, "I never should've broke my rule for you. You're nothing but trouble."

"Imagine my surprise," I smiled big at her.

"It's hard enough being a woman in this industry. Guys are so quick to flirt, I had to put Bradley and Darius in their places."

"They tried to get at you?"

"Bradley only tried once. It was a solid effort, but it was only once. Darius saw me turn Bradley down and he kept coming at me. I always felt he was in lightweight competition with Bradley. I wanted nothing to do with all of that. All of these men try it and I always shut them down. You didn't even try."

"You didn't seem interested. Imagine my surprise when you kissed me."

"Don't breakup with your boyfriend and drink." Then she kissed me, "thank you for understanding."

"Thank you for understanding too."

"I know you're in love with Torrie. I don't have time to bring someone new in."

"So why are you trying to disappear in the middle of the night? I still need you here." I pulled her into the middle of the bed with me. I unbuttoned her shirt; "you can go back to pretending that I've never tasted you later."

"Novian!" She moaned in defeat.

****

I walked around my house proudly. I liked my condo, but it really felt like a glorified apartment. I had my stereo turned up loud as I went from room to room cleaning and singing.

The ring of my phone on the floor next to me caught my attention. "Hello?" It was my mother, after I finally stopped chasing her. Part of me knew it was only a matter of time before she called me.

"You moved?"

"How do you know?"

"I went to your place and your name isn't on your unit."

"Good thing I transferred my phone number. What do you want?"

"Can I come to you?"

"He kicked you out? I called you and called you. Why didn't

you call me back?"

"I was with Eugene, he was keeping me from everything. I'll explain."

I exhaled, and then I gave her my address. When she hesitated I asked her where she was and then I told her I'd come get her. I decided to drive Torrie's gift car to pick her up. I don't drive it all that much. I did at first until someone scratched it in a parking lot and I about lost it over a barely there scratch. I made sure they had the proper insurance before my last video where I used my car. For now until, this car is my only baby.

My momma looked good when I pulled up to the corner store by the payphone she called me from. She had a nice and healthy glow to her skin, her stomach wasn't sticking out. Her clothes were new looking and she had a suitcase. I put her bag in the trunk and then we rode in silence. As we pulled up to my house she pulled a brown paper bag containing a bottle out of her purse. I took the bag from her and I told her to get out of the car. I put the cover back over my car and then I held the garage door open so she could go inside of the house. Her eyes were big as she looked around my big and spacious living room. I loved all the windows around the top floor. I showed her the kitchen, dining room and bathroom on this level. Then we went downstairs to the second level where the family room and three bedrooms and bathroom are. I put her bag down in the room I had for her. She started crying as she looked around. She asked me how I knew she'd be back. I told her I had a hunch. Then we went down to the third level, which is all my master suite. My house is on the side of the Oakland hills. I originally wanted a house that over looked the Bay until I saw this house. This house overlooks Tilden Park and it's not far from Chabot. Last night I laid in my bed looking out at the woods. My homeowners insurance is higher because of the fire risk. I feel like it's all worth it.

My mom smiled as I showed her around then I told her to have a seat on the couch. "I was calling you because I need answers. I know you don't want to tell me and I don't understand why. I never cared before, but it matters now. Is Bradley Caruthers my father?"

My mom stared at the brown bag in my hands as she hung her head. "It don't matter Novian."

"It doesn't matter to you cause you know. Imagine not knowing. Imagine what it feels like when someone says the man who promised to kill you the last time you spoke to him is the one. I need to know! Is Bradley my father?"

"No!" She said lowly.

"Are you sure? Cause when I look in the mirror I could see how he could be my father."

"Bradley and I weren't together like that in the beginning. He was like a little brother to me."

"But you did have a romantic relationship with him?"

"Eventually," she squirmed without taking her eyes off of the bag.

"Who is Briscoe Martinique?"

"Eugene's best friend. Who told you about him?"

"Brad said they were enemies, and then Mr. Dozier's reaction to him at the funeral."

"They don't get a long, never have."

"Is he my father?"

Her eyes hit the floor but she didn't say anything. "I need that bottle baby."

"Why would you drink this? You look good right now, better than you have in years."

"Too much reality!"

"What happened?"

"People always talk about a woman's heart. Men's hearts are just as bad. Eugene is in love with a ghost. She's been dead for years and he still can't let her go." She wiped a tear. "I left my husband, my children, everyone for him. I was so in love with him."

"Did he ask you to?"

She shook her head no, "I couldn't do both. I left everything for him. He always downplayed their relationship. It was too late by the time I realized who Pam was. I started drinking and everything spiraled out of control. I came between Eugene and Briscoe, and then Brad started trying to get at Briscoe. When Briscoe sent someone to deal with Bradley I was there. I thought I was going to jail for murder. That's when I sent you with your brother."

"You came between Eugene and Briscoe meaning one of them is my father?" She didn't respond as she stared at the floor. "Do you know who?" She still didn't say anything. "Tell me something please!" She kept her head down. I opened the bottle and went to the bathroom. I started pouring the liquor out. When my mom realized what I was doing she screamed and tried to stop me. "No! You deal with it. Deal with me! I need to know the truth and you're tapping out! I don't care how ugly it is. Tell me!"

"What does it matter? He doesn't care."

"I need to know!"

"Why? You're doing fine without him!"

"I'm not fine! I'm lost! I'm disconnected! It's not about you or him, it's about me."

"Archie!" She cried hard.

"What?"

"Archie was your father. He died a little after Pam did. He was Pam's man."

"Does he have family?"

"All I know is he had two girls. Some people say he had a kid with Pam, but I don't know if that's true."

"You just said it was between Briscoe and Eugene, now you're saying it's Archie."

"I told you I don't know for sure. You don't look like Eugene or Briscoe or any of their kids. You don't really look like anybody. I'm not proud of how reckless I became. Ruthless people surrounded me and I thought I could do it too. Giving birth alone was somewhat of a wake up call. Looking in the faces of three different men and all them screaming they're not the one. I named you Renee after Briscoe's father who died while I was pregnant."

I was quiet for a minute my head hurt. "Do you have pictures of Archie?"

"Not really, I'd have to look through my box at your brother's. He's holding onto a few boxes for me. He was Pam's man so it's not like we were ever out together like that."

"Who is Pam?"

"Once upon a time she was beautiful. She was eviler than a snake! She'd instigate fights and problems all of the time. Her name was always in the middle of some drama."

"She had two kids with Archie though?"

"No, they weren't hers. She took him from his wife. While she was rubbing my nose in her hold on Eugene, I snuck around and got to Archie."

"Was she with Briscoe too?"

"No, he was in love with her sister. Her sister wasn't anything like her. Briscoe is just a dog that'll lay with anyone. He only showed more depth at first to Pam's sister. She broke his heart when she went back to her husband. He tried for years to get her back, but she said he was too much of a dog. They say she had his baby, but I never saw it."

"Who is they?"

"Her husband before he died."

"How did all these guys die?"

"Street life, and they crossed Malcolm."

"Malcolm who? Black Malcolm?"

"Of course is there any other?"

"How is Malcolm involved in any of this?"

"Malcolm is Pam's son."

"But you said she's dead."

My mother looked me in my eyes, "you don't cross Malcolm."

"Who's Malcolm's father?"

"Nobody knows."

Torrie

I had the condo smelling delicious. I decided to continue to rent instead of hurrying to purchase something out here. I want to take my time and find something I really like. Meanwhile, I rent this beautiful condo in Beverly Hills. It's in a gated community. I don't know why it's not considered a townhouse. The doorbell rang right on time. I opened the door to a smiling Novian. I told my assistant to tell the driver when to be back. Novian hugged me tightly as he said it smelled delicious inside. When he started kissing my neck I told him we had all night. We needed to eat cause there wouldn't be real food at the after party.

Novian and I got caught up about the things that had happened since we seen each other last. He's really excited about his house. My smile dropped when he mentioned that his momma is staying with him. She doesn't like me and the feeling is mutual. Guess that means I'm not going over there any time soon.

My makeup and hair people came and I could hear my momma and Novian chatting up a storm about the different things my momma saw during my quick tour. Novian was dressed and waiting when I made my grand exit out of the room. He smiled so big at me and then he tried to come in for a kiss. I pointed to my lipstick and I told him they were on lock down until later on tonight. I could tell that irritated him, but he knows the drill.

Novian kept touching his pocket as if he was going to forget where his speech was in case he won. I sat back and admired him. I can tell by his hair that he went back to Camille. The hairdresser I found for him was fine, but obviously Camille knows his hair and how to work with it best. His hair was neat and nicely braided.

I held back my irritation as I saw Bonita arriving just before us. We haven't spoken directly since the hotel. Although that whole situation was ruled as food poisoning, come on! She threatened me and then I end up in the hospital. How could I ever prove that it was her? Next time Novian and I are going away. I'll wait until right before I'm showing and then we'll escape the states and lay up somewhere exotic until our child is born. She will not stop me from having my piece of happiness.

The on looking fans went crazy as Novian got out of the limo. He definitely was developing a following. I remember what it was like the first time I stepped on this carpet with tons of fans screaming for me. The energy gave me life that night, and my performance was amazing. When I stepped out of the limo the screams got louder. I saw Bonita look at me as she entered the building while Novian and I were being interviewed separately. Inside we mingled with the paparazzi, talk show hosts, and radio personalities as well as other celebrities. "GURL! Did you hear? Amber Wallace is coming and she's not coming with Dwayne." This woman who I couldn't remembers name said to me.

"I read that they broke up." I faked interest.

"You don't know for a fact? I thought you two were friends?"

"We haven't spoken since the incident, I think it was traumatic for everyone involved."

"Oh, right. Who would want to relive that? Well you look amazing sweetheart. Trauma does your body well."

I was so happy her dumb behind went for the topic change. The last thing I care about is who Amber shows up with. It's not like she's ever gone anywhere in public with Malcolm. He's her best-kept secret. Then I saw her, Amber glided in a little hesitant in her steps. I let out a slow breath as I took her in, in her dress. I tried my best to shake off my jealousy. I looked good tonight who cares what she looks like. Ramell on the other hand is looking almost as good as Novian. When I saw Novian do a double take at Amber it was time to go. He was trying not to obviously stare at her and it still bothered me. I told Novian it was time to find our seats. We were stopped by someone who was raving over Novian. I watched Amber and Ramell get escorted towards the center of the auditorium. I was relieved when the usher escorted us to the right.

The ceremony was going along good, the performers were great. Novian didn't win his first nomination but he had four more to go. Then it happened, suddenly the whole night was about Amber's love triangle. I watched Ramell perform his song *Unattainable Goddess*. The song was beautiful and you couldn't help but groove to his hypnotic melody that made you sway in your seat. Amber was sitting over there trying not to have a reaction, she's so fake! Always trying to play innocent when she knows she put it on Ramell and he's just responding to the voodoo. She better had stood up and clapped for him. He's keeping her relevant!

When Ramell came back to the seat Amber was trying to play cool and Ramell looked like a lovesick puppy. How does she get these guys so sprung? When Amber looked at me, I looked away. I didn't want her to see me watching her, but I was kind of sucked in. I wasn't the only one though, I saw others staring too.

When Dwayne and Gia took the stage, I caught myself before I reacted. Dewayne looked so GOOD! I guess once Novian gets a little more time under his belt he'll have a similar commanding presence. When Dewayne laughed I'm sure I'm not the only person who felt hot. I glanced at Amber and she had no shame about smiling at Dewayne. She's so disrespectful! As Dewayne and Gia announced the nominees I looked around. This was a complete setup. Amber was stiff; I guess she isn't completely dumb. Ramell had the nerve to grin a knowing look when they announced that he won. If you weren't looking at Ramell hug Amber, you were watching the stage looking for Dewayne's reaction. He kept his eyes on the screen showing Ramell hug Amber and Kimmy, and executive from my label. Dewayne kept his game face on as he congratulated Ramell. I watched Amber as the host made jokes about her ex and her next back stage together. She looked like she wanted to run away. Then she caught me watching her, again I wasn't the only person but she kept looking at me.

I was looking ahead when I glanced in her direction. I had to do a double take. I wanted to cry! Why was Malcolm here? Why was he now sitting next to Amber? He had his version of a happy face on as he spoke in her ear. With the exception of my debut party I've never seen them in public together. Malcolm was talking and she was all smiles now. She even kissed his cheek. I looked around, how come no one saw that? She looked up again and then Malcolm looked at me. He looked irritated and then he flipped me off. That's when I turned in my seat; this night was going downhill fast.

Novian was so focused on listening for his name that he didn't see any of this. We got down to his last nomination I'm sure he thought he was going home empty handed. When they called his name Novian shot up! He was so excited and he didn't try to hide any of it. I smiled at Novian remembering how it was the first time I won.

Malcolm and Amber were still talking; I doubt they even noticed anyone else was in the whole auditorium. I've watched Amber; I don't know what's supposed to make her so great that he would lose me for her. So what if she can dance, there isn't anything she can put together that I can't master. Maybe it's the white girl look that she's toting. It's not uncommon to see dark skinned guys with white or light skinned girls. Like they hate their skin so much that they don't want to see it in the women they date. However, Malcolm never acts ashamed of his complexion and the other women I've seen him with are either as dark as me or darker.

I found myself wishing I were Amber for one day. One day of having Malcolm interact with me like that would change my life. When Malcolm got up and walked away Amber smiled at him as he walked out. She was giddy and excited until Ramell came back to his seat. He looked pissed off, and Amber didn't seem to care. I don't blame her though. Novian came back to the seat grinning from ear to ear. He looked like he was floating on a cloud. He leaned over and kissed me deeply.

"Do we have to go to the after party?"

"Novian the after party is the whole point of this. You come here to be acknowledged, and you go to the after party to mingle and network. I know someone prepped you on the night." I smiled at him.

"I'm just anxious to get you home, and have our own celebration."

He probably thinks he's going to try to knock me up tonight. I don't have the heart to tell him I went back on birth control. I was gone for months; he can't think I was sitting in my hotel room lonely. "I'll be working here and there but I'll be here all week."

When we got to the party Novian was whisked away immediately. People wanted pictures and autographs. I walked away to let him have his time. When I saw Dewayne and his wife they both had on plastered smiles. He looked stressed, and I wished there was some way to have a moment alone with him. I was staring at him when my trainer Josie Kage hip bumped me. I smiled and gave her a hug. "I'm glad to see you're on good behavior tonight."

"The night's still young." I took a swallow of my punch.

"Listen, I've been leaving messages with your agent and she hasn't gotten back to me or even acknowledged that she's received the thousands of messages I sent her. I need a favor."

"Shoot," I said as I looked around the room.

"Sunday I'm shooting promotions for my workout video. I would love it if you would endorse my video."

"Sunday? I kind of promised Novian I'd spend time with him."

"We're shooting in San Francisco, fly out with me on Saturday, I'll have you home by Sunday night."

"Send the paperwork to my manager, I'll make sure they sign off on it."

Josie screamed excitedly as she hugged me. "Let's keep this quiet, deal?"

"Deal! See you at the airport Saturday morning." Then Josie walked away.

"Comfort! Comfort! I bet your win felt amazing tonight." I'm sure she had a microphone on her somewhere the way she leaned in on Ramell.

He looked sad even though he was trying to fake happiness. "Winning is the most amazing feeling out there. Please excuse me," he tried not to storm off to the bathroom.

When I saw Amber I took a seat in the corner to watch her, I didn't understand what she was doing. Ramell's a good guy; his raps are always about uplifting and respecting women. You could tell he really likes her. I don't know why no one sees through her innocent act. I know all about acting innocent when you're really not. I got excited as I watched Dewayne and his wife approach her. I was waiting for the slap or kick that Dewayne's wife would land that would start the fight. I couldn't hear what they were saying, but I felt it was more important to watch than to hear. By the way Amber walked away you would think they just shot the breeze about the weather and the wonderful events of the evening. When she looked at me I rolled my eyes and looked away. Why she keeps looking at me? Probably because I'm looking at her, but so what.

Novian

When I turned around the service elevator doors opened and Malcolm stepped off. Our eyes met and he squinted at me, as he looked me up and down. Why is Malcolm here? He scanned the room and then he looked at me again for half a second. When he walked towards me I extended my hand to shake his hand. He looked at my hand like it was covered in disease, and then he bumped my shoulder as he passed me. He looked at me but he didn't say anything.

I wish I knew what this fool's problem is. He walked up to Torrie's choreographer. If there was ever a time I wished I was Malcolm this was it. As soon as he touched her, her whole body went soft. She gave him the biggest smile as he spoke to her. Then they walked to the dance floor. I was watching them glide around the floor like no one else was here. That dress fit her like it was made for her, and I couldn't blame Malcolm when his hands rested on her big ole booty that could never be mistaken for anything but a product of the motherland.

Torrie was on the sideline acting up as I expected. She turned her back to their private dance. I looked at the rapper Comfort and he sipped his drink as he watched the dance floor looking pissed. I mean she came with him, I thought she was his woman. I would've at least gone down fighting. I guess he ain't stupid enough to challenge Malcolm.

I walked up to Torrie as she fussed; I took her by the wrist and led her to the dance floor. She resisted at first but then she came along willingly. She buried her face in my shoulder as we danced to the music. I kissed her cheek and I told her she was beautiful. Torrie grabbed me tighter as she cried into my shoulder. I don't exactly understand everything between her and Malcolm; however tonight I think he's made it pretty clear who matters to him and who doesn't. I watched Malcolm and the choreographer walk out as if they couldn't wait any longer for tonight to begin.

Torrie and I slow danced as the onlookers watched and started to ask each other questions about us. Torrie thanked me for the dance and then she walked away. I wanted to be irritated but I understood why she did that. She didn't want the drama of the media knowing about us. The music was loud and the bass was pumping when little miss freak nasty danced up on me. I stood there watching her do her dance around me for a minute. Then we tore up that dance floor. I was having a blast groping this nameless female all over the dance floor. When Torrie smiled at us and even cheered us on the buzz that was building quietly subsided. I got so hot dancing with this chick I took my shirt off and danced in my wife beater and jeans.

When I told her I needed a break to go get a drink she tried to look like she didn't need a break as well. I went to the bar and asked for water. As I waited someone touched me. I turned to see Adina; I smiled, and hugged her. I had no idea she was there. Adina wiped the sweat on my brow and said she was thoroughly entertained watching me do my thing out on the dance floor. I asked her where Matt was and she poked her lips at me as she said she came alone. I was drinking my water when she asked me what she had to do to get a dance. I knew Torrie wasn't going to see this as the same thing as me dancing with a random chick. However, Adina wasn't really giving me a choice in the matter. She pulled me out on the dance floor and started her slow wind up on me. I couldn't help it, this was so wrong that it made me blush. I stood there shy and stuck. Adina laughed at me as she told me to loosen up and stop acting stiff. Dewayne Reed and his wife were dancing next to us. He started instigating telling me I better not punk out after all the dancing I just did a few minutes ago. The rapper known as Comfort stood next to me as he looked at Adina like she was exactly what he needed for the night. Adina smiled at him, but then she turned her attention back to me as she told me to stop the shy act. So I danced with Adina for a couple of songs, but I did my best to keep our dance innocent. As I was dancing I glanced up at the people watching. Torrie was standing in the corner with her arms folded and she was not happy. It's ok to dance with a random chick, but it's never ok to dance with her cousin? I know I never addressed whether anything ever happened between Adina and I. I never press her for answers about Malcolm or any of the others. So she can take this.

"Why you holding back Novian? Dance with me!"

"Lee," I watched her eyes.

"Lee is married with a tribe of kids. That was years ago, you can dance with me today."

"I know you want to make Torrie squirm, mission accomplished."

"What did you tell her about us?"

"I never answered her questions, what did you say?"

"I don't talk to her period."

"I don't like being a pawn in your game Adina."

"We're all pawns in somebody's game." Then she exhaled, "thanks for the dance. Next time I'm going to need you to let go and just enjoy the moment with me."

"Um! Lee!"

"Um! Married!" Then she kissed my cheek and walked away.

As I watched her walk away I wondered if it even mattered to Lee anymore. Comfort walked up to me, "how you doing my man?" He put his hand up for a shake.

"I'm good, how about you?"

"I'm chill, I'd be nice if you told me that number that walked away is not yours."

"She's not mine, but I thought you were dating that choreographer?"

Comfort shook his head and looked at the floor. "That's a long and complicated story. As you can see she's not here and I'm looking to celebrate my win tonight."

Adina looked at us talking; she smirked like she knew what we were talking about as she walked away. "You got your A game on? You better strike before someone else steps to her."

"Later!" Comfort hurried to where Adina was.

When I turned around little miss freak nasty was back and ready for more. I danced with her a little, but four a.m. is my limit. I was tired and Torrie was drunk talking out the side of her neck. Instead of ending the night with a nightcap, I put her to bed and I passed out.

Torrie

I filled my week with the things I planned to blow off to spend time with Novian. Now, I'm irritated by the look of him. Whenever he tried to talk to me, I asked him if he slept with my cousin. He doesn't say anything he stares at me. And when I pressed real hard he said I should already know the answer to that. What am I supposed to know? Men are dogs and they will sleep with anyone. He tried to tell me that was the pot calling the kettle black. I kept screaming at him and getting in his face until he pushed me out of his way. He went in the bedroom and locked the door. I banged on the door screaming. My assistant walked into the condo unphased by my loud argument with Novian. She sat on the couch and started working like she tuned us out. It irritated me that she acted like this is something I do all of the time and she was used to it. Ok well maybe I do cut up from time to time, but still! Come on! I screamed at her and told her to wait outside until we were done arguing.

Novian came out of the room with his bags in his arms. He looked completely angry and I didn't stop yelling at him and pushing him. Novian reared up like he was going to hit me, and then he caught himself. He growled deeply, "leave me alone Torrie!"

"Where are you going?"

"Where do you think? I'm going home, I'm not staying out here so you can make sure I catch a case. You are really insane right now and I can't even deal with you."

"Just tell me, did you do it?"

"It doesn't matter what I did or didn't do. I don't ask you about your escapades that you let happen right in front of me. It doesn't matter!"

"Novian, I would never sleep with your brother!"

"That's probably only because you know my brother wouldn't go for you out of respect for me."

"You don't respect anyone that much. The only thing that matters to you is how Torrie is feeling. What Torrie's going through? You will not bully me into an answer one way or another. For once you will be me and dwell in the what ifs!"

"Oh so this is supposed to be some kind of payback?"

"No! This is me saying that I've had enough of you! My feelings don't matter to you! You've always strung me along! You've always done what Torrie wants to do with no regard for what I could possibly feel."

"When it mattered to talk to you, you weren't anywhere to be found."

"Why would I come around so you could act like my feelings didn't matter again? If I would've told you I wanted that baby it wouldn't have mattered. If I would've begged you to keep it, you would've laughed in my face as you always do! You don't get to know about this! You can ask until you're blue in the face, I'm not telling you!" Then he pushed past me and walked out of the door.

I looked out the window as my assistant got in her car to take Novian to the airport.

******

When he answered the phone I smiled to try to make my voice light and pleasant. "So you still mad at me?"

"Whatever Torrie, what do you want?"

"You!" He sucked his teeth, but he didn't say anything. "Look, I'm coming out there today. I want to see you tomorrow night."

"I'll be at home tomorrow night with my mom."

I closed my eyes to hold back some of my irritation. "That doesn't matter, I want to see you."

My assistant came to the door too happy to drop us off at the airport and get to her weekend off. My momma decided she wanted to stay in the condo over the next week while her sister and niece visit. I wanted nothing to do with that.

"Fine, come to my house when you're ready."

I took a pen out of my purse and I wrote down the directions to his place. When I hung up the phone I sat next to Josie. She smiled at me and asked if I was all set. I exhaled; I should've let it go. I was in my feelings about Amber and Malcolm and then I didn't want Adina anywhere near Novian. I was lost in my thoughts when Josie bumped me and asked who was approaching us. I looked up and gasped. Malcolm sat in the seat facing us. "Ladies."

"Malcolm!" I was so stuck! I thought he hated me.

"Who's your friend?"

"This is Josie, and that's my momma."

Malcolm looked at my momma like he was downloading her life story just by the look of her. "Going home?"

"Yep."

"Malcolm, what's a fine hunk of man like you doing in a place like this?" Josie tried to sound seductive.

Malcolm stared at her for a minute letting her feel completely small. "See you later." Then he got up and walked away.

I gave Josie the most annoyed look. I explained that Malcolm doesn't go for all that goofy, extra seductive stuff. My momma continued to stare at Malcolm until I asked her to stop. She looked scared when she said he was mean. When the First Class passengers boarded the plane Malcolm's seat was next to my momma and Josie was behind them. I told my momma to switch with me. Malcolm watched me for a minute and then he put his headphones on. He turned up his music so loud I could hear Michael Jackson clearly. He looked out the window most of the flight. As we approached our terminal in Oakland Malcolm took his headphones off. I looked at him and then I told him my number hasn't changed. I turned my face before I saw a *so-what* expression on his. The flight attendant gave me my carry on from the overhead compartment. As I walked away I saw Malcolm watching me walk out of the corner of my eye. I couldn't help it I smiled really big.

My euphoric feeling disappeared when our car was late. I was on the payphone going off until our car came. When we got to my place my momma put her bag in her room and then my uncle came to get her. Josie and I were going over our options for the night when my phone rang. I stopped breathing when I realized it was Malcolm. I did not see this coming. He asked what we were doing. I told him we were about to cook. He told me to come cook at his house. I told him I couldn't leave Josie behind, he told me to bring her. He told me to tell her to leave the corniness at home though. I got excited and I told Josie what Malcolm said. She smiled at me, "so what am I supposed to do? Watch TV while you two have a good time?"

"What are you saying?"

"Can you handle it?"

"Um, I ride solo!"

We had a good laugh at that. "Have you ever tried a threesome? They're a lot of fun. Why do you think he's open to both of us coming over?"

"You think he'd be in to it?"

"He's a guy isn't he?"

"Malcolm's different, you see how he reacted to your flirting. He doesn't go for the stuff that other guys go for."

"How about we just see how the evening goes. As long as you're ok with it, let's do it." We laughed and then Josie stood up, "I will have to stretch first. Malcolm has no idea of what I'm about to do to him." I laughed to myself cause she had no idea what she was about to see if Malcolm went for it.

Malcolm was his normal quiet as he watched Josie and I cook for him. I cleaned the kitchen before I sat down because I knew he would lose it if we left a mess in his kitchen. At the table Malcolm got Josie talking about her fitness business. For the most part he let her go on and on, he only interjected to ask her questions that made her think. I sat there quietly hoping that I didn't say or do anything to get thrown out. "What? No dessert?" Malcolm looked at me.

I smiled, "I brought cookie dough. Would you like some cookies?"

Malcolm lowered his eyes at me, "what are you offering me?"

I mimicked his look, "Malcolm. You can have whatever you like."

"Anything?" He looked at Josie.

"I'm all in," Josie smiled eagerly.

"Josie, let me show you to the shower. Torrie, make the cookies." He stood up.

When he walked away Josie put up both of her index fingers as she illustrated the assumed size of his imprint. I smiled because she was still way off.

I tried to focus on my task and not be jealous about anything that could be happening up there. When all the cookies were made, I cleaned up the kitchen I made sure everything was turned off and then I walked up the stairs. I HATE THIS PICTURE! It's like he has the picture here to taunt me. I've never been upstairs and automatically Josie gets to come upstairs? I followed the sounds of Josie's moans to Malcolm's bedroom. Josie was on the edge of the bed completely spread eagle. Malcolm had his hands around her neck and her light skin turned all kinds of red, purple, and then blue.

Malcolm backed up from her, he didn't even turn around he told me to come to him. He told me to get on my knees and then he walked into the bathroom. He flushed the toilet, and then he came back with a new condom wrapper in his hand. He put it on and then he told me to open my mouth. Josie scooted to the middle of the bed where she collapsed. She said ouch as she moaned as if she was hurt. I did what I do best and then Malcolm told me to get in the shower. I pinned up my hair and I got in the shower excited about what was about to happen. When Malcolm got in the shower he turned me towards the wall and then he pushed me to bend over. I didn't want to get my hair wet, but when he went in I lost the will to object.

I was trying to figure out if this man was mad at me or something. Just like last time he wasn't showing me any mercy. He wasn't stroking me, he was pounding me. This wasn't as fun as I thought it would be, I was hoping my yells of ouch would convince him to slow down. Suddenly the shower opened and Malcolm stopped moving. I felt him disconnect and my heart started pounding as I turned to look at who was standing in front of us. I was pulled out of the shower by my hair. Then what felt like fire hit me in the face.

All I could see was fist as it kept coming towards my face fast and hard. Then I heard Josie scream and it sound like she was rushing in. My hair was released, the shadow turned towards Josie and I heard her body hit the wall. As soon as she hit the wall the shadow came back. I knew whoever this was, was beating on me, but my body went numb. I mean, I couldn't move and I knew that I was being assaulted. I felt the side of my face open up and the warmth of my blood poured down my face. When I tried to get up I couldn't. I couldn't even open my eye and everything was fuzzy. I could hear yelling and screaming, but I couldn't make out anything other than I knew I was messed up. I passed out from the pain cause it was hard to catch my breath. I woke up to hearing Josie yelling telling someone to cover me up. People were standing over me, but I couldn't open my eye. When I lifted my head off the floor the smell of my blood was all I could smell. "Cover her up!" Something was dropped on me and it hurt.

"Malcolm what do you want us to do with them?" A guy's voice asked.

"I don't care, just get them out of here!" Malcolm roared in a defeated tone.

"Malcolm, she needs to go to the hospital." A man's voice said.

"That's not my problem, I just want her out!"

"She's bleeding everywhere!"

"That would make sense, she just got beat down. I don't want one drop of blood on my carpet! I'm going to have to burn that bathroom!"

"I don't even know how we move her, look at her."

"Bore someone else with the details! GET HER OUT!" Malcolm barked.

"Calm down Malcolm, she can't move and she needs medical attention. I think we need to call an ambulance. Both of them need stitches at least. This one probably got broken ribs too."

"Look! I'm over this! Call who you need to call, I don't care what you do!"

I laid there as they fussed over my body. Eventually someone else came, they picked me up carefully and laid me on a stretcher. I was taken to the hospital, but it's like they took me through the back. I kept going in and out of consciousness, I heard Josie going off about her face saying she was supposed to be filming tomorrow. I was given pain medicines after they stitched and bandaged me up. Josie took me home and I called my assistant and I told her to book a flight for me first thing in the morning back to LA. I was done with the Bay! In the morning I carefully walked to the bathroom and my face was so bruised and swollen, I didn't even recognize myself. Josie flew back to LA with me. When she started describing the person who attacked me. I expected her to say that it was more than one person. The description left no doubt that it was Amber. Amber alone had done all of this to me!

****

My assistant came in the room nervously, "Torrie. Novian's banging on the door and he won't go away. I told him you had unexpected promotions yesterday and so you had to come home immediately."

Even though I was hopped up on pain meds, rolling over to my other side so that Novian wouldn't see all the stitches and some of the bruises right away still hurt. Novian burst in to my room cursing and demanding answers. He stopped when he finally looked at me. I told him I was in a car accident. A bunch of emotions ran across his face as he looked at me. Then he asked me what happened. I told him I went out to eat Saturday night with Josie and we drank too much. I told him I shouldn't have driven. He asked what car was I driving, and I said I drove Josie's rental car.

Novian stared at me for a minute, "did Malcolm do this to you?"

"Malcolm? Why would you pull him out of the air?"

Novian stared at me. "I guess I was tripping."

Novian

I opened the door and took a deep breath as I watched him walk to my door. This man has got to have the coolest walk ever. I've seen it somewhere, but I just can't put my finger on it. He watched my eyes the entire time he approached me. I stuck out my hand, "thank you for agreeing to meet with me."

Eugene squinted his eyes at me, "you should be thanking me. You better be happy Ursula asked, I'm not a doctor, I don't do house calls."

"Doctors don't even really do house calls anymore either."

"What do you want?"

I stood to the side so he can enter. "Can I offer you something to drink?"

"Yeah! You can stop wasting my time with fake southern hospitality. What do you want?" He stood not too far from the front door. He glanced around the room once and then he kept his eyes on me.

"My mother said that you're the person to talk to when you're having problems with someone."

He squinted his eyes at me, "a man handles his own drama."

"My ship has finally come in, but I can't sit back and do nothing. I can't afford to get my hands dirty. I need this taken care of right."

"I can't believe Ursula called me for this. I AM NOT A GUN FOR HIRE! You better go find you a Pookie with a fix to satisfy." He took a step towards the door.

"I don't expect you to handle anything directly. I need someone who won't roll over when and if the police come knocking."

"Do I look like a run and tell that chump? Wait until I talk to Ursula!"

"I got six figures for whomever you name."

"Six?"

I shook my head yes, "a hundred grand."

"Is that supposed to be money to me? I can spend that in an hour just being me."

"I know it's nothing to you, but I figure it's enough to get the job done."

"Who you want gone that bad? What did they do?"

I looked around the room. "It's my girl, I let the first time he touched her slide. Her people tried to tell me that her face got messed up when her bodyguard saved her from an attack. I know she was on his turf and he had something to do with it. She won't admit it, but I can feel it. He saw us at an awards ceremony together, and he got mad and flipped her off. She came out here to be with me and then suddenly she got some stupid promotional gig she has to do, and then she up and flies home. Talking about she forgot about something she had to do. It didn't feel right to me, so I drove that night to LA. This fool did a number on her face, broke her ribs. She tried to tell me she was in a car accident. Her face is jacked, ribs cracked, I'm pissed! If she was in a car accident she would've called me not run back to LA. If it was anyone other than him she would tell me the truth. When it comes to him, she's always lying to me as if I wouldn't know the difference." Eugene stood there unmoved by my story. "He chose the wrong one."

"What are you not saying?"

I exhaled, "I've seen him in action. I know I'm no physical match for him. That still doesn't give him license to do whatever he wants."

"Cut the girl loose, she sounds like trouble."

"Only when he's involved."

"Why would I help you punk out? I personally have lost the speck of respect I could've possibly had for you with this conversation."

"Because I know you don't like him either, so I figure you'd at least want him out of your hair."

"Who is he?"

"Malcolm."

Eugene's eyes lowered to an evil squint, "Malcolm who?"

"I don't know, black Malcolm."

Eugene's breathing got heavy and he looked around the room. He walked away from me into the living room. I followed him, "who's here?"

"No one."

Eugene pulled his gun and aimed it at my chest. "You are the stupidest somebody I will ever know. YOU DON'T EVEN KNOW WHO HE IS AND YOU BROUGHT ME HERE FOR THIS! I SHOULD PUT YOU OUT OF YOUR MISERY!"

I put my hands up, "whoa. Calm down! You don't like him no more than I do."

"YOU COULDN'T POSSIBLY HATE HIM MORE THAN I DO! But it's ok if I HATE HIM! I'm his father and I have every right to hate my son! YOU HAVE GOT TO BE THE STUPIDEST PERSON ALIVE!"

My mouth dropped, "you're his father?" I looked over Eugene's everything looking for the truth in his eyes.

"You talking about that little tired singing trick who will

spread them for anybody? You want my son dead over some hoe?" He punched me in the side of my head. "She ain't anybody worth all of this!"

"She is to me!"

"You're just as dumb as he is. Why would you ever put faith and trust in any female? Women are disappointments! They will open their legs for anybody sometimes just to see what you will do. You want to give up your whole life's savings to avenge some trick who is only going to do it again if given the opportunity. You don't even ask the right questions. Why she won't leave him alone, why would she protect him after he beat her up like that? Oh and by the way, Malcolm doesn't go around beating on females like that. You need to get your facts straight."

"He beat her up before."

"You should've asked her instead of assuming that you know. You better check with that princess he mess with."

"Who's that?"

"Never mind! Ursula know who your target was?"

"Yes."

He smiled at me, "looks like your momma set you up." Then he chuckled. "Call her over here."

"Why?"

"She thinks she's so slick, call her now." He moved his gun, "I know she's downstairs. You can't even lie right."

I called down the stairs to my mom for her to come up. She came up the stairs with the guiltiest expression. "Eugene please," she said real tenderly.

"You think this is supposed to force my hand!"

"Please!"

"Please nothing! I should kill him right now. He's a waste of good hair."

"I'm not Pam, I don't breed soldiers."

"NO YOU ARE NOT PAM! You could never have been like PAM!"

"I love my son, and I've always been as good to him as I could be."

He smiled, "by being a drunk? You been so messed up you couldn't even raise him. You let your other son sacrifice his youth so you could run around drinking your life away."

"She was a junkie!"

"So drinking was supposed to be your way of competing? You let the booze take the life right out of you. Everything that you used to be is lost forever! You'll never look like you did when I met you. Where's that woman? What happened to her?"

"You are what happened to her!" My mother started crying. "I was a wife and a mother living the dream! Then you came along! Empty promises and a life full of regret!"

"Just like a woman, you need to take responsibility for your actions. If you never would've been out sneaking to sing, we never would've met. If you were so loyal to your husband, why you let me in so fast?"

My mother got angry, "I HATE YOU!"

"Oh you know how that's music to my ears." Then he looked at me, "go ahead and tell her."

"Tell her what?"

"How stupid she was for getting pregnant! For letting it happen, for…"

"LETTING!" My mother screamed.

"What did Brad do when you told him?"

My mother started shaking she was so angry. "I'm done with this trip down memory lane."

Eugene poked his lip out, "you going to pout because your little boyfriend is gone?"

"Brad loved me, he wanted to give me everything. You make the biggest issues out of nothing to try and hide what you really feel. For all your sobbing when Pam died you never once told her how much you loved her. You've never admitted to Malcolm what you just said to my son. You are the biggest coward that I will ever know. My son would never deny his child."

Eugene stared at my mother for a minute. "I outta kill both of you right now. Every time you put that bottle to your lips you bring yourself that much closer to death anyways. I might as well push you over the ledge." He looked at me, "you supposed to stand up to any man no matter if you go out fighting or what. You are a waste of a good nutt sitting over here like a punk. Brad was never this cowardly. What did you have him showing your son?"

"Brad is not my father!"

"Good to know you think you know that, but now whether or not you know the truth means nothing to me. Your brother is like his father, I guess you get your punk genes from her side. Now Malcolm may only pistol-whip you, but at least you could try to stand up as a man. If I even think you look in my son's direction too long I will put a bullet in your head so fast. I don't care how fine your momma used to be. You better continue to punk out or go talk to that man like a man. Congratulations Renee, you're now on my list. My list is the last place you would ever want to be."

Chapter 11

Torrie

"EXCUSE YOU! NO ONE IS ALLOWED IN THERE!" I heard the nurse yell out.

I watched the door and sure enough here came Bonita throwing her weight around. Her eyes got big as she looked at my face. "The same guy?" I didn't say anything I just looked at her. "You've got Novian, why would you need anyone else?"

"I don't have Novian, you won't let me have Novian. Every time things start going well for us, you send me away."

"So you do all this to rebel?"

"You're not my mother how would I be rebelling against you?"

"You didn't even want to help Novian just to spite me. Now you keep getting your face worked over by some guy who could careless about you. Doing him is one thing, this is another." I didn't say anything cause I wasn't going to give her the information she was looking for. "Does this have anything to do with your trainer Josie?"

"I don't know what you're talking about."

"I saw the paper work come across my desk for her endorsement deal. Everything was cancelled and now she's getting lawyered up like she's about to go for blood. At least she's not stupid enough to let some guy get away with stuff like this."

When the doctor came in the room, he told us that my scars were going to be really bad. I had damage to my eye socket and that part may never heal. He gave a referral for a top of the line eye doctor to go over options to save my eye. He said once the swelling went down we could consider laser therapy to minimize the appearance of my scars. He assured me that they would get my face as close as back to normal as they could.

When we walked out of the doctor's office I started crying. I told Bonita I needed real time off. She looked annoyed with my tears. She told me to suck it up, everyday working people don't get to make the world stop because they're going through something. She said they still have to work to make sure their bills get paid. She told me to stop acting like the world owed me something. I countered with the rest of the world wasn't in the public eye like I am. Every move I make is highlighted; my miscarriage was all over the world. People pressed me so hard wanting to know who the father was. The world may not stop when your average Joe is going through something. At least Joe could go home and escape the chaos. Bonita told me that I chose this life. I told her I was a child when I chose it, and I didn't realize that it would be this hard. Bonita sarcastically mimicked me and she told me to suck it up cause no one cared about my tears.

Novian

Camille was combing out my hair. "What do you know about Malcolm's family life?"

"The basics really, "he doesn't talk too much about anything why?"

"I was wondering about his parents."

"Speaking of parents, did you ask your momma about Brad?"

"She said it's not him. She said some guy named Archie."

"I have no idea who that is, she's sure Brad's not your father? I mean cause I could see how he could be."

"I do too, but it's not him. They didn't even get together like that until long after I was born."

Camille exhaled in relief, "well that's one less problem."

"Problem?"

"My nieces, Sandy has just about lost her mind. Baby girl is consumed with grief. They lost their father so it's hard for them right now."

"Father figure you mean?"

"No, I said it right the first time. My sister could have the babies I couldn't. Not that he was intentionally having children with her. It's complicated. Sandy always looked up to Darius as a father figure, and now he's in her ear about me. I never thought anyone could turn my baby against me. Darius is heartbroken and facing a life sentence. His accomplices keep coming up dead though. So I don't know if they'll be able to keep him in jail."

"If he get out, you think he's going to hurt you?"

She shrugged, "I can't say what he'll do. I don't know what to think anymore."

"My mom thinks Malcolm did it."

"I can't help what she thinks."

"Do you know a guy that goes by the name Eugene?"

"Should I?"

"He and Brad were enemies."

"Brad had a lot of enemies."

"I'm trying to understand all of this. Malcolm beat up Torrie for the second time."

"Torrie the singer?"

"Yes."

Camille shook her head, "I guess she must be stupid. Malcolm's never hit me. I've seen females try to push him there. He's snatched a couple up, but I've never seen him beat on a female as if he was a weak man like that. If he did do something like that she has to be stupid not to have learned her lesson the first time. Let's go over to the bowl."

I stood up, "I need you to go on this promotional tour with me."

"Go with you?" She raised an eyebrow.

"There's nothing keeping you here. I can't even deal with Torrie and her half-truths. We need time away from the Bay. Plus, I need my hair to be taken care of properly."

"Pass, I don't want a front row seat to watch you hook up with groupies on your tour."

I grabbed her hand, "I don't want a bunch of groupies. Trying to give me diseases and make babies. It'll be just you and me during this time. Torrie needs space and so do I. You can come back when you need to, but for the next few years it will be just you and me. What do you say?"

"Yes."

Torrie

"WHO IS MALCOLM?" Josie screamed at me as I let her in the door.

"Please tell me you're not still pursuing this?"

"She cost me millions of dollars! You are a fool to take this lying down."

"It's not my issue, Bonita is going on her own war path thanks to you."

Josie looked at me like I was a battered woman who was protecting my accuser. "Why are you washing your hands of this? I don't understand you."

"Malcolm never came after me and he kept warning me to leave him alone. I was the entitled idiot who has always gone after him."

"You didn't go after him this time. I was there, he called us over."

"I still knew better. I shouldn't have taken us over there."

"It's not even him that I want, I want her! Amber was having problems with him, that doesn't give her the right to attack you or me for that matter. She needs to learn to keep her hands to herself. We are adults. You can't walk around beating on people and think there will be no repercussions for your actions." Josie took off her shades and walked into my living room. She threw herself on the couch in frustration.

"What happened now? Did you get a new dog?" She came home one day a couple of weeks ago and her Doberman was dead in her yard. Her dog was in good health; there was no cause of death. Josie cried like a person died. I was going to get a little dog. After seeing her suffer the loss I decided against it.

"NO! I've been too busy trying to handle this. My assistant Caprice says she can get a better alarm system installed than the one I have. I just got off the phone with her."

"I thought you said Technology has flaws?"

"Yes, but I also don't have time to train a new dog and bond with it. If I get a new dog right now, it will be closer to my assistant than it would be to me. That doesn't sit well with me."

"Just take it everywhere with you. Don't leave it with her."

Josie waved her hand to tell me to stop. "You're taking me off topic. My assistant has a good point. She says I should sue you too. I'm conflicted because we go way back. I don't want to sue you, but if you keep protecting him, and he continues to protect her, you all leave me with no choice."

I couldn't hold back my anger! Who in the world is her assistant supposed to be to make such a suggestion? "What kind of assistant is that? She should be seen and not heard. Why is she advising you on anything? Unless you're asking her for information."

"Stop trying to change the focus of the conversation. Look at my face! Someone will pay for this, PLUS all the money that I lost. I will not run away like a dog with my tail between my legs."

"I'm just saying that my assistant knows better than to try to tell me anything unless I ask her. Trust me, I rarely ask her for anything like that."

"Caprice has a little edge to her, and I like it. Besides I have her doing all the leg work for me on this while I try to make back the money I've lost trying to heal my freaking face." Then she exhaled and looked around my place. "How long before you move?"

"The loan just funded, but I'm having upgrades made before we move in. It will be a few months. Why what's up?"

"My assistant says there's a waiting list, but she's going to try to get me bumped up." I noticed her hand shake as she put her shades on my coffee table. "Can I spend a couple of nights here? I can't go back there until the house is protected."

"What happened?"

"A man was in my room last night." She took a deep breath to calm herself.

I gasped! "Are you ok? Did he hurt you?"

"I've had that feeling a lot since Chomper died. You know that feeling like you're not alone, or someone's watching you. I told myself to grow some last night. When I was in the shower I heard a door close, it just about slam. I was so scared; I ran out of the shower into the kitchen and grabbed a knife. I went from room to room dripping water everywhere. When I realized all my bedroom doors were how I left them, I told myself to calm down. I got back in the shower and then I got in the bed. I woke up to a pillow over my face. The guy told me to stop trying to sue. He told me to let it go. He said my life depends on it. When I started freaking out again he put the pillow back over my face. When I woke up it was morning. I called the police. They said there was no forced entry. One officer pointed to my ashtray and asked me if I was sure I didn't hallucinate the whole thing. I didn't smoke last night for some strange reason."

"Could you see him?"

"I described him the best I could. I think he was white with long hair pulled back into a ponytail. I'll be out of your hair in a week tops."

"Ok."

"Who is Malcolm?"

"He's a nobody barber from Oakland."

"Well who is Amber Wallace? She supposed to be untouchable or something?"

I touched my face, "I didn't even think she could fight. I don't know who she's supposed to be."

Novian

"Hold on," Camille rolled over and then she put the phone on my ear.

"Hello?"

"Heeee…. Hey Novian, it's January."

"Hey girl, how you doing?" I tried to clear the sleep from my throat.

"I'm sorry for waking you. I I I'm in the lobby. Do you think you could come down?"

"You're here? I didn't know you were working my tour."

"I'm not, please come down. I need to apologize."

"Huh? Apologize for what?"

"Please come down Novian."

"Ok, let me brush my teeth. You could come up."

"You've got company."

"It's ok, come up." Then I hung up the phone. "My friend January is coming up, can you open the door for her?"

"Why she coming here?" Camille sat up.

"I don't know, I guess we're about to find out." I grabbed a hand full of Camille's butt and then I went to the bathroom to brush my teeth. I could hear talking as I finished up in the bathroom. As I walked out of the bedroom I heard a baby. I walked into the living room as Camille was holding a baby and smiling at it. January looked so nervous. "Hi?"

"Let me explain!" January said nervously.

"I'll show the baby the room, you two go ahead and talk." Camille walked back into the bedroom with the baby.

I looked at January but nothing would come out. "I sat on the fence about it for too long. I wanted to call you, but I wanted to know what I was going to do first. When it got to be too late I panicked and time stood still until my water broke. I'm sorry Novian; you know you are the last person I would ever hurt. I debated whether to tell you at all."

"Why wouldn't you tell me?"

"I'm not Torrie." Then she fidgeted.

I walked to her and I hugged her. "You gave me what Torrie can't! My firstborn!" I kissed her forehead. "What did we have?"

"A girl, I named her Ursula Jeanine Murphy."

I squeezed her tighter and then I kissed her. "Thank you! My mom is going to be so excited. Can I hold her?"

"Yes, but before you do we need to talk this out." She backed up a little bit. "Let's be fair and honest about how we parent. I met someone recently, I don't know. It could go somewhere, and maybe if not this guy, it could be another. I can't wait for you to get over Torrie. I won't put myself through that."

I hugged her again, "we got a daughter. I'm a daddy! I'm a dad! Thank you January! I do love you."

"Yeah well, we both know it's not the same."

Camille came out of the bedroom dressed and with her purse. "Novian, I'll be back tomorrow morning. You all need the day and night to bond."

"Camille you don't have to leave, we could spend the day together." January pleaded, "I did not come here to interrupt you all's routine."

"Honey, I need a break tonight anyways. You all need to put a cap on the night." Camille smiled painfully, "she's a beautiful baby. Congratulations."

"Camille," I called after her as she walked towards the door.

"No Novian, it's ok. I'll come back in the morning."

"Wait!" January hurried to her purse. "At least stay in my room tonight."

Camille smiled, "is it nice?"

"Not as nice as this suite, but you know I don't stay in anything basic." January gave Camille the card key. Then they hugged and thanked each other.

I walked into the bedroom where the baby was laying on the bed looking around the room. When I stepped into her eyesight she smiled up at me with my mother's eyes. January told me to hold her head as I picked her up. My baby girl started laughing at me as I smiled.

My Jenny-Bean loves her daddy already. I spent the entire day watching her every movement. Watching her sleep, watching her eat. I changed my first diaper in life. January laughed for a long time as she took pictures of that diaper. It was lop-sided and hanging off of her when I lifted her up. Like I was supposed to know that girls can only wipe from front to back. I didn't know there were so many rules, however I was loving every moment of this. January said she tries to nap whenever Jenny-Bean sleeps. That night with January was unlike anything I ever experienced. I have love for this woman; I'm just not in love with her.

In the morning just before noon Camille came back. Camille was so excited about the baby. She brought gifts for her and she said she left most of them in January's room and that she might want to have them shipped home. Since she wasn't back to work yet, January stayed on the road with us for the next few months.

Torrie

I looked at myself in the mirror. I looked good if I do say so myself. My makeup artist just left and my assistant was finishing up before her night off. "When are you flying out to meet up with my momma?"

"Tomorrow night, and then I meet up with her in the morning to fly back with her."

"Good, now leave before my friend gets here."

My assistant looked at me as if she thought I was joking. I stared at her to let her know I wasn't playing.

Josie buzzed at the gate, but I could see she wasn't alone. It's like she's joined at the hip with her assistant these days. She keeps saying Caprice says this and Caprice says that. In my opinion, she talks too much to be an assistant. My assistant was walking out as Josie walked towards the door followed by three other females dressed to go out. I blew irritated air. I don't do female crowds any more. When they got close to the door I folded my arms. "What the heck is this? Who are they and where are they supposed to be going?"

Josie waived me off, "stop playing. I promised Caprice she could come to the party tonight."

"Why would you make a promise you can't keep? I don't know her, and I don't want her at my party!"

"Torrie stop being like that."

I looked at the group she brought with her. They were all pretty, but that don't mean nothing to me. "Even if I could over look your assistant, that doesn't explain who the other two are."

"Oh these are my friends Brandy and Darlene." Caprice volunteered like I was even talking to her.

"NO! No! NOPE! Not happening, I'll go by myself! Good night!" Then I slammed my front door.

They stood out in front of my door for a minute talking, they started laughing. Then Josie knocked on my door. "Come on Torrie, you're wasting time."

I opened the door and pulled her in. "I don't appreciate this, send them home and then we can go to the party. I don't know them and I don't want to party with some girls I don't know."

Someone started knocking on my door. I opened it and told them to walk home, but the knocker pushed the door open. She was heck of strong. "Stop playing, I gotta pee!" She pushed her way in and then the other two followed behind her with big smiles on their faces.

"Torrie this is Caprice, that's Brandy, and that's Darlene."

"Like I could ever care!" I folded my arms.

"Um, the bathroom?" Darlene asked.

I looked her up and down without uttering a word. "Down the hall and the first door on your right." Josie told her.

"This is a really nice home you have." Brandy said as she ran her hand over the back of my couch.

"Josie her house is even nicer than you said." Caprice said touching my curio cabinet.

"Why are they touching everything? You all don't have manners? You don't walk up in a stranger's home and start touching everything."

Caprice stopped walking and her eyes flickered with evilness and then they smiled. "Oh I've got manners, I was just admiring your place."

"Besides we may be strangers to you, but you're Torrie Rowe. It's like I already know you. I work for Bonita, and I've been asking her for months to introduce me. She always has excuses for why we can't meet. I'm your biggest fan, and I can't believe I'm actually meeting you. If you never let me in your presence again I'm making imprints of this fabulous lifestyle that you have. I apologize if my actions seem rude, but I've never met a star on your level." Brandy smiled.

I calmed down a lot, "well it's rude to walk into someone's home and touch all over their things. I don't want finger prints all over my glass."

Caprice put her hands up and stepped away from my curio cabinet. "How about you give us a tour of your new house before we leave?" Josie suggested.

I didn't feel like taking them around my house no matter how flattering Brandy's little speech was. "Let's see how the party goes. If everything is cool I'll take you on a tour of the house."

The Brandy girl got excited, and then she asked me if it was ok to hug me. I wasn't in the mood but I agreed when Josie's eyes begged me to be nice to her friends. Darlene came back to the living room with the same excitement that Brandy had.

I pulled Josie to the side. I quietly read her her rights for assuming it would ever be ok to add groupies to my RSVP that I added her to. Josie looked embarrassed then she told me that she was trying to impress them and so she started talking about her celebrity client list. She said they all got excited when she mentioned my name and that I was also a close friend. Josie begged me to be nice for her. I asked her why she was trying to impress her assistant and her friends? Josie said that lately she feels safer in groups.

The guy at the door thanked me for bringing beautiful women with me. I guess I was too busy being annoyed by their presence.

Adina was there and not talking to me as usual. After all of these years I don't even miss her voice anymore. I remember how close we used to be, but she stopped talking to me behind a guy she doesn't even see anymore. She's been looking pretty cozy with the rapper Comfort even though both of them maintain that they're only friends. "Is that Adina Vaughn?" Darlene said excitedly.

"Yep!" I said unenthusiastically.

"Do you know her? Can you introduce me? I'm such a fan of her work."

"Sure, follow me." Adina had to keep up appearances just like I do. I tapped her on her shoulder. When Adina turned around her hair swayed with her. Showing off how well it's taken care of. "Adina, this young lady is a huge fan of yours. Naturally I had to bring her over to meet my cousin."

Adina flared her nostrils no doubt annoyed with my reference to our bond by blood. Then she turned on her smile, "nice to meet you. What's your name?"

"I'm Darlene," she blushed as she said.

"It's nice to meet you Darlene. A quick word of advice. If you want to keep a man don't let her near him. She's pretty ruthless, not even her family is safe."

"O k," Darlene looked embarrassed for me.

Then Adina walked away and continued to mingle.

After the party we went to this restaurant off of Sunset Blvd to get something to eat. I have to admit that Josie's group was a lot of fun. I didn't want this again after tonight, but it was fun. My days of running in a group are gone. Too many opinions and personalities. Sinclaire and her sister most likely ran through their settlement from their mother's lawsuit. I'm sure they're probably still looking for ways to get more money from me. I can't trust anyone anymore, everyone comes for something. If I didn't know Josie before the fame we wouldn't be friends either. She's actually my only friend, which is the ONLY reason I agreed to this whole set up. My bodyguard followed my limo back to my gate then he went home for the night.

I put on my slippers and then I showed the girls around my house. Brandy apologized saying that she communicated in touch. I guess that was license for all three of them to touch stuff in every room I showed them. I decided not to be annoyed cause I'd tell my housekeeper to wipe everything down tomorrow.

Caprice asked if I had anything to drink. I showed them my bar. Caprice volunteered to play bartender. She's such a lightweight though; she was giggling and silly real fast. When Darlene suggested we play truth or dare, I asked them how old they were. Josie said she was in and then I felt I had to play. I told them dares were limited to shots for me. I refused to do anything more than that. "Truth or dare Torrie?"

"Do you think you have a soul mate?"

I thought of Novian, "yes."

"Who do you pick?"

Josie knew I was going to pick her. However, I don't think she was ready for my question. "Josie, what happened that night with you and Malcolm? I only saw the end."

Josie deflated, "it was the best night of my life until that idiot showed up."

"Malcolm as in *THE Malcolm*?" Caprice asked.

"Yes, and I don't want to think about it."

"Aw come on Josie, everybody's been sharing. Tell us what happened," she got comfortable. "What made that night the best night of your life?"

She rolled her eyes, "he was big! He was strong! My body went into overdrive when he choked me."

"Choked you? You mean like he strangled you?" Brandy leaned forward.

Josie smiled, "I stripped in front of him and then I got in his shower. When I got out he was still standing in the same spot. I undressed him then it was on. Up against that dresser, in the middle of the floor. Explosion after explosion girls! When he finally laid me on the edge of that bed I thought I was about to die. Then he put his hands on my neck as he went completely savage!" She hit the floor as she shook her head, "that man is a beast. Like I said it was great! I was sore but so happy, and then that woman happened. I didn't hear her until she was beating on you and Malcolm was trying to tell her to calm down. It's too bad cause I could use a tune-up from all of the stress of trying to sue them." Josie stopped talking when she looked at Darlene who had a pillow over her face like what Josie said grossed her out. "What's wrong with you?"

"I can't hear this!" Darlene said from under the pillow.

Caprice marched over to her and snatched the pillow off of her face. "Grow up and get it together!" A couple of seconds ago I thought Caprice was drunk. Then she smiled at Darlene, "are you uncomfortable talking about sex?"

Darlene sat up, "talking ain't the same as doing. I was getting a visual and I don't want to imagine a woman I just met naked."

"I think you should strip!" Caprice smiled at her and then her drunken stammer was back. "You should show us how your first and only boyfriend does it. He lay on top of you dead weight pumping you. Giving you lazy sex cause he knows you don't know no better."

"He is just fine! Thank you very much!" Darlene snatched the pillow back from Caprice.

"HOLD ON! You only had sex with one person? Like ever?"

Brandy asked Darlene in amazement.

"Late bloomer I guess," then Darlene cut her eyes at Caprice. "You've got such a big mouth!"

Caprice looked at me and smiled, "is Murphy any good?"

I sucked my teeth, "I'm tired. I don't want to play this game anymore. You guys can leave now." I tried to stand up too fast and I got lightheaded.

"We're all wasted, we can't drive." Josie said as she yawned and stretched out on the floor.

"Call a taxi!"

"Come on! Stop…" Josie yawned again. "Stop being like that. We'll leave in the morning."

I stood up again and stumbled to the right. Caprice caught me and then she asked me where I was trying to go. I told her I needed to go to bed. Caprice kept counting backward from ten and even though she messed up she'd start all over again. I asked her what she was doing. She said that's how she checks herself to see how drunk she is. She laid me on my bed then she looked around my room. She asked me where my pj's were, and I pointed to my bathroom. I dozed off and then I saw her come out of my closet. I asked her what she was doing and she said looking for my pj's. I mean I know I was drunk, but I still saw her being nosey in my room. She was looking through my everything. I don't know if I dreamed it, but at one point all three of those girls were in my room talking and looking sober.

When I woke up in the morning there were blankets folded neatly on the couches and floors. Nothing was missing or out of place. My security camera showed them leaving early in the morning. Josie was still knocked out so they helped her walk to their car. They didn't steal anything, but I felt uneasy. Was Josie trying to set me up?

Novian

Jenny-Bean has become my life. I miss her when she's not with me, and I thoroughly enjoy my time with her. Camille seems to share the same excitement and affection for her as well. Jenny-Bean had very little hair at first. Then Camille started brushing her head and massaging it. Camille has growing hands cause my baby girl's hair has grown pretty long in this short period of time. January and Camille talk about my baby's hair all of the time.

The first time she called me daddy, and the first time she ran to me. I told myself to keep it together. It's like I've been in another world. A world where for the first time ever Torrie isn't the center of it. I thought about calling her and telling her about the baby. No matter how I sliced it she was going to be mad, so I waited. Meanwhile, January and I have become pretty close. Whoever the guy was when she came to me is no longer in the picture. She spends all of her time with me. She's now a part of my stage crew when we travel, while Camille and Jenny-Bean enjoy each other's company.

My mom is in love with her namesake. Looking at Jenny-Bean makes me realize how much I look like my mother. I don't think I realized how much I look like her before. Whenever the baby's around, my mom doesn't drink. So I stopped telling her my schedule or when the baby's coming for the moments I am home. I can't believe how much this is working, but she's looking healthier and healthier by the minute. I still don't give her money. I know the temptation would be too much for her. She stays between my place and Eugene's. One time Eugene came to pick her up while Jenny-Bean was there. My mom proudly introduced him to her granddaughter. He looked at the baby, and then he looked at me. "She looks like her father."

"Which means she looks like me! You always say he looks like me."

Eugene looked at her, "she didn't get Brad or Briscoe's nose."

"I guess she got yours." My mom countered right away.

Eugene looked at me, "don't even look at me like that! She's drunk!"

"I haven't had a drink in months." Then she stuck her tongue at him.

January pretended like she wasn't listening until they left. "Is that your father?"

"She said she doesn't know. I hope not, because that would make Black Malcolm my brother."

"Black Malcolm?"

"The one who used to be on set when that choreographer was working with Brad."

January was trying to remember, "Amber?"

"I don't remember, she got a big ole booty and she look Mexican or something?"

"Yeah, that's Amber. You don't look nothing like Malcolm."

"I know it."

"There's more than one way to find out. I mean if you want to know."

"She says it could be this other guy who died though, or Eugene's friend."

"Do you want to know?"

"Sort of, just to lay the mystery to rest."

"You could test with their kids to find out. I'll help you."

I looked at January; she's become a regular fixture in my life these days. I kissed her and I thanked her. Everyone says they've noticed a change in me lately. At first I kept saying that fatherhood has changed me. Looking at January right now I know it's more to it than just our child. I guess when you're chasing a Torrie you tend to miss out on women like January.

Torrie

I rolled over frustrated as usual. Marion and I were introduced by mutual acquaintances. He's a very popular Latin singer from Panama. My publicist thought it would be a good idea for us to be seen in public together. Then they thought it was a good idea for us to record a few songs together. We were together so much making the public believe we were a couple. I think we both lost track of whether we really wanted to be together or not.

Marion is pretty and the rumor about Latin men being small is not true. He just lacks stamina, after one round he's done for the night morning or day. There is no such thing as rounds with him. He could careless about whether I get mines or not. If he's tired it's not even worth it to bother with him. Marion and I fuss all of the time, we even came to blows one time. I guess he thought I was going to cower in the corner shocked that he slapped me. We tore that suite up and then we didn't speak for a few months. Until we were forced to appear in public.

Marion is the Latin male version of me, which is another reason we bump heads. His fans think he's the greatest just like mine. He's such a brat though and a whiner. His tantrums get on my nerves and that's when we start fighting. I tried to talk to Bonita about him, but she says he's what I get. Then she starts going off about the unresolved lawsuits.

Novian's been traveling the world. When he comes back for good I plan on finally giving him the chance to impregnate me for real. We can go away together for a while. Let the public think I'm still with Marion and then I guess they'll think the baby is Marion's. Novian will be so happy that I think he'll go a long with it.

Novian

Camille was unusually quiet; lately she's been having far off looks. She stares and when I ask her what's up, she shrugs. She took a deep breath, "are you and January going to get married?"

"Where did that come from?" I turned to look at her.

"You want more kids don't you? You two get along really well. She knows the business and she doesn't sweat you about the things you do on camera." I was quiet, even though I haven't talked to Torrie in these past few years. I felt wrong for wanting it as soon as Camille said it. "I don't know if you two are paying attention or if it's just you not opening your eyes. You need to start paying more attention to the things that surround you. That girl loves you and she doesn't stress you about drama. You'd be a fool not to."

"What about Torrie?"

"What about her? She strings you along, sleeps with everyone. I mean you don't marry that one." I looked at her, she started laughing. "Someone should've warned Brad and Darius for that matter. It could've saved both of their lives."

Sandy called Camille screaming and crying because she found out that Darius died in a jail fight. It took a little while for Sandy to come around, but Camille was overjoyed when they started talking again. With her babies back in her life she hasn't had as much time for me. January and I have been spending a lot of time together. My feelings for her have only grown; I just know she doesn't deserve to be hurt. "You still gonna do my hair aren't you?"

"Of course, call me when you need me. It's time for me to stay home. Thank you for getting me out of the house and not letting me go stir crazy while my baby girls decided whether to love me again or not."

"I love you Camille," I watched her face soften.

"Oh hush, I'm finally starting to feel my age creep up on me. I can't keep up with you two like I used to be able to. I need to slow down and take care of myself."

"Thank you for being my first woman. For upgrading me in every possible way. I feel like I owe you so much."

"Novian, I've watched you grow from a boy to a man. These last few years away from the Bay have really done you some good. Now don't go back tracking and forgetting who you've become."

I thought about that conversation the whole way home, I called my mom on my car phone from the driveway and told her to come take a ride with me. When she got in the car, she said January was cooking and Jenny-Bean would be waking up soon. I asked my mom what she thought about me asking January to marry me. My mom got so excited, she said she loves January. She told me with all of her heart she had my back. "I need to ask you a hard question." My mom nodded, but I could see her bracing herself for my question. "Why did you leave Mr. Dozier? Was he weak in bed? Did he keep you stressed about money? Did you really love him?"

"Leroy was good to me. He was a good provider, faithful, kind, and good. Even though there was a large age gap between us, he never threw it in my face that I was so much younger than him. I was overcome by selfishness. I've always wanted to sing, and I told myself that Leroy could be enough for me. For years I hid it deep down inside. I was a good wife, with two beautiful babies. That desire to sing wouldn't go away. The sad part is that Leroy never asked me to give it up. I knew I had to in order to be the kind of wife he needed. Things were tense but we were managing, until Eugene came along. One look at that man and all of my common sense went out the window. Suddenly I wasn't wholesome and good anymore. I became dirty and gritty. I hated myself for what I did to my family. Then I got so lost in everything. The worst feeling in the world is being pregnant and not knowing who to say is the father. Brad told me to pick one and tell him. So of course I picked Eugene, he denied me. Then I told Briscoe, he denied me too. As a last ditch effort, I told Archie and he ran screaming it wasn't him."

"See, I don't want to marry January and then put her through that. I can't deny that I love Torrie."

"Yes you can! Torrie has always done you wrong!"

"Well I got her back unintentionally. I got her pregnant, and didn't even check for her. I think I saw her like two years after that."

My mom frowned, "what is wrong with you? You should've used steel condoms just to look at that girl."

I laughed, "is this what you were like with Lee and Leona?"

My mom blushed, "I guess so." She patted my hands; "January got us to a place of understanding each other instead of just tolerating each other. I mean look at us. You came to me with a life changing decision. I mean I know we're on our way to your brother's, but you came to me first. Makes me feel like you love me son."

She was right, January has made just about every angle of my life right. "I guess I feel safe enough to love you now. Even though I wasn't enough for you to be sober for, the fact that you've gone above and beyond for my daughter is amazing."

"That's my baby," she smiled warmly. "I'm so honored that January named her after me."

"She thinks very highly of you." My mom blushed when I said that. "Most people do, even Malcolm."

"What do you have against Malcolm?"

"You should ask him what he has against me. When I met him he was like, *oh you're Ursula's son.* Back then you know I didn't want my name associated with you. I wanted to stand on my own. He hasn't liked me since."

"He probably lost respect for you. He doesn't have tolerance for anyone who disrespects me."

"Now you tell me," I chuckled. "Why does he hold you in such a high regard?"

She exhaled like she wasn't going to tell me, but then she started talking. "He's Pam's son, but she treated him so badly. I was friendly with her brother Macio. Macio loved music and would come by the club a lot to hear me sing. He was one of the few faithful male followers I had who didn't want anything from me other than to hear me sing. He always had Malcolm with him, and a few times Pam brought Malcolm to my place looking for Macio. He would always be underdressed and hungry. He was a quiet child; he would barely speak most of the time. I knew that was the pain of his life keeping him from speaking. Macio wasn't all that nice to him but he was way better to him than his own mother. He…"

I cut her off, "did you ever sleep with Macio?"

She looked embarrassed by my question, "no. He always told me that beautiful women were nothing but trouble. He just wanted to hear me sing as much as he could. Even when Macio stopped coming around sometimes Malcolm would just be outside my place. Whenever I saw him I'd feed him and warm him up if it was cold outside. He slept on my couch a few times. He wouldn't ever really say anything he'd just watch me. I didn't live near his momma, so if he was at my place it was on purpose. He was too young to be wandering around cold and neglected like he was. Even when you were born he used to come around."

"How come you never call him Eugene's son, why do you only say he's Pam's son?"

"Eugene rarely claims any of his kids. He denied Malcolm just like he denies any of his other kids. BUT LET SOMETHING GO DOWN WITH HIS KIDS NAME IN IT AND HE'S RIGHT THERE READY TO ATTACK AS IF HE'S EVER BEEN SOME KIND OF FATHER!" She cleared her throat like she was trying to pull back some of her emotion. "The night his son Leonard died," she swallowed. "I thought that was going to change things for him. Make him reach out to his remaining kids and possibly step up. BUT NO!" She turned towards the window as she wiped a tear. "I was there, we were at his place when suddenly someone was at the door in the middle of the night. He walked real slowly to the door, whomever was there barely spoke and I heard the door slam. It was silence and then I heard him cry out. When I came to him he said his son was gone. He was full of regrets for everything he didn't do for that child, including never coming clean with him. He was full of resolutions that night; I don't know what happened in between then and when the sun came up. By morning, he was quiet and no longer willing to discuss any of it."

"Does he claim any of his kids?"

"A few of them, but most of them no. Over the years he's lost more than a few of them for this reason or that one."

"What about Briscoe, he claim his kids?"

"Birds of a feather, Briscoe would at least send money for his kids. The ones he claims anyways. When one of his sons passed away a little while ago. He was a mess about it. Apparently Eugene had interacted with him and I guess kept him informed about that one. I guess that's why they're always saying that Pam's mom's kids bred soldiers. That son was a big deal, and it was something random that took him out early. Briscoe at least stepped up and started reaching out to his kids that were receptive to him."

"Why hasn't he reached out to me?"

"I think he honestly believes you are not his son."

"Looking at him I don't see how I could be. We don't look anything alike. He reminds me of the dad off of Good Times!"

My mom started cracking up, "we used to say that all of the time. He didn't want to believe me."

"Do you honestly think he could be my father?"

"No, not by the look of him. Sometimes you just don't look like your parents. My sister and I looked just alike and we didn't look like either of our parents. Sometimes your genes will make you look different."

"Be honest with me, who do you honestly think my father is?"

"Eugene, but that could be because that's what I want. You don't look like none of them."

"Did you look after Malcolm because of Eugene?"

"No, I didn't know about the connection until much later. He didn't admit it until Pam died and that was only once until he told you. Eugene is so twisted, I can't even give his ridiculousness anymore energy."

"So why did you look after Malcolm, but you sent me away?' I parked in front of my brother's house.

"The night I got arrested was rock bottom for me. I almost got you killed, because I was protecting Brad. I figured the only way to keep you alive was to finally give in to Lee's plea. As soon as he turned eighteen he went to work and asked me to send you. I kept telling him no, and that I was going to raise you. It was too dangerous to keep you with me at the time. You were so innocent and you deserved better. I could never forgive myself if something happened to you."

"I never thought of you sending me away to protect me. I

thought you wanted to wash your hands of me. Why didn't you look after me like you did Malcolm?"

She looked at the floor, "I gave you the best of me. I thought you knew that. The only thing that made me someone I poured all of that in to you. Music was the only time I mattered and I gave it to you. All of them used me for it, but I showered it on you. Look at you now! My baby is a star representing for my family. Your brother and your sister won't sing, but they like their bottles. You won't drink, but you're a star. Looking at your daughter made me look at things differently. You aren't like either of your parents. You love your baby, you love a good woman like January, and you know how to love." She shook her head, "you may even love that demon child who loves to try to play innocent. You still didn't let her stop you from having something good in your life. I know I'm just your mother, but you need to let that girl go. Look at my life."

"Let Eugene go."

"I'm too old to be letting people go now. I'll leave that to you." Then she patted my hand, "I love you son. I always have."

I hugged my mom, and then I kissed her cheek. She was so human now. Talking to her made me feel even more for January.

When we talked to Lee, he reacted just like my mom did. He said he liked the affect of January on me. My sister in-law interjected and co-signed with her husband. I told them I'd let them know as soon as I was ready.

Torrie

Ever since that night with her assistant, I was leery of Josie. I didn't feel like I could trust her. I couldn't tell for sure if she was my friend or my enemy. She called me crying not too long ago. She was begging me to be her witness and say that Amber attacked us. I honestly told her I didn't see Amber do anything. I told her she's always been the one telling me it was her. I told her to let it go. She said she's been losing clients and everything. She was freaking out and saying that everything was slipping away. I told her to calm down, I told her to let her assistant go, and let the whole lawsuit go.

Josie begged me to meet up with her. I didn't want to go. I just got home, and I planned on giving Novian a call since I haven't seen him in forever.

We met at The Vine in Los Angeles. Josie looked a mess. She had a scarf on her head to cover her uncombed hair. She had dark circles around her eyes like she hadn't slept in days. She was clutching a folder as she talked really fast. She had pictures of our injuries and doctors information for both of us. I asked her how she got my medical records. I know all of that is supposed to be confidential. She said Bonita gave it to her.

I sat there quietly brewing about Bonita having access to everything about my life. Is this how she knew I was pregnant?

Josie brought me back to the table by asking me who Yvette Bates was. I told her I didn't know. She flipped through papers. Then she pulled out court documents, showing mediations that have been ongoing. She asked me why I didn't know this lawsuit was still open? I told her I wasn't going to be a hypocrite and try to sue someone for doing what I've done. Josie was quiet for a minute then she looked at me. "I'm losing my everything because of you!"

"Me?"

"What goes around comes around. You've victimized so many people. No wonder you don't want to pursue this fight."

"So now you're the helpless victim in all of this? You were there because you wanted to be. No one forced you. You were the one up-selling me on a threesome. You're just mad that that specific orgasm came with a butt kicking. You're too prideful to let it go, and now here you are."

"Prideful? I lost money! MONEY TORRIE! I don't have money like you do. I can't blow off a couple million as if it's nothing. I don't have Torrie's glam team either. My face and my body is how I make my money. Since you're not with me Torrie, you're against me."

At that moment I felt so alone. It's not like I have friends outside of Josie. She's been my only friend. "Send me the bill. I'll see about getting the money you lost."

"Let's do this right, paperwork and everything." Josie ran her hand over her face. "I know you said he's just a barber, but his legal representation is on top of their game. I get the feeling there's more to him than just that."

"It doesn't matter, send the paperwork to my assistant." I picked up my menu, "what would you like to order?"

"Your treat? I can't afford this place."

I put my menu down, "things are that bad?"

"I lost my house, my car, the struggle has been real."

"How did you get here?"

"My old faithful Honda. Thank goodness, I got it fixed up and then I put it to the side. It's just about all I have left. I had to pay off the people I defaulted on. The legal cost from this battle have been expensive."

"I'd offer you my guest house, but I really don't want your assistant on my property. Wait how can you still afford her?"

"I can't, but she does what she can to help me out. She had to find a job somewhere else. When I need to meet up with her I could meet her at a coffee shop or something." She looked me in my eyes. Her eyes were red and the dark circles made her look so old. "I've been going through it."

"As long as you understand I don't want Caprice on or near my property."

"Understood, but why don't you like her? She's been my rock through all of this."

"She was going through my stuff after I fell asleep, the last time you were at my house."

"Why would she do that? Did she take anything?"

"I don't know why, she didn't take anything, but I did give you the side eye. I felt like you were trying to set me up."

Josie shook her head, "I'm your friend."

****

Bonita was late but she had a big smile on her face. "Time is money Bonita." I held up my watch.

"Whatever a mother's job is never done." She held on to her smile while mine dropped. "My baby makes me so happy! One day you'll understand when you have a child of your own." I stood up to walk away. "Sit down before I make you!"

I remained standing, "what do you want?"

"It's been a few years since you've seen Novian in person. I've exhausted my patience. I want another baby! My child will be going away to college soon. I want another one!"

"Aren't you too old to care for a baby?" I chuckled as I said it.

Bonita released her smile then she pointed, "sit down!"

"No! We are in a public place, I dare you to try it!"

Bonita's eyes turned evil as she stood up. "One of these days you're going to learn. I don't care who's watching." She walked in my face and thumped my forehead. "If you don't sit down I will embarrass you in this public place!" The gossip reels flashed through my mind. All the jokes about Torrie Rowe getting beat up in this public place. I sucked my teeth then I sat. "And people say you're dumb." Then she happily retook her seat. "We've got a lot of ground to cover and you want to be playing games."

"I'm supposed to be with Marion."

"You don't like him, he can take a pause in your rotation until you do this for me."

"I haven't talked to Novian in years. You are ridiculous!"

"I'm trying to get on his calendar now. He's so busy. Meanwhile your little save the day stunt with Josie is going to cost you. I want a meeting with this Malcolm guy. He's the gatekeeper to the woman who assaulted you two."

"I don't want to see him."

"Too bad! Our flight leaves in the morning. Stand me up and I'll make sure your endorsements and concerts suddenly fall through."

****

I couldn't sleep all night. At three I got up and started rehearsing the choreography for my upcoming video. I could already tell this guy wasn't going to workout. There's a difference between sexy and provocative. I sent my assistant a message telling her this guy wasn't going to work out. Yes, I can pop my booty, but with my years and talent I don't have to. These young girls trying to get on my level can do all that.

My momma was up and getting ready like we had discussed. Bonita almost missed the flight. She appeared at the door at the last minute. She looked upset, but I didn't care. We dropped my momma at her brother's and then I looked out the window as the car drove. Bonita and I sat in silence on either side of the backseat of the car. I recognized the bar as soon as the car stopped. "Why are we meeting here?"

"This is the address he gave us." Bonita got out of the car looking like a million bucks. Her weave had lots of body as it bounced with every movement. The driver walked her to the doorway under his umbrella. Unlike Bonita I didn't get overly dressed up. Ankle boots, slacks, and a sweater. Bonita had on heels, her makeup was done. I could only imagine the dress she paired with this trench coat. When we stepped inside the bar a man stepped to us immediately. "Ms. Fairchild, glad you could make it." A middle aged white man said to her.

"Charles, you're aware of Ms. Rowe." She said as she unbuttoned her coat.

"Yes, of course. Ms. Rowe, I'm your legal representation."

"Why are we meeting in a bar?" I didn't have time for this.

"This is where Mr. Latour agreed to meet us."

"Mr. Latour?"

Bonita chuckled, "you don't even know his name. Still a dumb kid no doubt."

A tall light skinned older man approached us. He didn't smile and he walked with intention. He reminded me of every old school description of a player. His cologne was nice and not overpowering. "Bonita Fairchild?"

Bonita looked him over, "and you are?"

"Vic Cardell, nice to meet you. Hello Ms. Rowe, and you are?"

"He's my lawyer, interesting venue."

"Thank you, please follow me."

Bonita looked him over as we followed. That woman was behind the bar watching us. I can only assume she was expecting us even though she looked like she wanted us out right away. We were led to a table in the back. All of the customers were on the opposite side of the bar. There was a wall with a window, an entry way but no door. The woman brought us water and bowls of nuts. She kept cutting her eyes at Bonita and I. When their eyes met they were locked in a stare down for a long time. Vic rubbed the woman's back as he thanked her for everything. Bonita sat back in her chair as she looked around. I couldn't tell what she was thinking; I just knew I didn't want to be here. The front door opened and then Malcolm walked through the door followed by two men. I felt scared at the sight of him; I wanted to be anywhere but here. Malcolm stared into the room with his death glare as usual. Bonita looked at me and I raised my eyebrows to confirm that was him. Her eyes got a little big when he entered the room then suddenly this woman is quiet. Malcolm started talking on the way to his seat, "this is my legal representation." One of the guys sat his phone in the middle of the table. "This conversation is being recorded. Federal law permits recording telephone calls and in-person conversations. As previously stated this conversation was only granted with the knowledge that this entire conversation would be recorded. Please state your names individually for recording. I am Malcolm Latour." Then he gestured to his legal team who all stated their names and then the rest of us stated our names. "Read your document out loud." Malcolm commanded. At first I could tell Bonita was looking at Malcolm like, why? He walked in this room about business and now I could see that she was intrigued. She followed along as her lawyer read his document then the debate began. "You have no proof that Amber Wallace was in my residence on this date. Your only witness has retracted her statement." He looked directly at me and I wanted to run. "Ms. Rowe can you positively state for a fact that you saw or even heard Ms. Wallace at my residence on said date?"

"No," how did he know I didn't see her?

"For the record Ms. Rowe should give her account of the

events of that day." Bonita's lawyer said.

The way Malcolm relaxed in his chair to tell me to speak made me nervous. "We saw Malcolm at the airport, a little after we made it to my place he called and invited us over to cook for him." I swallowed as Bonita leaned in like the details of this day suddenly mattered to her. "We made dinner and then Malcolm invited Josie upstairs. I baked the cookies and cleaned up while they were upstairs. I walked in on Malcolm and Josie as they finished."

"Was Ms. Kage injured when you entered the room?"

"No, she was tired and went to sleep in the middle of the bed."

"At any time did you see Mr. Latour harm Ms. Kage in anyway?" His lawyer asked.

"No, I didn't."

"For the record, can you describe your attacker?"

Bonita watched me closely, "I can't. I was in the shower with Malcolm when someone pulled me out of the shower suddenly and started beating on me."

"How do you know it wasn't Mr. Latour?"

"Because he was still behind me when the beating began."

The lawyers went back and forth for a little bit, while Bonita sat there listening and watching. "Here's my point gentlemen, at the end of the day these ladies sustained substantial injuries while they were in the Latour residence. As the property owner he is responsible for his guests, even if they trip and fall down the stairs. We are asking that damages are covered for our clients."

The figure I saw on the paper was beyond anything I knew Malcolm could pay. I don't know how he's affording these lawyers, other than Amber has to be chipping in with his legal fees. The lawyer looked at the paper and he passed it to Malcolm. Malcolm looked at the paper then he scanned the three of us. "Again! I've told you I'm not paying this. I agreed that I had sex with these two women in my home. I can't tell you how they were injured or how they made it to the hospital. It's my word against theirs. They can prove that they were in my home because that's where we had sex. They can't prove that these injuries happened in my house. It's my word against theirs."

Bonita cleared her throat. "Mr. Latour, I know you're tired of this just as much as I am. This has drug on and on for so many years. I need to ask you for my own peace of mind. Did you at any time raise your hand, beat on, or injure Torrie Rowe?"

Malcolm squinted his eyes at her; "don't play on words with me. You could technically say that having sex with her injured her. He pointed to Bonita's pictures, I did not do that to them."

"Can you prove that you didn't?" Bonita said strongly.

Malcolm held on to his squint, "you can't prove that I did. Otherwise wouldn't this have gone to court at some point? You aren't asking for a measly sum of compensation. Now, I'm tired of wasting time and money on this. We are done!" Malcolm's tone was final.

Vic stood up, "I'll show you to the door."

"No!" Bonita stared at Malcolm like he was her next meal. "I would like to have a conversation with Mr. Latour off the record. Please excuse us."

"That's cute, but when I tell you come on the first time you better get up." Vic started moving towards Bonita.

"It's ok Vic," Malcolm said looking just as annoyed as Vic.

We stood and walked out of the room. I walked to the bar where I could watch them through the window. I couldn't believe Bonita was this dumb. I've learned my lesson twice; I will never go after Malcolm again. Is she doing this to try and rub my nose in something else?

The annoyed expression never left Malcolm's face. I wished I could hear what they were saying. Then someone tapped me on the shoulder, "remember me?"

He looked familiar, but so do most people. "Vaguely, where did we meet?"

"The strip club in downtown Oakland." I still didn't remember. "You were looking for Malcolm, but you settled for me."

I still didn't remember, so much has happened in my life since then. "Oh right, what's your name again?"

"Vic," then he turned to the woman who was staring at me. "Can you bring the lady a cranberry and southern comfort?"

She sucked her teeth, "LADY? Please! Who's paying for it? I don't run a charity."

"I'm paying, thank you Bernie."

I tried harder to remember him. He knows my drink of choice. "Thank you Vic."

"So the tabloids say that you and Marion have been together for a couple of years. What's the truth?"

"That we're together for our careers, there's no love there."

Vic smiled at me as he handed me my drink. "Let me whisper something to you." When I brought my ear close to his mouth he said very lowly, "Malcolm is not the same person that you knew anymore. Your friend in there is very foolishly playing with fire. Because we had a nice little interaction all those years ago I'm going to warn you. Let this lawsuit go, tell her to drop it."

I turned my face towards his ear. "I've been telling her that for years. She won't listen to me. I don't want anything to do with this. She made me come out here."

Vic pulled back and looked at my eyes, and then he went back to my ear as he gently stroked my back. "So listen to me carefully. Some really unpleasant things are scheduled for you if you continue to pursue this. Distance yourself as much as you can from this woman if you don't want to deal with what's about to come."

"What does that mean?"

"Don't ride in cars with her, don't go to her house. Keep your distance."

I thought about Norie, "but she has a daughter. She's a teenager."

"This is not a game Torrie. Look around the room; none of these people in here are customers. You're not from Oakland, but the Cardell name isn't just another name around these parts. Distance yourself from this idiot. I make no guarantees about her child. I'll keep it in mind; convince her to leave Malcolm alone. Or else…" Then he kissed my cheek.

Malcolm's voice rumbled as he told Bonita to leave. She looked completely shocked by his response to her. As the driver escorted me to the car under the umbrella, suddenly I noticed all of the people watching us. I had the complete creeps. Bonita got in the car energized by the events of the day. "That Malcolm is a fighter!"

"Bonita please stop, I don't want to do this anymore. I've already made Josie whole, let this go."

Bonita sucked her teeth, "do you know how many millions of dollars we've paid out behind you. Don't forget that Bates woman is still threatening to go public with your fight information."

"Yeah, but you are getting off on the challenge of trying to take Malcolm down. I don't want any part of this. He didn't hit me."

"Oh I know he didn't hit you. I honestly didn't believe it until looking him in his face today. I know there's more to him than just a barber. The way he walked in that room spouting Federal law. A barber would know that why?"

"I DON'T KNOW! I DON'T CARE! I'M DONE! I JUST WANT THIS TO BE OVER! DROP ME FROM THE LABEL I DON'T CARE! I'M NOT DOING THIS ANYMORE!"

Bonita waived me off, "you're always a drama queen. This ain't even about you any more. I've never been attracted to someone so dark before."

"LOOK AT MY FACE BONITA! THIS WILL BE YOU OR WORSE! LEAVE MALCOLM ALONE!"

She ignored me as she looked out the window with a smile.

Novian

"You may kiss your bride." The audience erupted into applause as I kissed my wife. I kissed her deeply and then we were introduced as Mr. & Mrs. Murphy. January and I held hands as we led our procession towards the doors to go out on the beach and take our wedding photos. My mother brought her plus two's out for the family photos. I didn't care that she invited Eugene and Briscoe; I honestly didn't think they'd come. Since my mom was so dead set on them coming, I told her that I was inviting Camille and her nieces. After a day of having a fit about it, she gave in and said it was fine. I'm glad she thought she had some kind of control over whom I had at my wedding. January looked amazing, she was truly a beautiful bride.

When I proposed she hesitated to give me a yes. We had to talk out the whole Torrie aspect of my life. I was completely honest with her as usual. I convinced her that I felt confident in my ability to do right by her, by our family. I found myself falling more in love with her when she said yes.

Last night I thought about Torrie. I thought about calling her and letting her know about my wedding. If I called her she would throw a tantrum and try her hardest to talk me out of what my heart, mind, body, and soul were set to do. Torrie still has years of games and running to do before she could ever be what I need. My wife, MAN! I got to get used to saying that, my wife gives me everything I need today with no hesitation.

As usual, Mr. Dozier, Eugene, and Briscoe got into an argument over my mom. Same ole argument just a new day. Briscoe seemed to forget about their argument after awhile. He found his way over to Camille. As I watched that man try to run game on Camille, I didn't need some test to tell me. I already know Briscoe is not my father. It was still worth proving, so when January's Maid of Honor labeled Briscoe and Eugene's glasses, eating utensils, and napkins and then took them away. I prepared myself to finally know for sure.

Chapter 12

Torrie

      Sound seemed to cease to exist. Tears fell from my eyes like a waterfall as I read the article about Novian Murphy's wedding and happy family. JANUARY!?!?!? How in the world did this happen? January is a girl on the side at best! How did she marry my man? She was a beautiful bride, but ask me if I care. I told my assistant to find out when his next performance or interview was. On the first page it was a picture of Novian and January looking all love struck. When I turned the page it was a group photo with their families at the top. At the bottom was a picture of Novian, January, and their daughter. I painfully sighed as I looked at the little girl. She looked like Novian, he couldn't deny her if he wanted to. My eyes wouldn't move from this picture. Regret was all over me. I should've came clean years ago. Fame comes at a price! I don't even know what our daughter looks like. Did she look like this when she was a baby? That all too familiar depressing feeling came over me. I closed the blinds and I got back in my bed. I stared at the picture as I cried myself to sleep. How could he do this to me? After everything I've been through, he does this.

Novian

      People were talking to me as my wife stood before me fixing my tie. She took it a loose and started retying it. I was listening but I was staring at January's face that was starting to round out. The baby's due in August. We're both hoping for a boy, but it doesn't really matter. Sometimes I wonder how I could love one woman so much. Being faithful isn't as hard as I thought. I'm simply giving her what I expect from her. I never expected Torrie to be faithful to me. So I never really considered the concept. Let's face it; Torrie always had the upper hand in our relationship. With January she lets me think I have it. We both know there's a even playing field here. I kissed my wife as she reassured me that my interview and following performance would go well.

My interview went well, as I performed I saw her. Torrie was sitting in the audience trying to blend in when she would always standout to me. I pointed at her and told the usher to bring her to the stage as I sang. The audience ate it all up as we respectfully danced to my groove. "Torrie Rowe ladies and gentlemen!" For the people who didn't recognize her in her everyday appearance they went crazy. When we went to commercial I gave her a quick hello hug. Then I looked to the side of the stage and I told January to come. January looked uncomfortable as she approached us. "Torrie you remember my wife January." I grabbed January's hand and kissed it.

Tears were in Torrie's eyes, "yes. I read about it." She gestured towards me, "you couldn't have given me a head's up? You let me find out with the rest of the world."

"Calling you would've meant I was looking for you to change my mind. Since I had no intentions of walking away from this woman there was nothing to say. How's Marion?"

Torrie quickly grabbed the tear that dropped. "I don't even like him."

"I'm sorry to hear that." I looked at January who was watching me. "Thank you for coming out. That was a great surprise."

Torrie exhaled then she started openly crying. "Novian! I knew you when you were too afraid to sing in front of people. She doesn't!"

"She's also never made me jump through a bunch of hoops to be with her. She's never shut down on me and made me feel disposable." Torrie wrapped her arms around herself. "Look, let's not do this. I'm happy for you and all of your achievements. Please be happy for me. I'm the happiest I've ever been in my life."

Torrie turned on her heels and walked to the back stage area as she openly cried. January asked me if I was ok. I held onto her hand, as I stood there stuck. The real Torrie stood before me. Not the spoiled brat diva that she put on for everyone else. I hated to know she was hurting because of me, but did she expect me to spend the rest of my life wrapped up in drama just to be with her? I forgot we were in front of the audience who sat there like they were eating popcorn and sipping tea. January and I went backstage, but we didn't see Torrie anywhere.

That night January kept checking in with me to make sure I was ok. I told her I was ok; I called Lee just to talk it out man to man. We had a good laugh about how his wife went off on him after the funeral when Adina was there. He said he was holding his breath hoping I didn't invite her to my wedding. I did invite her, but she was filming so she couldn't make it. I'll always have love for Torrie. Things are not the same with me. I couldn't spend my life waiting for her to love me more than she loves herself.

Torrie

I was still in the bed; heartbroken and consumed with everything I've given up. I told my assistant to leave me alone. So when I heard light tapping at my door, I threw my pillow over my head. I heard my momma telling them to just go in. She knows better than to tell my assistant that, but I couldn't move. My momma opened the door. "Torrie baby, somebody's here to see you."

"I don't want to see anybody momma. Please send them away."

The door closed and then I felt both of their weights as they sat on my bed. "Torrie baby, just look!"

I sighed loudly and I threw my pillow at my headboard. I threw myself up ready to act ugly and paused as I saw Adina. Her eyes looked sad for me but she didn't say anything. I screamed as I started crying. "Auntie can you give us a little space to talk?"

"Ok," my momma hugged me and then she hugged Adina before she walked out.

"I'm sorry!" I offered right away.

"I think I know, but I need you to tell me everything as if I don't." I paused, "I can't figure out what Bonita has over your head."

"I didn't realize he was your man until it was too late."

"Why did you continue?"

I laid my head back in the pillow. "I was already hurting."

"That made it worse, you can't see that?"

I put my thumb in my mouth on instinct. "I haven't been able to see anything." Adina stared at me. "Norie!" I've never told anyone about her.

"Norie?"

"That's what I named her in my heart. I was pregnant when I came out for your audition. Bonita picked up on it. I told Lee I was going to have an abortion so he gave me money and I used that to come out to you, and live off. Bonita asked me to give her the baby. I tried to act like I didn't care and that it wasn't a big deal. I wanted my baby but I didn't know how to voice it. She didn't even let me see her. She's always threatened to end your career, to tell you everything, and the times that didn't work she'd beat me up."

Adina wiped my tears, "she only has the power you allow her to have. You should come to me no matter how bad it is. Torrie I knew you when strangers made you nervous. When you were a shy little girl with severe stage fright. On top of all of that we're family." Adina cleared her throat. "So I met this woman who hates you. I hated you too so I let things happen that I shouldn't have. She says you interfered with her and her man. She won't let Bonita buy her silence. She's been doing research."

I exhaled, "I guess I deserve whatever Yvette comes with. In my defense Malcolm was no more her man than he was mine."

"She found out who your father is. You have a sister trying to get into music. They're planning to pull some ole Jerry Springer type junk to get her name out there."

Anger shot up my spine and out the top of my head like a volcano eruption. "The idiot who took advantage of a mentally handicapped girl! That woman doesn't even know how she got pregnant. Then to add insult to injury, they don't even try to come to me! Bonita doesn't know about this?"

"Nope, I didn't care about the vengeful stuff. Springing your father on you was a bit too far in my opinion. Then I saw the Novian interview and performance. I could see it all over your face when you were dancing with him. The media leaked your whole conversation. It's doing wonders for Novian's career, people are asking for the background story. The context around the words you shared. Everyone's digging in trying to find out the back story."

I reached for the phone then I stopped. "I'm trying to decide if this is the life I want anymore. Maybe I want to fall back and have a family of my own."

"With Marion?"

"I only need him for one part. I could disappear with my baby and live happily ever after."

"That's your idea of happily ever after? What about love? The love you'd have for your child is not the same as love from a man."

"I have nobody! My momma won't live forever. Bonita has Norie, January has Novian."

"You got me. I understand how you feel cause I felt the same way. I considered having a baby by Comfort just to have one. I'm so happy I didn't. I met someone; he's an average working guy. He reminds me of Lee actually. Now that I know this, I can honestly tell you to wait. You need therapy Torrie. We'll figure this out but don't give up yet. Keep fighting!

******

If I leave my label most of Bonita's power ceases. In order to do this successfully, I need to build on my own. I started building my own legal team, assembling my own army. The firm that I decided to go with has assured me that I am in good hands. I had them look at my contract at the label. Imagine my surprise when they told me that legally I was free to go wherever I'd like to go. My current project with this label would be my last freebie.

******

"Hello Ms. Rowe this is Lisa Sadler, your assistant contacted me directly regarding a complete portfolio. I'd love to schedule a meeting with you in person to go over our projections and plan for you."

My head was killing me, the last thing I wanted to do was be worried about looking at a calendar. "Why didn't you set up the appointment with her?"

"I just spoke with her and she advised that you make all of your own appointments at this level."

I exhaled, "who do you represent?"

"Cooper Financial."

"RIGHT! One moment," I put her on hold as I drug my bones out of the bed to bring up my calendar on my tablet. My assistant has been acting like my money is monopoly money. I can't put my finger on how, because everything seems legit. I just happened to be paying top dollar for everything and I know I get thrown all kinds of perks for using certain vendors. My calendar was pretty full. "Where are you located?"

"I'm in Northern California, but we have offices all over the country. I can meet you wherever you'd like to meet."

The idea of traveling with such sensitive personal information did not sit well with me. I scrolled for a moment; I found openings in my calendar for my next visit to the Bay. I gave her the date and the timeframe that I would be available. She typed and then she said she had me booked for a meeting in their San Francisco office and she'd be there with a few of her coworkers.

******

"I just want to be able to take care of my animals." My momma said as she sat next to me writing her notes on her paper.

I had my shades on hoping that no one recognized me. I was not in the mood to play nice with fans today. It's been a minute since I got some and I was feeling completely pent up. "Ms. Rowe, right this way." The receptionist said as she showed us to the conference room,

"Hello Ms. Rowe, I'm Lisa. We spoke over the phone. This is my boss Andrew Wallace, and my colleague Ray Dutchnell, please have a seat. Would either of you like coffee, tea, soda, juice, or water?"

"Water is fine," I pretended to be interested in the decor. This guy seems familiar but I can't put my finger on why. He didn't seem all that enthusiastic about being in my presence. "Thank you for meeting with us. I want to set up some pretty aggressive accounts for my mother."

"Torrie bought a stable for me. I want to make sure that my animals are taken care of properly. I brought all of my papers if you'd like to see them."

"Misses?"

"I'm Rowe too."

"I'm Andrew nice to meet you. Please show me your paperwork and we will put something together for you." His cologne slapped me in the face as he walked behind me to sit next to my momma. It wasn't overpowering; I think it's just my sensitive nose.

Lisa and Ray made sure they pulled no punches as they spoke about my financial planning. When I went to the bathroom, I caught a glimpse of Andrew walking out onto the floor to speak with someone. When I came out he was still talking to that person. I walked up on him. "Why do you look familiar to me?"

Andrew cut his eyes at me, which I wasn't expecting. "You really don't remember me?"

Maybe I left him hanging and he's still smoldering about it. "Do you know how many people I meet daily? It's hard to keep everyone straight."

Andrew walked away and I followed closely behind. "Lisa's waiting for you. She will be your point of contact if you decide to go with Cooper Financial."

I couldn't take my eyes off of him. He's young and in such a powerful position, which means he has to be really smart. I signed all of Lisa's documents and then Andrew volunteered to walk us to the elevators. As we walked to the elevator he slowed down and smiled at me. I could see him looking at my scars as he smiled. I touched my face as I tried to smile. "Crazy fans! This is why I have bodyguards down in the lobby."

Andrew pushed the button for the elevator. "A fan?"

"Fans! More than one."

Andrew smiled big as he put his arm out so that we'd get on

the elevator. "You tell that story so much I guess you actually believe it." He pointed to my face, "my momma did all of that. I was there when she busted your eye open." Then he laughed as the elevator doors closed. Rude!

Novian

I looked at the letters, Briscoe is not my father. The results from the DNA test ran on Archie's daughter's show that we aren't related. I didn't open Eugene's letter. I told January I would be back. I drove to Malcolm's studio. Dame told them to let me in. He smiled at me, "what's up Superstar? I didn't expect you to ever come back after Malcolm knocked you around that time."

"Can you tell him I want to talk to him?"

"What I look like?"

"If I had any other way of reaching him, I wouldn't bother you."

Dame picked up the phone, "a smart person would go by the barber shop or something." He dialed then he put the phone to his ear. "Hey Ms. Laverne. How is the most beautiful woman in the world doing today?" Dame blushed then he remembered I was standing there. "I have someone here looking for Malcolm. What number should I call?" He smiled real big, "if that wouldn't be too much trouble.... nobody spoils me like you do... thank you Ms. Laverne. Tell your husband I'm coming this weekend to do the yard work... alright, thank you." Then he cleared his throat. I could hear the rumble of Malcolm's voice. "Malcolm, Ursula's boy is here asking for you." He looked at me, "he's grown up a little bit. It might be worth it... alright." He hung up, "he's nearby. Sit tight."

Two hours later Malcolm walked in the door. He kept scanning me as he walked up to me. "What do you want?"

"I'd like to talk to you in private." Dame smiled as he openly watched us.

Malcolm walked and I followed, he even walked like Eugene. It was slightly different, but it was the same. We went in an empty studio. Malcolm told me to sit and then he sat in the other chair. He locked his eyes on mine. "What?"

"First I want to apologize for misunderstanding everything. I get it now." Malcolm didn't say anything he continued to stare. "I'd like to start over." Malcolm didn't say anything. I stuck my hand out, "I'm Novian, Ursula's son and your little brother."

Malcolm rolled his eyes, "you supposed to be a long lost child of Pam's?"

"We have the same father."

"I don't have a biological father, my natural father died a few years ago and I know you are not his child."

"Neither do I, but you and I are related."

There was a big boom against the window. I jumped Malcolm didn't. "NO! DADDY NO! SAY IT AIN'T SO! NOOOO! DADDY!"

Malcolm's eyes turned evil as he looked at his son. "DARRYL!"

Darryl hurried in as he fake cried, "yes Poppa?"

"Get yourself together! I don't have time for this!"

"But daddy! This is all so sudden." I chuckled, "our little boy finally grew up."

"Your little boy?" I laughed.

"Darryl please!" Malcolm dismissed him.

"Do you ever smile?"

Malcolm looked at me like I asked a stupid question. "Van! One time he fell out laughing. I was a little boy so I thought the world was coming to an end."

"When was this?" Malcolm looked like his accusation was ridiculous.

"That time Drew threatened to hurt you if you hurt momma." Darryl started laughing while Malcolm smirked. "Malcolm fell out as if he's me or something. It was a great five minutes of laughter. My brother also known as Lil Malcolm came running out of the shower. Me personally, I was terrified. I never realized how white this man's teeth are. Malcolm you stand in the mirror twenty minutes a day brushing after every meal don't you?"

Malcolm returned his attention to me. "Does he know you're here?"

"No, are there anymore?"

"A few, some of them don't matter. The others only matter if you want them to."

"You matter."

"I always matter!"

Darryl stood there with his arms crossed as he shook his head in agreement while he cheesed real big. "We should have him over for dinner, he's grown so much."

"You can have him over if you want to. Nobody's stopping you."

"We'll see," he kept smiling at me.

"Are we done here?" Malcolm stood up.

"I want you to meet my family."

"I already know everybody."

"You haven't met my daughter."

"I've got a lot on my plate right now. Eventually."

"It was good seeing you Van, we'll see you soon."

Torrie

Adina was right, therapy has been wonderful. I even found a specialist for my momma. My first assertion of my power resulted in my cursing Marion out. I went off so badly that it was all over the news for a minute. I had my cousin back, Josie's business was picking up. My financial and career freedom was closer and closer on the horizon. We were all smiles. My assistant and my momma were in the swimwear section while Adina and I were trying on shoes. The shoes I had on were wicked and they made me smile. Adina was admiring her selection.

"Torrie, look! I got a two piece." My momma excitedly showed me.

A teenager and a woman walked into the seating area. The teenager was very excited about all of the shoes as she talked really fast pointing. She was pointing near Adina, she squealed when she saw her. I looked at my bodyguard who was watching the little girl as if she could be dangerous. "Mom! Mom! It's Adina Vaughn!" Then looked at me! She melted in her chair, "Mom! Mom! And it's Torrie Rowe!"

"That's nice," the mom said turning her nose up at us.

The girl paid her mother no attention. "I love you! All of my friends and I love your song."

I smiled, "which one?"

"I knew you when, and looking back. Angel and I are the only ones who believe that project has nothing to do with Marion. You broke up with him after that project was released."

"You're a smart girl."

The girl hopped around in her seat as she clapped her hands. Her blonde hair moved like she was underwater. An associate came over to assist them with their shoe selections.

I saw shoes on the far side of the section that caught my attention. I told my momma I'd be right back. As I looked at the wall of shoes another little girl joined our little fan. Her friend was black with long thick hair that she was wearing down. She was with a light skinned woman, most likely her mom, who had a very short and curly style. "Goodness Kimber you need to calm down!" The little black girl said as the blonde girl drug her towards me.

"Torrie, this is my friend Angel. She's the only other smart friend I have." She announced as she almost ran to me bringing her friend along. "She confirmed that those songs are not about Marion like we said."

Angel was beautiful and shy. "Pleased to meet you."

My momma walked over to us, and then she stared at the little girl like she didn't answer her question. "She reminds me of you."

"I'm Torrie, what's your name?"

The little girl blushed, "Angel."

"That's pretty, how old are you?"

"16," she took a deep breath. "We love your music. My mom works in the music business, but she's never able to get me tickets to any of your shows. That's so weird because she comes through on everyone but you."

"We bought our own tickets to your show in a couple months. Her mom couldn't get us backstage passes though." Kimber waited to let her words sink in.

"Kimber it's ok, stop that."

"But we're her biggest fans, we've got to ask."

"I'll need your names and I'll see what I can do." I signaled for my assistant to come over.

"I'm Kimber Nielsen and this is Angel Fairchild."

I did a double take as my eyes lost focus and then refocused. The woman that came with Angel hurried over. "Is this your momma?"

"No, that's Mimi my nanny."

"Angel, come on honey. We have to go." She had sweat on her forehead and she looked scared.

I looked at Angel; she was the product of my love. Here she was in front of me in flesh and blood. She had my nose, and Novian's eyes; she was average short like me. She was a little lighter than me, but I saw me and I saw Novian. "Wait! Why do you have to leave? Aren't you buying shoes?"

"We're supposed to be shopping for our outfits for the concert." Norie looked at her nanny, "what's wrong?"

The nanny looked like she wanted to cry, "nothing sweetheart. Enjoy!" Then she looked at me with sad eyes. She walked back to the seating area.

"Norie, I mean Angel what are you wearing to my concert?" I made mental impressions of her voice, her skin, her mannerisms.

"I'm finally old enough to wear the kind of shoes I want to wear. So I want them to be the stars of my outfit! That's why we're here today."

"Pick out any shoe you want, I'm buying them for you. Do you dance?"

"We've been in every type of dance since we were little. Ballet to West African, and everything in between." Norie said as she kept her eyes on the floor.

"Baby please look at me, you're too beautiful to keep your head lowered like this."

"She's just really shy."

I forgot about her friend, "that's ok. I used to be shy too. Sometimes I still feel shy. You two go pick out your shoes."

My hands were shaking as I looked at my momma who looked like she wanted answers. The girls happily scurried away looking at the possibilities! My momma crossed her arms as she waited. My assistant went back to their bags. "Who's child is that?"

Adina came over not knowing anything. "That's Bonita Fairchild's daughter." I watched Adina's eyes, as she jerked her head around trying to see whom we were talking about. I pointed to the girls and Adina took off.

"She's a big fan."

"Shoes? That's it? This whole store and you're only looking at shoes?"

"Momma I don't want to upset their parents."

My momma walked away as I caught the nanny watching me. I told her to come to me. She hesitantly walked over. "Please!" She put her hands up.

"You know?"

"Please!" She looked around to see who was looking at us.

"I need more time with her, please!" I pleaded from my heart. I looked over as Adina hugged Norie with tears in her eyes.

"Bonita is ruthless, she will kill me literally if she ever finds out about this."

"How do you know?"

"I just do ok. Please! I don't want any problems. I love that little girl and I want what's best for her." She wiped her forehead. "Give me your number and I'll call you so that we can meet up later." I gave her my number. Mimi the nanny wiped her face. She took a deep breath then she walked over to the other mom and started talking as normally as she could.

As I approached them Adina was talking, "ladies. If I can manage better tickets would you mind sitting with me during the concert?"

Kimber screamed, "yes!"

"What about our other friends, we can't."

"How many?"

"Three more! This is the first concert we're going to without our parents. We have to stick together or else my mom will never let me do this again." Norie reminded her friend.

"Who wants to give me their number so that I can let you know if I can get the tickets?" Both of the girls volunteered.

I wanted to ask Norie if she was happy. I wondered if she ever felt like something was wrong. I was stuck with the thought that someone so perfect and gorgeous came from me.

The girls picked out shoes. I heard Nanny Mimi tell Norie to tell her mom the shoes were from her if she asked. Tears ran down my face when they left. Adina hugged me as she said beyond a shadow of a doubt that was my baby.

Novian

Last night I dreamed about Torrie being pregnant again. January's convinced that it's my guilty conscience about Torrie's abortion. I wasn't around for Jenny-Bean's pregnancy. This is my first full-fledged pregnancy, and I've been nervous since she told me we were pregnant. I know when both of my kids were conceived. I will be there to catch this one when he slides out. I asked January if she'd want to have anymore after this one. She smiled and said, "definitely! I want a big family, can you handle that?" I love this woman so much! My brother and sister were good about it, but they're so much older than me that most times I felt alone. My children would be surrounded by their siblings. I was excited and couldn't wait. Malcolm hasn't come over yet, but it's fine. I know he's busy. I look forward to spending more time with him. Reviewing the things that make us similar.

I put the coffee pot on to get our day started. I heard the front door slam. Then a few seconds later the doorbell rang. I took a deep breath cause I knew this was my mom and Eugene fussing as usual. My mom sat down at the table in the dining room as she put her face in her hands. I opened the door. "Where's your mother?"

"Look Eugene, it's too early in the morning for all of this. My family is still sleeping."

Eugene frowned at me like something stank. "Tell Ursula to come outside and to quit playing."

His disregard of me irritated me. I closed the door in his face and I walked over to mom. "Do you want to see him?" She shook her head no. I walked over to my bookshelf and took out the envelope. I opened it and unfolded the letter. I didn't even look at it, I opened the letter flat and then I opened the door. I put the letter in front of his face.

His expression changed a couple of times then he squinted at me. "Is this supposed to mean something to me?"

"I don't want you doing me like you do Malcolm or any of your other kids. I would like to be acknowledged."

Eugene threw his hands up and walked away. My mom peeked around the corner. "What was that?" I gave her the letter. She put her hand over her mouth. "How did you do this?"

"Does it matter, now we all know for sure."

"I'm not sure what I'm looking at, but it says he's not your father."

"WHAT?" I snatched the letter! I exhaled, "you play entirely too much!" I laughed.

"I knew you didn't read it!" She smiled, and then she took the letter from me. "This is what I needed, now I'm complete."

Torrie

"Hello?"

"This is Mimi, is there somewhere private we can meet?"

"Come to my house, I'll give the guard your name. You'll need your picture ID."

Mimi gave me her full name and I gave her directions.

Mimi said she just dropped my Norie off at school. We went to my office and Mimi started talking fast. She said Bonita hired her as a nanny when she was married and undergoing fertility treatments. She said she was helping Bonita when her husband Matt left her. I needed to clarify that it was the same Matt that Adina dated. She said yes and that they were still married on paper. I felt so stupid; they used both of us as pawns in their game. Mimi said before Angel came Bonita joked about buying a baby on the black market. She said she didn't think Bonita was serious. She got nervous when Bonita's doctor friend started coming around. Bonita told her that her adoption was legal.

About eight years ago Bonita and her doctor friend fell out. She said the doctor interrupted their dinner one night. She heard my name and they were definitely talking about my Norie. The next thing she knew they were going to the doctor's funeral. She said that Bonita's been distracted lately.

"Ever since Angel was young my instructions have been to keep her away from you. I never had to question why, I have eyes."

"You think I can contest her adoption?"

"You have to have prove of adoption. The way her documents are set up, she had a home birth."

"DNA!" Shouldn't that be simple?

"Could she say you donated your egg?"

"I don't know. Is Angel happy with her?"

"Bonita is all she knows. What sixteen year old girl loves her mom?"

I thought about my momma. "I've always loved my momma. I take her everywhere with me. I also know my momma's situation is different. I want my baby, but only if she's open to me. Family is not something that I have a lot of. Angel is the last piece I have left of the man I loved."

"Let's see how the concert goes."

Novian

My mom surprised me today by picking me up at the airport. I was still smiling behind my performance last night on Saturday Night Laugh. I was the musical guest and a guest appearance on a couple of skits. They said I did really well and that they would look to have me back as soon as possible.

"Novian I need to ask you for a favor. Melanie Latour died last week. Her funeral is tomorrow and Briscoe is a complete mess. He's asked me to go with him, but I don't want any problems with Eugene. Can you come with me?"

"Why do you have to go?"

"I want to pay my respects to her family."

"How did she die?"

"She hasn't been herself since she lost her son. She tapped out really. They say all these medical conditions but we know it's her broken heart."

"Let me see if January feels up to going."

"I think she's going to be too tired, at the last minute she needed to stay home and rest."

"Why didn't Jenny-Bean come with you?"

"She's playing nurse to her momma. I left them to their bonding." My mom shook her head; "Briscoe is so in love with Melanie. I guess he thought he'd have more time. He has so many regrets. Do you think it would be ok if he came over for dinner?"

"What are you doing?"

"Nothing."

"Where's Eugene? I haven't seen him since that morning."

"He's not talking to me."

"You trying to make him jealous by having his best friend over?"

"No, Briscoe is my friend. He's hurting and I'm not going over his place. I want to invite him to yours so there's no confusion."

"As long as January doesn't lift a finger, it's fine."

"DADDY!" Jenny-Bean screamed as she ran to me happily. This greeting never gets old for me.

January had her feet up as she went over paperwork. She looked tired, but even her resting was work. I put my bags away then I sat by her feet and started rubbing them. January smiled at me and said that I did a good job last night. I thanked her, and then I told her about the collaboration ideas that the rapper Shameless and I came up with. Shameless suggested a duet with Chantel Shaw. January smiled and asked me if they were a couple. I told her Chantel wasn't there so I had no idea. Shameless lives in New York and since I was out there for the show I hung out with him and Dewayne Reed. Dewayne was telling both of us to get into film as soon as we can.

The wheels of January's mind were turning as I spoke. "Can you act though?" She smiled at me.

"I can take some classes."

My mom gave the housekeeper her shopping list. Then she took out the good China. Jenny-Bean was too excited to help my momma set the table. When the groceries arrived, first we heard my momma singing, then Jenny-Bean mimicking her, and the wonderful smells. The Ursula's wouldn't let us in the kitchen. It was cute as January and I sat on the couch. January bounced ideas off of me for concert productions and promotions.

When Briscoe arrived he had no smile on his face. His mournful demeanor was immediately visible. January hugged him and offered her condolences immediately. He thanked us and then he took his place at the table. My momma had music playing softly in the background. Briscoe thanked my momma for all of her efforts. My momma asked Briscoe to tell us about the woman who had his heart all of these years. It was gut wrenching as he spoke about all his regrets. How he messed things up time after time with her. How she refused to see him until he took on an active role in their son's life. He said he was afraid. He was afraid of being rejected or feeling like he wasn't good enough. When their son died he felt like the best part of him died too. He got choked up as he talked about how losing their son took the life out of Melanie. She projected all of her anger on to him, and she blamed him. He took ownership of her pain and blames himself as well. January and I held hands as we empathetically listened to him spout out his regrets. I thought of Torrie, although I've apologized for everything else. I feel bad about the way things ended. I should've given her a heads up.

****

The mortuary was packed out. I saw Malcolm, he acknowledged me with a head nod. His sons nodded at me as well. As the program began we were handed obituaries. Melanie Latour-Davis was a very beautiful woman. Briscoe kept tracing her face with his fingers. I doubt he even paid attention as the obituary was read. Her son's name was Troy Davis. Looking at the picture of him, I didn't really see Briscoe in his face. He looked just like his momma. When I looked at him he had a version of both of his parent's nose. His nose was similar to Briscoe's, but it didn't stand out on him.

Briscoe leaned over in his pew as he tried to get it together. My momma rubbed his back as she told him it was ok. When Briscoe said he couldn't take anymore and that we needed to go we stood up. My eyes caught Eugene's and he was looking like my momma and Briscoe were sexing before him. Like he walked in on them or something. Briscoe didn't care and my momma rolled her eyes at him as she held on to her friend as we walked out. We made it to my car when Eugene came charging towards us. "I knew it! You couldn't wait to find an opportunity to get at him."

"What? Eugene! You're being ridiculous!" My mom waived him off.

"Admit it, all this time you've wanted to go back to Briscoe. Now that Melanie's out of the way, you're going to take your shot. You..."

Briscoe growled cutting Eugene off. "MELANIE IS GONE! MY HEART! SHE'S GONE! You choose now to show all your insecurities? I'm not doing anything but bleeding out over here, and you want to fuss about yesterday? Stop! I lost my love I don't want to lose my brother."

"Eugene you're still in love with Pam. Dead or alive that's who has your heart. I'm too old to chase or beg you to acknowledge me. I'm done, I'm not playing your cat and mouse game no more."

Car doors closed then a man and a woman walked towards us. The guy didn't smile but the woman with him smiled big at all of us. "Eugene, other people." The guy said as a way of acknowledging us.

"Blu, since when you run late?" Eugene asked him.

"That's irrelevant, everything ok out here?" His eyes went from face to face.

"We're leaving," Briscoe said getting in my back seat.

My mom looked at Eugene, "you don't care anyways." Then she got in the front seat.

Eugene looked angry and betrayed. I looked at his friend who looked like he understood what wasn't said. I drove quietly as I tried not to stare at my mom. Was there any truth to what Eugene said?

That night I read the obituary to January as she did something to her hair. I stared at the obituary for a minute like my eyes were deceiving me. Troy's pictures were older and there was a current looking picture of Troy with locs. I was so confused January took the obituary from me. "This is his son, and that's his daughter. It says right here that she's survived by her Grandchildren Latia and Yussef Davis, and her Great-Granddaughter Yesmina Davis."

"MOMMA!" I ran out of the room, I knocked on my momma's door. She wasn't answering so I slowly cracked her door. The covers were pulled back on her bed but she wasn't in her bed. I figured she went to the kitchen. As I started hurried towards the kitchen I heard voices by the front door. I assumed it was Eugene, but the voice wasn't deep. I rounded the corner as they fell into a kiss. I dropped the obituary in shock. "Momma?"

My momma jumped, but Briscoe didn't. They looked at me like I was interrupting. "Renee, what do you need?" Briscoe said.

"I'm so confused!"

My momma held up her hand, "he just proposed."

"I don't understand."

"Eugene is a fool!"

"Momma, aren't you in love with him?"

"Tina Turner asked the question best. What's love got to do with it?"

"So his accusation was true?"

"No," Briscoe said.

I threw my hands up, "I give up! You guys are to old to be this goofy and confused." I stormed away back to my bed.

"What's wrong?"

"Briscoe proposed to my momma and she accepted. They're

too old to be this goofy. I don't get it."

"I get it," January rubbed my back.

I sat up, "please explain it to me cause I don't get it."

"They had unfinished business. She felt something for Briscoe, look at the meal she made him the other day. Both of them were focused on the people who were rejecting them so much that they held back what they felt for each other. Eugene could see it, but they were in denial."

"To ruin a lifetime friendship though." I looked at January, "would you marry Amos if I died?"

"No! He's good where he is."

Chapter 13

Torrie

I signaled to Adina to bring the girls up on stage. The girls screamed and spazzed out about being on stage in front of thousands. "Ladies, tell the world your names."

"Teresa!"

"Cher!"

"Cameron!"

"Kimber!"

"Angel!"

"Angel my angel! Isn't she beautiful?" The audience screamed louder. "They claim to be my biggest fans. Tonight I'm going to ask you to prove it." I pointed to start the song and everyone went crazy. "Sing it with me ladies!"

"*I knew you when, I knew you when, I knew you when! I knewwwww yyyyoooouuuu wwwwwhhhheeeennnn!*" The crowd scream, "that was great! Now I have a final test do you know the routine?" Then I backed up. Norie pointed to her shoes. "Camera man checkout these shoes. Aren't those *Torrie* shoes, my baby has exquisite taste. Well my love if you can't dance in them kick them to the side for a second." I cued the music and all of the girls started dancing. Norie closed her eyes as she danced. I remembered how scary it was the first time crowds of people were focused on me. "Go! Go!" I stood to the side while they did my moves. "Give it up for my mini-me and her friends." Norie and her friends were hysterical. "Thank you Los Angeles!" Then I told the girls to come backstage with me. They were excited and I saw the gossip folks scribbling as we passed them.

Novian

Lee sat over to the side watching our mom and Briscoe dance. I kept shaking my head, "January tried to explain it to me. I don't get it."

"They all met as a group, it's not like she met Eugene first. There was always something or someone in the way. I'm not surprised."

"Well I guess I'm the only one who's shocked by this then. I wish he'd stop calling me by my first name though. All I need is for someone to hear him calling me that. You know once the media gets a hold of it, it will never go away."

"There's nothing wrong with Renee."

"You weren't in a class with two other girls with the same name." Lee laughed, "name two girls named Lee."

"Jamie Lee Curtis, and Jennifer Jason Leigh." We cracked up for a long time.

Our mom looked so happy to be in Briscoe's arms. I mean it makes sense, why name me after the best friend's father unless there was something there. I just never would've saw this coming. Aren't they too old for this? January came over, "I can see you lost in your thoughts. Come dance with me."

"This is crazy!" I glanced at my mom and Briscoe again.

"It's great, they're in love. Stop trying to understand it, just accept it. You think people weren't confused when they found out we're together? No one saw us out together; we always kept things professional in public. I never mixed business with pleasure until you."

I smiled, "thank you for bending."

"Bending, folding, and stretching." She smiled at me.

"You trying to get knocked up before this one is born."

Torrie

"Give me a kiss before you go." He said as he sat up.

I kissed Myles and I tried to ignore the butterflies that were still in my stomach. I like this guy, and I try very hard to deny it. I turned on my biggest diva personality and he checked me. All I could do was say ok. He kind of reminds me of Malcolm except he's into me. It's so weird, but I'm loving the feeling. "I'll see you later ok."

"When?"

"I have something's to do today, how about tonight?"

"Come back and I'll cook for you."

I smiled, "you cook?"

"Oh, I throw down in the kitchen. You'll see tonight."

"I can't wait," I kissed him again.

I walked out to my car with a mile wide smile. I called Adina and we talked like we used to. We were both dating men who are not in the business and it's been really great. Adina met me at the high school where Norie and her friends started a philanthropy project for school. They've decided to turn it into a foundation. Of course I jumped on any opportunity to interact with Norie that I could get. When Mimi said that Bonita was distracted she wasn't kidding. My life has been manageable and bully free. I've been connecting with myself and the things around me in ways I never thought I could.

I sashayed down the hallway with a big smile on my face. My bodyguard was a few steps behind me as usual. I walked into the auditorium as I started to walk down the aisle. Bonita turned around when the girls got excited about me being here. The look of death that showed on her face gave me chills. I didn't hesitate I continued walking down the aisle. The girls all came running down from the stage to me. Bonita jumped out of her seat and ran to us. "NO! GET AWAY FROM MY CHILD!" Everyone paused and the Principal hurried over. "WHY DIDN'T ANYONE TELL ME THAT SHE WAS THE BIG NAME YOU GOT TO SUPPORT YOUR CHARITY?" Bonita screamed as she charged to Norie.

I started running to Norie, I put her behind me. "Bonita don't do this!"

"Mom! What's wrong? Why are you acting like this? Torrie has been great!" Norie thought she was helping.

"OH SO YOU'VE MET BEFORE?" The bass that came out of Bonita made the hairs on the back of my neck stand up. "GIVE ME MY CHILD!"

I blocked Bonita, "stop it Bonita! I can have this! You can't control everything!"

"Mom!" Norie said through tears, "what's wrong?"

"I'M PULLING MY CHILD OUT OF THIS SCHOOL! IF YOU CAN'T CONTROL WHO STROLLS IN HERE OFF OF THE STREET! THIS PROSTITUTE IS NOT A ROLL MODEL FOR ANYONE'S CHILD."

"MOM! WHAT ARE YOU TALKING ABOUT?"

I smiled at Bonita, thanks to her wonderful team the world has no idea of what she's talking about. "ANGEL LET'S GO! GET YOUR STUFF!"

"Bonita! Bonita! You're scaring everyone. You look crazy, take a deep breath and regroup."

"COME NEAR MY DAUGHTER AGAIN AND I WILL KILL YOU!"

I looked around the room at all the witnesses to Bonita's threat, and then I looked at her. "I guess the police will know who to lock up."

"WE'RE LEAVING!" She yelled at Norie.

"Mom?"

"GET YOUR STUFF NOW!" She pushed Norie.

Power I didn't know existed within me ran through me and I stuck Bonita in the face. As she fell backwards I grabbed Norie and I told the Principal to call the police. My bodyguard came forward and he grabbed Bonita as she tried to gather herself together. I threw my arms around Norie as I apologized to her. She kept saying she didn't understand what was going on. I guess the saying is true, when your child's in danger you find the strength to do things you normally wouldn't be able to do. I could never exert enough power to move Bonita when it was about me. Today however, I wasn't afraid of her and I was actually ready for whatever she brought. When the police hurried in I was impressed with their response time. The police never responded this quickly in Berkeley. I held Norie's sweaty hand as I told the police that we witnessed Bonita pushing my daughter, and I was certain that this was not the first time. Norie looked at me with big questioning eyes. "Don't worry honey, you're not the only person she's bullied, this ends today."

"Well yes, but what was the other part? Your what?"

Bonita started screaming and saying that I was lying and that she needed to protect her daughter from me. Everyone gave their statements, and then they spoke with Norie about everything. The officer asked if there was a family member that Norie could stay with until they investigated her claim? They advised that they would have to take her into child protective custody if no one stepped up. I raised my hand and said I was her mother and I wanted her to come home with me. Norie looked at me with tears as she asked me why I kept saying that. Bonita was screaming that I was spreading lies, and she begged Norie not to believe me.

Mimi hurried into the auditorium and straight to Norie. She hugged her and asked her if she was ok. Mimi identified herself as Norie's nanny. They asked her who employed her and she said that Bonita did. They said that I claimed to be Norie's mother. Mimi said she was hired to look after Norie since she was born. Mimi said she couldn't deny or confirm my claim.

My assistant showed up with one of my lawyers. They were passing out confidentiality agreements like they were flyers. When Bonita saw my lawyer she was stuck for a minute. I think she recognized her, and yes I hired the lady who was just as bold as Bonita. Child protective services took my information and they said they'd be in touch.

My lawyer was on her stuff and she was calling her family law partner.

Novian

Camille held my son up as she kissed his cheeks. "I just love babies! They smell so good, and they just want to love you and be loved. This one looks like his momma."

"Thank you! Please tell him that our son may be a junior, but he looks like me." January high-fived Camille.

"Please my son is a mirror image to me."

"Nope even your mom has said so. Sorry baby, that's my child."

"Jenny-Bean, come here baby." I sat her close to her brother. "Do they favor?"

"Yes, this is definitely her little brother." Camille answered.

"Jenny-Bean looks like me."

"She is your little twin."

"Therefore my son looks like me."

"I see your logic, but he looks like January."

"Camille, please don't tell me you're getting caught up on color as well. Just cause he's going to be browner than me you can't see the resemblance?"

Camille looked at Sandy who was sitting in the rocking chair almost across the room from us. "Come weigh in on this debate."

She shook her head no, "I don't want to."

"Aw! Come on Sandy, it will be fun to argue irrelevant points just for the sake of arguing."

"NO!" She crossed her arms and turned her head.

Camille lowered her eyes at her niece, but January spoke before she could. "Why are you here? If you didn't come to congratulate us you shouldn't have come."

Camille gave the baby to January and then she got up, "I'm sorry. I guess I missed something. What is your problem young lady?"

"You guys are disgusting, how could you allow your husband's ex whore to hold your child or even walk through the threshold of your home like nothing ever happened. Especially during your six week down time at that? You must want someone to steal him."

"SANDREEN!" Camille yelled in shock.

January moved her hand in a circle as she gestured. "Clearly you don't understand how grown women operate. I know my man; I know what he will do and what he won't. Camille has become a very dear friend to me, because of the friendship we've made I know what she will and won't do. You never asked me what I allow and what I don't. However, that's none of your business. Since you want to come in here all huffy about stuff that don't apply to you, you need to get all of your facts together before you act like you're supposed to be reading somebody." Then January smiled, "besides I saw you walking in here with your chest all poked out. I saw how disappointed you were when he didn't notice you. That's when you took your behind over there and started sulking. You need to grow up and get it together. At your age you need to realize that you most likely will not be the first person that your man has slept with. My husband and I know what's up, and you need not worry your pretty little head about it."

Camille looked at January and smiled, "well she is my mini-me." Then they started laughing. I didn't understand the joke. What I did understand is that my wife is always checking my reaction to other females. I wasn't mad at her for it, at least I was winning and I didn't know I was playing a game.

The phone rang, and I answered. "Hello, yes this is Sheila Barrymore of the Los Angeles County child protective services agency. I need to speak with you regarding the welfare of Angel Fairchild."

"Ok, but I have no idea of who that is."

Camille and January started laughing about something in the background. "I can tell that this may be a bad time. What would be a better time to speak with you?"

"No," I stood up and put Jenny-Bean down on the bed. "You said child protective services. I'll go somewhere quiet."

"Mr. Murphy can I verify some information about you before we proceed?"

"You can't call me asking to verify information. What is all of this about?"

"Mr. Murphy please give me your fax number. I will fax over the needed verification and confidentiality agreement. Once you fax your response we can discuss this case in detail."

I gave her my fax number and then I went to my office to receive the fax. As the paper work came over I looked up the office online and sure enough, the head of the department appeared to be the woman who called me. I returned the fax with a copy of my ID and signed documents. Sheila thanked me for responding so promptly. "So what's going on?" In my mind I knew it was some groupie claiming to have my child.

January walked into my office and closed the door since I had the call on speaker. She sat at my desk in front of me. "We currently have Angel Fairchild in child protective services. She was taken into custody after an incident where her mother Bonita Fairchild pushed her in public. Angel says that her mother has done worse to her."

"Ok, I know who Bonita Fairchild is. She's one of the board members at my previous label. I've never met her child."

"Currently we're going to determine maternity of the child, Torrie Rowe claims to be the mother." My mouth fell open as I looked at January. She stared at the phone but she didn't say anything. "Ms. Rowe claims that you are the father. Ms. Fairchild claims that she went to a clinic for fertilization. Have you ever donated at a clinic sir?"

"No, never."

"Is there any way that Ms. Fairchild could've obtained your semen?"

"I never had sex with Bonita."

"Not even oral compilation?"

"Not even that." The memory of being in Bonita's house as she showed me pictures of her little girl flooded my memory. I couldn't remember what the little girl looked like. I just knew I couldn't take my eyes off of her.

"If you are in fact the father of Angel Fairchild, we will need to have you sign away your parental rights or meet with our mediation team to determine the basics."

"How soon can we find out? I need answers."

"We have an accredited DNA facility in downtown Oakland if that is the most convenient location for you."

"How soon can I go, and is there additional cost to have the results expedited? I would like to get to the bottom of this as soon as possible."

"If you can go down there today, since this case is so high profile, we can have the results by tomorrow."

"Good then I'll fly out tomorrow."

"Mr. Murphy that may not be necessary and I think you should wait for the results."

"Something is telling me to book my ticket now."

"Tickets," January watched my eyes.

I wrote down the address and then I told January the few things she didn't hear. "Torrie was pregnant?"

"She told me she had an abortion. I don't know what's going on but I intend to get to the bottom of it."

"We need to get to the bottom of it. I know you don't think you're going to LA without me!"

"Baby, you just gave birth. Your momma will get you for

leaving the house this soon. What are we supposed to do, take the baby around all of these people?"

January stood up, "the choice is yours. You can either wait until you think it's a good time for me to travel to go. Or your take me with you. Either way you are NOT going without me!"

Torrie

My lawyer served the notice that I'm leaving the label. It has been interesting since then. My lawyer said I'm receiving invitation after invitation from other labels. Somehow a not so flattering video of me going off on someone started circulating. Once that one leaked a bunch of them started to mysteriously float around. I held my breath, as I just knew my career was over. Myles asked me if it was the end of the world if I couldn't be on stage singing and dancing anymore. At first it did feel that way. Now, it doesn't feel like the end of the world. I actually liked working on Norie's philanthropy project. I've been researching different foundations to find ones that would be good partners for Norie's foundation. I'm thinking about taking some courses, and seeing how I can help.

I know Bonita leaked those videos in an attempt to ruin me. What she didn't realize is that she created a monster. My publicist and her team were on top of it. They spun everything, and my likeability ratings started soaring. A lot of people said that they were tired of the nice girl act, and that they were happy to see me stand up for myself. I became even more powerful and lovable.

My family law lawyer called me as if she was waiting for the clock to say 8am. "We need to schedule a meeting, I will have the DNA results for you and Mr. Murphy today."

My heart dropped, "you mean you told Novian?" Everything got hot and I wanted to run, but there was nowhere to run to.

"Of course, if he is the father he has rights just as equally as you do. Since Bonita tried to pass Angel's birth off as her own there are no records filed for an adoption. There's no paper trail of an egg donation. I want to go after her for kidnapping and regardless she's going up for child abuse and child endangerment."

"Did you talk to him? Did he sound mad?"

There was a long pause. "I didn't speak with him personally. Child protective services did, I can imagine he was shocked. Wouldn't you think that's the appropriate response in this situation?"

"Do you have a number for him? I need to explain myself."

"Torrie, I need you to focus! You can worry about his reaction after you've taken care of business. Now, let's schedule this meeting."

I called Myles crying after my lawyer and I got off of the phone. I wanted to run and hide. Myles said he was calling in to work so that he could come be with me. I wanted to tell him not to do that, but I agreed.

Myles came with me to the lawyer's office as she revealed the results of the DNA testing. I wasn't concerned about that part, I knew the results since the beginning. I wanted to know when I would get my daughter and what Novian was going to do. My lawyer called child protective services, who brought Novian on the line. "Hello Mr. Murphy this is Sheila Barrymore calling from the Los Angeles County Child Protective Services office again. Do you have a moment to talk?"

"Yes," then he spoke in the background. "I'm putting you on speaker so that my wife can hear." I wanted to tell him she didn't need to be involved in this conversation, but my lawyer touched my hand as if she could sense my reaction.

"Mr. Murphy we have Ms. Rowe on the line as well as her lawyer. We have the results of the DNA test."

"Please proceed," I could hear Novian breathing. He was anxious and I know he's going to be furious with me.

"The results show 99.99% match for the maternity to Ms. Rowe. The results also show 99.99% match for the paternity to Mr. Murphy for Angel Fairchild."

Novian was quiet for a minute; all I could hear was breathing and mumbling. "Torrie!" Novian sounded so angry. Myles rubbed my back and shoulders as I lowered my head. "HOW COULD YOU LIE TO ME! YOU HAVE NO IDEA OF WHAT I WENT THROUGH AND SHE'S HERE! WERE YOU NEVER GOING TO TELL ME? WERE YOU NEVER GOING TO LET ME KNOW THERE WAS A PIECE OF ME IN THIS WORLD WHEN I THOUGHT I HAD NOTHING? YOUR SELFISHNESS KNOWS NO BOUNDARIES!" He was about to continue, but I could hear January saying something to him in the background. "I WANT MY DAUGHTER! WHEN CAN I COME GET HER?"

"Why do you think you deserve her over me?"

"BECAUSE WE'RE ON THE SAME PAGE! YOU AND BONITA CRAFTED THIS LIE AND WE KNEW NOTHING ABOUT IT! I NEED TO MAKE IT UP TO HER! SHE NEEDS ME! YOU'RE A LIAR AND SELFISH!"

Myles took a deep breath like he wanted to say something, but he was trying to hold his tongue. "Novian you don't understand!"

"WHAT IS THERE FOR ME TO UNDERSTAND? YOU CHOSE TO FORGET ABOUT MY FEELINGS WANTS AND NEEDS. ALL THESE YEARS AND EVERYTHING WE WENT THROUGH AFTERWARDS AND YOU SAID NOTHING! YOU SAT IN MY FACE AND HELD ON TO YOUR LIE! YOU WEREN'T PROTECTING ME, YOU WERE PROTECTING YOURSELF!"

"Mr. Murphy, we can understand your anger and your feelings of betrayal. I think you two should continue this conversation offline. Initially we're going to have the courts release

Angel Fairchild to Ms. Rowe. We can determine custody in a family court."

"We will get a lawyer to expedite these proceedings." Novian's wife said.

"Excellent, please provide my information to your lawyer so that we can move along." My lawyer said.

"WHERE IS BONITA?"

"She's running from the police at this moment."

"I WANT TO MEET MY DAUGHTER IMMEDIATELY!"

"Novian, stop yelling! You've already made your point you need to calm down."

"WHO DO YOU THINK YOU'RE TALKING TO? I'M NOT THE SAME PERSON YOU USED TO BOSS AROUND! I'M SO ANGRY AND DISGUSTED WITH YOU! EVERYTHING IS FLASHING THROUGH MY MIND RIGHT NOW, EVEN YOUR LAST OPPORTUNITY TO COME CLEAN AND YOU SAID NOTHING! I HATE YOU SO MUCH!"

"You hate me? You don't understand, you wouldn't…"

"Um! Again, I'm going to urge you two to take this offline." My lawyer said.

Novian

I paced back and forth, my breath felt like fire in my lungs. How could she do this to me! I can't believe that there is no limit to her selfishness. January sat there listening to me rant, but she didn't say anything. When I ran out of names to call Torrie I fell down on the bed. "I wanted her! I was a kid; I didn't know how to act. I would've stepped up, she didn't even give me a chance to."

"Novian let me get out of my feelings for a minute to play devil's advocate. I hear everything you're saying. You're right at some point she should've come clean. However, when she told you she was pregnant how did you respond?" I didn't say anything, "right cause you never responded. She had to have that conversation with your brother. Did you check for her even once after you got the news from your brother?" I didn't say anything. "I'm just saying I know how it is when you don't know what you're going to do. You were kids trying to make adult decisions. I'm not taking her side, but you need to calm down. You know first hand how difficult it was to get away from Bonita as an artist. Can you even imagine what she's gone through over these years? It sounds like Bonita played both of you, if you want to be mad at someone be mad at Bonita. Being mad isn't going to change anything about all of this. You've established your feelings, but now you need to think about your daughter, and what's best for her." January's voice trailed off. "I didn't give you your first born. This brings Torrie back into our lives."

My wife was trying to be strong for me. I noticed the crack, and I pulled her into my arms. "Jenny-Bean is still my first. You are my wife because we fell in love. I don't want to be with Torrie. You are my peace, my strength, and my rock. Torrie was my childhood obsession. What we have is real, and I owe everything I am and everything I have to you. Please don't second guess us." I kissed her face.

"So we're going to LA?"

"We're going to LA."

Torrie

Myles drove us back to his place. He sat on the couch and put his arm out for me to sit next to him. "How you holding up?" He rubbed my back as he waited.

341

"I'm not! Novian hates me! Norie is probably going to hate me too."

"Norie?"

"That's what I named her in my heart."

"Why do you care so much about people hating you? Everybody isn't going to like everything you do. You were a kid trying to do the right thing by everybody. Whether Novian sees it or not, he would not be who he is today if you didn't do what you did. What matters now is Angel and what she needs. You can't focus on Novian and whatever he's feeling. Leave that for his wife to sort through."

"You're right," I kissed him. "Thank you."

He rubbed my arm, "I'm sure this isn't the right time to ask, but I need to know. Do you want to have anymore kids?"

I couldn't answer that right now. "Myles right now all I can think about is Norie."

"That's fair, I guess I picked the wrong moment."

I heard the front door open and close. "Brutus is in the hallway, so that must mean the diva herself is here!" Mykai announced as he came around the corner. "What are you wearing?" He looked me up and down on the couch. "Jeans? I mean the blouse is ok, but what shoes are you wearing? And what's with your hair? Wha…"

"Mykai, it's been a long day. Leave her alone."

"I am the cure for a long day! Take me to the Vine and everyone will be asking who's that gorgeous man with Torrie. You will be the talk of the town for months."

"Mykai!" Myles' voice rumbled off of the walls.

"Ok! Ok! Forgive me for trying to bring some sparkle to both of your lives." Then Mykai went to his room.

"You want me to go with you tomorrow to pick her up?"

"You can't keep missing work, no. I think we'll need some time to sort things out."

Myles hesitated, "how much time?"

"I don't know, I can't say."

"You better not cheat on me."

****

My assistant called me as I pulled up to Mimi's place. Novian and his family checked in to their hotel and he was waiting for us. I dreaded facing him. She told me which room number he was in and for us to go there to avoid the public.

As I walked up the steps to Mimi's place Norie opened the door and came out to the porch. She looked really sad; maybe she didn't want to live with me. Maybe she feels like I abandoned her. "Hi."

"Hi," I stopped on the second step.

"I'm so confused. I have questions."

"Ok, I'm sure your father does too. He flew in with his family this morning."

She swallowed, and then she started crying. "I have a father!" She put her hands up to her face as she cried.

I hurried up the stairs and I put my arms around her. "Of course you do!" I kissed her forehead, "he didn't know about you though. Can I explain everything to you both at once? I'm sure he has questions just like you do."

As we put Norie's things in my car, I told Mimi that I wanted to hire her as well. On the car ride over neither one of us said anything. I looked over at Norie and she was quietly looking around with shades on similar to mine. I couldn't believe this moment was real. All these years I've wondered about her and here she is. I gave my car to the valet and then Norie and I took the elevator up to the top. There was a security guard just outside of the elevator. "Ms. Rowe," he nodded at me.

"Hi," I told Norie to come on. My heart was pounding, I was so scared. I knocked on the door and January opened the door. "Hi."

January's eyes went straight to Norie and she smiled. "Hello, I'm your stepmom January. Come in, come in."

A little girl came running to the door as we walked in. "I made a picture for you!" She announced as she ran to Norie.

"For me?" Norie looked so surprised as she smiled.

"My daddy said you're my big sister. I always wanted a big sister."

"You did?" January smiled at her daughter.

"Yep!"

"Since when?"

"Since we got on the plane to come see her."

Novian stepped into the walkway, "hi."

"MURPHY?" Norie gasped as she covered her mouth. "Murphy is my dad?"

Novian blushed, "I hope that's ok?"

"I'm so confused!" Norie said holding on to her temples.

"Your father has been saying the exact same thing. Torrie, I guess it's up to you to explain everything." January gestured towards the couches.

Novian didn't move when we started walking, he kept his eyes on Norie. When she got close he asked her for a hug. When they hugged Norie started crying hard and loud. She buried her face in his chest and they stayed like that for a minute. January put drinks out as we waited for Novian and Norie to come out of the hallway. I sat on the love seat thinking Norie would sit next to me. However when she and Novian finally came into the living room, Novian sat next to January and Norie sat under Novian. The little girl brought her pad of paper and crayons spread out in the middle of the floor. Norie and Novian had the same expression on their faces as they waited for me to say something. I don't think I've ever cared so much about my delivery than in this moment. I started at the beginning for Norie's sake. I could tell Novian wanted to go off again, but when he started breathing January bumped him and gave him a look. Novian took a deep breath and then he told me he could forgive me if I forgave him for leaving me hanging. January kept watching everything I did, and even when she walked out of the room to get the baby I know her ears were extended back in the room. Norie got excited holding her baby brother. Nobody cared that it was killing me to sit here with Novian and his happy little family.

Novian

"I saw your pictures one time." Norie was hanging on to my every word. "I was at Bonita's house and I couldn't take my eyes off of your pictures. I thought you were the most beautiful little girl I've ever seen."

"Did she look like me?" Jenny-Bean asked.

"Of course, you two still look alike." That made Jenny-Bean happy while Torrie looked like she wanted to say something smart about it.

"You came to my home?"

"Only once and you were still at school. I should've known then that there was something about you. I wasn't looking at your pictures looking for traces of me. I just knew you were gorgeous and I couldn't stop looking at you."

Angel's eyes continued to water. "She would get so mad when I ask about my father. I know she wanted Matt to fill that void, but we can't stand each other. Besides, I knew I wasn't white."

"How did you know?"

She held out her arm to me, "I'm too brown."

"Um, you're the same complexion as Halle Barry and Victoria Rowell, both of them are biracial." January shot me another look. I guess I was arguing the wrong point.

"I guess, but my point is that I knew he wasn't my father. I have so many questions for you. I can't believe Murphy is my dad. There's no way they can come back and say they made a mistake and take you away from me is there?"

I looked at Torrie; I could tell she felt some kind of way about Angel being so focused on me. "No sweetheart, I'm your father. You're stuck with me."

"Can I change my name, I don't want her name."

Torrie looked at the floor, "what name do you want to change your name to?"

"Yours of course! I want to get to know you as much as I can." She was so excited she was missing how any of her words were affecting Torrie.

January looked at Torrie then she looked at me. "What about

Murphy-Rowe?" I nodded at Torrie.

Angel's eyes got big when she looked at Torrie who was quietly sitting to the side in her feelings. She stood up putting junior on her shoulder, and then she walked over to Torrie's couch and sat next to her. She kissed her cheek and wiped her tear. "Why are you crying?"

"I feel like you guys blame me." Torrie started crying out loud.

Jenny-Bean got off of the floor and ran to me. January took the baby from Angel so she could hug her momma. "I'm going to live with you most of the time. I never had a dad; I have a lifetime of questions for him. This is weird but we'll figure it out."

Chapter 14

Jenny-Bean and I flew out to LA to pick-up Angel. I'm impressed with the level of self-control Torrie has been using with her personality. I guess I'm not the only person who has grown. I expected at least one diva fit when they came to our hotel that day. When I told January I wanted to come pickup Angel to bring her home, she took a deep breath. She didn't try to tell me I couldn't go, she simply said she doesn't trust Torrie not to try to pull at my heart when she has me alone. As a compromise I volunteered my babygirl to come with me and keep me honest. Besides I needed to make sure she didn't feel neglected during all of this. Jenny-Bean was so excited to go on an adventure as she called it with just me. Especially when I told her we were going to pick up Angel.

When the limo reached Torrie's front gate there was a car parked out front and Amos was standing next to it. I told the driver to pull over. I told Jenny-Bean to stay in the car and then I got out. "What are you doing out here?"

"I was told you're coming out here and to make sure you're cool." We hugged.

"Who told you that?"

"The big man himself, Big Vic Cardell."

"Why would Big Vic care about my life?"

"I don't have all those answers for you. Your flight doesn't leave until the morning; please tell me we're doing something fun. I don't want to watch you and Torrie fuss."

I smiled at my best friend; "I'm going to go in here real quick. Then I'm taking Jenny-Bean to Universal Studios. You wanna roll with us?"

"You bringing your daughter around Torrie. January is going to kick your butt! I'll wait out here, then you can follow me back to the hotel to drop my car off."

"That works, see you in a minute."

"AAAA! A quickie then lets go, don't have me waiting all day out here."

"Hey! I don't cheat on my wife."

Amos started laughing, "you get close enough is all I'm saying."

When I opened the car door Jenny-Bean poked her head out. "Hi Uncle Amos! Hi!"

"Hey baby girl!"

When we pulled up in front of the house Angel was outside excitedly waving at the car. I hurried and opened the door so that Jenny-Bean could rush her big sister and hug her. "Hi Dad, hi Ursula."

"You all packed and ready to go?"

"Mom wants to talk to you before we leave."

I swallowed; I didn't want to see Torrie. I prayed that she didn't say or do anything that would make me have to put her in her place. When I walked in the door I turned my eyes. She had on short shorts and a small top. "Novian my schedule changed, I'm going to need to stay in New York three extra days. Is that a problem for you? Cause if it is, you could bring her back to her nanny."

"No, it's not a problem. She can stay with us as long as she wants to." Then I turned towards the door.

"Wait, I don't get a hug hello or nothing?"

"Not dressed like that, you don't get nothing from me."

"Your wife got you that whipped that you can't even speak to other women?"

"Stop messing with me Torrie, keep this up and January will be the one to come pick her up and drop her off. I don't cheat on my wife."

"Oh so, I'm the only one who had the pleasure of the cheating Novian?"

"You want me to argue with you so you can try to emotionally pull me in. You don't even want me, you never wanted me. I was always an after thought to you. My life has gotten ten times better since January and I got together. After everything she has done for me and will do for me in the future, why would I jeopardize that for this? Everything with you has never gone anywhere. You…" she walked up on me and kissed me. I didn't want to kiss her back but my brain turned off.

"I'm sorry, I've been wanting to do that since you and Norie were sitting on the couch next to each other. We are her parents, we are bonded for life, and I will always have you no matter who's in my life. When you're ready for me, don't bring the kid." Then she walked away switching hard. "Norie's bags are in the living room on your left." She called out.

Even though she wasn't wearing lipstick I touched my mouth to make sure there wasn't any on my mouth. I took a deep breath and then I picked up the bags. This woman is going to be the death of me.

When Amos got in the car he looked stuck. I introduced Angel to her Uncle Amos and then I told him the story. He sat there blinking for a few minutes and then he said she looked like both of us. Jenny-Bean looks more like me than Angel does, but I see little pieces of me in her face. She has my taste buds though. She doesn't like any of the foods that I don't like.

Quite a few times Angel would just stare at me. Or she'd walk up to me and hug me. Jenny-Bean would wiggle her way in the middle of our hug. At the hotel we had a junk food spread in the middle of the floor. Angel asked me which candy was my favorite. I told her I used to love snickers, but I hadn't had one in years. I told her I had to keep up my workouts and over indulging in my favorites would cost me in the gym. Angel wanted to know everything about me. She kept asking me question after question.

I told her that we were having a family dinner and she was going to be our surprise guest of honor.

Angel looked at Jenny-Bean who was passed out in my lap. "How did you meet my mom?"

"Middle school, she was so nervous about performing."

Angel's eyes lit up, "please tell me the story."

I thought about it for a minute, I took a deep breath.

She was new to our school and walking with her cousins. She was trying to look tough like her cousins, but I could tell she wasn't. When I took my seat in my first period class she walked in nervously just before the bell. She handed her paper to the teacher. "Class this is our new student Torrie. Torrie, you can have that desk," she pointed to the desk next to mine.

Torrie sat down and then she looked around the room. When she looked at me, she looked me up and down then she rolled her eyes. She didn't even know me to be rolling her eyes at me, it made me mad. Then I noticed that her attitude wasn't reserved for just me. She had an attitude with everybody. It wasn't fair for her to act like that with me, she didn't even know me. I didn't like girls like her. They got on my nerves. At lunch I was with my friends, when Torrie walked in the lunchroom with her cousins it made me mad that I noticed her. Amos looked to see whom I was frowning at. He asked me who she was, and I told him she was a new student. He smiled at me and asked why she made me mad. I didn't know why she did, but she did. Jamesha her cousin walked over happy as could be to approach Amos. "Hey baby!" She had no shame.

Amos looked at her like she got on his nerves. "Whatever, who's your friend?"

Jamesha deflated, "that's my cousin Torrie, she's new here."

"Hi Torrie," he said ignoring Jamesha.

She looked at our small group of friends. All of the girls liked Amos. Then the rest of us were just his friends. Amos would tell us about the girls he messed around with. "Are these your friends?" I hated the way she wiggled her little finger around.

"Yes."

Torrie sucked her teeth, "oh man. I thought you were somebody."

All of her cousins started laughing at us. "What you trying to say?" Amos said now getting in her face.

She smiled up at him like she liked seeing him mad. "Show me who your friends are, and I'll show you who you are." Then she pointed at each of us. "Loser! Loser! Loser! Um! Double Loser!" She wasn't even phased by Amos' anger.

"Listen here HOE!"

"OOH!" We said to pump up what he said.

"HOE! HOE! HOE! Got me feeling like Santa in this piece. Nobody asked you what you think. You need to go somewhere with all that noise."

Torrie stood there smiling at Amos, "how you know my cousins are hoes?"

"TORRIE!" One of her cousins said.

"Jamesha and the rest didn't tell you about me?"

"Let's go!" Jamesha said pulling Torrie out of the cafeteria.

Torrie smiled at me as her cousin pulled her out of the cafeteria.

I looked at Angel as she processed my story. "So you liked her from the first time you saw her?"

I blushed, "yep. She didn't care, your mom has always been beautiful to me."

"Why are you married to January?"

"Torrie didn't really want me. January has always looked out for me and taken care of me. She helps me think things through, and she wants to be with me, build with me, and just love me."

"My mom doesn't love you?"

"In her own way she does, I've out grown the type of love she's offering."

"Ms. Fairchild was very strict about boys. She set all these goals for me to hit and failure was not an option. I feel so lost."

"What do you want to do?"

"I really want to continue working on my foundation. When I told her I wanted to join the Peace Corps she lost it. I want to help people in some way, money isn't everything."

"I want you to be happy and feel satisfaction in the course of your life. What did your mom say when you mentioned the Peace Corps?"

Angel smiled reminding me of a younger version of her mom. "She was excited and ready to do anything to help me. She's already been a tremendous help for my foundation. This is so weird, I feel like I have so much freedom now."

"Well, let's keep boys on the back burner for now. I don't know that I can handle that yet."

She smiled like Torrie, "would you get mad?"

"I don't know what I would do. Please don't put me in that situation. I know you're going to date **LATER**! Let's leave that for later. I love you little girl and I don't want some idiot messing up your life, and I don't want you bringing trouble to some unsuspecting fool."

She held on to her Torrie look, "yes daddy!"

******

"Renee, what's so important that we couldn't switch the date?" Briscoe said putting his arm around my momma's chair."

"Jenny-Bean wants to introduce you to someone." I had baby girl wait with Angel cause I know she couldn't hold water.

Jenny-Bean proudly brought Angel out by the hand. Angel looked around the table. "Lil Urs who's this?" Briscoe asked.

Lee's eyes bucked, "TORRIE OWES ME FOUR HUNDRED DOLLARS PLUS INTEREST!" He stood up as he announced.

"Torrie?" My sister said questioning Lee. "How you know this isn't that other girl he was dating' child? What was her name?" Leona snapped her fingers as if that would make her remember.

"Shay!" My momma announced as she moved around.

"Is she your daughter?" Briscoe asked me.

"Everyone this is my daughter Angel Murphy-Rowe. Angel this is my momma and her husband Briscoe. This is your Uncle Lee and his wife and those are your cousins. This is Leona and her husband. Their kids are over there too. This is Lee and Leona's dad, Mr. Dozier."

My mom stood up and walked towards Angel as she examined her. As if she didn't believe me. "I'm your Grand mommy Ursula, it's nice to meet you." Then she hugged her."

Everyone hugged her and introduced themselves personally. Briscoe said nothing as he sat to the side watching. "This is what you're talking about?" He asked my momma.

"Yes, it's not for you, it's for them. You won't be around forever, at least give them what they need to feel connected."

"Why won't I, Leroy is still here!" He pointed at Mr. Dozier who flipped him off.

Angel went over to the teenager table nervously as she said hi. The kids introduced themselves, and then everything was normal.

Torrie

My publicist held the article in front of me while he read. Every horrible thing I've done and even some made up stuff was in this article. This girl who claims to be my sister is claiming that I've blackballed her career because I'm upset about the tumultuous love affair her father had with my mother resulting in my birth. When he read that I was high when the gunmen shot at my group I knew Bonita was involved, especially with all of my business being out there and not one mention of Norie. She'd be the biggest bomb to drop. The article said I didn't know the guy who shot back, and I was there arguing with Amber about our love triangle. I leaned forward on the table as I grabbed my hair. The article named Amber Wallace

355

as my attacker in the fight that busted my eye. The article said that Amber comes from a family of hoodlums. Thugs and criminals known all around Oakland. I didn't know if that was true or not, but judging by the way she laid Josie and I out I wouldn't doubt it. Electricity shot up my leg as I thought about Malcolm. I hadn't let myself think about him for years. I told the publicist he had to make this go away. He snatched the papers up as he stood up. "This is a big mess!"

"This is why I pay you. You need to make this go away. There are untruths mixed in with truths. I need it to all go away! Do your job!"

"I'll call you!" He stormed out of the club.

I went out on the dance floor trying to dance my frustration away. Myles came and then he sat down for a while watching me as I kept dancing trying to clear my head. I didn't want to cry. I wanted it to all go away. I didn't want to think about Amber or Malcolm, or the guy who took advantage of my momma. I wanted to leave the past in the past. I needed to get my head on straight before Norie came home. When I needed water I went back to my table.

Myles came back to the table, "what's wrong?"

"Too much to talk about."

He looked irritated, "you know. Ever since your kid came you've been neglecting your man. I'm getting tired of this."

"Fine! Then leave! I can buy another one. Myles I don't have time for this."

Myles looked like he wanted to choke me. He stood up and walked away. I don't need to be here. I stood up to leave when my phone started ringing and it said unknown. I wasn't going to answer it but it could've been my publicist. "Hello?"

The deep voice said, "Torrie!" And everything in my body

came alive. This couldn't be.

"Yes, who is this?"

"You need to go somewhere so you can hear me!" Malcolm's voice was deep and unaffectionate.

I gasped and then I hurried through the crowd towards the back where I could hear clearly. Myles watched me for a minute but I didn't care. Malcolm was on MY PHONE! "Hello?" I said as soon as I reached the owner's back office.

"Torrie!"

I gasped again, "OH MY GOD MALCOLM!!! Where have you been? You completely disappeared! I was just...."

"This is not a social call!" I couldn't hold back my disappointment. "The tabloids are about to run some pretty damaging stories about you, what position is your publicist taking?"

"He called me a few hours ago, but I wasn't sure. I thought you were him." He wasn't calling me to free me from the nonsense.

"Call him now on three way!"

"Ok! Ok! Hold on." I brought my publicist on the line and they discussed in detail his plan of attack on the situation. My publicist asked why any of this mattered to Malcolm; he simply said this little rumor has bigger implications than we need to understand. When I hurried to get my plea in for Malcolm, he hung up in my face. I shook my phone like that would bring him back on the line. Call it a relapse, but I wanted the real thing in that moment. I wanted Malcolm. I stormed out of the club to my car. Myles followed me out. "Where are you going?"

"Away! Leave me alone Myles."

As I started to sit in my seat he looked at me with an evil look. "Who's Bonita?"

I stood up; I stared at him for a minute. "Blood sucking leeches!" I stomped my foot, "how much did she offer you?"

"She told me to name my price."

"For what?"

"For you, I needed to keep you here as long as I could."

"And then what?"

He shrugged, "I don't know."

I got out of my car, suddenly I thought of it exploding when I tried to start the engine. I threw my keys at Myles! "Keep it!"

I called Josie crying and scared. I told her about Bonita's threat through Myles. I begged her to come get me. I stood by the entrance in the direct light of the doorway. I pretended to flirt with the bouncer. I ran to the car in my heels when Josie showed up. If I didn't leave my momma at home I would've disappeared.

When we got to the house my momma looked confused. She said she thought I was home already. When I asked her why she said she thought she heard me in my room. I told my momma to come and we hurried out of the door. We weren't inside two minutes and all four of Josie's tires were going flat. I grabbed my momma's hand and I told her to get in the car. We locked the doors and I told Josie to drive. She said the tires were flat. I told her to ride the rims and I'd buy her a new car. The tires spun over the gravel but we made it out of the gate. You could hear the damage as metal grinded on the concrete. We slid to a stop, we were going nowhere fast. I told Josie to set off the panic button on her car. We weren't sitting for two minutes when police and the area patrol came. I told them there was someone in my home. When they asked me who I said Bonita Fairchild.

Novian

I looked at the clock and it was almost two in the morning. "Hello?"

"Novian! Please keep Norie with you, don't let her come home!"

Torrie's tears jarred me awake. "What's wrong? What's wrong?"

January looked at me as she tried to focus. "Bonita was going to kill me tonight. She was in my house. She wrote a suicide note and everything. In the note I was taking responsibility for killing Josie."

"She's dead?"

"No, but I called her to come get me from the club. The officer said Bonita didn't anticipate me telling Josie to ride the rims in her car that had four flat tires. I was supposed to be so distraught about the story that's going to run today about me that I killed Josie and myself. Novian she could've hurt my momma. She was going to kill me Novian!" Torrie cried hard into the phone. "Why do I deserve death? She was going to kill me!"

"Can you come out here?"

"Who is that?" January asked with sleep in her voice.

"Torrie," January shot up and waited for me to explain.

"I don't know what she had planned for me. I'm afraid of cars, I can't trust anything or anyone."

"Hold on Torrie, let me talk to my wife." I put the phone down as January kept taking deep breaths. "Bonita tried to kill Torrie tonight. She was going to make it look like a suicide."

"Novian we have a household to be concerned with. We can't

bring that drama here. Angel is safe with us. The police will put her in protective custody."

"I have to do something."

January kicked her feet angrily. She huffed for a minute. "Tell her to sit tight. Call Amos in the morning. He'll know what to do."

"Torrie, where are you?"

"At the police station."

"Stay there, we're going to figure something out."

Torrie agreed but she didn't have a choice. I called Amos right away, and he answered on the fourth ring. "Why should I care about what happens to her? As long as Angel is cool I don't care."

"Angel won't be ok if something happens to Torrie. Think about my babygirl and all she's been through. This would devastate her. Please help me, I don't know what to do that won't put me in harm's way."

Amos exhaled loudly in the background. Then his girl started going off about him waking her up. They went back and forth cursing each other for a minute. Then he cleared his throat and came back to me. He told me to let the sun come up and he'd have an answer for me.

I was restless the rest of the night. January fell asleep and I was left to my thoughts. Why is Bonita so evil? How could she convince the world that Torrie wanted to kill herself?

I popped up when my phone rang at almost eight in the morning. Amos said that Big Vic called him this morning before he could call him. He said Big Vic is sending his son to take care of Torrie. He told me to just know that she was in good hands.

Torrie

I awoke to this guy who looked familiar, but I couldn't remember his name, shaking my shoulder. "Good morning Torrie, time to rise and shine."

"Ok," I snapped my finger trying to remember his name.

"Vic, why don't you ever remember my name?"

"Do you have any idea how many people I meet on a daily basis? I can't remember everyone's name." I stood up.

"I'm Vic and this is my brother Rich."

I looked at the browner version of his face. Rich was just as tall and just as handsome. I smiled at him, "hello." Then I looked at Vic who was looking me over. "You're from Oakland right?"

"So you do remember me?"

"Of course I remember you, you're the one who gave me the heads up. I just couldn't remember your name."

"Ok good, so lets go."

I looked at my momma who was knocked out sleep on her cot. "Where are we going?"

"Your house."

Panic hit me, "we can't go back there. She knew how to get in my house past my security system and my guards. I don't feel safe there."

He put his arms around me, "my brother is top flight security. No one or nothing gets past him. His daughter bought a house and it's locked up like Fort Knox, can't nobody get in there without permission. We're going to re-secure your house and you will be fine. Come on."

I went over to my momma and I gently woke her up. I told her it was time for us to go. She looked from Vic to Rich and then she asked me who they were. I told her they came to help us.

In the car, I told Vic about the suicide letter that Bonita had planted in my room. He said he already knew about it, and he knew about the article that was supposed to be the reason why. There were men all over the grounds to my house. Rich explained that they took out the security system that I had, and they put in a new system. He said there were trips all over the property. When those alarms were tripped then the police department would be called and cameras would focus on that location. He said he could set the facial recognition to kill on site.

Rich spoke matter-of-factly, but he didn't look at me too long or hard. "Rich are you married?"

Rich looked at his brother like I irritated him. Vic smiled at his brother, "the lady asked you a question."

"No."

"You're in a relationship though?"

"It's complicated."

"Why you all up in my brother's business?"

"He's handsome, and I'm trying to understand why he's not checking me out."

Rich looked me up and down, "you fine but so what. Both of my brothers have hit and I'm not interested."

Vic smiled at me, "both?" I was lost.

He pointed at Vic, "and Malcolm. I'm cool!"

"Malcolm is your brother?" I couldn't hold in my curiosity. He looks nothing like Malcolm. Rich is tall, brown, with lighter brown eyes. His hair is wavy like Vic's. Rich and Vic have the same thin mustaches. Neither one of them look a thing like Malcolm.

"What did I say? Bottom-line I'm not interested. I know it don't take much to encourage you so if you can't handle being in my presence then go back inside."

"You wanna give some to my brother too?" Vic smiled at me.

"That's your perception of me? I'm a hoe?"

"Yes," he gave me an *and* expression.

Vic started laughing as he turned his back for a moment. "Come on man, be nice."

I smiled but that hurt. I know I've been reckless in the past, but I slowed down a lot. I went back in the house where a girl with a bucket explained that I had all of those bugs in my house. Bonita had been watching and monitoring everything I did. Thank goodness I never met with my legal team and new representation in my house. They checked my cars and everything out. All of my locks were rekeyed, security personnel were fired and new personnel replaced them. Rich suggested that I adopt ex police dogs as added security. He gave me the information for a couple of foundations locally. I needed to make sure the dogs would be compatible with my momma's barn full of animals. Her little mini farm.

My publicist called me and said the article didn't run. He said the company somehow got a virus in their system and everything has been corrupted. I exhaled, and then I told my assistant to find a detective. All of this drama had to stop. As Rich's team gathered their things to go I thanked him for everything. He told me to thank his brother and that this was business for him. Then he handed me the bill. Vic was finishing up a phone call as I approached him. "Thank you for everything. I feel safe already."

He touched my cheek with the back of his hand. "You're welcome Torrie, you need to stop playing and call me."

"Your brother acts like I have the plague."

"That's because you're off limits to him. Besides he's in love..."

"You're not in love?"

"Nope." He smiled at me.

"How do you know Novian?"

"His friend works for me. I don't really know him."

"When do you go home?"

"Tomorrow," he raised his eyebrows at me.

"Will you..."

"Yes! Of course! It took you long enough to ask. Let's get rid of my brother." He smiled really big as he walked away.

Novian

"Amos is she ok? Is she safe?"

"She's fine. Big Vic sent Vic out. He and his brother went over her security in the house and the grounds. Apparently she thought she had security, when in all actuality she was a sitting duck. She fired her security provider, they got her ducks in a row."

"Is my daughter going to be safe out there?"

"She'll be safe at the house. I can't tell you about the rest."

I put my car in park. "Thank you for helping me out. January was not going to go for her coming out here."

"Was she supposed to be any safer out here than out there?"

"Forget you! She would've been safe with me."

Amos laughed, "not after January got through with her."

We laughed together, "let me get in here and get this food."

"Where are you?"

"They voted for barbecue, so I'm in Jack London Square."

"Everett and Jones sounds real good right about now. Don't buy out the spot superstar."

I had a hoodie on with my braid tucked in the collar. I had a hat and shades on as I walked in the side door to pickup my phone order. No one paid me any real attention. It's the stupidest stuff. I get such a kick out of going out in public when no one recognizes me. Back in the day I used to make noise for attention. Now I try to slide in and out like I'm an undercover citizen. I gave the girl my name and I saw someone look up out the corner of my left eye. I paid and then the girl said it would be ten more minutes. Our order was huge cause January's family was coming over. I looked to the left and I smiled at Sandy. She watched my eyes as she jumped up and hurried to hug me. I don't know what she was looking for but her enthusiasm wavered. I hugged her anyways. "How you been?"

"Auntie Camille made me get a job." She rolled her eyes.

"What's wrong with that?"

"She just don't want me hanging out with Darius' family."

"Why would it be a good idea for you to hang with them?"

"Darius was more of a father to me then my dad ever was." Then she moved closer so I could hear her whisper. "Who is Malcolm Latour?"

I had a sinking feeling, "where'd you hear that name?"

"Around, Darius' brother has been looking for a way to get at him."

"Who's his brother?"

"Ramses, you haven't heard of him?"

I shook my head no, "why should I?"

"True! You are too square for your own good."

"Being square keeps me alive and drama free. How old are you?"

She smiled, "if you don't know I'm not telling."

"All I'm saying is that in your early twenties this may seem exciting. Give it time, you'll embrace a square life."

"You tired of your wife yet?" She stuck her chest at me and my skin crawled.

"Sandreen, you forgot we were almost brother and sister? I don't look at you like that."

"But we're not related," she kept trying to rub those things against me. I kept backing up, she was making me nauseous.

"Stop it! Don't ever disrespect yourself or me like this again. For one! I'm HAPPILY married! For two! Even though we're not related by blood you're family. You need to get your life right girl! Respect yourself enough to be about something more than just sex. You gonna end up used up and tossed to the side."

"My aunt didn't get tossed to the side."

"But your momma did, and your aunt got her butt kicked on a regular basis. If either one of those options sounds appealing, continue on your current path."

"Your order is ready," the girl called out. She looked like she wanted to let us finish before she interrupted.

They had to put my order in two boxes it was so large. A guy from the kitchen grabbed the other box for me. When I walked past Sandy I told her to grow up.

I called the barbershop and left a message. I said everything Sandy said. This must be how Eugene felt when I called him over. I wished I had a gun to smack her with.

Torrie

"How old are you?" I asked as I played with the hair on his chest.

Vic laughed, "I'm a lot older than you."

"That doesn't tell me anything."

"It's not supposed to." Then he patted my back. "You should…" a light flashed.

I looked around the room, "what was that?"

Vic popped up, "one of your alarms was just tripped." He put his shorts on then he marched into my closet. I grabbed my robe and followed behind him. He pulled up the monitor and the camera showed Bonita in dark clothes coming over my fence. She had a backpack on. When I said I was going to call the police, Vic told me it wasn't necessary. He told me to watch.

I felt all kinds of emotions as I watched Bonita enter my property as if she knew she would be successful. She took out keys and tried the lock on the side of my house. She really looked confused when her key didn't work. Vic told the guards to hold the police at the gate for a moment. Bonita kicked the door, and then she went to the door to the garage. Vic had his eyes glued to the screen as he asked me if I wanted to fight her? I asked him what he had been smoking. I told him that this woman has bullied me for the past eighteen and a half years. I told him whenever things got physical I was no match for her. He told me to speak now or forever hold my peace. When I didn't respond he sucked his teeth. He told me this is my only opportunity to be rid of her. She would never be this bold again. He said her obsession with controlling me ends tonight, unless I want to continue to let her get away with it. By the end of his sixty-second speech, I was pulling on exercise clothes, and pulling my hair back. He pulled on his pants and he brought his gun. As we walked past my momma's room, I peeked my head in. She was knocked out in the middle of her bed snoring peacefully. When we walked into the garage Bonita was kicking the door on the side from the outside trying to open it. Vic told me to be quiet then he handed me the baseball bat that was next to him against the wall.

Norie, my mom and I were playing baseball the other day and we left our equipment in here after we finished our game. Vic told me to stand by the door and when she walked in to give it to her. After five minutes and she was still kicking Vic looked annoyed then he whispered that they did a good job of reinforcing the door. He slowly unlocked the door, and when she kicked again he opened the door to make it look like she was successful. My heart was pounding. It was now or never. Bonita flashed a light in the doorway before she entered. I could hear her trying to catch her breath. She stood out there for a minute until her breathing calmed down. She started fussing to someone telling them she finally had the door open. I felt sad when I heard Myles' voice, he asked her if she thought I heard anything. She told him the garage was on the other side of the house and I never locked the door to the house from the garage. She told him she had the syringe, and for him to be ready when she came back over the fence. I watched her shadow as she picked up her backpack and then she came towards the door. As soon as she stepped in the door I hit her as hard as I could in the head. Bonita hit the door and then she fell, I went crazy. I was screaming as I kept hitting her. I screamed about Norie, I screamed about my unborn child that she took from me. I screamed about her costing me Novian. I screamed about everything. At first Bonita was kicking and trying to protect herself. Eventually she wasn't moving. Vic turned on the light and I kept hitting her. Blood was everywhere, but I didn't care. She actually thought she could come in my house the next night after she tried to kill me to finish the job. The balls on this woman. Vic told me to stop and then he told the guards to send the police up, he told them to grab whoever was sitting in a parked car on the Southside of my property. He told them the person in that car was an accomplis. Then police came up my driveway speeding with their sirens on. I led them to my garage where Bonita was laying unresponsive. I gave them the footage of her trespassing and her phone conversation before she stepped into the door. One officer jokingly said that Vic was of no help to me. Vic didn't respond, but I told her that I was only brave because he was here. As the sun came up, Adina and her boyfriend came hurrying over. She said it was all over the news that there was a fatality, and a woman was rushed to the hospital in critical condition as the result of a home invasion on my property. I asked Vic what she meant and he said when the get away car couldn't get away one of the people in the car shot and killed their self, and the other was injured. I asked who was injured and he said the guy's name was Mykai. Vic said the Santa Monica police were going to throw the book at Mykai as if he was the one holding the syringe. Vic stayed an extra night with me to make sure my mom and I were cool.

******

My lawyer explained that Bonita Fairchild was prematurely released from the hospital to go to jail. The paperwork said she died the first night in custody. I kept a straight face as I felt completely relieved that she wasn't going to come after me. The thought of her plotting on me for the rest of my life scared the daylights out of me. She wasn't afraid to do the things I couldn't. I didn't want to have to continue to fight her for the rest of my life.

Now I sit here preparing for the next fight. "Ms. Bates we've asked you to meet with to try to result this matter with you and Ms. Rowe once and for all." She was in all white looking flawless. I really can't stand how she's always on. I mean I really want to know if this woman looks like this when she's sick. Her short hair always looks freshly done. Her manicure looked like it cost hundreds of dollars.

Yvette slightly rolled her eyes as she looked to her representation to speak for her. "Ms. Bates cannot be bought."

"Well what do you want? A public apology? You want me to humiliate myself?" My lawyer shot me a look to tell me to be quiet.

Yvette put her hand up to gesture, "lets talk. You supposed to be from the Bay and you're coming at me with all this paperwork and lawyers. You know none of this means nothing to me. You crossed a line Torrie, and I'm the wrong one to ever cross. You were sitting over there shaking in your boots scared of Bonita," she rolled her eyes. "I'm your worst nightmare sweetheart, you can't dangle money in front of me and think I will slink away." A white man leaned over and whispered something in her ear. She whispered something back and they went back and forth while we waited. She adjusted in her seat and then she locked her eyes on the camera, which made it seem like she was staring into my soul. "So I've been advised to put it to you like this. Malcolm has Mitigated, and I have Access. Access gives you access to success. I will not be quiet, I will not fall back. I will make my presence known when it benefits me to do so." Then she grinned a little at me, "and when I come for you there will be nowhere to hide."

"Ms. Bates what exactly are you saying?" My lawyer asked.

"She's from the Bay, she knows exactly what I'm talking about. Stop sending your lawyers and paperwork to me cause I ain't signing!" Then she disconnected the feed.

My lawyer looked at me for a long time without speaking. "Gentlemen can you give us a moment alone?" She ushered the other two lawyers out of the room, then she locked the door. She shook her head and then she sat next to me. She lost her professional demeanor, "WHAT WAS THAT?"

"I'm still trying to understand."

"She is bold, she threatened you in a room full of lawyers. What did you do?"

"I interfered."

"With what? She walked in on you screwing her man?"

"That was Courtney, remember she thought she had that basketball player Desmond on the hook. Then in walks Torrie." I exhaled.

"She's not going to be satisfied until she kicks your butt girl. Make sure you tighten up security."

"My friend has been tightening up everything around me. I should be ok."

****

I tried not to feel emotional. I hugged Norie and then she hugged my momma. January was waiting next to her car with another swollen belly! How many babies is she going to have? Norie prefers to spend most of her time with them. She said it's not anything against me and she loves me. It's just that her father fills a void she's always felt. I wasn't surprised when she narrowed her school options to Stanford and Cal Berkeley. Norie lives with Novian, and January is the only person I see when my path would naturally cross with Novian. Professionally we may see each other but even then it's at a distance. Novian flirts with everyone except me. He barely speaks to me.

I watched Norie get in the car. Vic cleared his throat and asked me how long was I going to stand there looking pitiful. I walked towards Vic's car where my momma already got in the back.

I kissed Vic and I told him I missed him. He smiled but he didn't say anything. He took my bag as I got in the car. Vic smiled when he got in the car. "Momz, you sure you don't want to hang with us today?"

"Oh no thank you Victor. Both of my brothers and my sister are here. I don't see my other brother a lot."

When we pulled up to my uncle's new house, there was a group of people outside. At first I thought they were greeting someone until we got close. When Vic parked everyone looked at the car. Then the crowd started moving towards the car. My uncle's were trying to hold someone back. Vic told me to stay in the car and then he got my momma's bags out of the trunk. "Why is everyone mad Torrie?"

"I don't know." I watched my uncle push a girl by her face backwards. I took a deep breath. Vic opened the door for my momma, then everyone started yelling telling him not to. Vic closed the door and put one finger up to my momma. Then he walked towards the crowd. The girl who's face got pushed came forward hollering and carrying on. I immediately turned up my nose. That was my alleged sister. She was yelling at the top of her lungs about something. Then my uncle and a man started fighting. "Torrie! Torrie!" My momma tapped my shoulder as if she was a child. "I remember him, he used to give me this special juice. When my brother found out he beat him up. He told me not to take anything from him anymore."

I looked at the back of my uncle's head. At some point he cared. Vic took over and commanded the crowd. Whatever he said got everyone's attention. The outsiders started walking away. I saw the man who caused my birth. He was short and not attractive at all. I had to thank my momma for my beauty. As unattractive as he is, I could see he was the man. I hated him and his ugly daughter immediately. How in the world did she think she was supposed to be a star? Makeup can only work so much magic. I will never acknowledge them! Never! After they drove away Vic opened my momma's door. Everyone's eyes got big when I got out of the car. I hugged my uncle and then I got back in the car. He stood there looking confused. Vic asked me if I was ok. I dabbed my eyes as I shook my head yes.

Vic's parent's home was an old style Victorian house. There were people out front and you could see more through the window inside. A woman stopped on the sidewalk as Vic parked. She didn't smile she just watched us. "This is my big sister Vicky. Vicky you know who Torrie is."

"Vic? Since when you go trolling the playground for tricks?"

Vic lowered his eyes at his sister. "What am I supposed to be, old?"

"Those grey hairs would suggest that you are."

"Just cause you in denial covering yours means nothing. Stop being evil and say hello."

"Hi," she said unenthusiastically.

Vic kept introducing me to all these women who were his sisters and a ton of nieces and nephews. I remembered his father as we greeted each other. Then he introduced me to his momma. "Enna, this is Torrie. Torrie this is my momma."

A girl cleared her throat. Vic told the girl he didn't see her. "This is my niece Sasha."

Vic's momma looked me over, "nice to meet you."

Sasha bumped her grandmother as they stared. I didn't know what their problem was. "Nice to meet you both."

"We've met before, but it's ok. I know you meet a lot of people." Sasha watched my eyes.

"Thank you, you look familiar."

Sasha grinned, "I'm Amber's niece. I used to come to the practice sessions in LA on occasion."

My smile dropped and they laughed. Vic's family is huge and everyone was nice enough. I didn't make any new friends or bonds.

That night when we got to Vic's place I walked around looking at his pictures and artwork on his walls. "Why don't you have any kids?" Vic shrugged. "Do you want one?"

"Sure, you offering?"

"Yes, my clock has been ticking like you wouldn't believe."

Vic looked at me, "you're serious?"

"Forty is coming, I don't want to miss my chance."

"This is an awfully lighthearted conversation about something so life changing."

"In the end, it's just a yes or a no answer."

"So you're not going to attack Novian anymore?"

"His wife is blocking for real. I don't even get to see him."

"Sounds like she's not stupid." Vic pulled me in close. "You sure?"

"Yes, you understand what family is, and I feel safe with you. We'll work everything else out."

Vic pulled me in tighter, "if you choose me you can't choose someone else. I will kill you if you cheat on me. That's a promise!"

"Understood, and I have no desire to cheat. Best sex ever!"

Vic smiled and then he kissed me.

******

Vic's soldiers marched to do their duty. I got pregnant probably that night. Life has been so much easier without Bonita in it. I'm taking the next couple of years off to be with the baby once it's born. Meanwhile, I've been writing and I may give some of these songs to a few of the artists doing their thing right now. I'll never admit it, but I love Chantel Shaw's music. Her sound is very soulful and her range is amazing. I'm so happy I was out long before her. She don't dance like I do, but she opens her mouth and the show is on.

Norie is excited to have more siblings. Every time I see her she has her little sister with her. Little Ursula, who acts just like her Grandmomma. She doesn't like me and I try to tolerate her.

My momma keeps staring at my stomach as it grows. "Torrie, do you have a baby?"

"Yes momma, my baby will be born in five months."

My momma's eyes got big then she sat down. "Are you ok? Do you want to cry?"

It looked like my momma's mind drifted away. "I'm very happy momma. You're going to have another grand baby."

"About that," she leaned back in her chair and took a deep breath. "Where did Angel come from?"

"You remember that Novian is her dad?"

"Yes but how?"

"I fell in love with him. Bonita took her from me. I didn't tell Novian that he gave me a baby. Now he's married and giving his wife baby after baby. It's like he's trying to have as many as he can before she can't have anymore."

"Did Victor give you that baby?"

"Do you like him?"

"He's nice, he let me help him make you breakfast. I don't like when you argue."

"I'm sorry about that momma. I'm a very spoiled brat, and I need a lot of attention."

"I know," she nodded her head in agreement.

I started laughing, "how do you know?"

"My momma used to tell me to put you down cause I carried you everywhere. She would always tell me to stop doing stuff cause I was going to spoil you."

I sat next to my momma, "did you?"

"No, that's why you're spoiled now." Then my momma started laughing.

I put my arms around the only consistent person in my life. "Thank you for always spoiling me. Thank you for loving me."

"I will always love you, you're my caterpillar." Then she kissed my forehead.

Novian

"Hey Renee how's it going?" Briscoe said as he opened his front door.

"Why do you insist on calling me that?"

Briscoe looked me in my eyes, "it's your name isn't it?"

"Yeah, but man!"

"You were named after my father, he was a good man. He…"

"Then what happened with you?" I stood there and waited to see if he slammed the door close.

Briscoe flared his nostrils and then he stepped out of the door and closed it behind him. "I am more man than you will ever dream of being. Don't believe me ask your momma!"

"A man takes care of his family, he doesn't run from them."

He threw his hands at me. "I'm not your father, you need to bring this drama to Eugene."

"You knew the possibility was there, she named me after your father!"

"I've already apologized to my wife, I don't owe you nothing. Eugene is your father."

"Your wife is my momma, that makes you my stepdad and still you have nothing to say to me. You told Mr. Dozier you've always been around. Funny how I never met you nor Eugene until my adult life. You had me at war with my own brother. No sense of family other than what Mr. Dozier provided and I'm supposed to regard you as a man because you married my momma? You still haven't come to me like a man about nothing." Then I remembered, I remembered the fact I was going to tell my momma when they sprung this whole wedding thing on me.

"I don't need to come to you like anything. I don't owe you anything. You still crying about what happened when you were a kid. You're a grown man with a little tribe of your own seeds. Just concentrate on being good to them."

"So you've reached out to your kids?"

"Yes."

"All of them?"

"YES!"

"What about the ones from Melanie?"

The mention of her name made him angry. He started breathing heavy. "MY son died!"

"What about your grandchildren?"

"My what?" His eyes got big and his fist started balling up.

"Your son has children. You didn't look at the obituary did you?"

"Renee, I'ma bust you upside the head if you don't quit messing with me!"

"When you get a chance, look at your obituary. I know you still got it. Melanie was survived by siblings, nieces, nephews, and grandchildren."

While Briscoe held that devastated look on his face I walked in his door. My momma had music playing and she had Angel and Jenny-Bean singing with her. When I walked into their family room, they were playing a karaoke game on their gaming console. My son was on the floor playing with his toys oblivious to anything going on. Angel stopped smiling and looked at me. She asked me what was wrong. Briscoe stormed past us. My momma asked me what was going on, so I told her like I just told her husband about his grandchildren. My momma hurried to her husband. After a few minutes Briscoe returned with red eyes and a wet face. "You knew about this these last couple of years and you didn't say anything?"

"I honestly forgot, but what difference does it make when you knew my whole life, who my father was, who I was, and you never said anything? What comes around goes around!"

"Pops, what's wrong?" Jenny-Bean asked Briscoe.

"I have grandchildren I don't know." Then he went to the phone. He dialed a number. He hung up and called again. He hung up and then he called again. "YOU KNEW I HAD GRANDCHILDREN AND YOU SAID NOTHING???"

I could hear the other person yell back at him, "I DON'T OWE YOU NOTHING! ESPECIALLY AFTER YOU MARRIED **HER**! THERE'S NO MORE LOYALTY BETWEEN US RIGHT?"

"YOU ARE SO CHILDISH! YOU KNOW WHAT THIS MEANS TO ME! I NEED TO TALK TO MALCOLM!" Eugene hung up in his face. Briscoe growled as he slammed the phone. Then he pointed at me angrily, "HOW DO I GET IN CONTACT WITH YOUR BROTHER!"

"I haven't spoken to him in a minute. I leave him voicemail messages."

"DOES HE GET THEM?"

"I don't see why he wouldn't."

"CALL HIM!"

I dialed the barbershop number on his phone and then I gave it to him. I told the kids to come on cause January and I had a surprise for them.

When we got to the house January had luggage waiting by the door. She was running around making sure she had everything.. "Murphy family, we're going on a family vacation. We packed sun tan lotion."

Angel grabbed one arm while I picked up Jenny-Bean. "What about my mom Torrie? She was expecting me to come home." Angel squeezed tighter.

"She'll be fine, we'll just call her and tell her that you're spending a little more time with us.. She's probably working on her next album or promoting, it'll be fine."

"But she's pregnant and she can't just..."

I felt like my baby girl shot me. "SHE'S WHAT?"

Angel looked up at me, "she's pregnant." I tried to take the devastation off of my face, but Angel's reaction told me I was not successful. I took the bags out to the car and I found myself grumbling to myself. I told myself to get myself in check, I've moved on and so should she.

When we got to the airport I reached out to touch January and she barked at me telling me not to touch her. She was mad about my reaction to Torrie's news. I didn't think she'd try again. I didn't think she'd have anyone's child other than mine. I did my best to suck it up. I didn't want Torrie back, but I also didn't want her to have someone else's kid. I didn't have a choice; I had to let it go. I guess that was the closure I needed. I kissed my wife's butt until she was over it. I assured her that I had a momentary slip up.

Preview

~

Novian

"Malcolm! I didn't know!" I pleaded.

Malcolm looked at me with hatred in his eyes. "Do you think your lack of knowledge is supposed to gain mercy from me? I have no heart when it comes to you. Your only saving grace is not here." Malcolm held back the others.

I took what felt like my final swallow in life. "I'm not against you! There's still time to save him. I can help you! Please Malcolm!"

Malcolm was considering my offer. "MALCOLM! YOU BELIEVE HIM? HE'S BEEN BUTT HURT OVER TORRIE ALL OF THESE YEARS! LOOK AT THE BOARD! WE CAN'T TRUST HIM! WE'RE WASTING TIME! KILL HIM AND LETS GO! URSULA WOULD UNDERSTAND!"

The other guys shared similar thoughts. I closed my eyes cause I knew this was it. My final breath, my final moments. Then a raspy voice called out, "Malcolm!"

"TWO FOR THE PRICE OF ONE!" Darryl said as he turned his anger towards him.

"I know who has Yussef! It's not what you think." Eugene said stepping between me and the wall of villains demanding my life.

Closing thoughts

Hello all, thank you once again for allowing me to entertain you for a brief moment of your time. SO... What did you think of Malcolm's little brother? Nothing like his big brother huh... Well they seem to have the same taste in women.

So my Beta Reader/Rough Rider said she had a hard time hating Torrie after reading about her. Did you feel the same way? I tried to humanize her as much as I could. Just like Toya and Nellie, I always feel like there's a reason why a person is the way they are. Sometimes the easy answer is that they're just evil. Most times it's a little more complicated than that.

As I sit on my bed writing this quick note to you I haven't done all of the editing I need to do on this book yet. I need to decide whether Bonita lives or really dies. I'm currently working on the finale to the Together We Are Strong series, "What Comes Next!" I can't wait for you to read that book. You're going to briefly see Malcolm in action. Also that question, also known as a cliffhanger, at the end of this book. The answer will be in the Together We Are Strong series, BUT you can't read it if you haven't read the other books. The TWAS will make no sense to you without the other books in the series.

If you are new to my books, I stuck this book somewhat towards the beginning of the series line up. Although each story is written as a standalone. They're all pieces to the much bigger picture. The story of the Wallace's and the Latour's. One thing you HAVE to do is leave the TWAS (Together We Are Strong series) at the end. Otherwise you won't understand the significance of all of these players and the things that are happening.

Even some of you who have read the series will have to say... WAIT A MINUTE! They'll go backwards however many books and say, "how did I miss that?" I love doing that can't you tell?

Anyways, I wanted to say thank you for reading and I cant wait to catch up with you in the Finale.

MORE FROM THE AUTHOR

Thank you for allowing me to entertain you. I hope you have enjoyed reading the Wallace Family Affairs Series. If you have not read any of the other books within this saga, please do so. Stay tune for more to come shortly. Follow my Author Page to keep up to date with my new releases Carey Anderson.

At Last

Tracy's Complications

Distorted Mirrors

Sometimes Love Isn't Enough

Love Is Just Enough

Just A Friend

Invisible

I Knew You When

Look Beyond Your Eyes

Abandoned

Second Chances

No Regrets

First You Laugh Then You Cry

A Heart That's Taken

Last Words

Present

Secret & Lies

www.ingramcontent.com/pod-product-compliance
Lightning Source LLC
Chambersburg PA
CBHW030240030726
47493CB00023B/263